VLAM

THE HOUSE OF THRONES

MW 2007

THE HOUSE OF MYSTERIES

THE HOUSE OF SPIRITS

Londoner Mike Wilks is an award-winning artist and
bestselling author of *The Ultimate Alphabet* and
The Ultimate Noah's Ark. His paintings, which have
been described as 'meticulous and eye-bending', can
be found in public and private collections in Europe
and the USA. *Mirrorscape* transports the reader
into Mike's compelling inner world.

www.mike-wilks.com
www.mirrorscape.co.uk

Other books by Mike Wilks

Pile – Petals from St. Klaed's Computer
(With Brian Aldiss)

In Granny's Garden
(With Sarah Harrison)

The Weather Works

The Ultimate Alphabet

The Annotated Ultimate Alphabet

The BBC Drawing Course

The Ultimate Noah's Ark

The Ultimate Spot-The-Difference Book
(Metamorphosis)

Mirrorscape

MIKE WILKS

EGMONT

For Lucy Jane Wilks
(wherever you are)

EGMONT

We bring stories to life

Published in Great Britain 2005
by Egmont UK Limited
239 Kensington High Street, London W8 6SA

Text and illustrations copyright © 2007 Mike Wilks

The moral rights of the author and illustrator have been asserted

ISBN 978 1 4052 3349 1

1 3 5 7 9 10 8 6 4 2

A CIP catalogue record for this title is available from the British Library

Typeset by Avon DataSet Ltd, Bidford on Avon
Printed and bound in Great Britain by the CPI Group

Pre-Publication Acclaim for Mirrorscape

'An endearing hero, a cast of incredible characters and a plot that will keep you breathlessly turning the pages. *Mirrorscape* is magical and enthralling' Jenny Nimmo, author of the Charlie Bone series

What young readers are saying...

'The book has excitement and thrill around every corner and it's so imaginative you actually believe you are there with Mel sharing his art ambitions and adventures. I couldn't put it down again' Nadine (11)

'I like this book because it is full of magic and mystery. It keeps you attentive, you want to know what happens next. It is very adventurous and imaginative . . . I can imagine it becoming a film' Nicola (12)

'I enjoyed every single page, and didn't want to stop reading it! It's packed full with adventure, mystery, and lots of excitement . . . I like the way it's like a jigsaw puzzle, with all the mysteries slotting together perfectly. I can't wait for the sequel' Holly (10)

'A really imaginative book that had lots of clever and enjoyable twists to the story. I thought that the whole idea of people owning pleasures was clever and I really liked some of the disasters that Mel and Ludo and Wren got into' Joe (14)

'An enthralling and extremely clever book . . . The story is thrilling and makes you want to read on forever; I picked the book up and only put it down to eat and sleep' Daniel (14)

'The reason I love this book is because the plot is so mysterious . . . not a bit in the book is boring' Ryan (13)

'It made me laugh, want to cry and scream because it was very scary! . . . I can't wait for the next book' Rachel (11)

'I would definitely recommend this book to any reader' John (11)

'I really really really enjoyed [Mirrorscape] and I've never read anything quite like it. I kept on reading until midnight to finish it (don't tell my mum). I liked the idea that you could paint a painting and then go into that world' Lucy (10)

Contents

Prologue

It should have been darker than the darkest night, as black as Indian ink. But it was not. He held his hand in front of his face and could clearly distinguish its outline in the feeble light. It was both a blessing and a curse. If he could see, then he could also be seen.

He quickened his pace. There was little risk of stumbling now with the increasing light, but where it was coming from he could not yet tell. The echo of his footfall and the even floor told him that he was indoors, and the darkness that he was deep underground.

Then there was the smell. A smell of damp and decay laced with something sour and feral.

And sounds too. Sounds that could only be footsteps somewhere behind him, getting closer. Periodically they stopped, and he was sure he heard sniffing.

There was a sudden movement to his left and the man froze, his heart pounding. Had it found him so soon? He turned his head slowly and so did his watcher. With an audible sigh of relief, he saw it was his own reflection. He approached the mirror. Its ornate frame was cracked and festooned with cobwebs, its glass scabby with age. But the shadowy reflection was his sure enough, even if his own mother would not have recognised him. The gaunt features and the malachite green skin of the fugitive stared back at him. Escaping from the Island of Kig had been the easy part. It had only taken him a matter of hours to travel the hundreds of miles from the horror of the mines to here – wherever here was. But when he finally emerged, fumbling, into the pitch darkness he found a new peril. It soon became clear he was being stalked by something every bit as cunning and murderous as his former captors, the Fifth Mystery.

As the man hurried on, water splashed underfoot. The light gradually increased until he discovered its source. A forgotten gallery stretched before him, one long wall hung with many paintings. But these were unlike any paintings he had ever seen before. These paintings had been there so long that they seemed to have become bored of being confined within their meagre two dimensions. Weird vines and plants had become real and spilled out of the images and on to the gallery floor. The branches of gnarled trees, originally crafted in oil paint, had left the paintings to snake and intertwine overhead. Streams that once were formed by deft brushwork and pigment now splashed their way out of their pictures and meandered along the gallery floor. In the distance they could be heard as they erupted into cataracts when they encountered unseen stairwells. The light was leaking from these pictures and illuminating the space at regular intervals, casting rectangular pools on the bare, stone floor. It reminded him of a deserted city street at night, lit by the windows of many shops.

The green man walked down the long gallery, staring at the canvases open-mouthed. He stopped before one. In a clearing in the heart of a nocturnal forest overflowing with extravagant plants, slept a band of travelling players. They were dressed in gaudy costumes and masks. The scene was illuminated by thousands of candles that littered the floor of the forest and the branches of the trees. It was as if the troupe were dreaming a collective dream that materialised into the forest around them as they slept. Dark spaces between the trees suggested shadowy forms that lurked beyond the light of the candles, only waiting for them to burn out before they became substantial. In the foreground of the picture were strange, nocturnal creatures the size of small marmosets and covered with piebald fur. They had wrinkled, pink faces peppered with minute tattoos depicting signs of the zodiac. One had left the picture and was scampering around in its pool of light on the gallery floor. The man knelt and picked it up.

Then the smell was suddenly stronger. Behind him he heard a sound and without looking he knew what it was. His stalker had finally found him. Its nightmare form slowly emerged from the darkness beyond the gallery and into the light. It stood erect on immensely muscular hind limbs that could clearly propel it faster than he could ever hope to outrun. In front of its spine-covered body was its huge head, which was mostly comprised of enormous jaws filled with needle-sharp teeth as long and transparent as icicles. It had huge, pale eyes as big as tea trays. From between them extended a long, curved barbel with a luminous tip like that of a deep sea fish. For a long moment they stood staring at each other. Then it flexed and folded its long wings and charged. As it hurtled towards the man, it uttered a blood-curdling roar and the glowing barbel thrashed from side to side.

The green man thrust the small creature into his rags, turned and sprinted down the gallery, his feet splashing in the watercourse. He knew from his pursuer's composition and fine detail that it was the work of Lucas Flink, and therefore exceedingly dangerous. But this was not the moment for the finer points of art appreciation.

Ahead, an interruption in the receding patches of light betrayed the presence of a painting with its surface still intact. There was no time to examine the dark canvas closely; he had to trust that the seal remained unbroken. He came to a halt and rapidly made a complicated gesture with his hand. With a faint smile of satisfaction, he saw the surface ripple as if it were a vertical wall of water kissed by a soft breeze.

Then he vanished!

Flink's creature let out a howl of frustration and skidded to a halt in front of the canvas, its wicked jaws closing on thin air and its claws tearing great gashes in the floor. It sniffed the air but its quarry had gone. It approached the painting and sniffed again but inhaled only dust and sneezed loudly, spraying pellets of foul, black mucus on to the canvas. As these slid slowly down the picture, they reflected back dozens of tiny, distorted images of the creature as it searched back and forth over the canvas for its lost prey. The pale light from its barbel illuminated first one small section of the painting and then another. If its uncomprehending eyes could have understood what it was looking at, it would have perceived a snowy landscape with bare trees leading down to a group of lamp-lit dwellings nestling in a hollow, their strange forms softened by the snow. Misty, blue mountains graced the skyline silhouetted against the setting sun. If it had been able to examine the picture more closely it would have seen a trail of footprints leading from the foreground down towards the village. And if it had followed that trail to its end it would have seen the beautifully painted form of a ragged man with a skin of malachite green cradling a tiny, piebald creature in his arms.

He was looking back out of the canvas and smiling.

The Messenger

The hare lay perfectly still. As a breeze stirred the long grass, her silky fur would ruffle and her whiskers twitch. Once, when a bee lifted off from a nearby gentian, she gave a quick flick of her long ear to send it on its way. Mel looked more closely and could see the nervous movement of her tiny nose as she sniffed the air for danger. Her bright eyes remained motionless but she was aware of everything around her. There was no sound except the faint buzz of insects and the whispering susurrus of the trees.

Mel had skived off to his favourite spot on the outskirts of the village. He had been dying to try out his new drawing materials ever since he had prepared them two days before. Lately he had been experimenting with different kinds of ink. His first attempts had been soot mixed with water, but even when he was able to dissolve this smoothly and without lumps the resulting ink was thin and soon faded to a sickly yellow-brown when he drew with it. His brainwave was to boil the sooty liquid until it concentrated the same way his mother thickened the broth. This ink was much more like real ink of the kind Fa Theum used to pen his sermons. For his pen Mel had a fine goose quill made from a long wing feather. With his father's sharp knife he had stripped away all of the feathery part and cut a fine point that he split to hold the ink. It was light – feather-light in fact – and responded to the slightest movement of his hand.

Mel sat in the sweet-smelling grass with the warm midday sun on his back, resting his mother's chopping board on his knees. On this was a precious sheet of paper that he had begged from the Fa.

He drew slowly but carefully. All the while, he looked more than he drew, only putting the quill to the paper when he was certain that he understood what he was looking at. It was absorbing work, but he found the same old frustration gnawing at his concentration. If only he had colours to match the vivid splendour he saw all around him. The grey-brown of the hare, the green of the grass, the blue gentians, the yellow buttercups, the rich colour of the soil. But colour was out of the question. He might as well wish for a mansion to live in or velvet and silken clothes to wear.

'You haven't finished it, Mel.'

The hare streaked away, its stillness instantly transformed into a flash of movement. As startled as the wild creature, Mel spun round. Indistinct, with the sun directly behind his head, creating a kind of nimbus, stood the figure of Fa Theum. Relieved, Mel squinted up at the old priest. 'Nearly, Fa. I was thinking that if I had some colours I could make it better. You know, more lifelike.'

'It looks very lifelike to me. But that's not quite what I meant.'

'Sorry, Fa. What did you mean?' asked Mel, puzzled.

'Why, you've forgotten the most important part, my son.'

Mel stared back blankly.

'Your signature! All great works of art should be signed by their creator. Come on, Mel. Like I taught you.'

Mel smiled at the compliment. He tilted his little

pot, dipped his pen in the last of the ink and slowly and carefully, with his tongue pushing out his lower lip in concentration, wrote in the bottom right-hand corner *Melkin Womper.*

'And the year,' prompted Fa Theum.

Mel slowly wrote *Spen 21* in his unpractised script.

'That's it.' Then, after a pause as he continued to admire the drawing, 'I guessed I'd find you here.' With a grunt, the elderly priest eased himself down to sit alongside Mel and absent-mindedly plucked a blade of grass to suck. He looked again at the drawing, thoughtfully stroking his grey stubbled chin with his long, bony fingers. 'That's a fine sketch, Mel. You have a rare talent. But it's not your usual subject matter, is it?'

'No, Fa. I really like to draw, you know, *imaginary* things.' It was his favourite word. 'But sometimes when I want to draw an imaginary thing I can't see it clearly enough and I need to find an outside thing and use it as a starting point. Like, if I want to draw a creature with . . . with an owl's body and a hare's head, I'll need a drawing of an owl and another of a hare so that I can join the two up.'

'We call such creatures "hybrids".'

Mel tried out his new word. 'Hybrids.'

'You know, Mel, in the House of Spirits – the Maven's palace in Vlam – in the great library, there is a rare book called a bestiary. And in this book there are descriptions and pictures of all manner of beast from every corner of the world. There are also fabulous creatures – unicorns, mermaids, gryphons and manticores – and there are hybrids. There are cameleopards, hippardiums, allopecopithicums. And there are armadillos and lots more besides. Do you know what they are?'

So many strange and new words, Mel could only shake his head in bewilderment.

'Well, you know that when a donkey mates with a horse, their offspring is a . . .'

'Mule,' finished Mel.

'That's right. Now, according to the bestiary, when a camel and a panther mate they create another kind of creature altogether – a cameleopard. But if that same panther were to bear the offspring of a horse, well that would be a hippardium. The offspring of a fox and a monkey would be an allopecopithicum and that of a hedgehog and a tortoise an armadillo.'

'Do such creatures really exist, Fa?'

'Possibly, possibly. But there's something just as interesting going on here. You remember what a symbol is?'

'It's something that means more than itself. Like your diaglyph.'

The old priest touched the tarnished pendant slung around his neck that rested on his shabby, brown cassock. A triangle within a square within a circle. He smiled at his quick pupil. 'Just so. This is a symbol. A symbol of my maker and of my faith.'

Mel nodded, eager for the old man to continue.

'So, a mermaid might symbolise temptation and a unicorn purity. As for the hybrids, well they might symbolise two things at once. A fox is cunning and a monkey full of mischief, so an allopecopithicum would have both those qualities. A kind of cunning rascal.'

'Yes, but do they *really* exist?' insisted Mel.

'When I was a young priest in Frest, I met some sailors who swore that they once saw a mermaid and had travelled in a land where unicorns and other strange creatures lived.'

'Mermaids and unicorns sound better than an owl with a hare's head,' said Mel, disappointed that he had come up with such mundane components for his imaginary creature.

'Well, there you're wrong. According to ancient folklore, the owl possessed wisdom and the hare was the messenger of the moon. So your hybrid might symbolise a wise messenger.'

Mel thought about this for a moment and smiled. 'And do you think that my hare might have been bringing me a message, Fa?'

The priest smiled and looked down at Mel and saw the way his large, blue eyes almost glowed with wonder. He took in the tousled fair hair and the way the tips of his large ears protruded from under it, the ink-stained fingers and the faded, dun-coloured clothes that had been patched many times. He was shorter and slimmer than most boys of his age but compact and wiry and somehow more alive than the others. There was something else too, something difficult to define. It was as if he carried with him more wisdom than could be accounted for in his thirteen years of life. The boy liked to be on his own, he was comfortable in his own company, unlike the gang of village boys who liked to play and create mischief together. Sometimes they tried to pick on Mel but mostly, perhaps recognising his solitary character, they left him to himself. Then there was this yearning that he had for things outside of himself and his environment. *There is a real thirst for knowledge in this boy,* Fa Theum thought, *and a great talent. What I have done is right.* Then, out loud, 'Come on, Mel, let's go home and see your parents. There's something very important we must discuss with them.'

A wave of panic swept through the youngster. 'It's all right. I'm not skiving. I've done my chores; they know I'm out here drawing. They said I could come,' he quickly lied.

'Don't fret. Come on, take my hand and help me up.'

Mel clutched his drawing and materials to his chest and the two headed back over the fields towards Kop.

As Fa Theum and Mel made their way up the village street, the boy began to drag his feet, reluctant to reach home and the inevitable price he would have to pay for his truancy. The rutted, unpaved street was now dusty in the summer heat and their footsteps raised puffs of pale dust. An unpleasant smell rose from the central gutter where all manner of waste flowed. The low, single-storey houses that lined the street had roofs of thatch and walls of wattle and daub. Some had once been whitewashed but most were faded, with the dun, mud colour of their construction showing through. The entire village seemed to be painted in shades of sepia, alleviated only by the green backdrop of the distant trees and the grey smudges of smoke from cooking fires drifting slowly upwards from the chimneys into the clear, azure sky. Everywhere, the doors and wooden shutters were thrown wide to allow the warmth of the day to circulate and air the cramped dwellings.

The Womper cottage was on the far side of the village. It was little more than a shack with a lean-to at one side. The ceiling was low, the tiny windows unglazed and the floor was of hard, packed earth scattered with dried rushes. There was a main room where Mel's father, Willem, worked incessantly at the wooden loom that filled most of the space. What little was left was occupied by the plain family table and chairs and by Willem's fireside chair. Next to a small, mud-brick hearth hung around with a collection of pots and pans, there was a settle where Mel and his mother would sit of an evening, and in the far corner the straw pallet where Mel slept. The remaining accommodation was no more than his parent's tiny bedroom and some storage in the lean-to.

As they approached, a gang of the village boys with anxious looks on their pale faces raced past them in a great hurry to escape something. Fa Theum looked down at the boy. 'Mel, before we go in and see your parents there is something I must tell you.'

Mel was not listening. He had sensed from the fleeing gang that something was wrong. Everything was quiet where there should have been the steady clackety-clack of his father's loom. What had started as a sense of unease grew in Mel's heart to one of trepidation. He broke away from Fa Theum and ran the last few steps to his door.

The priest shouted after him, 'Mel, wait!'

But Mel did not hear him. As he burst in, his young eyes quickly adjusted to the gloom and he stopped dead as his eyes fixed on an object of horror. Seated in his father's chair by the hearth was a monster, its vast size dwarfing the room. Its leathery head slowly turned and its single eye fixed itself on the intruder.

Dirk Tot

The creature slowly rose from the chair and would have stood erect if the ceiling had been high enough to accommodate its great size. Eyes wide, Mel uttered a cry of abject terror, turned on his heels and fled back the way he had come, dropping everything in his panic. He collided heavily with Fa Theum, who blocked the doorway.

'Mel, Mel, whatever is the matter?'

The boy could only whimper as the priest held him fast, preventing his flight. He looked up at the old man and was astonished to see that he showed no fear. Instead, he was actually smiling across at the monster. Mel half turned and was even more astounded to see his father and mother in the shadows, calmly sitting side by side on the settle. His mother was smiling nervously at him but his father shifted uncomfortably as if he were embarrassed at Mel's behaviour. He glared at Fa Theum.

Then the monster spoke. 'Hello, Mel.' The voice

was deep and resonant but surprisingly gentle and his Vlamian accent refined.

Slowly, Mel turned to confront the dreadful sight and a strange thing happened. He began to look at the creature in the same way he looked at a subject he was about to draw. Almost at once, his fear and preconceptions fluttered away like so many moths shaken out of an old blanket. What he now saw was not so much a monster as a man; a very tall and powerful man dressed in the finest clothes Mel had ever seen. And, what's more, they were *coloured*. He had never met anyone before who was not dressed in tabby. The monster wore a long, sleeveless garment made from fine, richly embroidered purple brocade trimmed with tawny fur, beneath which was a deep blue velvet doublet. Where the sleeves of his doublet were slit in many places the white silk of his shirt peeped through. Mel's sharp eyes even noticed fine gold stitching around these slits that matched the gold of the heavy chain he wore around his neck. He carried a plumed, flat velvet hat and he had a jewelled reticule at his side, attached to his ornate belt. His black leather breeches were tucked into soft, high boots. He made a dazzling contrast to the drabness of the cottage as if he were bathed in a strong light while all around him was in shadow.

But, the wonder of the colours aside, it was his ruined face that held Mel's attention. Yet, as he studied it, this became less an object of revulsion and more one of fascination. The whole of one side – the right side as Mel looked at it – seemed to be made of wrinkled leather. But not quite like leather. As his keen eyes studied it even more closely he could see that it seemed to have melted like candle wax. Set in this was what would once have been his eye, but was now no more than a milky dome. There was a deformed lump where Mel supposed his ear had been and on that side of his head there was no hair at all. The man-monster turned his head for a moment to look at Mel's mother and father and Mel was surprised to see that when the ruined half of his face was turned away he looked perfectly normal. In fact, he was even handsome. By this time, Mel's initial dread had almost completely vanished.

'Mel, don't stare,' admonished his mother,

clearly embarrassed by her son's gawping.

Mel lowered his eyes momentarily, but surreptitiously raised them again as the stranger bent down to pick up his drawing from where it had fallen. The stranger straightened up, forgetting the low ceiling, and bumped his head, sending a small shower of dust cascading around him that sparkled like stardust as it passed through a beam of sunlight that penetrated the gloom. Mel stifled a laugh.

'*Mel!*' His father was angry at this.

'I'm . . . I'm sorry,' stammered Mel sheepishly. He looked up at the stranger to see that he too was suppressing a laugh. He rubbed his head where he had bumped it and Mel noticed something more. His left hand was made entirely of silver that was covered in finely chased engraving. It was artificial but beautifully crafted, even down to the articulated joints. Mel was staring again and his mouth had dropped open.

The stranger was quite used to the initial effect his appearance had on others and pretended not to notice. He looked down at the drawing of the hare he held in his good hand. 'I can see that everything I've heard about you is true, Mel.'

The stranger had heard about him!

The man looked at the drawing again, holding it first closer then further away, and then turned to place it on the table, where Mel was surprised to see lay many of his other drawings. 'You are industrious too, I can see.'

'Mel, this is Dirk Tot. Say hello,' said Fa Theum, as he stood behind Mel with his hands resting on the boy's shoulders.

'Hello,' and after a sharp squeeze from the priest added, 'sir.'

'Come here, Mel,' said Dirk Tot. Clearly discomforted by the stooped posture the tiny room forced him to adopt, he sat down again in Willem's chair. The chair complained with a loud creak as he settled his great bulk. Hesitantly, Mel approached. Dirk Tot smiled his strange half-smile and Mel smiled back. 'How long have you been drawing?'

'I don't know in years,' Mel answered. 'Ever such a long time, as long as I can remember.'

'What do you like to draw best of all?'

'I like to draw *imaginary* things best of all,' Mel replied instantly.

A smile flitted across the undamaged side of Dirk Tot's face and then vanished. He was all business again. 'Tell me, Mel, which do you think is the best of your works?' He gestured towards the drawings scattered on the table.

Mel quickly sorted through them, some in charcoal and some in ink. 'This one,' he said, passing Dirk Tot a picture of a set of bagpipes with dancing human arms and feet and the head of a nightingale with its beak open wide.

Dirk Tot studied it. 'Why do you think this is good?'

There was a short silence before Fa Theum prompted, 'Come on, Mel. Don't be shy.'

'I like it because it's more than just an ordinary picture. You know, an ordinary picture of a thing.' Mel looked at his interrogator who stared back at him, obviously expecting more in the way of justification. 'It's a picture that means two things at once.' He shot a quick glance at Fa Theum, who nodded almost imperceptibly. 'It's a symbol.'

The old priest smiled the faintest of smiles.

'You see, it's a picture of a bagpipe, which makes a certain kind of noise, joined up to a picture of a nightingale, which makes another kind of noise – a noise much sweeter than the pipes. And the arms and legs are dancing – as if to the music. So, even though there's no sound, you can make believe there is. But you're not sure what kind of sound it is, bagpipes or bird, or both. And you wonder why he's dancing. Is it because of the music or because of something else?'

'Where did the idea come from?'

'I don't know really, it was just there when I sat down to draw.'

'Are your ideas always there?'

'Usually. Inside in my head. But if I ever can't think of one, I look at the shapes and get a new idea from them.'

'Shapes? What shapes?' asked Dirk Tot.

'Just shapes. Sometimes I look in the hearth, at the ashes, and I see pictures there. Or in the flames in the fire. Sometimes I see them in the clouds or in the stains on the wall. I see people and animals and monsters with . . .' he nearly said horrible faces '. . . strange landscapes.' Mel could feel everybody's eyes on him. He hated being the centre of attention.

Dirk Tot sensed his awkwardness and quickly asked in the same steady tone as before, 'Tell me, how often do you make mistakes?'

Mel thought about lying, but he realised this man knew too much about drawing. 'Not very often. Well, sometimes . . . Quite a bit actually.'

'Every artist makes mistakes; it's nothing to be ashamed of. Only people who never try anything new never make mistakes.'

Dirk Tot sat forward, resting his elbows on his thighs. 'Now tell me, which is your *worst* picture?' he asked.

Mel was surprised at this question and it raised a murmur from his parents. He shuffled through the drawings a couple of times and then handed the man an ink portrait. 'This one, I think.'

The stranger studied it. 'Tell me why.'

Mel thought for a while before answering. Should he point out the mistakes or tell him how the pen kept clogging up or how lumpy the ink was or how dark it was when he made the drawing? As Mel rehearsed these themes in his head they began to sound like excuses. Eventually he said, 'Well, you see, it's a picture of Fa Theum – but it's not like him.'

'You're wrong, Mel, it is the very image of him,' interrupted Dirk Tot.

'It *looks* like him – at least I hope it does – but it's not him. Fa Theum talks and laughs and does lots of things that my drawing can't show. He can read and write and say sermons and he tells funny stories and –'

'Well, I'm glad *someone* thinks they're funny,' interjected the Fa.

Everyone laughed – everyone except Willem.

Dirk Tot continued. 'You know, Mel, there is more to being an artist than being able to carry a likeness. A true artist knows the difference between what is good and what is bad and, more importantly, between what is merely good and what is great. Sometimes great masters make paintings that are bad – not as often as bad artists, but occasionally – and do you know what they do to these bad paintings?'

Mel shook his head.

'They destroy them.'

Dirk Tot had expected this remark to shock the boy but after a while Mel slowly nodded. 'So that the bad apple doesn't spoil the others in the barrel.'

Dirk Tot fixed his one good eye on Mel and stared so hard that the boy began to feel uncomfortable. Mel lowered his head and shifted his weight from one foot to the other. After what seemed an age, Dirk Tot grunted, turned to Fa Theum and nodded once emphatically.

'Mel, gather up all these drawings now and come over to the fane with me,' said Fa Theum. 'We need to put them back up on display so that the rest of the village can admire them.' This drew an alarmed look from Dirk Tot that the priest pretended not to notice. 'Besides, Dirk Tot has things he needs to discuss with your parents.'

After a glance across at his father who nodded his assent, Mel did as he was told.

Almost as soon as the pair were out of the door the questions started. 'Who's Dirk Tot, Fa? Where's he come from? What's the matter with his face? What happened to his hand? What's he doing here in Kop? Why was he asking me all those questions? What's he going to discuss with Dad and Mum? Why can't we stay? What were all my drawings doing there?'

'Slow down, Mel. All in good time.'

'But, Fa, why . . .?'

'Mel, please.'

'Why can't –?'

'Mel! Hush now.'

Seeing that he was not going to get any answers until Fa Theum was good and ready, with great difficulty Mel suppressed his curiosity. He could not contain his excitement, however; he was virtually pulling the old priest towards the fane in his impatience. The gang of village boys who had been frightened away now had their attention fixed on Dirk Tot's fine carriage and coachman in their matching liveries of deep blue where they waited in the grounds of the fane. The couple pushed past them and entered. Mel rearranged his pictures around the vestibule in record time. After straightening Mel's hasty and haphazard arrangement – and noticing that his 'worst' picture was absent – Fa Theum said, 'Let's go inside where we can sit and be quiet.'

They entered the cool, whitewashed interior and genuflected to the large diaglyph on the altar before sitting down on one of the scrubbed, wooden pews. Sunlight slanted in through the small windows, creating patches of amber light and shade on the bare stone floor. Mel was bursting to ask his questions all over again but the old man held up a pre-emptive finger.

'Sit still. Listen carefully to what I have to say.'

What Fa Theum had to say began a chain of events that changed Mel's life, and, ultimately, the lives of everyone in Nem, for ever.

Hopes and Dreams

Some time later, Mel left the fane almost in a state of shock. Then, as he began to understand, he started to smile and then he began to run. He ran faster and faster, back through the village, until his breath came in gulps. He reached home and burst into the tiny room. The stranger had left and his parents sat side by side on the settle, deep in conversation.

'Is it true? Is it true?' Mel shouted excitedly as he struggled for breath.

His father said nothing. He did not even look at his son as he rose, walked over to his loom and began weaving again, his face set like stone. He wove at a frantic pace, violently stamping on the treadles and dashing the shuttle carrying the weft from side to side through the warp with a speed Mel had never witnessed before. He turned to his mother and noticed that her eyes were red. She had been crying.

'Mum, is it true? What Fa Theum told me?' A great crash rang out as his father applied himself to his weaving even more violently. If he carried on at this rate Mel feared that the loom would shatter.

'Come outside with me, sweetheart, and help me pick the vegetables for supper,' said his mother softly.

When they were alone in the vegetable patch, Mel asked, 'What's the matter with Dad?'

'Leave him be. This whole business has come as a bit of a shock. He needs to adjust to the idea. We both do.'

'It's true then.'

'Yes, Mel, it's true.'

'Fa Theum told me that –'

'Yes, I know what Fa Theum told you.'

'Then I am to go and –'

'Nothing's certain yet. Please don't get your hopes up.' She gently caressed his cheek. 'The gentleman had to continue his journey but he will return this way in a few weeks. There's a great deal to be discussed before then. It's best if you don't dwell on this too much.'

An impossible request; from that moment on he thought of nothing else.

That night, as he lay in bed, Mel turned over the

momentous events of the day. Earlier, in the fane, Fa Theum had explained to him that he had written to Fa Marten, an old friend in the Maven's household, to ask if he knew anyone in the capital who might be interested in commenting on Mel's artistic gift. He had recently received a reply that exceeded his wildest expectations. He had produced the thick sheet of paper from inside his cassock and unfolded it with a soft, crackling sound.

'The first part does not concern you, Mel, but this bit surely does.' Fa Theum turned the page.

'"I found the story of your young protégé fascinating and the boy's precocious talent is amply demonstrated by the drawing you enclosed. I took it at once to show to Dirk Tot, steward to Ambrosius Blenk, the greatest artist in the Seven Kingdoms. You will remember how we used to marvel at his fantastical canvases in the Maven's collection when we were novices together in the seminary. Dirk Tot was as impressed as I was and took it at once to show to the great man.

"Now, you may know that Ambrosius Blenk's studio employs many apprentices and is almost like a factory for producing paintings. What you may not know is that these apprenticeships are usually purchased for large sums of money by wealthy families, keen that their sons study with the great man. What you almost certainly do not know is that very occasionally the master will offer a free apprenticeship to someone who is too poor to pay but who shows truly exceptional talent. I am pleased to report that your boy is so considered. However, as Dirk Tot made clear, artistic ability alone will never be enough to make an artist. Quite apart from a skill in draughtsmanship, the boy would also need a discerning and inquiring mind, the right attitude and, above all, a great passion for art if he is ever to succeed."'

Mel did not hear the rest of the letter or Fa Theum's caveat that any apprenticeship depended on the agreement of his parents. He had been in an almost delirious state of excitement ever since, despite his father's odd behaviour. Willem had not spoken another word to his family all day and, as soon as he had finished work, went to bed without a glance at his wife and son.

Now Mel tossed and turned on his straw pallet. His entire universe seemed to have spun on a great, invisible pivot and now faced in a totally different direction. At breakfast he had been a happy enough boy who was good at drawing and who would grow up to become a tabby weaver like his father. By supper time, another magnificent vista had opened up that held the promise of becoming an apprentice and, eventually, an artist who would spend all day, every day, doing what he loved most – making the most wonderful pictures. Mel's deepest wish, a wish he had scarcely dared to admit even to himself, had actually come true.

Obviously his parents could not sleep either, and he was aware that they were having a heated conversation as their muffled voices rose and fell in the bedroom. Mel lay there in the darkness, looking at the fan-shaped patch of light on the floor coming from under their bedroom door. From time to time, shadows moved across it. It was no good; his curiosity was too great. He just had to know what they were saying. He rose from his bed and crept towards their room.

'. . . not so loud, you'll wake Mel,' he heard his

mother say as he placed his ear to the door.

'But how can you bear to be parted from him? If he went away we might not see him for years on end.'

'It's just as hard for me as it is for you, but think of his future. He would get away from here, make something of his life.'

'And what do you mean by that?' shot back Mel's father. 'Suddenly being a weaver isn't good enough for him. Is that it? Perhaps I'm not good enough any more. Let me remind you that weaving puts food on the table. Weaving keeps a roof over our heads. We've done all right by weaving, despite the scrotting Mystery. He might go off to Vlam, spend years playing about with paints and whatnot and never make it as an artist. Have you considered that, Mab?'

'Will, you know as well as I do how talented he is. And Fa Theum, he wouldn't have gone to all that trouble if there was no talent there.'

'Don't talk to me about that interfering old priest, after he's gone behind our backs like that. Why didn't he discuss it with me first? I could have put an end to this nonsense then and there.'

Mel knew how stubborn his father could be when he took against something, but he also knew that his mother often got her way by subtler means. She would let her husband rant on at length until much of his anger had spent itself before she began a quiet campaign of being reasonable and considerate.

'Mel's shooting up,' continued his father. 'Soon his legs will be long enough to reach the treadles. I'll build him his own loom. He can weave alongside me. Think what a difference that will make. Double the cloth, double the income. Why, we would be able to move out of this place into somewhere larger, with better light. I could buy the Pleasure to make finer cloth and we could have the things we've dreamed of.'

'You think I would want that rather than Mel's happiness?'

His father blew out loudly through his nose in exasperation before beginning on a new tack. 'And then there's Vlam. Do you know what goes on there? There's drinking dens and there's . . . there's worse. Do you know that?'

'No, Will, and neither do you. Neither of us has

ever been more than ten miles from Kop.'

'But I've heard stories. I've got ears.'

'All I'm asking is that you think about it. Just think about it. Can you do that, Will?'

'There's nothing to think about. My mind's made up.'

Then the argument seemed to start again from the beginning. Mel stole back to bed. His mother would get her way. She always did. Well, nearly always.

Eventually he dropped off to sleep and his dreams were full of fabulous hybrids romping about in the most glorious colour. In the morning he awoke with a wonderful feeling of elation and anticipation. There was something else as well. Mel felt more than a little guilty at being the cause of his father's anger and the disharmony between his parents. Was he being selfish to want to be an artist? Was he more than selfish to be so delighted about going away to distant Vlam?

His father's black mood lasted all the next day and into the one after but it did not dent Mel's joy.

By the fourth day following Dirk Tot's visit, Mel sensed that things were beginning to return to normal and he and his father managed to exchange a few words here and there. He took this as a sure sign that his mother had won the argument.

One week later, with normality more or less restored, as they sat around the table after supper, there came a knock at the door. Mel, in the highest of spirits, rushed up and opened it.

'Fa!' he exclaimed to the visitor, his face beaming.

'Good evening, Fa,' said Mabin as she gestured for the old man to enter. 'Please join us. Will you have something to eat? To drink, maybe?'

'Thank you, but no.' The old priest sat down. 'Willem, Mabin, Mel,' he looked at each in turn. 'It's been over a week now and Dirk Tot will be returning this way soon. I realise that there has been much for you to think about. We really must have an answer for him.'

Willem looked at his wife and then back at their visitor. 'Fa, this apprenticeship is wonderful, there's no denying it. I know opportunities like this rarely come along – and never to the likes of us. This has made our decision so very difficult. At first, I was confused and angry that you had done this thing. That you had approached someone else about Mel's future. A future that would mean us living apart. You should have discussed this with us first.'

'I know, Willem, I apologise. But there was no certainty in this matter. I took it upon myself just to find out if Mel's work was as good as we all think it is. That Mel should be asked to join Ambrosius Blenk's studio was as much a surprise to me as it must have been to you both. And what a wonderful surprise!' The old priest smiled.

Willem paused and lowered his eyes. Then, turning to Mel, he said, 'I'm sorry, son. We're simple folk; artisans. This thing isn't for the likes of us. Surely you can see that? You can continue to draw in your spare time but this apprenticeship is out of the question.'

Mabin sighed and leant over to hug her son. There was a tear in her eye. 'Your father's right, Mel. I know it seems hard now but it's for the best. This apprenticeship was a dream – for both of us – but now we must wake up. You'll stay here with us, just like it's always been.'

'But Mum, Dad . . .' The words died on Mel's lips. He wanted to argue about how unfair this all was but he recognised the tone of his father's voice, which told him it would be futile. Willem's mind was made up. Mel felt an almost overwhelming desire to break into tears but he fought these back as the disappointment settled on him with an almost physical presence.

'Is there nothing I can say to make you change your mind, Willem?' said Fa Theum. His face betrayed a regret almost as bitter as Mel's.

'Nothing. This is how it must be.' Willem turned again to his son. 'Mel, I know how hard this must be for you but you'll get over it. Weaving is a fine trade. Why, it's almost an art in its own right. In a few months none of this will matter. It will all be forgotten. What do you say?'

Mel could say nothing. He just smiled the feeblest of smiles that trembled slightly and barely curled his lips. It contained no joy whatsoever.

That night when he was tucked into bed and the candle had been blown out, the tears did come. Tiny trickles eventually gave way to small, persistent rivers and silent sobs racked his small body as he cried himself to sleep. That night he did not dream in colour. He did not dream at all.

The Pleasure and the Pain

The world did not end. As one week stretched into two, Mel gradually became more resigned to his future. His desire to create slowly returned and he eventually found the time to draw the view of Kop that he had planned when the hare turned up. In fact, the landscape turned out so well that he felt eager to take it at once to show to Fa Theum and to pin it up with his other works in his impromptu exhibition.

When the fane came in sight, he saw that there was a magnificent carriage waiting on the sward outside. Unlike Dirk Tot's, this one was a vivid scarlet and ornamented with fine carving embellished with gold leaf. It positively throbbed with colour. It occurred to Mel that he had seen more colour in the last few weeks than in his entire life. Four huge, black horses with hairy fetlocks looked up from their grazing at the boy. They were steaming, and pale sweat streaked their flanks and froth hung around their mouths as if they had been driven hard. Hitched to the back of the carriage was a trailer with what looked like a large, domed bird cage on it. Mel could not imagine what kind of bird it was intended for though, as it was easily big enough to hold a man. Hanging from the thick bars were stout chains and manacles. Mel's first reaction was simply to stand there and gawk. This was shortly followed by a strong desire to draw this marvellous sight. But it was his curiosity that won and he walked towards the fane wondering who Fa Theum's visitor might be.

As he reached the door, it struck him that the village boys were not around. No one was. He would have expected people to be irresistibly attracted by such a spectacle. Even the birds had stopped singing and, when he scanned the trees, there were none to be seen anywhere. It was as if everything had fled.

Mel hesitated for a moment and then pushed open the door.

'Ah, and this must be the artist.'

There were three of them, the one who had spoken, and who was obviously the leader, and two other armed and powerful-looking men who held Fa

Theum between them. The old priest stood in a pool of his own vomit and was in a pitiful state. He was bleeding heavily from a deep scalp wound that matted his grey hair, and his left eye was so swollen that it was completely closed up. The lower half of his face was encrusted with blood and snot and he held his right hand at an odd angle to his chest. Fa Theum tried to say something but only succeeded in uttering a feeble croak that blew a bloody bubble from his mouth.

His captors were dressed in long, scarlet robes that brushed the floor, with a large, black eye emblazoned on the breast. They wore many jewelled rings in rows like knuckle-dusters over their red gloves. All had abnormally white skin and straight, jet-black hair that hung to their shoulders. This was shaved in a strange tonsure so that the front of their scalp and everything in front of their ears, including their eyebrows, was completely bald. Their leader was taller than the others and cadaverously thin. He had reptilian, grey eyes with irises so pale they were only a shade or two darker than the surrounding whites. They were deep-set above a tiny, upturned nose, and radiated menace. The man held a long, multi-coloured staff with an ornate, gilded boss on top. It was obvious that this was a mark of his office. He sneered at Mel, revealing uneven teeth, made to seem even more yellow in contrast to the cosmetic whiteness of his skin.

'So these are your masterpieces,' he said sarcastically as he made an expansive, sweeping gesture towards the drawings decorating the vestibule with his staff.

Mel, too frightened to speak, nodded.

'I thought as much. Seize him!'

One of the men left Fa Theum to the charge of his companion and grasped Mel roughly by his arms from behind. His new drawing fell to the floor and was trampled underfoot.

'Leave the boy alone,' Fa Theum managed to croak.

'Keep quiet until I tell you that you can speak! Unless you want another beating,' said the leader abruptly, jabbing his staff maliciously in the priest's ribs. The old man gave a gasp of pain. 'And *you* . . .' he said, stooping so that he was eye to eye with Mel,

'. . . will tell me who gave you permission for this exhibition.'

His fetid breath made Mel wince. Up close he could see where his white make-up was cracked around his thin lips and pale eyes.

'Well, I'm waiting. Who said you could display these pictures?'

'It's got nothing to do with the boy. It was my idea,' rasped Fa Theum.

'I thought I told you to keep quiet!' he bellowed, making Mel jump and showering him with beads of foul-smelling spittle. Then, to Mel, in a whining, ingratiating tone, 'Well? What's the matter? Forgotten how to speak?'

'Can't you see he's terrified?' said the priest, fighting back his own pain.

'You're not frightened of me, are you, sonny?' the man said, grabbing Mel's hair so hard that a clump was torn out. Mel screamed but the man grabbed him again and pulled him even closer. 'Do you know how many laws you've broken with your pathetic little exhibition here? Do you realise how much trouble you're in? Such deep, deep trouble,' he sneered.

'Aaaaghhh! Stop hurting me,' screamed Mel. 'Stop it!'

'So it can speak, after all. Well, now that you've found your voice, answer me. Or would you like another hairdo?'

'Mel, say nothing,' came Fa Theum's voice.

'I'll not tell you again, skeg-breath.' Turning to his henchman holding the priest, he said, 'If he interrupts me again, hurt him. Hurt him badly.'

'Leave him alone!' said Mel through gritted teeth.

Yanking his hair even harder, his interrogator said, 'Don't try and tell me what to do, *Smell*. That is your name, isn't it?' He sniffed theatrically and wrinkled his nose as if smelling something nasty. 'You have no rights in this matter. None at all. You, Smell, and this disgusting old man, are mine. I will do with you exactly as I please.'

'Don't hurt the b–' the priest's protest was cut short by a backhanded blow across the face.

'You have no idea who I am, have you, Smell? Not the faintest idea. You don't know the significance of my robes, or of this here, or this.' The man touched the emblem on his breast and then his staff of office. 'Have you ever heard of the Mysteries? Of course you have. Even out here in Feg, this stinking cesspit of a backwater. Well, I am the High-Bailiff of the Fifth Mystery.' He expected this information to impress Mel. When he saw it did not he continued. 'All you need to know is that as far as you and this old man are concerned, *I* am the Fifth Mystery. And as the Fifth Mystery, it is *me*, and no one else, who says what goes and what does not go, as far as pictures are concerned. Not that I'd grace such ugly scribbles with so noble a title as *pictures*.' He spat the last word as he prodded Mel's dropped landscape with the toe of his boot before grinding it underfoot as if it were a verminous insect.

Mel could feel himself trembling and losing control of his body. He was scared that at any moment he would wet himself. His scalp hurt terribly where his hair had been yanked out and his arms had gone numb where they were being held from behind in the man's vice-like grip. What had he done wrong?

'As you seem to be ignorant as well as stupid, Smell, let me explain some things to you. Are you listening? Good. Are you wondering why I am dressed in this beautiful, rather fetching shade of scarlet, while your clothes are the colour of farmyard slurry? Eh? Of course you're not. You're too stupid ever to think such thoughts. Well, let me tell you. It's because I, and my fine fellows here, have the Pleasure of colour and you do not. That particular Pleasure belongs to the Fifth Mystery. And Pleasures must be bought and paid for. Including the Pleasure to display pictures which also belongs to the Fifth Mystery. And do you have the Pleasure to display pictures? No, you don't. How do I know? I know because if you and the rest of this ugly, squalid, pitiful, little village were to sell everything you possessed ten times over you would still not have enough to buy the Pleasure to display pictures.'

At that moment there came a shrill whistle from deep within the fane.

'Ah, we're ready. Bring them both inside,' announced the High-Bailiff. 'Now we'll get some answers. Soon you'll both be eager to talk.'

The men dragged their prisoners through the double doors that separated the vestibule from the main body of the fane. The bench-like wooden pews had been hastily pushed aside but two, placed close together to form a kind of bed, occupied the centre of the space. Fa Theum was roughly thrown down on to this on his back and his hands and feet were tied to the legs. To one side, two more pews had been pushed together to make a low table. This had been covered with a scarlet cloth upon which stood an ornate chest with many drawers and compartments that folded and concertinaed out. Alongside it, set out in a neat row on the cloth, were a variety of vicious-looking metal instruments. They were being arranged by a stocky dwarf no taller than Mel and dressed in an identical uniform to his companions but proportional to his stature.

'Are we ready, Mumchance?' asked the High-Bailiff.

In answer, the dwarf took a silver whistle attached to a chain around his neck and blew a hesitant note.

'No, you're quite right, of course we're not. We need some fire.' The High-Bailiff snapped his fingers at the henchman standing over Fa Theum. The man grabbed a spare pew and dashed it down hard on the stone floor, shattering it. He did the same with a second and heaped the debris together in a rough pile beneath a window. With his tinder box he set light to this. Thick smoke began to billow and the High-Bailiff shouted 'Chimney!' The man grabbed another pew and hurled it at the window, smashing it and allowing the smoke to escape.

Mumchance selected a couple of his instruments and approached the fire. Squatting down, he blew into it. Satisfied with the glow, he inserted his tools into the hottest part.

The High-Bailiff walked across to Mel again and bent down, grabbing his hair once more. 'Now, Smell, don't flatter yourself that you are the only artist here. My Mumchance is also an artist. A most exceptional artist. Aren't you, Mumchance?'

The dwarf looked up from the fire and smiled a smile that turned Mel's stomach. He twisted his tools in the glowing coals with his tiny, gloved hands.

'You have one last chance, Smell. Tell me, who gave

you permission to display these drawings? Let me hear it from your own lips.'

Mel gazed at the helpless priest, who feebly raised his head and shook it.

'Not going to answer me? Fine. Let's add another drawing to this little exhibition. Let's create an original Mumchance, why don't we. Are we ready yet?'

The mute dwarf blew a more positive blast on his whistle and withdrew one of his implements from the fire. It was a branding iron, its business end in the shape of an eye and now glowing red-hot. He spat on it and it sizzled.

Fa Theum's blood-stained cassock was ripped open by his guard, baring his pale and skinny torso.

There came a noise from the doorway. 'Mel, Fa, what's going on?' said Willem, come to search for his truant son. He was followed closely by his wife, fearful of the confrontation between her angry husband and Mel. They looked with horror at Fa Theum where he lay bound. Willem looked back at his son held there by the strangers and pulled Mabin to him.

'Ah, an audience. There's nothing I like more than

an audience,' said the High-Bailiff. 'Are you the father of Smell here? The resemblance is uncanny. There's something of the festering cesspit about both of you. A family trait, I'll warrant.'

'Let go of them. You have no right.' There was a tremor in Willem's voice.

'*No right?* On the contrary. I have *every* right. It's you who have no right. The only one who has less right than you is Smell here.' He jerked Mel's head hard.

Mabin stifled a sob.

'W . . . What are you going to do?' Willem had difficulty saying the words.

'What am I going to do? Well, first I am going to watch my little man here create his work of art. Then . . .' He released Mel's hair and looked at his hand quizzically before wiping it on his robe as if he were cleaning off something unpleasant. He placed a long, gloved finger to his pallid face and rolled his eyes in a showy gesture. '. . . Mmm, let me think. What *shall* I do? Shall I have this pair of miscreants nailed to a tree and whipped and let it go at that? No, that would hardly fit a crime as serious as the theft of a Pleasure.

Shall I hang them? No, not that either. Leniency was never my strong point. *I know!'* He held up his finger, pretending he had just had a brainwave. 'I'll send them to the mines on Kig! That's what I'll do. The old man won't last long, not in his present state, but Smell here,' he jerked Mel's head up by his chin, 'might last for years before the Coloured Death takes him. Who knows, he might even last long enough to pay for this stolen Pleasure. Not that it will matter to him. Not after a spell on Kig. Maybe I'll take you as well. And your woman. Make it a family affair. There's always room for more in the mines. The more the merrier, I say.'

Willem hugged his wife even closer. 'All the boy did was to pin up a few of his pictures.'

'All the boy did was to steal a Pleasure. And whose Pleasure did he steal?'

'Ambrosius Blenk's Pleasure,' came a deep voice. 'Let the boy go.'

Escape

'Dirk Tot,' said the High-Bailiff, recognising the voice and turning to regard the newcomer. 'I was wondering when you would turn up.'

'Adolfus Spute, you have no jurisdiction over these two. Release them at once.' Dirk Tot strode into the fane. His deep voice carried great authority and he seemed even larger and more imposing than Mel remembered. Mel's captor released him and retreated with the others towards the rear of the fane.

Adolfus Spute alone stood his ground. 'I represent the Fifth Mystery here and these . . . these *vermin* have stolen one of our Pleasures. They must be made to pay. Even the great Ambrosius Blenk must pay for his Pleasures. That's the law.'

'Oh, I quite agree. But, you see, Ambrosius Blenk has already paid for this Pleasure.'

'Poppycock!' Adolfus Spute dismissed the notion out of hand.

'Let me explain so that even your addled, pea-sized

brain can understand. This boy is one of Ambrosius Blenk's apprentices. And everything that Ambrosius Blenk's apprentices create belongs to Ambrosius Blenk. So, you see, this is actually my master's exhibition. Arranged, with great kindness I might say, by the good Fa. The same good Fa who you are treating so abominably. You are here on a fool's errand. Which seems fitting. Now let them go.'

The High-Bailiff sneered at Dirk Tot just as he had when he first saw Mel. Mel thought that was something he did to intimidate people but it was clearly having no effect on the giant. Mel's parents seemed mesmerised by the confrontation. The men-at-arms were in a state of indecision, caught between supporting Adolfus Spute and making a hasty escape. The tension was palpable.

'Let – Them – Go.' Dirk Tot enunciated the words very slowly. The two men stood like statues staring at each other. 'My outriders are with me. Shall I call them?'

The High-Bailiff narrowed his pale eyes and made a rapid calculation. On one side of his equation stood his intense loathing of this man. On the other, Dirk Tot's powerful master, the vast sums of money

Ambrosius Blenk paid the Mystery for his Pleasures and the influence he had with the Maven and the King. To that he added the outriders. Adolfus Spute blinked: the balance tipped. All he could do now was to try and save face. He rounded on his men. 'Why wasn't I told this Pleasure belonged to Ambrosius Blenk?' he bellowed. He kicked Mumchance in the ribs, sending him flying, and lashed out wildly with his staff at the others. 'Which one of you scrot-brained, cretinous, half-wits organised this excursion?' he screamed, the tone of his voice rising an octave as he became more and more incoherent in his rage. 'Which one?' His men, all too well acquainted with his vile temper, were retreating backwards as he advanced on them.

Willem went over and cut Fa Theum free. Mabin rushed to her son's side and held him close.

Mel was distraught. 'It's all my fault. It's my pictures that brought those men here. I nearly killed Fa Theum.'

'Hush, Mel, hush.' His mother hugged him closer.

'There's not a moment to lose,' Dirk Tot said to Mabin quietly. 'Take Mel out to my carriage at once.'

Mabin stared at the man, uncertain what to do.

'Now! Before it's too late. If we don't act at once all will be lost. Mel's life depends on it. Willem, do you know of a place where the Fa will be safe for an hour or two?'

Willem nodded.

'Good. Take him there and have someone tend to his wounds.' He looked towards the back of the fane where the furious High-Bailiff had cornered his men and was laying into them with his heavy staff.

'Come on, Mel, we must do as the gentleman says,' said Mabin as she tried to usher her son towards the door.

Mel turned to look at Fa Theum as his father helped the old man to his feet. *I shouldn't be leaving at a time like this. Leaving everyone to take the blame for what I've done.* Then he caught sight of the chest resting on the scarlet-draped pews and shrugged free from his mother. 'Wait, there's something I need.' He gazed in at the tools of torture and made to grab one for himself. He needed a weapon to make him feel less vulnerable. But they all looked somehow inappropriate, too specialised for self-defence. Then he spied a bodkin. *That's the one.*

'Mel, hurry.' His mother tugged at his sleeve.

There came a pathetic whistle from the back of the fane and, as everyone turned towards it, Mel grasped the bodkin, but as he tried to lift it out it became wedged. '*Come here!*' he tugged it hard and it knocked against the inside of the chest as it came free. There was a soft metallic ping and a secret drawer sprang open. Inside was a small decorated box. Without thinking, Mel grabbed that too and stuffed them both into his shirt.

'Mel, come *on*,' said his mother as she pulled him more forcibly towards the door and out to the carriage, which was now surrounded by villagers drawn by the screaming and the smoke pouring from the fane's windows.

Behind them, Dirk Tot followed them from the fane. 'Put Mel inside and make your goodbye quick,' he said to Mabin.

'*Goodbye?* But your outriders, surely they'll protect us?'

'I don't have any outriders,' confessed Dirk Tot.

'There's just me and my coachman. We only have moments before Adolfus Spute realises I was bluffing.'

'But you can't snatch Mel away from us like this,' said Mabin.

'Look, there's no choice. You saw what was happening in there. Mel must come with me to Vlam. It's the only way he can survive now. Say goodbye. As quickly as you can.' He turned away and said something quietly to his coachman, before disappearing back into the fane.

'Oh, Mel,' said Mabin as she helped him into the carriage. She cradled her son's face between her hands and wiped away the tears that were forming in his eyes with her thumbs. She pressed her handkerchief to his torn scalp. 'It shouldn't have been like this. Not like this.'

'I'll be all right, Mum,' Mel said, sounding braver than he felt. He gazed at his mother standing there and noticed a grey hair among her blonde tresses. *Why haven't I ever noticed that before?* He looked beyond her at the fane and the group of villagers, people he had known all his life. *They all look different too. Now that I'm leaving everything looks different.* 'Mum, you know that –'

'No time. We must be gone,' interrupted Dirk Tot as he joined Mel in the carriage, which dipped and groaned on its springs under his great weight. 'You will probably want these,' he said as he tossed the drawings from Mel's exhibition on to the opposite seat. He then sat alongside Mel, with the damaged side of his face towards him.

Mel's artistic eye no longer seemed to be working and he only saw the monster he had first encountered.

'Mabin, you and the villagers make yourselves scarce until those men leave. I'll send word as soon as we're safe in Vlam.'

'But Mel has no food, no clothes, no money. How will he survive?'

'Fear not. What he needs will be provided. Yan, drive on!'

Mabin held on to Mel's hand, running alongside the carriage until it was moving so fast that she had to let go. Leaning out of the window, Mel watched the familiar figure of his mother through the dust as she became smaller and smaller. He saw the tiny figure of his father join her. He attempted to see the expression on his face, to read him, but could not before they diminished as the carriage sped away. He wished he could have spoken with him to dispel the tension that had grown up between them. He saw his parents clutch each other, and his mother waved until they were eventually lost against the background of Kop. Soon, that too became so small it was impossible to discern individual houses. Then it vanished behind the trees.

The Mysteries

Mel had never experienced such a complicated flood of emotions as he then felt. There he was, hastening off in the finest transport he had ever seen with a rich and important man to begin a new life. A life where he would learn to do the thing which he loved the most. *Now that my dream's come true, why do I feel so wretched?*

'Here, Mel, let me look at you,' said Dirk Tot. 'Are you hurt? I can see some bruises and a nasty wound on your scalp. Any broken bones? You belong to the master now. He won't want damaged goods.'

Mel shook his head. He suddenly realised the danger he had been in and then, with a shock, the danger his parents and the whole village were still in. 'Those men . . . what are they going to do? Mum and Dad, will they be all right?'

'You've had quite a fright. Take some deep breaths.' Dirk Tot placed a reassuring hand on Mel's shoulder. 'Better?'

Mel nodded.

'Good. Now, I don't think that your parents – or anyone else – are in any immediate danger. If I know Adolfus Spute, as soon as he has vented his rage on his men he will be hot on our trail.'

Mel looked alarmed.

'But he won't catch us. Not without these.' He opened his good hand to reveal two greasy linchpins. 'I had Yan remove them from the rear wheels of his carriage. I reckon he might get as far as ten miles before they finally fall off. The only spares in Feg would be in Arpen and it would take a fast rider a day to make it there and back.'

'I don't understand any of this. Those men, what did they want?'

Dirk Tot turned his good eye to look at Mel. 'What do you know about the Mysteries?'

'Everyone knows about the Mystery. It controls weaving. Dad says that if he had more money he wouldn't have to make tabby. He could buy the Pleasure to weave fancy cloth.'

'That's just the First Mystery. The Mysteries do

rather more than that. Long, long ago, when Nem was just beginning to become rich and prosperous, all trade was unregulated and unscrupulous traders began to take advantage of their customers. Wine was watered, flour was bulked up with sawdust and all manner of shoddy goods were passed off as genuine. The honest merchants and artisans of Nem decided that this could not be allowed to continue. So they banded together and formed the Mysteries. If you wished to trade or produce any kind of goods, anywhere in the realm, then you had to be a member of your particular Mystery. Your work was carefully inspected before you were admitted and at regular intervals thereafter. The Mysteries only asked that their members pay a small tithe each year to cover the cost of seeking out the frauds and charlatans and policing the trade. Within a few years, the fraudsters had all but disappeared, the customers grew content and bought more and more goods from the members of the Mysteries.'

'If the Mysteries are so good, why does everyone in Kop always moan about them? And I still don't understand what this has to do with those men back there.'

'Well, over the years, things went wrong. In life there will always be men who only think in terms of profit, never in terms of value. Men who have no interest in what they claim to represent. I doubt if you will be able to find a single weaver in the entire First Mystery. Eventually, such men came to dominate all the Mysteries and under their control the Mysteries became increasingly corrupt. The tithes they demanded became bigger and bigger. When this form of income no longer satisfied, they came up with the idea of Pleasures. The bigger Mysteries began to gobble up the smaller ones until, eventually, only a few remained.

'Today they regulate all life in the realm beyond the bare necessities by their control of Pleasures.'

'So if Heck the baker wants to bake a new kind of cake he has to buy a Pleasure?' asked Mel.

'That's right. Or if a seamstress wishes to decorate a garment with a new kind of stitch, then she must buy that Pleasure.'

'So how many Mysteries are there?' Ever since he was small, Mel had always vaguely known that everyone's life in Kop was regulated by some shadowy authority far away.

'There are five, and each controls one of the senses. The First Mystery has dominion over touch and it controls, among other things, the production of cloth and tailoring – but that you already know. The Second Mystery rules over the sense of smell, and thereby the production of such items as perfumes and cosmetics. The Third Mystery concerns itself with the sense of hearing, and so with regulating all entertainment in the land. The Fourth Mystery is concerned with the sense of taste and its power lies over agriculture and the production and supply of food and drink.'

'But everyone eats food. I've never heard of the Fourth Mystery.'

'That's because the kind of food you would have been used to in Kop – bread, water, home-grown vegetables – doesn't come under their auspices. If things don't change, they probably will soon.'

'But . . .' Mel paused, confused. Suddenly the world

seemed huge and hostile. 'I still don't see what those men wanted.'

'That brings us to the Fifth Mystery, which you have just had the misfortune to encounter. Its domain is the sense of sight. It controls the use of colour and anything to do with it with an iron fist.' Dirk Tot's brow furrowed and his good eye narrowed. Beneath the scarred flesh of his face his jaw muscles clenched and unclenched. 'You will be seeing a lot more of it in the years ahead. The Fifth Mystery is the largest, richest and most powerful of all.'

'More powerful than the Fourth Mystery? You can't eat colour.'

'Oh, colour was just the beginning of its power. Its rise to power began when it discovered deposits of pigment on the island of Kig.'

'That's where that man said he'd send me.'

'Yes. And he meant it. Anyone who crosses the Fifth Mystery can end up there. On Kig the Fifth Mystery became expert at mining – and not only pigments. It discovered gold, silver, precious stones and other valuable minerals, which increased its wealth further.'

'I've heard they're valuable but you can't eat them, surely.'

'There are things even more valuable than gold, silver and gems. It expanded its mining operations and discovered the coal and gas that powers Nem today. When we get to Vlam you'll see what I mean. The Fifth Mystery's wealth is fabulous – certainly greater than the King's, the Maven's and the other four Mysteries combined.'

'So you're telling me the Mysteries are all bad?'

'Bad? As things stand, yes. There are a few, a very few, within the Mysteries who still hold true to their original ideals but their voice is weak.'

'But none of that explains why the Fifth Mystery came all the way to Kop. How did they know about me?'

'You flatter yourself, Mel. Adolfus Spute didn't know you existed before today. He came to Kop looking for me.'

'But why . . .'

'That's enough questions. You must be hungry.'

Mel had never imagined that there could be food

like the delicacies that the giant then pulled from a wicker hamper. There were richly coloured and delicately smoked slices of ham cut so thin they were almost transparent when Mel held them up to the light, and a great loaf of fluffy bread with tiny pieces of fruit in it. Even the water was alive with thousands of tiny bubbles that danced on his tongue as he drank it.

'Enjoying the picnic? We'll stop for something more substantial this evening.'

Mel's eyes widened. 'More substantial? That's the best food I've ever tasted.'

'You can eat very well in Nem – if you can afford the Pleasures.' Dirk Tot's tone had a bitter edge at the mention of Pleasures.

Afterwards, Mel began to doze, lulled by his full stomach, the warm day and the steady rocking motion of the carriage as it made its way across the rolling countryside towards Vlam.

Suddenly, he was jolted awake as the carriage stopped abruptly. They were in the middle of a thick wood and he realised he must have slept for some time.

The door opened and Yan stood there. He looked at his master meaningfully and then twitched his head, indicating something over his shoulder.

'Wait here and keep quiet,' said Dirk Tot sharply. 'Don't try and follow me.' He ignored Mel's questioning look and drew down blinds that blocked the view from the windows. 'And don't look out. You belong to the master now and must do as you're told.'

Mel was taken aback at the man's terse tone of voice. Was this the same man who had spoken so encouragingly about his drawings?

As soon as Dirk Tot slammed the door after him, Mel felt very alone. Sitting in the darkened interior, he became fearful that the High-Bailiff and his men had caught up with them. He remembered the bodkin he had stolen and fished it out of his shirt. He touched the box he had taken and explored its shape with his hand but left it where it was. That could wait. He grasped the sharp dagger firmly and sat very still, straining his ears for sounds of activity. One minute turned into two, and then two into five, and still Dirk Tot did not return. Mel gingerly lifted a corner of the blind. He saw only a green world full of trees. He strained his ears even more but heard only the wind. He slowly turned the handle and opened the door a crack. Seeing nothing, he opened it fully and stepped down. There was no one in sight; the road was deserted. Then, Mel caught the faint sound of voices on the wind. Mustering all the courage he could, he patted the horses and set off down the road towards the sound.

After a few yards, he came upon an overgrown track on one side of the road, leading into the wood. He heard the voices again, louder now, and turned down the track in their direction. He soon saw a ruined building ahead. Even though it was now decrepit and had obviously not been lived in for years, it had clearly once been much grander than anything he had ever seen in Kop, with fluted columns supporting the door and windows, and the still recognisable remains of coloured tiles set into the walls. He began to creep towards it. The walls were still upright and covered with ivy and brambles but the glass in the windows was missing, and only blackened, bare rafters showed where the roof had once been. He sensed movement inside and edged closer still. At the window he saw what he dreaded most. Three men, dressed in scarlet, were confronting Dirk Tot and Yan.

The Road to Vlam

Mel stood as still as a heron, his whole body tense. He strained his ears but heard only the wind whispering through the trees and the song of birds. His senses were now as alive as they were when he was drawing, aware of everything around him.

He edged further round the ruin until he saw the doorway. He felt sick with fear. He crept closer and saw that there was a sixth figure inside, dressed in the same deep blue livery as Yan. He appeared to be on their side. The odds seemed better now, but the Mystery men were sure to be armed and Dirk Tot still might need his help. He watched as Dirk Tot unfastened his reticule, withdrew what Mel guessed was a bag of money and some kind of folded document and handed them over to the men in red. *They're robbing him.* Mel struggled to control his too rapid breathing. He readied his bodkin in his sweaty hand and prepared to attack. Then, in a gesture that shocked Mel, Dirk Tot embraced first one man and then the others as if they were old friends.

The meeting broke up abruptly. Mel ducked down. There was no way he could get back to the carriage before the others. He let them pass his hiding place and then set off back through the wood at an angle he calculated would bring him out near the carriage. When it came in sight through the trees he saw that the three men were already there. Thinking quickly, Mel unbuckled his belt and emerged on to the road refastening it.

'Mel, where've you been?' asked Dirk Tot. 'I told you not to leave the carriage.' There was suspicion as well as anger in his voice.

'Just in there,' Mel lied, indicating the trees with a jerk of his thumb over his shoulder. 'That food was much richer than I'm used to. I had to go.'

Yan and the new man exchanged a smile but Dirk Tot stared hard at Mel. Then, as if giving him the benefit of the doubt, he said, 'Mel, this is Hennink,' indicating the other man. 'We just stopped by his house to pick him up so that he could share the driving with Yan. We've a long way yet to go. We'd best be cracking on.'

Mel did not feel quite so guilty about his deceit now that Dirk Tot was lying to him too. As it turned out, his was only a half lie, as shortly after their journey recommenced he felt a stirring in his bowels. The food *had* been rich. The steady rocking motion of the carriage that had so lulled him before had an altogether different and unwelcome effect now.

As evening approached, they halted at an inn and Mel was at last able to relieve himself. In his brief absence, Dirk Tot had arranged rooms for them all and ordered supper. The inn itself was bigger than Fa Theum's fane and much better furnished. The other customers looked at the odd-looking new arrivals with thinly veiled distrust. Mel also viewed them warily. Strangers rarely came to Kop and those that did were invariably dressed in tabby, the plainest, uncoloured cloth. There was tabby to be seen here but augmented with brighter, better-made garments. To Mel, tabby meant friend while coloured clothes increasingly meant foe.

Mel felt even more ill at ease as he sat down at the dining table. Dirk Tot looked at him as if he could read his thoughts. *Why had he said such bad things about the Fifth Mystery when he was one of them?*

When the hot food came Mel wolfed it down. 'Can I go to my room now?' he asked.

Dirk Tot nodded. 'It's been an interesting day – for all of us. We won't be long from our beds. There's another four days of hard travelling ahead of us.'

Mel had never had a room of his own before, nor a bed as large as the one in it. He could not believe how soft the feather mattress was and he was tempted to just lie down on it and sleep in his clothes but knew his mother would have disapproved, so he undressed. As he pulled off his shirt, the bodkin and the tiny box fell to the floor. He retrieved them, placed the dagger on the small table next to his bed and examined the box by the light of the candle. He remembered seeing something like it before. The factor who collected his father's cloth had one similar, although not nearly so ornate. It had contained a brownish powder that the man pushed up his nose to make him sneeze.

This box was made of some veined material that he had never seen before. Overall, it was as dark as old pewter but with murky swirls of colour. They seemed more natural than man-made, like the colours formed by oil on water. But they were not so natural that he could not discern the picture that was frozen within – the tiniest picture he had ever seen. It represented the inside of a cave, looking outwards. There were sharp rocks on the floor pointing upwards and others on the ceiling pointing down. Beyond the mouth of the cavern he could see a landscape, veiled in mist, stretching away to jagged, snow-capped mountains. There were stars in the evening sky but they described no constellation that he could recognise. On the cave floor a strange plant grew and in the folds of its leaves nestled an egg. Mel was astounded at the fine detail within the seemingly random swirls and tried to imagine how the material had been crafted to retain the image.

He turned it over in his hand but could see no way of opening it. He was about to give up when he pressed both ends at once and the lid popped open. There was powder inside it, all right, but this stuff was every colour of the rainbow all at once and glowed with a beautiful iridescence as he turned the box in the candlelight. *Perhaps I'm supposed to sniff this as well.* He raised the box to his nose experimentally but could detect only a faint, metallic odour. *Maybe it's something to eat, then?* It did not look especially appetising, but Mel licked his finger and dipped it into the powder. He put this to his tongue and tentatively tasted it. It was bitter. *Perhaps it's poison.* With horror, he remembered where he had stolen it from. He cried out and immediately spat it on to the floor. Mel then watched in amazement as the blob of multicoloured spit swirled this way and that on the bare boards and then seemed to writhe more purposefully. It began to form a miniature picture all by itself: a view of Kop! Mel felt a fleeting pang of homesickness. Incredulous, he grabbed the candle so that he could examine this marvel closer when there came a knock at his door.

'Mel?'

Mel just had time to snap the box shut, hide it behind his back and place his foot over the gently moving stain before Dirk Tot's face peered around the door.

'Are you all right? I thought I heard you call out.'

'Oh, it was just a spider. It startled me, that's all.' Mel was becoming a practised liar.

The giant looked at him for a few moments more and glanced around the low-ceilinged bedroom. 'You're not in Kop any more, Mel. You've got some growing up to do and you'd better do it fast. Goodnight.'

Hurt and angry, Mel wanted to answer back, *don't talk to me like that, traitor or I'll tell* . . . Who? He was not in Kop any more. He was all on his own.

As soon as the sound of Dirk Tot's footsteps had vanished down the hall, Mel removed his foot. There was now just a many-coloured smear on the floor. *Did I imagine it?* He was puzzled but also weary. He blew out his candle and climbed into the soft, clean-smelling bed. Sleep overtook him almost instantly.

In the morning there was no trace of the stain left.

Mel would have liked to examine his box and its strange contents further but the inns they rested at each night were busier so he had to share rooms with Yan and Hennink.

After they had been travelling for five days, there came a rapping on the roof and Yan's voice shouting 'Vlam ahead, sir.'

Mel looked out of the window. What he saw took his breath away. They had crested the brow of a hill, one of a long chain of hills that spread away in a great loop on each side all the way to the horizon. Nestled in the hollow within this vast natural amphitheatre were many farms, fields and orchards that became more and more numerous as they approached the centre. There, right in the middle, like an immense magnet drawing the world to it, lay their destination. Roads snaked towards Vlam from every direction, vanishing into the city walls through grand arches. These thoroughfares were crowded with people and vehicles – smaller than ants at this distance. The buildings that flanked these roads became denser as they neared the city until they actually appeared to climb up the walls in places. A wide river and many smaller canals entered through other, broader openings. Mel made out barges and sailing ships on them, going about their business. Yet more boats sailed high above them, entering on tall, stilted aqueducts over the city walls. Spaced at intervals around the walls were tall towers, on top of which were peculiar machines with articulated arms that moved up and down, left and right in odd, purposeful patterns. At the side of the road the carriage was on was a similar tower that seemed to be answering with movements of its own arms. They had passed others on the way there, too.

When he finally found his voice, Mel said, 'I never imagined anything could be so *big*. Vlam must be very old.'

'Some say it's half as old as the world.'

'Are all cities like Vlam?'

'I've travelled throughout the Seven Kingdoms but I've never seen its like.' Now that they were in sight of home, Dirk Tot's mood had lifted. 'You see those towering palaces?'

'Palaces,' repeated Mel. He never dreamed he would ever see a real palace.

'Those are the three Great Houses. To the west stands the House of Thrones, the palace of the King. You can see his purple banner. And there to the east, crowned with the golden diaglyph, is the House of Spirits. The other one to the north, the biggest of all, is the House of Mysteries.'

'Who lives in them?'

'King Spen lives in the House of Thrones and the Maven in the House of Spirits.'

'What, all on their *own*?'

Dirk Tot laughed. It was a deep, rich sound. 'No, Mel, not on their own. The King and his entire court and council live within the House of Thrones. The realm doesn't govern itself. The Maven is the spiritual leader of Nem. He has the Hierarchs, the Fas Major and lots of Fas Minor to keep him company. As for the Mysteries, well, there is a vast bureaucracy needed to keep *that* House and all its machinations functioning.'

Mel could make out the five banners of the Mysteries fluttering from a tower so tall it seemed to scrape the underbelly of heaven itself. The topmost banner, bigger than the rest, was scarlet, emblazoned with the same black eye emblem that Adolfus Spute and his men had worn. To Mel's mind the city did not appear man-made at all, but rather as a collection of weird structures built by colonies of insects, or accretions of seashells that seemed to owe allegiance to neither the laws of architecture nor gravity. These soaring, man-made wonders each stood atop a steep hill. From the flanks of these hills the rest of Vlam seemed to tumble down, its headlong fall only checked by the city walls, which seemed to hold it in and prevent it from spilling out into the surrounding countryside.

Unable to take his eyes from the spectacle, Mel asked, 'What're those hills called?'

'The hills are named after the palaces that stand on them. The Hill of Thrones, the Hill of Spirits and the Hill of Mysteries.'

As they descended the steep road, more and more of the architectural wonders became clear. Mel's flood of questions slowed to a trickle and finally ceased, so enthralled was he by the splendour of Vlam.

Little by little, the daylight leaked from the world and by the time they reached the city gates it was evening and lamps were being lit everywhere. The guards at the gates recognised Dirk Tot's carriage instantly and respectfully ushered him through, holding back the hoi polloi, who craned their necks to peer in at the occupants. The music of the wheels changed as they rumbled over the cobblestones of the city.

Mel had never seen so many people before in his entire life, and they all seemed to be busy rushing this way and that as if there was no time to lose. There was not a scrap of tabby to be seen on anyone. All of the streets were lit by lamps that burned within glass globes on top of tall, intricately fashioned posts. He saw buildings with their lower storeys open to the street. They were especially brightly lit.

'Why haven't those bright houses got proper walls?' he asked, baffled.

'They're shops, Mel. You know what shops are? They sell things.'

'Shops? I've never seen shops before. In Kop we make everything ourselves or barter with the other villagers for what we need. Once a year a tinker visits with pots and pans and stuff. We usually pay him in tabby. The people here must be very rich.'

'Some are, but not everyone.'

Mel rapidly became disoriented by the frequent twists and turns as they navigated the steep hills. At one point they crossed a wide river, although the bridge was so lined with shops and inns that at first Mel thought it was just another busy street. But from wherever he was in the city, Mel saw that the three Great Houses were always visible above the rooftops.

'Mel, come away from the window,' said Dirk Tot suddenly.

'Why?'

'Those men are from the Fifth Mystery. It's best you don't draw attention to yourself. And look, those others are members of the Fourth Mystery. And those are from the Second.'

From the darkness within the carriage Mel studied the people Dirk Tot had pointed out. People with the same arrogant air as the High-Bailiff but dressed in other colours and with different hairstyles. Mel saw that the citizens of Vlam would deliberately cross the street to avoid the men from the Mysteries and one man spat disgustedly in the gutter at their passing.

At length, their carriage turned into an imposing

square with tall, many-storied houses on each side and a huge, elaborate fountain at its centre, its many jets gurgling musically. The carriage aimed for the far side of the square. That side had narrow houses of five, six or even seven storeys, brilliantly lit from below by gas lights set into the walls. The architecture was intricate and made much use of herring-bone brickwork, tracery and coloured tiles. The steep, gabled roofs in particular were tiled in extravagant, geometric patterns with tall, barley-sugar chimneys in parti-coloured brickwork. The roofline was punctuated here and there with pointed spires and turrets and another of the odd towers with movable arms that Mel had seen earlier. Fierce-looking stone gargoyles projected from the carved eaves. At the centre was a building larger than its neighbours, the upper part of which was mostly devoted to an enormous clock surrounded by a multitude of small doors and windows. At that moment the clock struck the hour with a great, musical peal of bells. A procession of small, brightly painted mechanical figures appeared in the windows and filed out from the doors. As the clock chimed, minstrels played instruments, maidens danced, knights fought each other or chased dragons from one side of the timepiece to the other. Above them, bright planets and constellations whirled and pirouetted until the chiming ceased and they all disappeared back into the clock face. Mel, whose sole concept of time was gauged by the height of the sun, was awestruck.

'What's *that*?' asked Mel.

'It's a clock. It's one of the wonders of Vlam.'

'Who's it belong to?' Mel craned his neck to keep it in view as the carriage drew nearer.

'It's Ambrosius Blenk's clock. It's his house.'

'What about the others?'

Dirk Tot smiled his half-smile. For a moment he saw the mansion through the new apprentice's eyes. Everything must seem overwhelming and so very different to his life in Kop. 'All of the houses on this side of the square belong to the master. The other houses on the block behind belong to him, too. It's now one big mansion. The master has a large household, Mel, as you're about to see.'

Beneath the wondrous clock was a set of gilded

gates. They were obviously expected and as they approached the gates swung open and the carriage entered and passed through a tunnel into a large courtyard. Sure enough, what had seemed to be a row of individual houses from the outside was revealed as the facade of a single dwelling that occupied the entire side of the square. The courtyard was surrounded by a cloister and planted with low box hedges and flowering trees interspersed with stone sculptures. More lamps burned there, turning the twilight to noon. Servants in the same deep blue livery as Dirk Tot and his coachmen hurried to and fro. More could be seen busy within, silhouetted behind the tall windows. Grooms appeared and took charge of the horses. A footman opened the door and touched his forelock to the new arrivals.

Dirk Tot stepped out of the carriage but Mel held back. Now that he had finally arrived, he felt nervous and painfully aware of how shabby and unsophisticated he was. Everything was so grand, so alien, so coloured. *I look like a scarecrow. I'm never going to fit in here.*

'Come on, Mel. It's late.'

Mel swallowed hard, grabbed his precious drawings and stepped down from the carriage. Dirk Tot snapped his fingers impatiently. Mel held his drawings in front of him to hide his threadbare clothes and followed. He was so captivated by everything around him that he did not notice when he stepped in a mound of horse dung, before following Dirk Tot up a low flight of steps, under a pillared portico and into the mansion of his new master.

The long hall they entered was in the clock tower and rose above them the full seven storeys to a brightly painted and intricately beamed ceiling. The floor was paved with pale tiles in a huge, circular design now tainted with Mel's filthy footprints. The entire mansion was illuminated by gas lamps that burned with a gently flickering light in brackets attached to the walls. Before them rose a wide staircase that branched and divided into galleries around the space all the way to the top.

Then, in an instant, Mel's world changed. For the first time he came face to face with a great work of art. He had listened to Fa Theum's descriptions of paintings, but nothing could have prepared him for the raw thrill of actually seeing one. It seemed to him that it was not just lifelike but was even more real than the concrete objects all around him. It was as if he could step through the canvas and enter the immaculate world depicted there.

As he stared, he felt a great happiness enfold him. That happiness was deep but also scary as he felt the borders of his life expand until they stretched for ever. He knew then that he had come home.

The Apprentices

Mel stood transfixed at the foot of the stairs. There, just above him, at the head of the broad, first flight, on a great crystal throne, sat an enormous, robed figure with the head of a giant eagle. In its clawed hands it held a golden harp and an uprooted fruit tree with roots formed from writhing snakes. To one side stood a priest with the head of a boar and on the other a priestess with an ox's skull. Gathered around the feet of this trio prowled a multitude of fearsome, hybrid creatures. Among them was a many-spined fish that sprouted bat's wings, a giant mouse with a scorpion's tail, a multi-hued kingfisher with a human head and a part-toad, part-unicorn monster. Above them soared more strange and wonderful birds and insects than Mel could count. They all gazed down at the new arrival with a piercing, unblinking and malevolent stare.

'One of Ambrosius Blenk's. Impressive, isn't it?' Dirk Tot's voice jolted Mel from his ecstasy.

'The master did that? *Really?*'

'Really. Look, Mel, it's late and I must report. Minch will look after you now.'

As Dirk Tot strode away through a side door, Mel looked up at the fat servant. He did not need to be told that Minch did not like apprentices – it was evident in every pucker of his sour expression.

'Shoes,' said Minch curtly.

Mel tried to lower his drawings and hide his scarecrow shoes.

'*Shoes.*'

He followed the man's imperious gaze down to his own feet and, with a sinking feeling, saw the muck he had trailed into the mansion. 'Sorry.' He blushed and quickly removed them.

'Follow,' ordered Minch as he set off up the stairs. With his back to the new apprentice, he smiled to himself at the lad's discomfort.

Mel padded after the liveried servant in his bare feet. As they reached the painting he paused to examine it more closely. The technique was so perfect it was hard for him to accept that it had been created by a human hand. Up close there was even more detail visible than from below. There was no trace of brushwork or of anything to distinguish it from the texture of the reality he saw all around him. He lowered his gaze to his own drawings which, in comparison, seemed pitiful and meagre.

Movement attracted his eye. At the foot of the stairs he saw a young girl, probably no older than he was, on her hands and knees with a bucket and soapy scrubbing brush, attacking the mess he had created on the tiled floor. She looked daggers at the boy who had caused her this unwanted and unpleasant work.

'*Boy!*' snapped Minch and gestured brusquely for Mel to follow. They climbed the stairs and turned down one corridor after another until Mel was hopelessly lost.

'Stop,' ordered Minch. 'Wait.' He produced some keys and unlocked a store room. He looked Mel up and down before pronouncing, 'Small.' He entered the room and soon emerged with a pile of clothing. 'Kit,' he announced as he piled a shirt, doublet, hose and boots in the household colours on top of the drawings Mel cradled..

Mel stood for a moment with his jaw hanging open. 'Are these for me?'

Minch sighed. 'Come.' He set off again at once, Mel half-running to keep up. More corridors and more stairs followed until they arrived at a door through which Mel could hear the murmur of many voices. Minch pushed open the door and, in what was for him a great flood of verbosity, announced, 'Refectory. Apprentices,' before turning and leaving.

Mel found himself looking into a long, brightly lit room with a coloured mural running around the walls. This depicted a panoramic scene of harvesting, fruit-gathering, hunting and fishing. Here and there were comic alterations by various hands – a hunter with a hugely elongated nose, a plough-horse with five legs, a haystack with doors, windows and a chimney and so on. Running down the centre of the room was a long oak table, around which sat a dozen apprentices on wooden benches with their half-finished suppers before them. They all wore anarchic additions to their livery such as coloured caps or patterned scarves or sashes. All of their clothes bore paint stains. There was an evident hierarchy in the refectory, with the younger apprentices at the end of the table nearest the door and the older ones at the other. Seated in the place of honour, furthest from Mel at the head of the table, was the eldest of all. He was skinny and much taller than everyone else, his spotty face in need of a shave. He alone sat on an ornate, upholstered chair.

As Mel stood in the doorway the conversation ceased. All eyes were upon him. The head apprentice took a long draught from his goblet and wiped his mouth with the back of his hand. He wore a bright red bandanna tied around his head, from beneath which escaped strands of dark hair, and there was a large wine stain on his shirt beneath his open doublet. He had a rat-like, pointed nose and tiny grey eyes, above which ran a long, single eyebrow. Slouching back in his throne-like chair, he asked in a slurred voice, 'What've we here? Wash your name?'

Mel smiled and introduced himself, 'Melkin Womper. But everyone calls me Mel. Pleased to meet you.'

There was a moment's silence and then they all bellowed with laughter.

'A Fegie, we've got ourselves a Fegie! We've never had a Fegie before.'

'I do believe you're right,' sneered the eldest apprentice. 'Our very own country bumpkin. Look at what he's wearing – it's *tabby*. And he's barefoot. Have you ever seen anything like it? And where did a shoeless, tabby-wearing Fegie get the wherewithal to buy an apprenticeship with old Blenko?'

'I didn't buy it. It was a free one,' answered Mel.

'*It was a free one,*' mocked the other in a poor imitation of a Fegish accent. 'And what makes you so special? What're those?' He had spotted Mel's drawings and pushed his right-hand companion roughly. 'Bring it here, Bunt. Let me see.'

'It's not bad, Groot, it's actually not bad,' said Bunt admiringly as he retrieved a charcoal portrait of Mel's mother from under the new clothes Mel carried and handed it to the head apprentice.

'You don't know what you're talking about, Bunt. It's rubbish,' proclaimed Groot, giving it no more than a cursory glance. 'Fegie there wouldn't be capable of producing anything but rubbish. I doubt if his hands have held anything finer than a plough or pitchfork. Still, it's nothing that a few strokes from a real artist couldn't improve.' He dipped his finger into the gravy on his plate and childishly wrote 'Fegish rubbish' across the drawing.

'Hey! Don't do that.'

Groot ignored Mel's plea. 'There now. What do you think?' He held it up for the other apprentices to admire. When no one answered him he grabbed the nearest apprentice viciously by the throat and asked again, 'Well, Jurgis?'

'It's Fegish rubbish, Groot,' answered the lad in a strangulated voice.

'Let's hear it from all of you,' said Groot, releasing Jurgis.

There came an unenthusiastic murmur of 'Fegish rubbish' from around the refectory.

'It's better than you can do,' mumbled a boy about Mel's age, sitting at the foot of the table.

Mel looked down at the mumbler. He had very pale

skin and dark hair. His hazel eyes had a dejected look that matched his hangdog expression.

'What did you say, Ludo?' asked Groot. 'Let's all hear it.'

'I said it's probably the best he can do.'

'That's right . . . What's that smell?' asked Groot.

Bunt approached Mel again and saw the shoes he was carrying. 'It's Fegie, Groot. His shoes are covered in scrot.'

'Ugh, that's *disgusting!* But what more can you expect from a Fegie?' Then to Mel, 'Perhaps you're used to that smell where you come from but it's not allowed in *my* refectory. Ludo, take him out and get him cleaned up. I don't want to see either of you again until he's dressed properly and smelling like a human being. Here, *Fegie*, take this with you,' he said, flinging Mel's defiled drawing back at him before taking another great swig of wine and belching loudly.

'They call me "Fegie" as if it's an insult,' said Mel, balancing his new clothes and drawings as Ludo led him away. 'None of us have the choice where we're born.'

'Think yourself lucky. It could have been worse. They could have smelt your shoes before they heard your accent.'

Mel laughed. 'I guess Fegie doesn't seem so bad, after all. So those are the other apprentices. I can't say I think much of them.'

Ludo laughed with him. He was taller than Mel and his demeanour was lighter now that they were out of the refectory. 'They're OK, once you get to know them. But they're scared of Groot. He's a bully and a snob. Watch out for him. And his sidekicks, Bunt and Jurgis. They can be vicious – especially when they're drunk.'

'Isn't he, you know, a bit old to be an apprentice?'

Ludo gave a dismissive laugh. 'Tell me about it. He should have graduated years ago. But when the time comes each year to present the master with his apprentice piece he always comes up with some excuse or other.'

'What's an "apprentice piece"?'

'It's a painting that we all must produce on our own at the end of our apprenticeship, before the master passes us as journeymen.' He looked at Mel. 'You don't know what a journeyman is, do you?'

'Afraid not.'

'It's like a junior artist but without apprentices. The truth is, Groot's not that good. He's lazy too, prefers to spend his time boozing and gambling rather than working. The master would like to boot him out but the trouble is, he's a Smert.'

'What's a "smert"?'

'It's not a thing. It's his name. Groot Smert.'

'What's so special about that?'

'Don't you know anything? The Smerts are only one of the most powerful families in Vlam, that's all. They're related to the Brools and the Sputes.'

'Not the High-Bailiff?'

'The same. Groot's his nephew. What's the matter? You've gone as white as a sheet.'

'It's . . . it's nothing. It's just that I've met Adolfus Spute.'

Ludo and Mel mounted some stairs. 'So the master gave you a free apprenticeship then. You must be good. May I see?'

'I don't know. Groot said it's rubbish.'

'You don't get it, do you? If it *was* rubbish he would have ignored it.' Ludo took some of Mel's new clothes so he could look at a drawing. 'Wow! This is great, Mel! Groot couldn't draw like this until he'd been here years.'

A broad grin cracked Mel's face.

Ludo pushed open a door. 'This is the dormitory. You can sleep there, next to me.' He indicated a vacant bed in a kind of compartment formed by three low, wooden walls lined with shelves and cupboards. There were identical units along the length of the room. 'You can stash your stuff in there,' he said, opening one of the cupboards and placing the clothes inside. 'And look here.' He knelt down and showed Mel where a board was loose at the back, revealing a shallow space. 'Great for hiding things you don't want the others to see.' He winked at Mel. 'You can pin your drawings up next to your bed, we all do. I'll fetch some drawing pins while you get changed.'

Mel quickly discarded his coarse tabby garments and changed into his new livery. They were indeed the finest clothes he had ever worn. The shirt and the hose were made of white silk, the doublet of the softest deep blue velvet and the ankle-boots of supple doe-skin. He stroked the velvet, relishing its luxuriant texture.

Mel folded his old clothes and placed them inside his cupboard. As an afterthought, he secreted his bodkin and little box in the cache he had been shown, pushing the box especially far down so that only an arm as small as his could retrieve it. He laid his drawings on the bed, placing the defaced portrait of his mother to one side. It was ruined beyond repair. With a few strokes of his hand the malicious Groot had turned a thing of beauty into no more than a piece of stained paper. It was as if he had assaulted Mel's mother. Mel felt a stomach-churning mixture of rage and sadness.

'Don't you look smart? Almost like one of us,' said Ludo as he returned. 'But you need to add something of your own that sets you apart from the other servants. Like this here.' He touched the olive-green and gold sash around his waist. 'It's the colours of the Cleefs – my family's house.'

'Your family has its own colours? You must be awfully posh.'

'No, not really. Certainly posher than Groot – not that it counts for anything round here. Not while he's in charge.'

'I know!' said Mel. He reached inside his cupboard, pulled out his faded, tabby breeches and tore off a wide strip. Tying it around his waist, he said with a sense of pride, 'It's the Womper family colours.'

'Great! That's one in the eye for Groot.'

The two of them pinned his drawings up around his bed.

Ludo picked up the portrait of Mel's mother. 'I'm really sorry, Mel. That was a squity thing to do. Even for Groot.'

Mel could not respond because a great lump had formed in his throat. He placed the drawing in his cupboard. He felt tears forming but did not want to embarrass himself in front of his new friend. Changing the subject, he said, 'I'm starving.'

'I guess you don't want to go back to the refectory. Let's sneak down to the kitchens. It's strictly out of bounds but Wren will give you something to eat. But first, I think we'll get rid of these.' He picked up Mel's smelly shoes and, holding them at arm's length, dropped them out of the open window. 'If only Groot was as easy to get rid of.'

'There she is. Psst! Wren. *Wren*,' called Ludo softly from their hiding place. Heat and bright light radiated out of the bustling kitchen into the cool, dimly lit storeroom, washing a long, orange-tinted patch on the flagstones.

'Who's there? Is that you, Ludo?' came a girl's voice from beyond the door.

'Wren, this is Mel. He's new here and he's missed his supper. He's starving – could you find him something to eat?'

'You know it's not allowed, Ludo. You shouldn't be down here. And if they catch me then I'll be out on my ear. We both will.' She peered cautiously over her shoulder and, seeing that she was unobserved, stepped into the storeroom. 'And who's this new . . . *you!*'

It was the girl Mel had seen earlier, cleaning up the mess he had created in the hallway. She was slim and wore a long cloth wrapped around her head like a turban. A strand of auburn hair had strayed from this and she tucked it back with a work-reddened hand. She had green eyes and her cheeks were bright with exertion. Over her long dress in the Blenk household blue was a soiled, white pinafore. *When she's not scowling she might be quite pretty,* thought Mel. 'Uh, hello,' he said sheepishly. 'Sorry about the . . . the you-know-what.'

'Why should I risk my job to get anything for *you* – after all the work you made for me?'

'But, Wren, he's really hungry. *Please,*' pleaded Ludo.

Wren glared at Mel, but after a moment her expression softened and she said, 'Oh, all right. You look half starved. Wait here. And keep quiet. If they catch you there'll be big trouble.' She disappeared into the kitchen and returned shortly with a generous sandwich containing a thick slice of succulent beef and an apple. 'I must go now. We're rushed off our feet at the moment. Just stay out of sight.'

Mel had only ever eaten beef once before, at a village feast. It tasted even better than he remembered but he only managed one bite.

'Caught yer, thief!' A plump woman grabbed him by the scruff of his neck and held him fast. 'Minch, Minch! Come and lend a hand. I've caught a thief.'

Mel looked round quickly for Ludo. Shelves around the walls were stacked with large earthenware crocks and glass jars containing all kinds of preserved fruits. The elongated, stick-like reflections of Mel and the cook were mirrored in them. Garlands of onions and garlic hung alongside dried peppers threaded on strings. There were pungent cheeses as big as grindstones and pyramids of eggs. Large sacks of root vegetables and flour were stacked against the walls and from the ceiling hung great hams, dried sausages as big as Mel's arm and brightly feathered poultry. The storeroom was packed with everything: everything except Ludo.

'What're you looking fer? Is there more of yers down here, stealing from me? *Eh?*'

Mel shook his head. *Where was Ludo?*

Minch emerged from the kitchen, wiping his greasy mouth on his sleeve. He grabbed Mel's arm. ''Prentice,' he said. He snatched Mel's sandwich away proclaiming, 'Proof.'

'It's off to the steward with you, my lad,' said the cook. 'This could mean prison. I've seen people sent to the mines for less. Yer no better than a guttersnipe. The gutter's where yer belong and that's where yer'll be before tonight's out. Mark my words.'

Mel's heart sank. *Ludo, please help.* A great feeling of dread overtook him. *Arrived and expelled on the same day.* How could he face returning home with so great a shame hanging from his shoulders?

As he was marched away between Minch and the cook he looked around and just caught sight of the toe of a boot as it withdrew behind some sacks. *Ludo.* The first sign of trouble and he'd left Mel alone to face the music.

Mel was marched up to the steward's office. Minch knocked and they entered.

Dirk Tot looked up from his papers. 'Yes?'

'Thief,' said Minch, pushing Mel forward. Then 'Proof,' as he slapped the illicit sandwich on to the desk and 'Witness', indicating the cook with a jerk of his thumb.

'Is this so?' asked Dirk Tot, addressing the cook.

'Yes, sir. Caught him red-handed, I did. Freshly baked bread and some of the best beef, straight from the spit. An' this!' she said triumphantly, producing the apple as if it were the clinching piece of evidence.

'Is this true, Mel?'

Mel hung his head and nodded.

'Very well, Cook, Minch. I'll deal with this. Please return to your duties.'

'Just so long as he gets what's comin' to him,' said the cook as she left.

''Prentice,' said Minch with a sneer, as if it were an insult. He cast a last, longing look at the sandwich and closed the door after them.

Dirk Tot fixed his withering one-eyed stare on Mel and said in a stern voice, 'Is there anything you want to tell me, Mel?'

Still staring at the floor, Mel shook his head, 'No, sir.'

'Was there anyone else involved?'

Mel said nothing.

'Mel, there have been hundreds of apprentices through the studio in my time, and more than a few of them have stood where you're standing now for all manner of misdemeanours. But not after so short a stay. That's some kind of a record, I must admit. I cannot really believe that after only a few hours in this household, you made it all the way down to the kitchens, found where the bread was kept, helped yourself to a fat slice of the master's best beef, from the spit in the very heart of the kitchen and then found yourself the means of preparing this sandwich. All on your own. Come on, Mel, who else was in this with you?'

Mel raised his head. *Scrot to you, Ludo.* 'No one, sir. I just found my way there by . . . by accident and took the food. All on my own.'

'Very well. You've disappointed me, Mel. Cook wanted you punished and punished you will be.'

Lord Brool

Later, Mel found his way back to the dimly lit dormitory. Everyone was busy retiring for the night and paid him no attention. From the far end, where the elder apprentices slept, there came the sound of heavy, drunken snoring. As Mel sat down on the edge of his bed, Ludo's face appeared over the partition that separated their compartments.

Great. Now *he turns up.*

'Sorry, Mel, I tried to warn you when I spotted Cook coming,' Ludo whispered sheepishly. 'I only just had time to hide myself. It was a close thing, I can tell you. There was no point in the two of us getting caught, was there? It's not as if the punishment would have been halved if two people had to suffer. Besides, you're new here. They'd be bound to make allowances. You didn't say I was involved, did you?'

'Don't worry, Ludo, I didn't mention you.' Ludo had let him down but he was still the only friend he had in that strange new world.

'Thanks. You're a pal. If my family ever heard of this I'd really be in for it. By the way, what did you get? As a punishment.'

'One month's loss of privileges and stipend, whatever they are.'

'Privileges are permission to go out and about in the city every Sunday. The stipend's like pocket money. It doesn't amount to much though, only one silver piece per year.'

One silver piece sounded like a fortune to Mel, who had only ever seen copper coins – and never too many of those either.

He undressed and climbed into bed, feeling miserable and betrayed. Then he thought about his parents and Fa Theum and hoped that they had not suffered any more at the hands of Adolfus Spute following his flight. He was still puzzled by his father's behaviour. He wished he had had time to talk with him before Dirk Tot had whisked him away. And then, perhaps a little too quickly to be wholly comfortable, his thoughts turned to his new life. He would have the opportunity to study the many paintings that hung around the mansion. One day he would even create some of his own. In spite of his hunger, he drifted off to sleep with a smile on his lips.

At the same time, high in one of the lofty towers of the House of Mysteries, a heated meeting was taking place. Adolfus Spute and his dwarf Mumchance, both weary and travel-stained, cowered before the huge bulk of Lord Brool. The Lord-High-Master of the Fifth Mystery sat, toad-like, at his desk. Behind him, the window overlooked the still-busy city a thousand feet below. A single lamp illuminated Lord Brool's face grotesquely from beneath with its flickering, yellowish glow. This served to emphasise his warts and the gross features that seemed too big for his already substantial face. His huge shadow loomed on the ceiling above him, making him appear even more massive. The corpulent Master was angry; very angry.

'*Lost it!* What do you mean, *lost* it?' he bellowed. Flecks of spittle hung at the corners of his mouth. His complexion almost matched that of his scarlet robes and somehow managed to seep through the thick cosmetic whiteness of his face. The silver goblet of wine he was holding buckled in his grasp.

'It was definitely with us when we arrived in Kop. Wasn't it, Mumchance?' Adolfus Spute glanced nervously at his diminutive companion for support.

Mumchance raised his silver whistle to his lips to pipe his assent, but only got halfway before he thought better of it and merely nodded.

'Yes it was. But after we packed away the Instruments of Interpellation it no longer seemed to be there, in its hidey-hole. It was, in a word, *gone*,' the High-Bailiff confessed.

'It was such a simple task, Spute; I could have sent a child to do it. Perhaps I *should* have sent a child. An infant could not have made more of a mess than you incompetents have done. All you had to do was pay a visit to that meddling fool Floris and persuade him to return the Fifth Mystery's property. He's no longer the governor of the Coloured Isles and no longer a member of the High-Council. He had no right to keep our property.'

'Just so, cousin.' Adolfus Spute hoped that playing

on their kinship might help to mitigate his superior's ire. 'But, if I may be so bold as to venture a thought, a mere observation; Lord Floris was most reluctant to be parted from the substance. He needed to be persuaded to within *an inch of his life*. Could a child have achieved that, I ask myself?'

Lord Brool was unimpressed. His tiny eyes bored into his subordinate. 'Your persuasive powers, Spute, are not in question. That is, after all, your job. What *is* in question is your trustworthiness. To *misplace* such a treasure. That seems to me more than careless, more than unfortunate. It seems to me almost disloyal. Disloyal to the point of treachery. The Fifth Mystery expects more from its servants. It expects much more. Do I make myself clear?'

Adolfus Spute's mouth was moving but no words were coming out.

'So, seeing as it was you who lost it, it only seems reasonable to expect that you should restore it before the next meeting of the High-Council. Otherwise, we might review your current position.'

'But, my lord . . .' Finding his voice again, Adolfus

Spute began to protest, but then recognised that he was in no position to object. 'As your lordship wishes.'

'And you have yet to explain exactly what you were doing in such a god-forsaken province as Feg in the first place. If I thought that you were pursuing your own, private ends – your personal vendetta against Dirk Tot, perhaps?'

Adolfus Spute's mouth dropped open.

'Oh, I know all about the history between you two, Spute. I know that you've been trying to entrap him for years. I also know that he's thwarted you at every turn. It must be galling to be bettered by only half a man. It makes you seem such an ineffectual High-Bailiff. Perhaps I should also bring this to the attention of the High-Council. We would take a very dim view of such dereliction of duty on the part of our High-Bailiff.'

Adolfus Spute swallowed hard with an audible gulp.

'Do I make myself clear, Spute? I'm sure I do. Now, get out! And don't let me see you again until you have it back.'

As he reached the relative safety of the anteroom

and his two waiting henchmen, Adolfus Spute rounded on Mumchance and kicked him viciously, bowling him over. 'You were in charge of that, you snivelling fraction of a man. How could you have let it out of your sight?'

Mumchance picked himself up and raised his whistle to his lips.

'No, I don't want to hear it. There's nothing you can say in your defence. It may have been hidden but it wasn't hidden well enough. Was it? It's gone and that's all there is to it. And it's me that is to be held responsible – *me*.' He chewed at the fingers of his glove in frustration.

Mumchance blew a note.

'Yes, it had all been going so well. We expected Floris to be reluctant to surrender the substance, didn't we? Did you see his face when we started to smash his precious tick-tocks? He was almost in tears – over a collection of *clocks* of all things. It was so gratifying. I almost thought that you wouldn't need to spell out exactly what would happen to his family if he didn't surrender it. But you did. And he did.'

Mumchance blew a trill that might have been laughter.

'What? Of course I was going to keep some for myself. It's me who should be Lord-High-Master, not that beslubbering, toad-featured scut in there.'

Mumchance's tiny eyes twinkled and he blew a triumphant note.

'You're right, "*Lord* Spute" does have a certain ring to it.' The High-Bailiff bared his yellow teeth in a smile. The effect was repulsive. Then it vanished and his face darkened. 'But now I'm right back at square one. I need to get my hands on it all over again.' He looked down at Mumchance. 'Now, where do you suppose it went?'

The dwarf blew a positive blast.

'Yes, that's what I thought, too. There are only two people who could have taken it and my money's also on Smell. If Half-Face had it then we'd know about it by now. Oh yes. Half-Face would never be able to resist using such a powerful weapon against me. So it's all down to the Fegish runt.'

Mumchance piped a tuneless warble.

'Succinctly put, my murderous midget. There's no chance of getting our hands on Smell while he's under Blenk's protection. That old fool's too rich, too powerful and has too many important friends. He's been a thorn in the side of the Mysteries for far too long. So, the question is, how do we prise that particular winkle from its shell?'

Mumchance's whistle blew again.

'Great minds think alike, my little man. The Fegish boy might be induced to leave the mansion if I chose the right bait.' He turned to his henchmen. 'Unfortunately, I need this malodorous cretin here with me for the time being. But you two are looking a bit peaky, a trifle run-down. I think you could do with a holiday. In the country, maybe. I hear Feg is rather lovely at this time of year. And while you're there, why don't you look up some old acquaintances of ours in Kop – the Womper couple and that disgusting old priest, Theum. I'm sure they would love to see their darling little boy again. We'll organise a family reunion.'

Ambrosius Blenk

The sound of the great clock striking eight echoed through the mansion.

This is it! The start of my new life as an apprentice. Mel smoothed his hair, straightened his smart new livery and peered around the studio door. Morning light flooded the large, whitewashed space from several skylights highlighting a multi-coloured pox of paint stains on the bare floorboards. There were working drawings pinned around the walls, along with several small canvases depicting details of the large unfinished paintings he could see propped on the massive easels at the far end of the room. Most of the apprentices he had met the previous evening were busy, the elder ones at easels and the younger ones at workbenches. Even at that early hour the studio was a hive of activity. Despite this, hardly anyone spoke and the air of concentration was palpable.

'The master will be here soon,' said Ludo. 'I need to get on with my work. Take a look around until Groot gets here and tells you what to do.'

Mel stood in the middle of the room, drinking in the goings-on and the intoxicating, alien smells. The other apprentices acknowledged him with nods of their heads. One even smiled at him.

Emboldened, Mel approached and looked over his shoulder. 'Did you do that?' he asked in a tone of awe.

The boy stopped working and swivelled the drawing of a unicorn round so that Mel could see it better. 'I wish. No, it's one of the master's. Don't touch it. It's not fixed yet. My name's Henk, by the way.'

'My friends call me Mel.'

Mel watched full of admiration as Henk confidently drew a grid of small squares all over the drawing like a net, dividing it up into many regular boxes. Next to him, on his workbench, he had a much bigger sheet of paper with a grid of the same number of correspondingly bigger squares drawn on it. Into these he carefully copied the contents of each of the smaller boxes, and soon had a larger version of the master's original sketch.

'I wish I was that quick,' said Mel.

'You will be soon. It's just practice. This is called graticulation,' explained Henk.

Graticulation. It instantly became Mel's second-favourite word.

'Using this technique you can enlarge a drawing to any size you like.'

'Or reduce it,' said Mel, instantly seeing the possibilities.

'Turn the squares into oblongs and you can even distort things.'

'That's *amazing.*'

Mel wondered what task he might be given. *Probably something simple like mixing paints.* He could see another apprentice near the door shaking some green powder into a mortar. He began to grind it with a pestle.

'What's this?' Mel raised and examined a glass jar containing the bright pigment.

'It's malachite. It must be ground really fine before –'

Just then the door burst open, sending Mel flying, and spilling the colour in a great, long slash across the floor. He crouched there, the dot at the end of a green exclamation mark.

'*Fegie!* I might have known it. You clumsy little scrot!' snapped Groot. 'Do you realise how much that pigment's worth? You won't last long around here. Not if I have my way.' He looked pale and sickly.

'Clean it up, Fegie. I can see that you're going to be a *great* help in the studio,' said Jurgis. 'Jump to it!' He aimed an unsteady kick at Mel, but missed and almost lost his balance. He looked no better than Groot.

'It wasn't his fault,' said the apprentice with the pestle.

'Oh? If it wasn't his fault then it must have been yours, Teck. It certainly wasn't mine. Perhaps you should clean it up, eh?' said Groot, grabbing the boy's ear and twisting it cruelly. 'So, whose fault was it?'

'It was Mel's fault,' said Teck, grimacing with pain.

'*Whose* fault?' Groot twisted his ear harder.

'Fegie's fault.'

'That's better,' said Groot, releasing him. 'Now, clean it up, Fegie.'

'That's servant's work. Let the cleaners do it,' said Teck as he nursed his sore ear.

'Thanks for reminding me, Teck. That kind of work's only for household scum. I expect you'd much rather be using a brush, wouldn't you, Fegie?' asked Groot.

'Yes,' answered Mel. 'I thought that's why I'm here.' He set the empty jar back on the workbench.

'I'm so sorry, Fegie. Do forgive me.' Groot half bowed to Mel. 'Bunt.' He snapped his fingers. 'Fetch the new apprentice a brush, if you'd be so kind.' He winked at his crony.

'Here you are, Fegie,' said Bunt, returning with a domestic brush and pan. 'You fit the bill of household scum, all right. Now get on with it. Do as you're told, unless you want to feel my boot.'

Mel sighed and knelt and began sweeping the spilled pigment into the little pan.

'Hung-over. *Again*,' explained Teck in a low voice as Groot and his cronies sauntered down the studio and took up their positions in front of the easels.

'The master's coming,' said Henk.

The master! At last, I'm going to meet him. Mel hurried

to finish collecting the expensive pigment. He decanted it back into the jar, then noticed some he had missed. He disappeared under the workbench on his hands and knees and came face to face with a tiny pink face surrounded by a shock of pure white hair. The face stared at him with wild pink eyes, bared its pointed teeth and hissed loudly. Startled, Mel jumped up and banged his head hard against the underside of the workbench. The glass jar tottered and then fell, covering one side of the snowy white monkey, for that is what it was, in bright green pigment. Mel saw a pair of stubby hands with thick fingers and jewelled rings appear and grasp the monkey, gently lifting it.

'Albinus, my lovely, what has he *done* to you?' said an agitated woman's voice.

Mel gazed out from under the table. All around, the apprentices were staring at him, horror-struck. There, right in front of him, stood Dirk Tot with a group of important-looking people Mel had never met before. The agitated woman was stout, and so richly dressed that Mel instantly thought of a midwinter tree bedecked with glittering glass baubles and tinsel. An enormous, stiff lace collar framed her face, atop of which sat the biggest hairdo he had ever seen. Yet more jewels were interwoven into her red curls. Her face was thickly made up and her cheeks heavily rouged. She cradled her now parti-coloured pet in her arms. It was divided almost exactly in half, one side white, the other green. *What have I done? She must be the master's wife!*

On her left was a woman in the household blue, whom Mel assumed was her lady-in-waiting. To her right stood a liveried secretary who carried a kind of small desk in front of him suspended from a strap around his neck. Between them stood the man Mel knew must be the master.

Mel's first impression of Ambrosius Blenk was that he looked very old and very young, both at the same time. He was tall and slim and had a long grey beard that hung over his elegant black robe like a hairy waterfall. The garment was covered with arabesques of fine silver embroidery that sparkled as they caught the light. Around his waist was tied a sash in the deep household blue and he wore a tight-fitting black skullcap that extended over his ears. He also wore a white, stand-up collar but one less flamboyant than his wife's. From beneath busy eyebrows two of the most piercing, blue eyes Mel had ever seen darted back and forth between him and the monkey, finally coming to rest on the new apprentice. Then, to Mel's astonishment, he winked at him.

All the while, the master's wife was becoming more and more agitated as she fussed over her pet. 'So you are the Fegish boy,' she said. 'Well, Green-Knees, what have you to say for yourself? What do you mean by mutilating my beautiful Albinus, eh?'

Mel gazed down and saw that his new white hose was stained by the pigment he had knelt in. 'I'm . . . I'm very sorry, Mistress,' he stammered as he got to his feet. 'I can bathe him, perhaps it'll wash off.'

'Wash off? Wash off! That is the finest Kig malachite. It costs its own weight in gold. It's not intended to merely *wash off*! If it did we'd want our money back, wouldn't we, Ambrosius? It's permanent. He's stained for life, thanks to you.'

Mel looked around anxiously at the many faces

staring at him. He came to rest on the master's face and was sure he saw amusement in his eyes. He might even be smiling beneath his beard.

'By my giddy aunt. Quite remarkable. Womper, isn't it?'

'Yes, Master.' Ambrosius Blenk – *the* Ambrosius Blenk – was actually speaking to him!

'Tell me, Womper: are you familiar with the southern rainbow-ape? Related to the harlequin-mangabey? From the Pyrexian jungles, the home of the carnivorous butterfly and the tree-dwelling crocodile.'

As Mel heard the names of these exotic creatures, ideas – dozens of them – began to ricochet around in his imagination; ideas for a whole new menagerie of fantastic creatures.

To the master the outward signs of inspiration were unmistakable. He *was* smiling beneath his beard. 'No? Never mind. I have a likeness of one in my bestiary. You must take a look at it sometime. There's much else in there that will appeal to you. You'll find basilisks and catoblepas and chichevaches and cockatrices and the crocotta and –'

'Albinus, you're rambling again,' interrupted the mistress.

'Sorry, my dear. Now, where was I? Oh yes, the rainbow-ape. Well, this creature has a most singular pelt. The patterning is remarkable. It has a russet crown with a parti-coloured body. In particular, the under parts and the tip of the tail are pale whilst the rest of the body is blue-black. In mature specimens the under parts often become stained with tree moss, giving it a greenish tinge – hence the name. But I have never seen a monkey with such colouration as this.'

'I'm truly sorry, Master. For the accident.'

'Sorry? What on earth are you sorry for? This is pure serendipity, Womper. We must talk more when I have time. I've seen your work; it's interesting stuff. Very promising. Once you get some technique at your fingertips you'll flourish. Here's a silver piece for you, you've made my day with this happy accident.' The master patted Mel's arm and looked over to another of his apprentices. 'Ah, Henk, how's my unicorn? Grown up, has he?'

Mel stared at the silver coin in his palm.

'What are you gawping at?' said the mistress. Then to Groot, 'Put this . . . this, *mutilator* to work at once. Before he creates any more damage. And keep him away from the paintings until he has found at least a modicum of coordination.'

'As you wish, Mistress. I'll see that he understands his duties and doesn't get into any more mischief. Come along now, young fellow, let me show you how you can help.' The head apprentice placed a protective hand on Mel's shoulder and led him away.

When they were out of earshot, Groot leant close to Mel and hissed, 'Oh, you've really done it now, Fegie. Albinus is the mistress's favourite pet. You've really landed yourself in her bad books. Just because old Blenko's taken a shine to you, you needn't think you'll be getting an easy ride. And give me that. All gratuities belong to the head apprentice.' Groot snatched Mel's gift away and dug his nails viciously into Mel's shoulder. His tone changed as the master and his entourage approached. 'Well now, young Mel, what can I give you to do to help?'

When they had gone, Groot said to everyone, 'OK, you scrot-stains, the show's over.' Then to Mel, 'All right, if you're so good let's see how well you can draw. I want you to draw water.' Mel's face betrayed the briefest flash of hope. 'Oh no, Fegie. You can forget all about doing *that* sort of drawing. I want you to take that bucket over there down to the little courtyard behind the kitchen and draw enough water to fill it. Then, I want you to carry it up here and begin to clean all of the stains off of this floor. When it's clean to my satisfaction I'll see about the next stage of your *education.*'

Mel soon found out that artists' colours made stains that were almost indelible. Throughout the long day he toiled down the mountain of stairs between the studio and the pump in the mean little courtyard and then back again. Every time Ludo managed to get close to Mel to offer him encouragement Groot would order him back to work. On each visit to the courtyard Mel had to pass Cook, who could not hide her delight at his treatment. On one of his trips he caught sight of Wren but she, too, was being kept busy and could only exchange a sympathetic smile as their eyes met.

The great clock struck six as Mel reached the top of the stairs at the end of yet another knee-trembling, arm-numbing climb and was met by a thunderous wave of apprentices as they hurried from the studio.

'Come on, Mel. Supper time,' shouted Ludo. 'I'll meet you in the refectory.'

Mel felt as limp as his mop-head. As he tidied away his cleaning tools, he heard a noise coming from the storeroom that opened off the studio. Curious, he crept over to the doorway. Mel had caught tantalising glimpses of this room during the day. To him it seemed like an Aladdin's cave, packed as it was with every imaginable type of art instrument and material. There were large chests with shallow drawers containing paper in a great variety of colours and weights, and shelves crowded with exotic oils and pigments. Large pots contained every kind and size of paintbrush arranged in fans like flower displays, and long rolls of canvas and stacks of wooden stretchers leant against the walls.

Mel saw all this again but only with his peripheral

vision, for amongst all of this was Groot. Mel crept into the room and hid himself behind a chest. From his hiding place he watched as Groot fiddled with a cabinet mounted on the wall. He had a long, bent piece of wire which he was poking into the tiny keyhole. After several attempts he managed to pick the lock and open the door. Arranged on shelves inside the cabinet were small glass jars of pigment. Mel guessed that they were amongst the most costly of colours kept under lock and key on account of their value. On a table to one side there were several small sheets of paper. Groot took one of these and rolled it to form a cone. He took one of the jars and shook a quantity of pigment into the cone before folding the top and bottom over to make a parcel. He repeated this with other pigments. When he had finished he closed the cabinet and manipulated the wire until it was once again locked. He concealed his parcels inside his doublet and, pausing to make sure no one was around, he left, closing the door to the storeroom behind him.

He's stealing pigment! Mel stood up from his cramped hiding place and flexed his aching legs. He approached the cabinet to examine it more closely, then heard the noise of footsteps outside. He turned to see the door handle turning slowly and the door begin to open with a soft creak.

The House of Mysteries

Mel only just had time to hide again before the huge form of Dirk Tot entered the storeroom. He went straight to the cabinet and unlocked it. He took down one of the glass jars and shook it gently, examining its level. He then took a phial containing a similar pigment from his reticule and tipped it into the jar. He repeated this several times with other coloured pigments, replenishing the material Groot had taken. This task complete, he relocked the cabinet and left.

Mel did not understand the scene he had just witnessed. *Groot's a scrotty thief. No surprise there. But why is Dirk Tot covering up for him?*

Mel was the last to arrive in the refectory. He ignored the Fegie-baiting from Groot's end of the table and sat down. A plate with a huge portion of rabbit stew was placed before him, much larger than everyone else's. He turned and saw Wren serving.

She leant close and whispered, 'Thanks, Mel. For not telling on me. I can't afford to lose this job. Now, eat up. You look like you could use it.'

Mel noticed that Ludo did not seem pleased with the supper menu.

'What's up? Lost your appetite?'

Ludo looked sick and pushed his plate aside. 'Rabbit for supper always spells bad news for the junior apprentices.'

'I thought rabbits were lucky. Their feet, anyway.'

'If you think scrubbing the floor's bad, just wait till tomorrow.'

Puzzled, Mel glanced at Henk and Teck for an explanation. They said nothing and just smiled knowingly to each other.

The next morning, the weather had changed and a dense fog clung to Vlam. With the omnipresent landmarks of the three Great Houses hidden in the thick, swirling greyness, the narrow streets became anonymous and labyrinthine.

Mel awoke on that dismal morning and looked forward without enthusiasm to the prospect of continuing his cleaning of the studio floor. Against all the evidence of his aching limbs, he had hardly made any difference. However, when he and Ludo arrived in the studio, Groot, who was on time for once, had something else in mind for him.

'Leave that, Fegie,' he ordered. 'I have something that's more urgent for you and Ludo. Get on down to the kitchen courtyard. Ludo knows what's to be done.'

Ludo groaned. 'Told you supper was bad news.'

Perplexed, Mel followed his morose friend down to the courtyard where some servants had built a fire. Above it, suspended from a stout metal tripod, was a large, iron cauldron filled with water that was slowly heating.

'Well, you wanted to be given something to do with making pictures and it looks like your wish has come true. We're to make size. I hope you're happy,' said Ludo.

'What's sighing got to do with pictures?' asked Mel, puzzled.

Ludo rolled his eyes. 'Not sighs, *size!* It's a kind of glue. Before a canvas is ready for painting it must be prepared with a coat of size, so that the paint won't soak into the fabric. Then more size is mixed with gypsum to make gesso.'

Mel looked confused. 'Gesso?'

'You know, the white ground on the canvas. It also helps to fill in the weave so that it's flatter and easier to paint on. They must have run out,' he added gloomily.

Mel could not see why Ludo was so disheartened. 'So, what do we need to make size?'

Ludo took out his handkerchief and tied it around his nose and mouth. He lifted the corner of some old sacking that covered a pile in the corner. 'This,' he said.

A cloud of flies rose up and the two boys reeled back at the sickening smell of a large heap of rabbit skins.

'That's disgusting!' Mel took out his own handkerchief and copied Ludo. From all around the courtyard came the sound of windows and doors closing.

'The water's boiling,' said Ludo. 'Grab a pitchfork and help me transfer the skins to the cauldron.'

When the nasty task was complete, Ludo handed

Mel a paddle. 'Here, you must stir the brew. Just keep it moving.'

'What about you? Aren't you going to help?'

'I've got to clean this mess up.' Ludo grabbed a broom and a bucket of water and began to scrub the gory stains from the cobbles.

Mel's arms were already beginning to ache. 'How long must I keep stirring?'

'Till it's done. Use the ladle to skim off the scum as it forms on the surface. It needs to be the consistency of syrup before it's ready. And make sure you keep the fire fed. It must be kept boiling. I've just got something to finish in the studio. I'll be back soon,' said Ludo as he left.

Within a very short time, Mel wished he was back scrubbing the studio floor. The rank steam from the cauldron got into his hair and into his clothes until he was dripping wet. Stirring the ripe brew as it thickened made his arms ache far more than any scrubbing could have.

Ludo only reappeared at midday.

'Where've you been? I thought you were supposed to help me.'

'Sorry. Groot found something urgent for me to do in the studio. Here, I got you a sandwich.'

Mel was not altogether sure he believed him. He raised the sandwich to his mouth and lowered it again.

'What's the matter? Aren't you going to eat it?'

'It stinks! It smells just like the size.' Mel threw it, untouched, on to the fire.

'Ludo!'

The boys turned to see Dirk Tot standing in the doorway, a handkerchief covering his mouth. 'Take over, will you? Mel, come here. I have an important errand for you.'

Mel smiled to himself.

'First, go and see Minch. Tell him I sent you and that you're to have a new set of clothes. Then you must wash – try and rid yourself of that smell. You're to go to the House of Mysteries and present this warrant for cinnabar pigment at the commissary. Guard it well, it's very valuable. Now, is that clear?'

'The House of Mysteries?' The idea of another meeting with the Fifth Mystery filled Mel with dread. 'How do I get there?'

'You must take a tramcar. A number sixty-one. Here.' He knew that Mel was nearly illiterate so he had inscribed the number clearly on a sheet of paper. He told him where to find the tram stop and gave him the fare. 'You can't mistake the House of Mysteries – it's the biggest building in Vlam. If you get lost anyone can point you in the right direction.'

A little later, Mel, washed and dressed in his new clothes but not smelling very much sweeter, found himself in the foggy square outside the mansion. He made his way to the busy tram stop and boarded a tram with a number that matched his piece of paper. After he had travelled only a few stops he had the entire car to himself as the other passengers had dismounted, driven away by the strong smell that clung to him. Only the conductor remained, behind his glassed-in driving position. He occasionally looked back at his sole passenger with annoyance.

Mel listened attentively each time the conductor rang the bell and shouted out the names of the various stops but he did not hear the name of his destination. He soon lost all track of time and imagined himself exploring the city once he had regained his privileges.

'All change. End of the line.' The conductor's voice shook Mel from his reverie. He looked up just in time to see the conductor step down from the cab and disappear into the fog. He was quite alone and absolutely unsure of where he was. He stepped off and looked around for someone to ask directions from but the place appeared to be completely deserted and in no time at all he was totally lost in the narrow streets. Mel sat down on a doorstep to think what to do next when he heard footsteps. He caught sight of two strangers wearing red robes emerging from the fog. *Fifth Mystery men!* He shrank back into the doorway and the two men walked past without seeing him. In a flash, he realised that they must be going to the House of Mysteries. Cautiously, he began to follow them.

Sure enough, they soon approached the veiled form of a huge building, punctuated here and there with faint points of lemon yellow where lights from windows penetrated the swirling greyness. They were reflected palely on the damp cobbles of the street. It was easily the biggest building Mel had ever seen. A larger rectangle of light briefly appeared when a door was opened and closed as the two Mystery men entered the building. Mel dashed up after them but found the door locked. *At least I've found the House of Mysteries*, he thought.

It seemed oddly deserted for such an important place. Mel began to follow the wall, hoping to find the door to the commissary. Eventually, a thin sliver of light appeared, which resolved into a door standing ajar when he reached it. Mel pushed it open and stepped inside.

The deep, repeated boom of a drum filled the air. Mel found himself standing on a gantry halfway up the wall in a cavernous building. Below him, he could see many men in scarlet robes milling about. In the very centre, and occupying most of the vast area, were two giant treadmills powered by a great many men inside. The towering wheels were rotating in opposite directions and hauled fat cables that wound around their circumference. Periodically, exhausted men were freed from the treadmills and others took their place without the speed of rotation diminishing. All the while, the drum boomed monotonously, dictating the pace of the wheels. Mel instantly realised that these men and the treadmills powered the trams. He shuddered as he looked closer and saw that the men were chained hand and foot and were prisoners.

'Oi, what're you doing here?' Mel spun round at the sound of the voice. Confronting him was a tall man dressed in the uniform of the Fifth Mystery.

Mel backed away involuntarily. 'I'm sorry but I'm lost. I'm new to the city. Please, is this the House of Mysteries? I'm looking for the commissary.'

'I don't believe you, you're miles from the House. You're a spy. What're you really doing here?' The man grabbed Mel roughly by the arm. '*Yargh!* You smell dreadful.' He released him quickly and reached for his handkerchief.

'No, honestly. I'm looking for the commissary. See, I've got a warrant here for some pigment.' He withdrew the document from his doublet and showed it to the man.

Whether the man was convinced of his explanation or simply wanted to be rid of the obnoxious smell, Mel was escorted brusquely to the door and pointed in the direction of the Great House. He began walking and soon heard a clanking sound, followed before long by a subdued groaning as a line of chained men in ragged clothes materialised from the fog, headed in the direction of the building he'd just left. Mel stood aside to let them and their scarlet-clad guards pass in the narrow street. They were obviously replacements for the poor wretches in the treadmills.

'Hey, you there,' said a quiet voice. 'Apprentice. Blenk's boy.'

'Silence. No talking back there!' yelled one of the prisoners' escorts.

Mel looked around for who had addressed him.

'Yes, you,' said the voice even more softly. One of the prisoners was looking at Mel from the corner of his eyes. He was trying to speak without moving his lips. He was filthy with matted hair that might have been auburn underneath the dirt. He had a scar across the bridge of his nose. The half-starved prisoner stared at Mel with hollow, haunted eyes.

'How did you know I'm one of the master's apprentices?' asked Mel.

'You're wearing the most famous livery in Vlam. Do you know Wren? She's about your age, works in the kitchen.'

'Yes,' said Mel, surprised. He fell into step with the line of prisoners. 'She's my friend.'

'Tell me, is she well? How's she looking?'

'She's well. But how do you know her?'

'Can you take her a message —?'

'Who's talking back there?' One of the guards was walking briskly back down the line.

The man began to speak quickly. 'Tell Wren I love her. I think of her all the time. Tell Wren her father said to . . . to look in the night.'

Mel took to his heels and ran off at the guard's approach. Behind him, he heard the sound of a man being beaten. Shaken, he ran on blindly until he saw some lights appearing through the fog. He was back at the tram. The conductor had returned from his tea-break and was climbing into the cab. 'Excuse me,' said Mel, slightly out of breath. 'I thought that this tram went to the House of Mysteries?'

The conductor paused and climbed back down.

'Not this tram, son. From here at the South-East Winding Shed to the river. That's my route.'

'But I was given this number. Look.' He showed the man the paper Dirk Tot had given him. 'It's the same as yours.'

'So it is, number nineteen, right enough,' the conductor said, examining it. 'But wait a mo; it could also be sixty-one.' He turned the note upside down. 'Now, a sixty-one goes right past the Mysteries. Hop back on. I'll tell you where to change.' He caught a whiff of Mel. 'But do me a favour, son. Ride on the running-board outside, will you?'

Mel fretted about the delay in getting the urgent pigment during the two tram journeys that eventually set him down outside the House of Mysteries. The scale and splendour of the structure was obscured by the fog, otherwise he might have lost still more time ogling the man-made wonder, which he had only seen from afar until now. He ran up the steps towards the imposing entrance.

'And just where do you think *you're* going?' A doorman barred his way.

Mel showed him the warrant.

'Side door. The commissary's at the *side* door. How many times do they have to be told? I don't care if you are one of Blenk's apprentices, civilians are not allowed in the front. Whatever next?'

Mel reached the side door and entered. He found himself in a long corridor punctuated with arches that overlooked the city. The corridor curved upwards in a sweeping incline around the outside of the building. Presently, he came to an open door and entered it to find himself in a long room lit from high above by a row of gas chandeliers. All along one wall was a long, continuous bench seat of mahogany beneath a wall-length mirror. On the bench sat customers awaiting their goods. Facing it was an equally long and high counter of the same dark wood, lit by more gas lamps. Behind it, on shelves that reached up to the ceiling, were arrayed thousands of huge glass jars in weird designs, containing pigments of every imaginable colour, including a few that the fascinated apprentice had never guessed existed.

As Mel advanced into the commissary, the

customers waiting on the bench slid away from the unwelcome odour surrounding the newcomer.

'Yes?' The man in charge eyed Mel over his half-moon spectacles.

'I'm to give you this,' said Mel nervously. 'It's for some pigment.'

'The young scut here says he wants some pigment. Have we got any pigment in at the moment?'

'All gone. Tell him to come back tomorrow,' said his assistant, as he measured out a quantity of orange pigment into a complicated set of brass scales.

'What's all that then?' Mel pointed to the shelves where another man rolled back and forth on a wheeled ladder. 'Please, it's really, *really* urgent. I've got to . . . You're teasing me, aren't you?'

The man in charge shook his head. 'Give it here then.' He leant forward to take the proffered warrant. '*Poo!* You smell worse than you look.' He snatched the document and quickly retreated. 'Go and wait outside. You'll be called when it's ready.'

Mel went out into the corridor to stand by one of the large arches, open to the air. The first puffs of a breeze that threatened to blow the fog away ruffled his hair and made him feel less uneasy about being there in the headquarters of the Fifth Mystery.

That same breeze wafted along the corridor, insinuating its invisible tentacles into clefts and crevices and into the ventilation shaft feeding fresh air down through the building into the chambers below. In one such chamber, which might be blackly described as Mumchance's studio, the breeze oozed out of the ventilator, carrying with it the disagreeable odour of rabbit-skin size. It swelled to fill the room.

'What's that smell?' asked Adolfus Spute, wrinkling his stubby nose.

A negative note from his whistle indicated that Mumchance did not know either.

'It can't be our friend here,' said the High-Bailiff as he lifted the terrified head of a securely bound man, Mumchance's latest sitter. The hapless clerk had taken to adding an extra flourish to his normally plain copperplate script without having bought the Pleasure. 'We haven't even begun on him yet.

Men!' He shouted for his assistants.

Mumchance's whistle.

'Yes, you're quite right, of course I did. How forgetful of me. I sent them to Kop to collect our guests, didn't I? We'd best go and find out for ourselves. What *is* that stink?'

'Red mercuric sulphide!' The completion of an order was announced in the commissary. 'Where is the wretch? Red mercuric sulphide!' When no one came forward the man bellowed at the top of his lungs, 'Red mercuric sulphide! Cinnabar for Blenk!'

Mel realised that they were calling for him and rushed back in. 'That's for me!' A parcel was pushed down the counter. He tucked the valuable pigment into his doublet and hurried back the way he had come.

'It's getting stronger. It's definitely coming from this direction.' The High-Bailiff and his companion hurried along the corridor leading up to the commissary. 'Whatever is that . . . *Smell!* How nice to see you again.'

Mel froze. The High-Bailiff and Mumchance stood there, blocking his way. He suddenly felt very cold.

'So we meet again. Just when we thought that we faced a dreary afternoon, you've brought some colour into our lives.'

Mumchance wiggled his eyebrows and fingered his scarlet robe.

'You're an artist, come on down and inspect Mumchance's studio, why don't you? Come and sit for your portrait. We've got a nice, comfy chair for you to sit in. He won't recognise himself after the sitting, will he, Mumchance?'

Mumchance smiled and piped a long note on his silver whistle. He and the High-Bailiff moved closer.

Mel wished he had his bodkin or some kind of weapon. *But I do have this!* He withdrew the parcel and flung the powdered cinnabar in their faces. Adolfus Spute screamed and Mumchance doubled up, both coughing and clawing at their eyes. Mel turned and began to run back up the corridor, but the commissary servers emerged and barred his flight.

'What's all this? Where do you think you're going?' they said.

Mel looked to his right, at the open arcade, but escape was impossible that way. It was high above the street; the fall would surely kill him. To his left was a closed door. In desperation, he lunged at it and it swung inwards. It opened on to a stairwell with one flight of steps that led upwards and another down. There was a scuffle of feet behind him as his pursuers reached the doorway.

With no time to think, Mel took the down staircase as a hand grabbed his collar. He half-turned and saw the High-Bailiff's face, now stained red and contorted with an inhuman fury. Two bloodshot eyes beamed hatred at him. 'I know you took it, Smell. It's mine, you thief. It's mine, and I want it back.'

Terror supercharged Mel's energy and he wrenched himself free and plunged down, the sound of feet close behind him. He reached the foot of the stairs and turned left, right, left again as he tried to throw his pursuers off his trail. *They mustn't catch me. They simply mustn't.* Mel had a fleeting vision of a long row of

Mumchance's surgically sharp instruments laid out on their blood-red cloth. They glinted, pain-bright, in his mind's eye. *No!* Mel forced the image from his mind. He ran down a long, dimly lit gallery hung with large paintings. He stole a look over his shoulder. He could see no one in the gloom but he could hear the drumbeat sound of running feet coming ever closer from behind. The tattoo merged with the pounding of his own blood in his ears. Then he heard more running feet, this time from in front, doubling the rhythm. *I'm trapped.* He skidded to a halt in front of one of the paintings. Panting, he pressed his back to it. *There's no way out. It's all over.*

Secrets

Everything went black as a sack was thrust over his head. Strong arms grabbed him and heaved him backwards. Abruptly, the sounds of pursuit ceased and were replaced by birds singing. He could hear wind blowing through trees and, somewhere nearby, the gentle tinkling of a stream. He felt the warmth of sunshine and, beneath his feet, grass. This sudden transformation was, in its own way, as frightening as the High-Bailiff and his pack.

'What're we going to do with him now?' said a man's voice.

'Shut up, I'm thinking,' said another.

'*Yech!* Have you smelt him? We should have left him out there,' said the first voice. 'We don't need this. He's not our problem. Let's slit his throat and dump him back. One more body in the House of Mysteries won't matter. They wouldn't even notice.'

There was silence for a while. All Mel could hear was the sound of his own rapid breathing, which was getting faster.

'Listen to him, he's hyperventilating. He's going to croak soon anyway. Let's slit his gizzard and be off.' It was the first voice again.

'I told you to shut up.'

The sack was whisked off Mel's head and he received two sharp slaps to his face in rapid succession.

'Are you all right, lad?' said the other voice.

Mel was blinded by the sudden light, but the shock of the blows did what it was intended to and slowed his breathing. He blinked rapidly and gradually came to his senses. Then he wished he was back inside the sack. He screwed his eyes tight shut. *I'm in the dormitory. I'm in bed; I'll wake up in a moment. I'm having a dream – a very, very weird dream.*

But he was not.

When he opened them again he was still in a forest glade serenely lit with beams of clear, golden light. In the distance were snow-capped mountains, and birds with bright plumage wheeled overhead. Nearby, a unicorn grazed – a *real* unicorn. It looked up briefly and blinked its languid eyes at Mel. He was in a perfect landscape. Not just perfect, *more* than perfect. There was not a leaf or a blade of grass that was out of shape. Everything was in exactly the right place and perfectly lit. Mel shook his head. It was all too much. His legs turned to jelly and he collapsed heavily on his bottom.

'What've you done now? He's seen where we are. We'll have to kill him.'

'Are you all right, lad? Speak to me.'

Mel looked up. *It's not a dream. I've gone mad.* The man bending over him was green: the colour of grass. His hands and his fingernails were green. His skin and his hair were green, as were his teeth. Even his eyes were a paler shade of the same green, with dark green pupils. This was so bizarre in itself that Mel did not notice his strange clothes or the weird piebald creature with a tattooed face clinging to his shoulder.

'He's in shock,' said the second man. Mel looked at him. He was blue. *This isn't possible. I'm hallucinating.*

'Of course he's in shock. So would you be. What's your name, lad?' the green man asked.

Mel just looked at him, uncomprehending.

'Your name. Who are you?' He spoke softly and shook Mel again gently.

'M . . . Mel. Melkin Womper.'

'How long have you been Ambrosius Blenk's apprentice, Mel?'

'How do you know . . .?' He then remembered the livery he was wearing. 'Just a couple of days. I got a free one.'

'What's he talking about, "a free one"? He hasn't been there long enough, he can't know anything. Now he's gone and seen us. Let's do him and dump the body back out there. We need to get out of here,' said the blue man, drawing his knife.

'No one's going to do anyone. Not while I'm in charge. Put that knife away. If Adolfus Spute and the Fifth Mystery are after him, then he's on our side. Can you stand, Mel?'

Mel nodded. Unsteadily, he got to his feet.

'Well done. Now we're going to take you somewhere where it's safe to release you but I'm going to have to put the sack back on your head. It's for your own good.'

Mel briefly fought back panic as he was blindfolded again. The last thing he saw before the sack was placed back over his head was a softly shimmering and undulating wall of mist that rose up, sheer, from the grass to the sky just a few feet from him. Then they began walking rapidly, Mel guided by the firm hands of the two coloured men.

They walked for what seemed like a long time across country. They climbed hills and clambered down steep inclines, picking their way over fallen branches. Once, the temperature dropped suddenly and they skidded across a broad expanse of ice. Then it became warmer and they were in some inhabited place where he heard music and the sound of many voices. And then back into some countryside. Eventually, they halted.

The green man spoke. 'Right, Mel. I'm going to let you go now. When I take the sack off you won't be in the House of Mysteries, you'll be somewhere else. You won't be in any danger but you mustn't linger. You must go straight back to Ambrosius Blenk's mansion. Do you understand?'

Mel nodded.

'And you can never talk about this. Not to anyone.

Otherwise my mate really will slit your gizzard. OK? Now, close your eyes.'

Mel was gently thrust forward. He felt a tingling sensation all over and he sensed that the air around him changed again. The sack was lifted off his head.

'Goodbye, Mel. And remember, not a word.'

Mel opened his eyes. He was standing in a strange room. In front of him was an open door with a short flight of steps leading down to a busy street. He turned around and saw that he was standing in front of a large painting. Before he had a chance to study it he was interrupted.

'I'm sorry, my son, but the House of Spirits is not open to visitors.'

The House of Spirits? I'm back in Vlam! Mel turned to see a young, brown-clad priest walking towards him. He was smiling and his shining diaglyph sent reflections dancing around the walls.

'I'm sorry, Fa . . .'

'Ah, I see you're one of Ambrosius Blenk's apprentices. Well, we sometimes allow you to come here and study the Maven's paintings but you must make an appointment first.'

'Excuse me, Fa. I'm new here. I only arrived in Vlam a couple of days ago. I'm lost. I must get back to my master.'

The priest escorted him to the door and pointed across the wide, man-made valley at where the rooftops sloped down from the three hills to the centre of the city. 'Ambrosius Blenk's mansion lies at the very heart of Vlam. The fog's lifted now and you can see the Great Houses. When they're equidistant, you'll be near home. Now take care.' The Fa waved him goodbye.

It was long after dark when the footsore boy arrived back outside his master's mansion. Above him, the clock chimed midnight and no amount of knocking brought anyone to answer the door. The gates to the courtyard were also locked. Weary to the point of exhaustion, Mel walked around the block, trying to find someone to let him in through one of the side doors. He felt hopeless as he began a second circuit. Then he heard his name being called.

'Mel. Up here.'

He looked up and saw Wren at a second-floor window.

'I'll come down and let you in.' A short while later, he heard bolts being shot and a nearby door opened. Wren was not wearing her pinafore or turban and her long auburn hair hung loose about her shoulders. She looked altogether different. Less like a servant and more like she lived in the splendid house.

'Mel, where've you been? You look done in. The house has been in turmoil. They were on the point of calling the Watch to go and look for you. But I knew you'd come back; I waited up for you.'

'Wren, you won't believe what happened to me. First I got lost and then I was chased and *then* –'

'Slow down.'

'But I have a message for you.'

'For me?' She laughed nervously.

'From your father.'

'My *father*. You can't have met him. He's . . .'

'A prisoner of the Fifth Mystery. Honestly, Wren. I'm not making this up. He has a scar, here, on the bridge of his nose,' said Mel, touching his own.

Tears welled up in Wren's eyes. 'Oh, Mel, did you *really* see him? Where?'

'Near the South-Eastern Winding Shed. He was with some other prisoners and I think they must have been taking him to work in one of those big wheels that pull the trams about. He looked . . . OK.' Mel could not tell his friend that her father looked wretched.

Her crying changed into a sad-happy smile. 'This means that he hasn't been sent to the mines. There's still hope.'

'Why's your father a prisoner? What's he done?'

'Done? What do you have to do to fall foul of the Mysteries? *Nothing*, that's what! You know the great clock on the front of the mansion? Well, my father made it *and* the one at the House of Thrones *and* one for the Governor of the Coloured Isles *and* others. He's made clocks for all sorts of important people. He's the greatest clockmaker in Nem! The Mysteries – all of them – hated him because time didn't belong to any of them. You can't touch it and you can't smell it. You can't hear it, taste it or see it.'

'There's no Pleasure attached to it.'

'None. No one could make a profit from time. So they made up some kind of crime for his not having the Pleasure of time. No one ever knew what it was or which Mystery was responsible. They just came and took him away one night, about three months ago.'

'I'm sorry, Wren, I had no idea. I didn't mean to upset you.' He touched her arm in a gesture of comfort.

'We used to have a nice house, not far from here, and two servants, and now we have nothing. My mother has to work in a laundry and I have to work here, in the kitchens.' She was crying again but she fought back the tears and raised her head proudly. 'So what's this message my father gave you?'

'He said that he loved you and thought about you all the time. And then he said something else that I don't understand. He said that you should "look in the night".'

'Look for what? Which night? Tonight?'

'I don't know. That's all he had time to say.'

The great clock chimed the half hour. 'Come on, Mel. I need to get you back to the dormitory.'

'But, Wren, there's so much more to tell. You won't believe what's happened to me since I left to get the pigment.'

'What pigment?'

'That's what I need to tell you about.'

'It can wait until later.'

'Later? Later's when I'm going to be kicked out. I haven't got the cinnabar. Dirk Tot will be furious.'

'Stop worrying, Mel. You need to lay low until the morning. Things will look better then. Stay here, I'll be back in a moment.' Wren disappeared down a hallway but returned very shortly, holding a candle and a small key. 'OK, here's something you 'prentices don't know about. Even I'm not supposed to know. I *borrowed* a key.' Wren winked and led Mel to some carved panelling on the wall, fitted the key to a tiny keyhole and opened a door Mel never even suspected was there. The oak panel swung open and Wren stepped inside. 'Come on.'

Mel followed her. 'A secret passage!'

'*Shhh!*' Wren closed the panel behind them and lit the candle. Her green eyes twinkled in its soft light.

'This is a service passage. The mansion is riddled with them. Most of the rooms can be accessed from the passages. It allows the senior servants to come and go without having to clog up the normal corridors. Come on, this way.'

Mel followed Wren along the passage, which had others branching off it at intervals. They climbed uneven stairs and sometimes cobwebs brushed their faces. As they proceeded, Wren whispered to Mel what lay beyond the various doors they passed.

'That leads to the servants' hall and that one over there to the scullery. Here's the door to the linen store.'

'You must have a good memory. To remember all the doors like that.'

'No, not at all. The rooms are all written on the doors. Look.' She held the candle up to one. 'What's that say?'

Mel was silent.

Wren held the candle closer. 'There, surely you can see it now.' Then the truth dawned on her. 'You can't read, can you?'

Mel hung his head and shook it. 'No. Fa Theum,

the village priest, wanted to teach me but he didn't have any books in Nemish.'

'I've got some books. I can teach you.'

'*Really?* You'll really teach me to read? I can write a bit.'

'Then I'll teach you to write more. I'd like that, to have something better to do after work than to gossip with Cook and the others. It would be fun.'

Mel smiled for the first time that day. 'Look, Wren, thanks for everything. If you hadn't waited up for me I'd still be wandering round outside. You're the only friend I've got in here.'

'What about Ludo?'

'Ludo . . . He's . . .'

'Selfish?'

Mel nodded.

'He's not really; he's just a bit thoughtless sometimes. It's his upbringing. Ludolf Cleef comes from a very well-to-do family. His father's Lord Cleef. They used to be very rich – still are by anyone else's standards. But they love their Pleasures a tad too much. He's the youngest son and his parents dote on him. The truth is, he's spoilt. They bought his apprenticeship for him. Probably with money they don't have. They're counting on him being a successful artist one day. He was bullied a lot when he first arrived. His life never prepared him for an apprenticeship under Groot.'

'I don't think *anyone* could be prepared for that,' said Mel with feeling.

They continued onwards and upwards. Once or twice, Mel had the uneasy feeling that they were not alone in the passage and imagined that he heard faint footsteps following them. But he dismissed the idea. After that day's adventures he was bound to feel on edge. At length, at the top of a steep flight of especially rickety stairs, they reached the dormitory.

Wren opened the door a crack. 'All's clear. Just get straight into bed. You can deal with this mess in the morning.' She held the panel open for him and Mel slipped through. Wren closed it after him and made her way back through the passages in the direction of the servants' quarters. She imagined that she smelt the sharp tang of a recently snuffed candle but thought no more of it. She was also tired. It was long past her own bedtime and she hurried on, taking the passage that led to her own room.

In the silence after she had passed, a flame flared as a candle was relit. It illuminated the face of a man: a green man. He made his way down a different passage. When he came to the door he sought, he raised his candle to read the inscription: *Dirk Tot's study*. He knocked softly and entered.

More Secrets

'Six months' loss of privileges and stipend. You're ever so lucky, Mel,' said Ludo.

'*Lucky?* What does *un*lucky earn you around here?'

'No, really you are. Apprentices have been thrown out for much less. It can only be because you're so talented. And the master likes you. I was here for six months before he even spoke to me. That's going to make Groot angry. He's bound to try and get back at you somehow.'

Ludo was right. The following morning, Mel was given a final warning by Dirk Tot. He was then put straight back to work scrubbing the studio floor. Groot, Bunt and Jurgis would periodically pass by, splashing fresh paint on parts he had already cleaned or kicking his bucket over. At lunch his food was sabotaged with a dead mouse and he left the refectory hungry. Then, in the afternoon, when he went to use the privy he found his precious drawings scattered around. This time they were smeared with something worse than gravy.

Back in the dormitory, shreds and tatters of his drawings hung from the pins from where they had been ripped. Mel was devastated. *That's it! That's enough, you vicious, scrot-brained pig. You're going to pay for this.* He opened his secret cache and withdrew his dagger. He crossed the dormitory to Groot's sleeping place. He stood there, looking at the head apprentice's drawings pinned up around his bed. His fingers tightened on his bodkin.

The door opened and Ludo walked up the empty dormitory towards him. 'I thought I'd find you here. I saw what they'd done. Are you going to shred his drawings? I would.'

Mel hesitated. He tucked the bodkin into his doublet. 'No. It would just drag me down to his level.'

Ludo was quiet for a moment and then said, 'Look, Mel, things will be different from now on. You'll see. You covered up for me when you got caught in the kitchen and you're the only one here, apart from Wren, that treats me like I'm a human being. You're my best friend. I'll make it up to you, OK?' He offered Mel his hand.

'OK,' agreed Mel, touched by his friend's concern as they shook hands.

'But there must be some way you could strike back at Groot. You could tell Dirk Tot what happened. He hates bullying.'

'No, I can't do that.'

'Why ever not?'

'There's something you don't know about Dirk Tot. He's –'

The door opened again and Wren entered. 'Mel, I heard what happened in the refectory earlier. Here, I brought you some cheese. You must be starving.'

'That's not the worst of it. They . . . they destroyed his drawings,' said Ludo.

'Just wait till I'm serving again in the refectory. I'll give them a taste of their own medicine.'

'No, Wren, they're not worth it. Thanks for the cheese.' Mel gratefully took the food. 'Look, there're things I've got to tell you both. Important things. I've kept them to myself for too long. I wish there was somewhere private we could talk.'

'Maybe there is,' said Wren. 'Come with me, you

two.' They made their way to the grand entrance hall. On one of the galleries that surrounded it, about halfway up, she approached a panel.

'Is this another one of your secret passages?' said Mel.

'What secret passages?' asked Ludo, intrigued.

'We'll tell you later. Just a minute.' Wren looked about to make sure they were not being observed and then ran her hand around some moulding, pressing a hidden switch. There was a click and a small door, only half their height, sprung open. 'Mind your heads and follow me.'

'We're inside the great clock,' said Mel as he gazed around in astonishment.

The entire space was evenly lit by the light penetrating the translucent glass of the huge clock face. Its hands and back-to-front numerals were clearly silhouetted against the daylight. All around them moved gears and pulleys, and a large, brass pendulum swung back and forth. Coiled springs contracted and expanded. Escapements and well-oiled ratchets rocked to and fro and large counterweights hung suspended.

The whole machine ticked and tocked with a loud but friendly voice. Racks of bells, in strict order of size, waited in tiers to announce the hours.

'How did you know how to get in?' asked Ludo, touching the rows of brightly painted automated figures that waited to parade across the clock face each time the hour struck.

'My father made this clock. And I designed and painted all the figures.' Wren ran her hand lovingly over the machinery.

'*You?*' said Ludo.

'I wasn't always a kitchen girl. I used to help my father in his workshop.'

Up close, Mel recognised several of the faces on the figures. A scrawny dragon bore the unmistakable features of Adolfus Spute and a tiny, horned devil that of Mumchance. 'Their faces. They look like . . .'

'Yes, they do. It was our way of poking fun at the Mysteries,' said Wren. 'Great, aren't they?'

'They're *amazing!*' said Mel. 'So you can draw, too.'

'Almost as well as you, I imagine. But girls aren't allowed to be apprentices so I just worked with my father until . . .' She looked away and changed the subject. 'Look, now that you know how to get in, why don't we meet here every evening, after work. It can be our secret place.'

'*Great!*' said Ludo and Mel together.

'Now, we must all get back to our duties before someone misses us. Especially you, Mel. You can't afford another mistake. I'll see you both later.'

'So what's all this about secret passages?' asked Ludo.

Supper had finished and the three friends were back inside the clock.

'*Service* passages. Later,' said Wren. 'Right now I think Mel's got something more important to tell us.'

So Mel took a deep breath and started to tell them of all the things that had happened to him. He began with his meeting with Dirk Tot in Kop and his encounter with Adolfus Spute in the fane. He told of their flight to Vlam and the meeting he had witnessed between Dirk Tot and the Fifth Mystery on the road. He recounted how he had seen Groot stealing the pigments from the storeroom and how his crime had been covered up – by Dirk Tot.

Suddenly, they were interrupted by a whirring noise.

'What's that?' said Ludo.

'The clock. It's about to strike the hour,' said Wren. 'Watch.'

All of the machinery around them came alive. The bells, struck by an army of small hammers, pealed their familiar carillon loudly in the enclosed space. All of the figures began to spin and jerk their limbs, and the belt they were attached to began to move. The friends jumped up and watched in delight as the figures filed out of the small door at the right of the space and their shadows danced across the glass clock face. Then they rushed across to watch as the figures returned through the left-hand door. Above their heads the stars and planets did the same.

Laughing loudly, the friends collapsed on to the floor as the performance ended.

'You know, that's the first good laugh I've had since I arrived in Vlam,' said Mel.

'Come on, finish your story.' Wren was as eager to hear it as Ludo.

When the noise died away, Mel detailed his visit to the House of Mysteries, his escape from the High-Bailiff, his strange encounter with the coloured men and their journey through who-knows-where. His tale ended with Wren taking him through the secret passage back to the dormitory. The only thing he left out was the tiny box and its mysterious contents. If he told them about it he would have to admit that he was a thief.

'That's quite some story,' said Wren.

'We had no idea,' said Ludo.

'But I just don't understand any of it,' confessed Mel.

'Well,' said Ludo, 'Groot's a thief. That's no surprise. He must be stealing the pigment to pay for his drinking and gambling. You've got something on him now, Mel. Something you can use against him.'

'And the coloured men,' said Wren. 'They must be fugitives from the mines on Kig. The pigment gets into their skin and eventually it colours them completely. Not many ever escape. The pigments are toxic and it usually kills the miners after a while. It's called the Coloured Death.' Her voice trembled slightly. She could not help but think of her father.

'What I can't work out is why Dirk Tot should be working with the Fifth Mystery,' said Mel. 'Do either of you have any idea?'

'No,' said Wren, shrugging her shoulders. 'He always seems so dead set against them.'

'Me neither,' said Ludo. 'But I bet we could find out if we explored the secret passages.'

'The *service* passages,' corrected Wren.

'But what do you think about the strange journey that the coloured men took me on?' asked Mel.

'Let's start with the things we can find an answer for,' said Wren. 'Then, perhaps, we'll find out a bit more about the other things.'

Mel knew she was right. 'I don't have a better idea.'

'So we're going into the . . .'

'Ludo,' warned Wren.

'. . . passages then. No time like the present,' said Ludo.

'I thought you might say that, so I brought these.' Wren produced the little key and three candles from the pocket of her pinafore. 'I think we should start with Dirk Tot's study.'

'What are we waiting for?' said Ludo.

Opposite the clock, just across the gallery, was an entrance into the passages. After the door was closed behind them, the three friends lit their candles. The normally busy sounds of the mansion were shut out and they felt enclosed in their own parallel world. The air was very close and the yellow light cast their shadows tall and grotesque on the wall.

'Now, keep it quiet. Remember, there are rooms with people just the other side of the panelling,' warned Wren. 'I just hope we don't meet anyone while we're in here.'

'What, you mean like monsters or ghosts?' joked Ludo. '*Whooooo!*'

'*Shhhh!*' said Wren. 'No, silly. I hope we don't bump into any of the other servants. Now, come on.'

Mel and Ludo followed Wren but could not help casting the occasional uneasy look behind them as they threaded their way along in single file.

'Dirk Tot's study is just up here,' whispered Wren. She carefully began to mount the uneven stairs.

Halfway up, Ludo stumbled into Mel who stumbled into Wren. They froze and listened to hear if they had betrayed their presence. Mel's heart was pounding so loudly in his chest that he thought the whole mansion must hear it. A stair creaked loudly in the silence as one of them shifted their weight. They held their breath. Nothing happened. After a while, they breathed out and continued until they stood outside the study. Wren put her ear to the door. She turned to her friends and shook her head, indicating back down the stairs.

'There was someone in there. We'll have to come back some other time,' she said.

'Where to now?' asked Mel.

Before she could answer, they heard the sound of footsteps coming their way. Wren pushed the two boys down a side passage. They blew their candles out and waited in blackness darker than any of them had ever known.

Please don't let us get caught, thought Mel. *Not now. Please, please, please.*

Slowly, a rectangle marking the end of their short passageway paled and grew brighter as the footsteps grew louder. Then the space flared brightly for a moment as Minch, carrying a candle and a silver tray, passed by, whistling tunelessly. They heard him mount the stairs and rap sharply on the study door. They caught some muffled conversation and then the sound of the door closing and footsteps descending the stairs. Minch, empty-handed except for his candle, passed them again and the passage became dark once more. A few moments passed before Wren said, 'OK, I think it's safe to light our candles again.'

'Let's get out of here,' whispered Ludo.

'I thought you wanted to help us find out what's going on,' said Wren.

'It's too risky.'

'We're in here now,' said Mel. 'We might not get another chance for ages.'

'Please. Let's go on for a bit longer,' said Wren, 'or we're never going to find anything out.'

They both looked at Ludo.

'I suppose so. What's down there?' he asked, indicating a new direction.

'That the way to the master's private studio,' said Wren.

'No one's ever allowed in there,' said Ludo, 'not even Groot.'

'Let's just take a look,' said Mel, his excitement winning over caution.

'OK,' said Wren. 'But let me lead. *And keep quiet.*'

They set off towards the studio. Eventually, Wren signalled for them to halt. She put a finger to her lips and then pointed into the darkness ahead of them. A tiny sliver of light indicated where a door stood slightly ajar.

If I never get to see anything else in my life, I've got to see this, thought Mel.

They crept up to it. Then, Mel crouching, Wren standing and Ludo on tiptoe, each put one eye to the crack.

The master stood before a painting on a large easel that dominated a spacious, whitewashed room lit by gas brackets around the walls. From their hiding place, the watchers could not see what the canvas depicted. Mel took in the bright tapestries hung here and there and a number of large, unframed paintings that leaned against the wall. He noticed several tables stacked with tottering piles of books and artist's materials, and a huge, richly coloured rug that covered most of the floor. In the far corner he saw a bulky cage in which several strange creatures chattered and swung to and fro. With surprise he realised that they were white monkeys like Albinus but coloured in different ways – one striped, one in harlequin quarters, one spotted and another patterned in rainbow hoops.

As they watched, the master raised his hand in front of the canvas and moved it in an elaborate gesture as if he were tracing a complicated design in the air. He moved closer to the canvas and –

The trio gasped. 'He's vanished!'

The Fugitive Garden

The friends were so astounded by what they had witnessed that they fell headlong through the door into the studio and landed in a heap. Their candles were extinguished in the fall. The patterned monkeys began screeching loudly and jumping around inside their cage, rattling the bars.

Wren picked herself up, rushed to the main door and looked out into the corridor. 'All clear.'

'Quiet, *please* be quiet,' pleaded Ludo with the monkeys.

'You've a knack with animals,' said Wren as the shrieking died down. 'I'm impressed.'

'It's nothing, really, when you know how.' Ludo smiled to himself. 'Hey, Mel, the master must have liked what you did to Albinus so much that he's tried something similar on these guys.' A sketch of the newly green and white pet was pinned to the wall next to the cage.

But Mel was not paying attention. He was studying

the canvas. 'Come here, you two. There's something you have to see.'

The canvas depicted a landscape in the unmistakable, hyper-real style of Ambrosius Blenk. It was so finely painted it seemed to glow. An ethereal blue sky was studded with white clouds that clearly resembled faces smiling down on the undulating landscape below. In the foreground grew odd, alien trees that had spiral trunks and ripe, speckled fruit hanging from their branches. A variety of brightly coloured, hybrid creatures grazed contentedly in the shade beneath them and on the lush pasture that led down to a placid lake. On a small island, right in the centre of the lake and reflected perfectly in it, stood a weird building that seemed to have crystallised out of the rock on which it stood. It looked like a giant, misshapen head. It had an expansive, thatched roof that resembled shaggy hair, peppered with random plants and the occasional stork's nest. Thick ivy grew around its face like a beard. There were two great windows for eyes, above which projected shallow, sloping roofs like brows, and the entrance was in the form of a gaping mouth. A portcullis appeared like teeth, reinforcing the carefully crafted illusion. From the shore of the lake, a tongue-like bridge, built from red brick, spanned the waters and disappeared into the entrance. On the bridge, dressed exactly as they had seen him moments before, was the perfectly painted form of the master.

'It's beautiful,' said Wren.

'It's completely different from anything that he sends across for us to work on,' observed Ludo.

'You don't understand,' said Mel. 'A moment ago, the master was depicted here, in the foreground. Now look.'

The master had moved further along the bridge.

'How did he do that?' said Ludo.

'I don't know. Look again.'

The master had gone.

'Now he's inside the building,' said Mel.

'What're you saying? That it's painted with some kind of vanishing paint?' suggested Ludo.

'No. I'm saying that I think the master's somehow managed to get inside his picture.'

'How can you get inside a painting? It's ridiculous.'

Ludo prodded the surface of the picture. It was still wet but as solid as any other stretched canvas.

'You saw the master vanish,' said Wren. 'We all did.'

'Yes! And remember I told you about the coloured men, the ones that kidnapped me? Well, before they put the sack back over my head, I had a moment to look around. The landscape was different from this one but it feels the same. The way everything's perfect. The way it's lit. It's special; it isn't like nature at all. Just before I was whisked out of the House of Mysteries I had my back to a painting. And when I was released, there was a painting there as well. I know it sounds crazy, but I think I was inside a picture with them.'

'Which picture?' asked Wren. 'The one in the House of Mysteries or the one in the House of Spirits?'

'I don't know. Both of them perhaps. Or maybe they're all one big picture. I just don't know,' said Mel, shaking his head.

'That's impossible,' scoffed Ludo. 'Even if you could get inside a picture – which you can't – how could you be inside two pictures at once? Look, there must be a trapdoor here somewhere and the master used it when we weren't looking.'

'But we *were* looking, Ludo,' said Wren. 'We never took our eyes off him.'

'You're both talking rubbish. There's a trapdoor. I bet it's under the rug.' Ludo relit his candle from one of the gas lamps and began inspecting the floor. He crawled behind the easel.

'Look!' Wren and Mel gasped.

'Leave the candle there and come and look at this, Ludo,' said Wren.

With the picture illuminated from behind by the candlelight, the under-painting became discernable. All of the complicated brushwork that underlay the master's technique, that made his pictures seem so real, was revealed. But more than meticulous brushwork was visible. In the centre of the picture, and painted in some denser medium that rendered it opaque, was a motif. It was a circle within which other lines twisted and whirled, creating a knot-like design.

'What is it?' asked Ludo.

'I think it's a symbol. Like a Fa's diaglyph,' said Mel.

'What do you mean?' said Wren.

'It's something that means more than itself. Maybe it's got something to do with the master vanishing.'

'But he *didn't* . . . Look, it's just a shape,' said Ludo. 'It can't actually *do* anything. It's just a paint stain.'

'The painting wouldn't look like it does without the under-painting. So maybe this is a part of the illusion as well. You saw the master trace something in the air just before he vanished. It must be this symbol.'

'Come on, Mel. Are you telling me that it's magic?'

'No, it's *art*. Fa Theum says that's the only type of magic that exists in the real world.'

'But art's about things we can see,' insisted Ludo.

'You can no longer see the under-painting,' said Wren. 'Or the skill or time it took to paint – but they're all locked up in there, too.'

'That's different.'

'Is it? My guess is that this thing's an important part of the picture,' said Mel. 'I'm going to make a copy. See what else you can find.'

Ludo shrugged and began sorting through the piles of books with Wren. 'There's a book full of drawings of animals here. I've seen some of these before in the master's pictures.'

'It's his bestiary,' said Mel. 'Remember the master said I was to study it. I'll have a look, as soon as I've finished this.'

Ludo wandered over to inspect the large paintings stacked against the wall. 'These must be in the master's private collection,' he said as he sorted through them. 'Wow! There're a couple here by Lucas Flink.'

'Really? They must be worth a fortune,' said Wren.

'Who's Lucas Fink?' asked Mel absently as he concentrated on his copy.

'*Flink.* Only the greatest master of fantastic paintings – along with our master, of course.'

'Does he have apprentices too?' asked Mel.

'He might have had once, but he's been dead two hundred years. That's odd. This canvas is still wet. How could the paint on something this old not be dry yet?'

'*Quiet!*' Wren crossed to the door and placed her ear against it. 'Quick, someone's coming.'

Ludo snatched his candle from the floor and followed her to the service passage. '*Mel*, come on!'

Mel hastily finished his sketch and stole one last look at the canvas, which appeared normal again now, with no trace of the hidden design. He joined his friends and they closed the door to its former crack just as Dirk Tot entered the studio. They watched as he sniffed the air. He looked suspiciously about the room. Then he shrugged and approached the painting. He looked at it and smiled, before withdrawing some phials of pigment from his reticule and arranging them with the master's other painting equipment. He took another look around the room before turning on his heels and leaving. They heard him turn the key in the lock after him.

'Wherever there's a mystery, he turns up,' said Wren.

'Is that mystery with a small m or a capital M?' said Ludo.

'Well, we've learned something this evening. If you know how, you can get inside a picture,' said Mel.

'No, you *can't.*'

'Ludo, what's it going to take before you accept what your eyes told you?' said Wren.

'Look, if you're so certain that you can get inside a

picture, then there's one way we can find out for sure,' said Ludo. 'We can make one of our own.'

The next morning the master visited the apprentices in their studio to inspect the progress on the large paintings. Mel looked up from his scrubbing and studied him as he and his entourage strode by. They exchanged smiles and Mel detected a wave of jealous hostility from Groot and his sidekicks. Mel contrived to clean a patch near Ludo so that they could talk.

'He looks OK,' said Mel in a low voice as he scrubbed back and forth with his holystone. 'Wherever he went hasn't done him any harm.'

'That's because he hasn't been anywhere. Meet me in the clock after supper and I'll prove it to you. Watch out.' Ludo made himself look busy as Groot scanned the studio, looking for Mel.

During one of his many visits to the courtyard to replenish his cleaning water, Mel noticed that a door that was normally closed stood open. He looked about him. *Should I risk it?* He approached it and entered. The door led, by way of a short covered passage, to the strangest garden he had ever seen. Along one side of the high-walled space were several beds of brightly coloured flowers. One contained only the primary colours, of red, yellow and blue, and another the secondary colours – green, orange and purple. Yet another held an entire rainbow spectrum. Not only were there red, orange, yellow, green, blue, indigo and violet plants, but between them many intermediate shades, so that the whole effect was of a rainbow laid out on the ground. Still another bed contained earthy, tertiary colours and one more was planted with unusual, achromatic plants ranging from black to white, with every shade of grey inbetween. As if all this was not strange enough, the opposite side of the garden contained the mirror image, except that the plants there were made of carefully crafted and painted wood. Some of the colours were as vivid as their natural counterparts, others less so. Kneeling there, tending these artificial plants, was Dirk Tot. Without looking up from what he was doing, he addressed Mel. 'Skiving off from your cleaning, Mel?'

'No, I . . .' He could not think of an excuse.

'It's all right. Can't say I blame you. If I had my way you'd be doing something more useful than scrubbing floors. I know the master feels the same – but Groot's in charge of the apprentices and we won't interfere. Don't be downhearted, though. All apprentices start out with a few days of menial labour. It never lasts long.'

Mel knew Dirk Tot was mistaken in this. He would never be given anything useful to do while Groot was in charge.

Dirk Tot looked up. 'This is my Fugitive Garden. Fascinating, isn't it?'

'What's it all for?'

The giant rose to his feet and dusted some dirt from his knees with his good hand. 'It's a kind of on-going experiment. You see, all artists' colours are fugitive to some extent. That means that they fade when they're exposed to daylight. Some are highly fugitive and fade rapidly while others are less so and hardly fade at all. Look here.' He pointed to some brown artificial flowers with his silver hand. 'Generally speaking, those that are painted with earth-like colours are the most permanent, and others – like those faded pinks over there – the least. I take a sample from every batch of pigment that we use in the studio and paint one of these wooden plants. The real plants, over there, are our control group, the ones I compare them to, so that I can gauge the extent of the fading. It's important to know how a painting will age. They're likely to be around a lot longer than you or I. Some pigments are more expensive than others, as you have already learnt to your cost, but the most precious is this one here.' He indicated a deep blue.

'That's the household colour,' said Mel, fingering his own doublet.

'It's called ultramarine. It's made from ground-up lapis lazuli, a semi-precious stone. The master likes that colour as it impresses his patrons, makes them aware of how rich and successful he's become. How much his pictures will cost them. It's good salesmanship.'

'He must be very rich to have us all dressed like this.'

At that moment, a gust of wind blew open a gate at the far end of the enclosure. Mel caught a fleeting glimpse of another garden beyond. It was also planted with artificial flowers but they seemed to be much less faded than the majority of those in this. Dirk Tot was not aware of the open gate at first, as the undamaged side of his face was towards Mel, but the boy's expression must have betrayed his curiosity and the giant turned to look at what he was finding so interesting. Immediately, Dirk Tot dashed over and hastily closed the gate.

He spoke gruffly. 'Shouldn't you be working? Run along. That floor isn't going to clean itself.'

Reluctantly, Mel left, wondering why Dirk Tot did not want him to see the other garden.

After supper, Mel, Ludo and Wren gathered inside the clock. Ludo had smuggled some sheets of paper from the studio storeroom and had glued several together until they formed a sheet about as big as the master's painting. He had also brought a small pot of gesso and a paintbrush. They pinned the paper up on to the wall and Mel carefully copied the knot-like design on to it from his sketch. The gesso rapidly dried and the white on white symbol was invisible.

'That's the first part done,' said Mel. 'What have you got for us to make the picture with?'

'These are all I could nab.' Ludo held up a bunch of pencils apologetically.

'They're no good,' said Mel. 'The master's landscape, and the one where I was kidnapped, were both coloured. And as real as here and now – realer.'

'Mel's right,' said Wren.

'Yeah, but what I was thinking is that paintings are usually made for other people to look at. They *have* to be detailed. If the picture was just for us, then we'd know what colour everything was supposed to be. Like, if we drew some grass, then we'd know it was green, or that the sky was blue. Wouldn't we? That way it wouldn't matter that it wasn't as perfect as the master's. It's only us that are ever going to see it.'

'Then why did the master make his picture in colour?' asked Wren. 'I bet he's the only one that's ever going to see it.'

'There's no way we could get enough paint and canvas and stuff to make a picture like that. Everyone would know it's missing,' said Ludo. 'And we'd need an easel and everything. Anyway, it's only a test. It's just to find out if it works – which it won't.'

'All right, but let's keep it simple. Just a basic landscape. Ludo, you start that side and Wren the other. I'll begin in the middle. We'll make it up as we go along.'

They had only been drawing for a minute before Mel and Ludo stopped and stepped back.

'That's really good, Wren,' said Ludo. 'You weren't lying when you said you could draw.'

'I think it's unfair there're no girl apprentices,' said Mel. 'You're far better than Groot.'

'And prettier too.' She fluttered her eyelashes. 'Now, get a move on or we'll never finish.'

By the time the light began to fade, they had not made much progress between them.

'Look, tomorrow's Sunday and we don't have to work,' said Ludo.

'*You* don't have to work,' corrected Wren. 'The kitchen will still be busy.'

'Yeah, but Mel and I can carry on with the drawing

first thing and you can join us when you get the chance. We should have it finished by the afternoon.'

By the time Wren was able to free herself from her duties the next day, the picture, such as it was, was complete. 'I don't think much of that,' she said critically.

What she saw was a crude landscape in shades of grey. In the foreground was a stunted tree standing amid hastily scribbled grass. The middle and background were smudged and vague, with just the merest suggestion of hills and valleys. A roughly drawn building occupied one of the hilltops. The sky was an all-over uniform grey and there were odd blotches everywhere where they had inexpertly rubbed out mistakes.

'It's not very good, is it?' said Mel. 'Perhaps we should begin again?'

'It'll do. It's not as if it's going to work, after all,' said Ludo.

'I don't know, Ludo.' Mel looked concerned.

'You're being a perfectionist. Just think of it as a working drawing if that'll make you feel any better. Let's try it. Are you staying to watch, Wren?'

'I can't. I've got a mountain of pots and dishes to wash up. Good luck. And, if it works . . .'

'No chance of that.'

'. . . be careful. Promise?'

'What do we do now?' asked Ludo after she had gone.

'We copy the master.' Mel sounded unsure. He held his sketch of the symbol up in front of him. 'Here goes.'

'Wait! If you do that you might go into the picture but I'll be left standing here on my own,' complained Ludo.

'I thought you said it wasn't going to work.'

'It won't. But just in case it does.'

'Why don't we link arms? That way we'll both go.'

'OK, I'm ready.'

'Now I can't hold the sketch *and* move my hand.'

'Try it the other way round. Change hands.'

'Oh, this is impossible!' said Mel. 'The master must have the symbol memorised.'

'I've got an idea.' Ludo unpinned the drawing from the wall and, with a couple of dabs of glue, stuck it to the translucent clock face. They could see the symbol underneath the drawing clearly silhouetted against the daylight. 'That's more like it.'

'*Brilliant!* Right, here goes. Take my arm.' They looked at each other, nodded and each took a deep breath. Then, hesitantly, Mel traced the design in the air in front of him.

The Ill-Conceived World

Nothing happened.

'What did I tell you?' said Ludo.

'Maybe I wasn't trying hard enough. Let's do it again.' Mel screwed his eyes tight shut, willing it to happen. He traced the design in the air. *Come on, come on, come on, come on.* He opened his eyes.

They were still inside the clock.

'It's never going to work. We're wasting our time.'

'It's got to. I *saw* it work. There's something I'm not doing right. Think back, which hand did the master use?'

'His right!' said Ludo confidently. 'No, his left. At least I *think* it was his left.'

'No. It was his right hand. The one nearest to us. Then what?'

'Then he . . . I can't remember. Why don't you try starting at the top? Make a kind of spiral, like a whirlpool. Whirlpools suck things into them, don't they? And look, some of the lines are drawn on top of the others. That means that the bits underneath were made first, before the other bits were laid on top.'

It took a bit of working out but soon Mel had it. He glanced up at the clock face. Its back-to-front hands indicated that it was midday. Behind them, the works began whirring as they prepared to chime. 'All right. Clockwise or anticlockwise?'

'How should I know? Oh, *clockwise!*'

The boys linked arms again and took another deep breath as Mel traced the motif. The drawing shimmered and seemed to rotate, just like a whirlpool. The world around them – the real world of the clock and the mansion – grew indistinct and distant. They felt a sensation like pins and needles all over as they were drawn forward. Everything seemed to blur for a moment. When they regained focus, they stood, side by side, inside their own, newly created world.

The friends looked at each other.

'*Scrot!*' exclaimed Ludo. 'It *does* work!'

'That tingling feeling,' said Mel. 'It was the same as I felt before.'

They looked behind them. There, close by, rose

the undulating wall of mist that Mel remembered seeing before.

'That must be the surface of the drawing,' said Mel.

'The master calls it the "picture plane",' replied Ludo.

'It's the way back to the real world.' Mel touched it but it felt strangely resistant rather than misty.

They turned again to gaze at their world. Everything looked particularly sketchy and unfinished and very, very grey.

'It doesn't look very, you know, *real*,' said Mel.

'Maybe if we imagine the colours that'll help. I'll try with the grass.' Ludo narrowed his eyes and dramatically pointed at the grass like a stage magician. 'Alacaboozle.'

'*Alacaboozle?*' Mel stifled a giggle.

The grass remained grey.

'I felt I had to say *something*. Maybe it needs the two of us. Come on, Mel, both together now. Imagine it's green.'

'OK, but without all the hey-presto wizard stuff this time, it's daft. Just imagine we're painting it.'

The boys concentrated and slowly the grass took on a definite greenish tinge, like a grey sponge sucking up coloured water.

'Did we do that?' Mel was astonished.

'You're not the only one with ideas,' said Ludo, delighted that it had worked.

'Just imagine if we could do that in the real world. We could put the Fifth Mystery out of business. Now let's try the sky.'

The sky became bluer but the grass lost some of its previous greenness. 'And the tree,' urged Ludo.

Soon they had coloured their world.

'Doesn't it look a bit washed-out to you?' asked Mel.

'It's so difficult to keep the colours there,' complained Ludo as the colours started to fade away. Beneath everything, the rough texture of the pencil drawing showed through.

'It works while we're concentrating, but as soon as we think of something else they start to fade again. It's as if we can only imagine a certain amount of colour between us. It's not enough to spread over the whole world.'

'OK, it works. You've proved your point. Now, how do we get back?'

'But we've only just arrived. We must explore a bit. No one's ever been here before. We're the very first people in this world.' Mel folded his sketch of the symbol and tucked it inside his doublet.

'I don't know . . .'

'Come on, Ludo. Just imagine what Wren will say when we tell her.'

They approached their tree. Mel reached up to grab a leaf but it turned to dust in his hand, leaving a dirty green smear that rapidly turned grey like powdered graphite. Disappointed, he wiped it clean on his sleeve. 'Come on, Ludo, let's go and visit the house.'

But walking was hard work. Their scribbled grass was more like a low-lying vine that snagged their feet and tugged at their ankles. They had to raise their feet higher than normal to avoid being tripped up and their legs began to ache. The house did not appear to be getting any nearer. But they did reach it and they found that, rather than being full-sized, it was tiny and barely reached up to their knees. It was no bigger than when they first saw it.

'That's *really* odd,' said Mel.

'It's the same size as it was in the drawing. Perhaps if we knew more about the laws of perspective, things would behave like they do in the real world. It's not much of a house either, you can't get inside.' The doorway and windows were simply hollows in the surface. He kicked it and the tiny house crumbled like a sandcastle into grey dust. 'The colour's going again, Mel, concentrate.'

'It's getting harder all the time. I think we're using up all our concentration. And, I'm getting a headache.'

The world slowly began to colour up but not as much as before.

'OK, explorer, where to now?' asked Ludo.

'I think you're right. There's nothing much to see here. Let's go back.'

'Er, Mel. Which way?'

The wall of mist had vanished. Everything looked the same in all directions except for the tree, which had not diminished in size at all even though they had walked away from it. Their eyes told them that it had grown enormously.

'That way,' said Mel, pointing to it. 'The way out's right next to the tree.'

But it wasn't. Their eyes told them the tree shrank as they approached it, but, in fact, it remained the same size.

'What's going on, Mel?'

'I don't know. I think it's because we drew it big, in the foreground, to make it seem closer.'

'Or maybe this world's got laws all of its own. We should have worked them out before we came here. I bet the master did with his world.'

When they reached the tree the landscape still looked exactly the same in all directions. There was no sign of the mist wall anywhere.

'I just don't understand any of this,' said Mel. He leant against the tree and fell on to his back as it crumbled to dust, just like the house. There was no landmark left in their world.

'What now?' asked Ludo.

Mel picked himself up and dusted his clothes. 'I

don't know. The way out has got to be around here somewhere. Maybe the wall of mist is only visible from a certain angle.'

'What's that? Something's moving out there.' Ludo was pointing into the distance, or what passed for the distance in their topsy-turvy world. An amorphous shape was thickening and solidifying. 'It looks like one of your mistakes that you rubbed out.'

'It could be one of yours. You made as many as I did.'

As it came nearer it began to assume a form, and a most unwelcome one at that. A smudge near the bottom began to grow legs: three of them. The centre flowed and solidified into what looked like a skeletal rib cage. Scrawny, finger-like wings unfurled from behind and spread wide. For the moment the top could not decide what it wanted to be and hovered as an indistinct blur before it resolved into a cloud of buzzing flies. Then, two eyes formed within the cloud as sinister dark slits.

'Run!' shouted Mel.

The scribble-grass caught Ludo's ankle and he

fell headlong. Mel helped him to his feet. The creature was getting nearer or, if not, it was certainly getting bigger. The buzzing of the flies grew louder and the creature loped towards them with its awkward gait, like a one-legged man on a pair of crutches. Neither of their minds had any room left for anything except their immediate peril, so the last traces of colour bled from the landscape. The only colour that remained was the two apprentices in their grey, ill-conceived world.

Mel looked desperately around the nondescript landscape. It looked somehow thicker in one direction and the pair set off that way, hoping it was the wall. But it was a mistake: literally. This hastily erased error was transforming itself into a second nightmare creature. It grew long, long legs, upon which sat an insect-like carapace. Antennae, as slender as whips, sprouted from the top in place of eyes, and two mantis-like arms hung down in front.

'Come on, Ludo. This way.' The boys changed direction yet again.

The scribble-grass grew bigger and thicker. It

became more like roots, as thick as rope, that knotted and intertwined, slowing the boys further. Ludo stumbled again. Mel made a grab for his friend and the two overbalanced and tumbled down through the oversized undergrowth, which parted and then closed over their heads to form a kind of imperfect, interwoven roof. They lay there breathlessly on their backs and watched as the two Mistakes stalked backwards and forwards above their heads.

'Now where are we?'

'Who cares,' said Ludo. 'We're safe from your Mistakes for a bit.'

'More like yours. Come on. We can't stay here. Those things will find us in a minute.'

They got to their feet and found themselves in a maze of low tunnels beneath, and formed from, the undergrowth. Under their feet was flat, dirty-white ground that Mel associated with the surface of the paper. He looked up and saw that a third Mistake had joined the other two. It was like a huge spider with a long, barbed trunk, which it stabbed down through the undergrowth at them. The boys ran down one of the tunnels as the Mistakes above followed the sound of their footsteps.

'This way,' said Mel as he branched off to the left.

'Mel, *help!*' Ludo had caught his ankle in a loop of undergrowth projecting from the tunnel wall.

As Mel turned back to help him, the barbed trunk shot through the canopy, tearing Ludo's sleeve and grazing his arm. Before Mel could reach his friend, it flashed down again, wounding Ludo in the leg. Mel drew his bodkin and slashed at the trunk as he freed Ludo's foot with his other hand and dragged him away. The vicious trunk, spraying arcs of grey blood, continued to stab at the space where they had been and was soon joined by the multi-jointed arms and the thrashing antennae of another Mistake probing cruelly down into the tunnel.

'Can you walk?'

'Sure I can.' Ludo tried to stand but fell as his leg collapsed under him. 'Or perhaps not.'

'Here, grab hold of me.' Mel helped his friend to his feet. 'Use this.' He hacked off a length of undergrowth to use as a stick.

'Why's this so solid when the house and tree turned to dust?'

'Good question. Perhaps we were pressing harder when we drew it.'

Ludo looked around. 'What now?'

'Let's keep moving. The roof seems to give us some protection. Come on, this way.' They set off slowly down another tunnel. Mel glanced behind and saw the thin trail of Ludo's blood quickly turn grey as it soaked into the ground. As they moved through the tunnels Ludo became weaker.

'This is no good,' said Mel. 'We could be going round and round in circles down here. We need to get back to the surface.' He eased his friend to the ground and began snapping off pieces of the undergrowth until he had created a hole big enough for them to escape through. Cautiously, he raised his head and peered out. Some distance off, he had no way of telling how far, he saw two of the Mistakes stabbing and probing the undergrowth where they imagined their prey might still be. The third Mistake, the one with the long legs, was prowling in a circle around them.

Mel looked around. 'The going seems easier away from the Mistakes.' He ducked back down and helped Ludo through the hole. The two made their way as fast as they could, Ludo leaning heavily on Mel. The size of the undergrowth grew less until it was like the previous low-lying vine. The going was easier but not easy, and a soupy grey-white mist began to rise from the ground. Ludo was rapidly becoming heavier and less able to help himself. As the mist thickened it made everything seem even greyer.

Ludo cried out in pain. 'Mel, I think that barbed trunk thing must have been poisoned. I feel cold.'

The Mistakes had heard Ludo's cry. They were coming towards them. Mel gazed at his helpless friend. The colour was beginning to leave him. He and his clothing were slowly turning grey.

'I can't go on any further, Mel. I'm sorry.'

Mel shot a worried glance towards the Mistakes.

'Don't leave me here.'

'Don't worry; I'm not going to leave you. The way back's got to be around here somewhere. Come on, Ludo. Ludo . . .?'

Ludo did not answer.

Mel heaved his semiconscious friend on to his shoulder and stumbled on, away from their pursuers. He began to fight hard for his breath. The mist started to thicken and clot in front of him. The clots began to resolve themselves into trees. *How could that be? The world we drew had only the single tree.* A sparse wood opened up around him as he hastened along. Their drawing had taken on a life of its own.

Mel stopped for a moment and lowered his friend to the ground. He eased Ludo's wounded arm from his doublet and tore his shirt, revealing the gash. With revulsion he saw that it was crawling with tiny grey worms. The maggots were eating Ludo's flesh and, as they ate, more colour drained from him. Mel tore Ludo's hose and saw the same thing on his leg. With a rising sense of disgust, he picked as many as he could off the wounds but they seemed to be multiplying. For every one that he picked off another took its place.

He looked about him desperately. *Which way, which way? If only I could see a landmark.* All he saw were the Mistakes searching for them. He heaved his friend back up on to his shoulder and staggered on, but after only a short way had to rest again.

Thin, icy tendrils snaked towards them along the sketchy ground, like shabby skeins of gossamer being drawn to and fro by unseen hands. And beyond them . . . nothing, just grey, ever more indistinct shapes dissolving into the fog. Only the few trees nearby had any substance and even those were changing themselves as he watched. They were now more like giant, many-fingered hands. Corpse's hands, knotted where there would have been joints, thin, mean and cruel. Here and there the grey bark fell away like rotting flesh to reveal not bare wood but sinew and bone.

Mel regretted drawing the grass so casually. He had thought it would be so much quicker than drawing in every single blade. *How could I have been so stupid?* He should have realised they might need a landmark or two, to give a sense of direction in this world.

Then, very faintly and at the limit of his hearing, he heard a familiar tune. It was the sound of the carillon in the clock. It was coming from behind him, from where they had been. He must have been walking away from it all this time. Then he thought about the strange, distorted laws of this world. Perspective didn't seem to exist and only relative size remained. Where the grass had become thicker, where it had seemed as thick as rope, must be near the front of the drawing. That's why it did not break like the house and tree. They *had* pressed harder with their pencils to make it seem darker and nearer the foreground of the drawing.

'We're near to the picture plane and the wall of mist, Ludo,' said Mel.

With great effort he heaved Ludo up on to his shoulder again and half-ran, half-staggered in the direction of the music. The bells became louder, the undergrowth thicker. Then, just as he thought he could carry Ludo no further before his lungs would burst and his legs collapse under him, he saw it. The wall of mist shimmered and undulated gently, silver against the dead grey of the landscape. This ray of hope summoned the last of his energy. Just a few more steps, just a few more moments and they could return to their world. Their world of colour and sunshine and music. Their world of safety.

'Nearly there, Ludo. Just a little further.'

Then, out of the fog they stepped, barring the way. The three Mistakes stood in a line in front of the wall, awaiting their prey.

The Uninvited Guest

Mel lowered Ludo to the ground. The chiming of the
bells continued from beyond the wall and the creatures
cocked their heads as they listened to the first music
ever heard in their world. Mel reached into his doublet
and withdrew his bodkin. He doubted that it would be
of any real use against the three towering monsters but
it was a comfort to hold it. He knew instinctively that
this was not a problem that could be solved with cold
steel. It was a problem for an artist's hand and mind.
He had inadvertently created this perverted world and
these malformed creatures with bad art. He could now
only save himself with good. He remembered his father
chiding him when he had made a mistake threading
the heddles on his loom as he set it up to weave a new
bolt of cloth. 'If you leave it like that, son, the whole
bolt will be ruined.' Willem had patiently undone the
botched job and shown Mel how to do it correctly.

No sooner had Mel formed these thoughts, than
the Mistakes seemed to grow less formidable. *They're*

only mistakes. I just need to correct them. But how?

The problem, he realised, was that he was still thinking in terms of the rules of the real world. Such rules did not exist here. So, he reasoned, the creatures he was looking at were not so much things as stains, clumsy marks that had been made on a piece of paper. He had used stains in the past. The shapes he had seen in the stains on the wall back home in Kop had suggested monsters to him. Now the situation was reversed. Back there he would have taken the raw shape, looked at it to see what it suggested and then altered it until it became something else.

'Hey! Errors! Botched Jobs! Blunders! Here I am! Come and get me!' He darted to the side and led them away from Ludo.

The Mistakes began to move slowly towards him. Then the spider-creature, its hairy body glistening, lunged at him with its venomous trunk. Mel tried to sidestep it, but snagged his foot in the undergrowth and fell. He felt the whoosh in his hair as the barbed weapon shot over his head. He quickly rolled over and stabbed at its long legs with his dagger, but missed.

Then, from where the first creature's head should have been, a swarm of flies flew towards him like a black, chiffon scarf. A great, buzzing cloud thronged around him, temporarily blinding him and inflicting cruel bites. Mel swiped wildly at the attacking flies but his bodkin was useless. It was like trying to cut smoke. He reached back with his free hand in an effort to push himself to his feet and touched something powdery. The remains of the tree. He grabbed a handful of the graphite dust and flung it at his attackers. It made a great arc in the air that hung there suspended, as if it had stuck to a sheet of invisible glass. The long-legged Mistake rushed at him, but as it touched the dust its legs became entangled and then fused together. It toppled down and landed with a great crash, shattering into powder and sending up a great, grey cloud of dust. Mel rolled towards it and, as he did so, the flies moved with him. As they encountered the cloud, its mass added to theirs and they began to coagulate and form a single, large accretion like pools of quicksilver flowing together. It became one big fly-thing too heavy to take wing. Mel rose and jumped on it with both feet and it exploded in another cloud of dust that slowly drifted to the ground. The bulk of the Mistake, now deprived of its head, also crumbled away.

The final Mistake advanced towards him on its eight, hairy legs, swinging its barbed trunk before it like a swordsman entering a melee. Mel kicked a pile of dust into the path of the approaching creature. Its trunk scythed through the cloud, shredding it into streaks. As it swung back, the streaks attached themselves to the trunk and transformed into hissing snakes. They opened their many mouths wide, revealing sharp fangs that Mel knew contained yet more venom. *I've just made it ten times worse!* He backed away but the undergrowth snagged his feet yet again and he toppled backwards. If only the scribble-grass was as friable as the other artefacts of this world.

That's it! He grabbed and tore up handfuls of the undergrowth as he scrambled away from the Mistake. When he had an armful he flung it at the creature like a retiarius gladiator tossing his net. As it flew, the grass spread and flattened in the air into a shaggy pancake and as it fell it enveloped the creature, weighing it to the ground, where it struggled wildly to free itself. The many snakes struck about in their frenzy, biting anything they encountered. This included itself. The creature screamed and writhed in pain and then, like the other Mistakes, exploded into a cloud of dark grey dust.

Mel dashed back to Ludo. His friend felt cold and lifeless. 'Ludo. Ludo, speak to me.' *What've I done? It's all my fault this has happened. We wouldn't be here if I hadn't insisted.* The familiar musical carillon continued through the barrier. 'Come on, we're going home.' He lifted his friend in his arms and walked towards the wall of mist, but as he neared it he felt resistance. He could only get so close but no closer. For an instant the dreadful prospect of being trapped there forever flitted through Mel's mind. He quickly dismissed the thought. *Come on, think!* Just as some powerful force kept people out of pictures the same force must be keeping them locked inside. He had needed to unlock the picture to get in so he must unlock it to get out. He laid Ludo back down, withdrew his sketch from his doublet and unfolded it. Making sure he was touching his friend, he traced the design in the air. He expected to feel the tingling feeling and to be drawn back into the real world but nothing happened. He tried again but without success. *Think,* he told himself, *think!* He recalled how they had got there and imagined the drawing stuck up on the clock face. He could see it clearly with his mind's eye. The drawing illuminated from behind by the great face with its back-to-front numerals. *That's it!* The symbol would be reversed. He traced the design anticlockwise in the air. Then came the spinning, the tingling and they were back, collapsing on the floor of the clock.

The carillon reached its crescendo and ceased. The animated figures completed their motions and returned to their resting places. The door to the clock opened and Wren ducked in, clutching two apples.

'*Mel! Ludo!* Whatever's happened?' She stared down at her two, colourless friends. Ludo such a pale grey and Mel so dark he almost seemed black.

'Help me.' Mel eased Ludo's doublet from him, exposing his wounded arm, which writhed with the tiny worms. He began plucking them out of the gash.

218

Wren knelt beside him. 'What're *those?* How did this happen? I only left you a moment ago.'

'We've been in the picture.'

'But you can't have been . . .'

'We *were*, the symbol worked. Ludo was attacked. He's dying. *Help* me.'

They quickly picked the worms off Ludo's arm and then his leg. As they threw the obscene maggots aside, they squashed them with their hands into mush. They were brightly coloured inside.

'*Yuk!* They must have been drinking Ludo's colour,' said Mel.

'His colour's beginning to come back,' said Wren.

As each worm was removed, a little more colour seeped back into the boy. Soon Ludo's wounds were free of them.

'What happened to you in there, Mel?' asked Wren.

Mel caught sight of himself reflected in a shiny brass counterweight. The graphite dust covered him from head to foot. His blue eyes stared back at him – the only colour on his black body. 'It's a long story.'

Ludo moaned.

'He's coming round!'

'He's so cold,' said Wren, rubbing his hand. She rolled his doublet and placed it beneath his head for a pillow.

Mel took off his own and placed it over his stricken friend.

Ludo opened his eyes. Suddenly coming to himself, he tried to sit up. His eyes shot about him in panic. 'Mel, Wren, what . . .?'

'It's OK, Ludo. You're safe now. We're back home,' said Mel.

Ludo forced himself up on his elbows. 'I've just had the strangest dream.' He looked up and saw the drawing hanging on the clock face. 'Except, it wasn't a dream, was it? Look, Mel, the drawing's changed.'

In place of their ill-conceived world there was a misty landscape dotted with the vague forms of stunted trees and, in the foreground, several large piles of grey dust.

'And what's all this mess? It's like the studio floor.'

'Nothing, Ludo,' said Mel. 'Just take it easy.'

'This is all crazy,' said Wren. 'There's not enough

time for anything to have happened. As soon as I got halfway down the stairs I remembered I'd forgotten to give you these apples. I came back at once and found you like this.'

Mel looked up at the clock. Sure enough, it was barely past midday. 'But we've been gone ages. Time must be different inside the picture.'

'Look, you'll have to tell me later. I've got to get back to the kitchen before I'm missed.' With a last, concerned look at Ludo, she left.

Mel inspected Ludo's wounds again. Now that they were free of the maggots they were healing visibly. 'It's like magic.'

'I'm OK, Mel,' said Ludo, standing up, although Mel could see that he was badly shaken.

Mel ripped down the drawing and tore it into many pieces. 'That's somewhere we won't *ever* be going back to.'

As the two boys left the clock, neither noticed a tiny worm hidden under the machinery. After the door had closed behind them, it crawled out of its hiding place and began to eat the coloured remains of its kin. Then, its hunger unsatisfied, it found a crack in the floorboards and fell through. From there, the slimy creature slithered its way on through the mansion.

The night was stifling. Even though all of the dormitory windows were open wide, no air seemed to circulate in the stuffy room. Mel moved about on his bed, trying to find a cool spot so that he might sleep. After a while he gave up and lay on his back staring at the ceiling, feeling small rivulets of perspiration tickle his body like crawling centipedes. Shadows, cast upwards through the trees by the gas lights in the courtyard below, danced above him. For a time they formed innocuous, familiar things such as a hare and a nodding flax plant, but after a while his overheated imagination began to turn them into more sinister shapes. Bats and fat spiders cavorted, and then the unmistakable form of a tall man accompanied by a dwarf holding a bodkin appeared. They seemed somehow more substantial than the other fleeting silhouettes. The dwarf-shadow lowered the bodkin-shadow towards Mel. He felt a scratch on his arm and found that he could not move. He thought he heard sinister laughter. Movement attracted his attention and from the corner of his eye he saw a hand appear over the sill of the open window and then a man haul himself into the dormitory. Another followed him and then another until a dozen or more stood there in the dim light. They were all dressed in grey robes and were obviously members of a Mystery he had yet to encounter. They wielded fat spears shaped like pencils and two were carrying a long, rolled bundle. They formed a semicircle around his bed. The bundle was unrolled, revealing a huge, colour-eating maggot. It was manhandled towards his paralysed form. The shadows above him solidified and the dreadful, grey face of the High-Bailiff leant close. Mel could smell his vile breath.

'Smell, you thief. It's mine. Your colour's mine. All the colour in the world's mine. You stole it and now I shall have it back,' he hissed.

Mumchance's shadow beckoned to the others and the maggot was brought forward towards Mel's face. Nearer and nearer it came. Mel struggled to rise but only managed a few feeble movements from side to side as it was brought closer, its drooling, colour-sucking mouthparts squelching, and pursed as if for a kiss. Mel struggled harder against his paralysis.

'Mel, wake up! Wake up.'

Someone was shaking him. Mel slowly surfaced from his dream and blinked. He looked anxiously around the dim dormitory for the intruders as his nightmare faded. 'Ludo? What time is it?'

'It's dawn. Mel, come and look at this. I think we're in deep trouble.'

The Vermiraptor

Mel climbed out of bed, followed Ludo to the window and looked down into the courtyard. Even in the thin light of early dawn, they could see that the far corner beneath the clock tower had lost its colour.

'It looks just like . . .'

'Our drawing,' completed Mel. 'There's something moving down there. Come on.'

By the time they had hastily dressed and hurried downstairs through the still-sleeping mansion, the full extent of the damage was evident. Many of the flowering trees and low box hedges were completely grey. Some of the marble statues near to them had lost their delicate pale pinks and blues and a small gilded fountain now looked as though it were fashioned from a particularly dull and lifeless metal more akin to lead than anything precious. The ground writhed with a carpet of slimy, grey creatures.

'It's the *worms*. But it can't be. Wren and I pulled them all off you and squashed them.'

'*What!* You mean those things were on *me*?'

'The ones that attacked you were tiny. These are huge. Some are as big as cucumbers.'

'You must have big cucumbers in Feg. They're more like marrows.'

Now that the maggots were bigger their features were more defined. They were covered in fine hairs and trailed sticky mucus behind them. Bulging, pale eyes stared sightlessly. Their mouthparts had slug-lips like gaping wounds, and they made an ominous sucking sound as they fed.

'They're drinking the colour from everything.'

'I think they're multiplying.'

'What're we going to do? The servants will be up and about soon. It won't be long before this is discovered.'

'If anyone finds these we'll really be in trouble.' Mel began stamping on the mucus-covered worms that were squirming about ankle-deep. They made a squelching noise underfoot and a satisfying *splop* when they burst and their coloured innards shot out.

'This is revolting. I feel sick.'

'You must help me, Ludo. No one must know about this or we'll both be kicked out.'

After a short while, both of the boys were skidding about on the slick, multi-coloured surface of the courtyard. Their boots were thick with the coloured residue of the squashed worms and their white hose was splashed with bright stains below their knees. But the maggots kept multiplying.

The task seemed hopeless to Mel. 'We need help. Go and find Wren.'

By the time Ludo returned with Wren, the oversized maggots had increased visibly.

'I thought a broom might help,' said Wren.

Ludo took it from her and began frantically brushing yet more worms from the trunks of the trees and from the statues. Wren hitched up her skirts and joined in the stamping but it was a lost cause.

'We need more help,' said Wren. 'I'll go and get the other servants and one of you go and wake up the 'prentices. *Get off!*' She kicked one of the larger worms that had sucked her shoe, leaving a grey patch.

'No, we can't do that. We'd be thrown out for

sure,' said Ludo. 'This is all our fault.'

'We must do *something*,' said Wren. 'The mansion's full of the master's paintings. Just imagine what would happen if they get inside. And what if they escape into the city?'

'She's right. We'll never wipe them out on our own,' said Mel. 'But no servants. I've got another idea. Wren, can you get the key to the passages?'

'I've got it here.'

'Will the master be in his studio this early?' Mel asked her.

'No, he never starts work until after his morning rounds.'

'Good. Come on, you two.'

The friends raced through the service passages to the master's studio.

Mel asked, 'Where's the bestiary you found the other day, Ludo?'

Ludo rummaged around and soon found it. 'Here it is. What're you thinking?'

'I was hoping that we might find a creature in the bestiary that could help us fight the maggots and that we might find that same creature in one of the master's paintings.' Mel nodded towards the master's canvas.

'Sounds like a pretty feeble plan to me,' said Ludo.

'I still think we should get help,' said Wren.

'But we *can't*,' said Ludo.

'Do you have a better idea?' said Mel.

Ludo sighed. 'OK, let's try your idea.'

The richly illuminated bestiary was a large tome bound in worn, tan leather. It was tooled with fine gold designs on its cover. It had reinforced metal corners and hinges and a heavy iron clasp holding it shut.

'Lay it down here,' said Mel as he cleared some space on one of the tables.

'Where do we start?' asked Wren. 'There must be hundreds of pages.'

There *were* hundreds of pages and each one featured several creatures painted in bright colours. The illustrations were obviously by many different hands and the older ones, near the beginning, were faded.

'I recognise some of these,' said Mel. 'That's an elephant and that's a lion.'

'Come on, Mel. Your natural history lecture can wait,' said Wren.

As they turned the pages, the beasts depicted on the crinkled vellum became stranger and stranger.

'These are hybrids. That looks like a –'

'*Mel!*'

In the later half of the book the illustrations were fresher and the creatures became weirder still. Next to each was a handwritten inscription in sepia ink.

'What's that one?' Mel pointed to a likely looking brute. 'It looks like it might eat worms for breakfast.'

'I don't know. It's in some strange script,' said Wren. 'Can you read it, Ludo?'

The fierce growling defends itself with its sharp tusks and antlers. It spends its days half submerged in swamp where the tufted carbuncles of its shell resemble floating islands of bog debris. Any flying megaphine that is unwary or foolish enough to approach is seized and dragged into the depths of the mire, where it is left to decompose for several days before it is devoured by *the grotling. The eggs of the grotling resemble green, spiked balls. In the absence of flying megaphires the grotling has been seen to consume its own eggs or, on occasion, small parts of itself.*

'No, I can't. It looks like you should be able to read it but when you try it doesn't make any sense. I'll tell you what though; it's the master's handwriting.'

'Perhaps it's in code,' said Wren.

'I'm sure it's in Nemish, but I still can't read it,' said Ludo. 'There's something odd about it.'

'Why does everything have to be so difficult?' said Mel in frustration. 'Even getting back from the picture was hard. Everything was back to front and I had to –'

'Wait! Hang on . . .' Ludo looked about the studio. 'Yes!' He unhooked a small mirror from the wall and held it at an angle against the book. 'Can you read it now?'

'Ludo, you're brilliant,' said Wren. 'It's mirror writing.'

'The fierce grothling defends itself with its sharp tusks and antlers. It spends its days half submerged in swamp where the tufted carbuncles of its shell resemble floating islands of bog debris. Any flying megaphine that is unwary or foolish enough to approach is seized and dragged into the depths of the mire, where it is left to decompose for several days before it is devoured by the grothling. The eggs of the grothling resemble green, spiked balls. In the absence of flying megaphines the grothling has been seen to consume its own eggs or, on occasion, small parts of itself.'

'It sounds gross. What do you suppose a megaphine is?' asked Ludo.

'It doesn't matter. It says they fly, which the worms don't,' said Mel. 'What about that one?'

Wren tilted the mirror. 'It's a "thringle". It seems they feed on things called "fustinbules".'

'What're *they*?' asked Ludo.

'Wait.' Wren turned to the back of the book.

'There's an index here. Let's see – here it is – "thringle".'

Neither "thringle" nor "fustinbule" looked promising. They tried several more creatures but with the same result.

'We're wasting time,' said Wren.

'Wait a minute. What's that? I've seen it before,' said Mel, pointing to a white-scaled, lizard-like beast.

'Where?' asked Ludo. 'In a bad dream?'

'No,' said Wren. 'He's seen it there.' She pointed to the master's painting. Sure enough, in the foreground, beneath a tree, lazed the selfsame creature.

The friends looked back at the bestiary and studied the beast. It had a triangular, crested head with large eyes rimmed with lemon yellow, a stout body and a long, thin tail that curled up over its back in a tight spiral. Wren read out the annotation in the mirror.

The vermtraptor is normally docile but has been seen to enter into a frenzy after feeding upon chromophages. On no account should the vermtraptor be approached during such a frenzy.

Vermiraptors are normally solitary and inhabit rocky wasteland, only venturing to richer climes when they have the need to drink or seek a mate. The beast depicted here is an immature female but the adult can become aggressive and grow to enormous size should sufficient food be available.'

She looked up 'chromophage' in the index. There was no illustration, just a brief note that said,

Chromophages are pernicious worms (probably mythical) thought by some to inhabit the half-worlds. If such entities exist they are probably formed within the saliva of such creatures as the hogfire and arachnophant.

Wren drew her finger down the index. 'Harpy . . . Hippogryph . . . Humbata . . . Hyrda . . . There's no hogfire here.'

'How about "arachnophant"?'

She flipped back. 'Ajatar . . . Allopecopithicum . . .'

'That's a . . . sorry,' said Mel.

'. . . Amphisbaena . . . *Yes!*' Wren turned to the indicated page.

Ludo gasped. 'It's the spider creature that wounded me.'

'Well, we've found our creature,' said Mel. He approached the canvas and studied it more closely. 'You two wait here, I'll go into the painting and fetch it.'

'Are you sure?' said Wren.

'It doesn't look as though it'll be too much to handle.'

Mel stood up straight and composed himself. He traced the unlocking symbol in the air and Wren and Ludo saw the surface of the canvas gently ripple. They watched Mel vanish, only to see him reappear almost instantly. He was panting heavily. His hair was dishevelled and his doublet was muddy.

'Too much to handle?' asked Wren with a smug grin.

'It's bigger than it looks,' he gasped. 'It doesn't seem to want to leave. I'll need a rope or something.'

'Here,' said Ludo, taking a length of velvet cord that held back the curtains.

'That should do the trick,' said Mel.

Almost as soon as he disappeared, there was a loud thump and the strange creature appeared on the studio floor immediately in front of the canvas. It looked just as it had in the painting except it was about as big as a small crocodile and much fatter.

'Get this great lump off of me,' came Mel's muffled voice. One of his arms appeared from under the vermiraptor.

Ludo grabbed the velvet rope attached around the beast's neck and tugged, while Wren helped Mel out from under it.

'She's a stubborn brute,' he said, rubbing his bruised ribs. 'I had to chase her for miles. I don't know about a vermiraptor, she's certainly a *surly*raptor.'

'We'd best get her down to the courtyard right away,' said Ludo, tugging gently on the rope.

'Careful, she's vicious. She tried to bite me.'

'I think I'll call her Munchie. You're not going to give me a hard time are you, Munchie?'

Munchie looked up at Ludo with her big, long-lashed eyes and blinked mildly. If a lizard could be said to smile that is certainly what she was doing to Ludo.

'I don't believe it,' said Mel.

'Just like the monkeys,' said Wren.

Ludo led the unresisting vermiraptor towards the door to the service passage. She moved with a comic, exaggerated waddle, her pot belly dragging on the floor. They entered the passage and Wren lit the way. When they came to some stairs, Munchie was reluctant to descend.

'You two are going to have to carry her,' said Wren. 'Give him a hand, Mel.'

'*Me?* She hates me.' Mel took Munchie's tail, keeping well clear of her head as she twisted and hissed and spat at him.

'Munchie. Stop that,' cooed Ludo.

Munchie complied.

They heard the great clock striking the hour. 'Hurry! Everyone will be up and about soon,' urged Wren.

In their absence, even more of the courtyard had lost its colour. There was now a distinct chromatic gradient from the wholesome, coloured part, through gradually desaturated sections, to the part that was entirely grey. Munchie had seen the chromophages and was straining at her leash.

'OK, Munchie. Let's see what you can do. Grub's up,' said Ludo, releasing her. He turned to his friends, evidently pleased with himself. 'Grub's up. Grub? Get it?'

Munchie's funny waddle became more purposeful. When she had covered half the distance towards the maggots she rose up on her front legs, uncurled her tail to balance herself, and her incredibly long, sticky tongue flashed out and returned to her open jaws with the speed of a piece of elastic snapping back on itself, cleaning a wide swathe of the courtyard of the maggots.

'I'm glad I'm not on the receiving end of *that*,' said Mel.

'That really was an inspired idea of yours, Mel,' said Wren as Munchie collected and swallowed whole scores of the fat worms.

'What about me?' said Ludo. 'Munchie wouldn't be here if it wasn't for me.'

'Well done, *both* of you.' Wren shook her head. '*Boys.*'

'Er, Wren, Ludo. Look at Munchie. She's changing.'

The first thing they noticed was that her scales began to swell. Before, they had lain sleek and flat against her body but, as the friends watched, they became globular like pearls. They then elongated into sharp spines until she was covered in them like a sea-urchin. The crest on her head transformed into a sharp horn and the loose skin around her neck became a broad frill that also bristled with spines. Long spikes grew from the end of her tail and she used powerful, uncoiling flicks to impale yet more worms on the mace-like tip. These she picked off with backward flicks of her tongue over her shoulder. Her white complexion vanished, to be replaced by vivid streaks of colour that flashed over her hide in rapid succession. The play of the moving patterns was hypnotic as they constantly changed shape. Her eyes lost their appealing, doe-like quality as they narrowed, and sharp teeth appeared in rows in her jaws. She was certainly not smiling. Munchie grew visibly as she ate more and more of the fat maggots. She was no longer like a small crocodile; she was like a very big crocodile. Along with her size, shape and colouring, her demeanour changed into something decidedly unpleasant. Within a short space of time, there were no more worms left but Munchie was obviously still hungry. She cast her eyes around the courtyard and they came to rest on the friends. She stared at them balefully.

'I've a funny feeling that getting rid of the worms will turn out to be the least of our worries,' said Ludo.

'Uh-oh, she's coming this way,' said Wren.

'Back away slowly,' said Mel. 'Make for the door. Try not to make any sudden moves.'

'Scrot to that. *Run!*' shouted Ludo.

Munchie broke into a lumbering gallop.

They just made it to the mansion before a fat, sticky tongue splashed against the jamb. They slammed the door behind them and braced their backs against it, holding it shut as Munchie rammed it.

'What do we do now?' asked Wren.

'We have to get her back inside the picture somehow,' said Mel. 'She still has the leash attached.

Ludo, you're going to have to grab it and lead her back to the passageway.'

Thump! Munchie rammed the door again. The friends lurched under the impact.

'*Me?*'

'You're the only one with any control over her,' said Wren.

'It was Mel who fetched her; he should take her back. It was all his idea.'

Thump! The door shivered.

'Ludo, we're all in this together,' said Wren. 'If we don't do something very soon, we'll be caught. I'll lose my job and you and Mel will be thrown out.'

Thump! The door opened a fraction under the impact but the friends' weight closed it again.

'Getting thrown out may be better than being ripped to pieces by —'

Ludo was cut short as the door finally gave way. It exploded inwards and the friends were hurled down the corridor. Silhouetted against the shattered doorway, and eyeing them malevolently, was Munchie. She advanced towards Wren as she got back to her feet.

'Wren, your pinafore!' shouted Mel.

Wren looked down and saw several pale chromophages still attached to her.

She flapped her pinafore in front of her and the maggots flew off, to be instantly captured by Munchie's long, sticky tongue in a whiplash motion before they touched the ground. 'You two. There're more on your hose,' cried Wren.

Mel and Ludo quickly brushed them off. The chromophages instantly disappeared on the tip of the vermiraptor's long tongue.

'Looks like she's still hungry,' said Ludo.

Munchie continued to move towards the trio.

'Spread out,' said Mel.

Hissing, the vermiraptor stalked towards Mel.

'Mel. *Run!*' shouted Wren. 'Here, catch!' She tossed him the little key. 'Ludo, grab the rope!'

Wren and Ludo seized the leash Munchie was trailing and attempted to slow her down, but the beast was too strong and pulled them off their feet.

'It's no good. It's only Mel she's interested in,' said Wren as Munchie dragged them along behind her on their stomachs until they were forced to let go.

Mel made it to the door to the passageway and opened it. He grabbed the still-lit candle from the small table where they had left it. Once inside, he retraced his steps, shielding the candle flame from the draught with his hand as he ran. He could hear Munchie rapidly padding after him, and a rending as she banged into the sides of the passageway, which was only just wide enough for her in her new form. She gouged deep groves in the panelling and shaved sharp splinters with her spines as she raced after him. The new Munchie no longer had any trouble mounting the stairs as she pursued Mel, gaining on him rapidly. Every now and then, her long tongue would flash out and, once, caught Mel a wet blow on his back. He could feel his doublet being tugged back by the sticky projectile, but he only slowed for a second as his momentum carried him forward.

He was looking back over his shoulder to gauge how near she was getting when he stumbled into another flight of stairs and dropped his candle. He blinked and found that he could dimly see the stairs in front of him. He then clearly saw his hand as it found the candlestick. He turned and found the source of the light. Munchie was only a few yards behind him and she was glowing. As she spotted Mel, the light increased spectacularly and she gave off wave after wave of brilliant flashing colours of such intensity that it hurt Mel's eyes. The patterns on her hide changed from random, abstract shapes into threatening mask-like faces and fearsome beasts that moved like characters in a shadow play as he watched.

Mel threw the candlestick at Munchie but it was snatched out of the air by her dexterous, prehensile tongue and hurled back, barely missing him. Mel ran, chasing his own shadow along the passageway. He would have been easily caught by Munchie if her bulk had not hampered her in the narrow passage.

He reached the master's studio and burst in. He went straight to the painting and prepared to unlock it using the secret gesture. Mel turned. The service door into the studio was alive with flashing colours as Munchie arrived. She saw Mel and let out a great croaking howl that curdled his blood. It rattled the windows and toppled some articles from a nearby table. Her breath was rank and filled the cool room with a sulphurous reek. Her tongue lashed out and connected with Mel's doublet just as he formed the symbol and was drawn into the canvas.

Munchie penetrated the canvas with a powerful bound that carried her past Mel and further into the land beyond. He was counting on this and, as she flashed past him, he grabbed her trailing leash and wound it several times around the nearest tree, wedging its end into a cleft. He knew this would not hold her for long and quickly went to the misty wall, performed the reverse gesture and jumped through.

Mel stood back in the master's studio, panting and gagging at the atrocious smell. He looked at the canvas. Everything appeared the same, except that the image of the gentle, white vermiraptor that had lain so contentedly beneath the tree was now that of a multi-coloured monster with a terrifying mien. There was no way it was going to go unnoticed. He touched it with a fingertip and found that the paint was wet, while everything else on the canvas was dry. He opened the window wide and took a deep breath. He snatched a spare candle from a table, relit it, entered the passageway and made his way back to his friends.

Another Piece of the Puzzle

Later that day there was much conjecture in the household as to the cause of the baffling events in the mansion. Some thought that the grey courtyard was the result of a prank by the apprentices. Cleaners set to cleaning off the supposed grey paint but without success: there was none. It was as if all the colour had been bleached away by magic. Dirk Tot dismissed the idea of a prank. He knew that such a feat was beyond the capabilities of any apprentice and probably beyond those of Ambrosius Blenk as well. Another theory ran that the plants had been infected by some obscure, botanical disease, but that failed to explain why the statues and fountain had also been affected. Most were agreed that the coloured sludge that covered the ground had fallen from the sky. Supporters of this theory could not explain why the sludge had only fallen in that part of the courtyard where the colour had vanished and not elsewhere. It was as if the colour had somehow coagulated and dripped off its hosts on to the ground – but that was preposterous and, as such, did not deserve a theory of its own. And, no one could deny that it stank dreadfully, as if something had died.

But everyone was in complete agreement as to the cause of the shattered door: burglars! The only thing that could not be accounted for in the entire household was a cord used to hold back the curtains in the master's studio. This seemed to be an improbable item of loot but the Watch was summoned and alerted. Assurances were received that the nightly patrols about the district would be stepped up. As to the confused mass of coloured footprints just inside the door, there was again a difference of opinion. Had the burglars trudged through the coloured sludge before breaking in? If so, why had they paused to dance? The same apprentice stunt was held by some to be more likely while a small group held to the improbable notion that because the floorboards were made from unseasoned wood, the summer heat had caused coloured resin to leech out.

Whatever the cause, the effect was unwelcome, as putting things to rights involved lots of additional work for everyone. Gardeners uprooted the 'diseased' plants and replaced them, the fountain was re-gilded and carpenters were brought in to repair the shattered door and replace the ruined floorboards. Nothing, alas, could be done to rectify the colour that had disappeared from the statues.

However improbable the theories about the court-yard were, the master and Dirk Tot were much more concerned about the change to his painting and its implications.

'By my giddy aunt, this is all most perplexing. Is it possible that someone else knows the secret?' asked Ambrosius Blenk.

'No, Master. The only people in the household who know are you, me and the mistress. Are you certain that the painting hasn't deteriorated in some way?'

'Now you're sounding like the servants. It's just not possible. Look, the vermiraptor is clearly by my own hand and the alterations are deliberate.' The master offered Dirk Tot the magnifying glass he had been using to inspect the painting.

'So it *has* been altered?'

'Undoubtedly. But not by me.' Ambrosius Blenk moistened the corner of a rag with turpentine and wiped away the creature's tail. 'There's no original image underneath. It's just changed of its own accord.'

Both men knew this was impossible.

'Could it have anything to do with the arrival of Womper, the Fegish boy?' asked the master.

'I can't believe that. He's talented but not *that* talented. Besides, he's only been here a few days. He can't possibly have found out anything.'

'All the same, I think we should keep an eye on him. He reminds me very much of myself when I was his age. He's very sharp.'

'Very well, Master.'

The riddle of the courtyard aside, work for the apprentices continued as normal. For Mel that meant more scrubbing, and for Groot it meant finding new ways of tormenting the object of his hatred. The end of the working day came as a welcome relief to Mel.

After supper the friends reassembled inside the clock.

'Do you think we've got away with it?' asked Ludo anxiously.

'I don't know, Ludo. There're all kinds of ideas floating around the servants' hall but none of them are anywhere near the truth,' said Wren.

'That's just as well,' said Mel. 'I think Dirk Tot suspects something though. He's been giving me funny looks whenever I see him. And the master must have seen the new addition to his painting. My guess is it won't be as easy for any of us to go there again.'

'I don't want to go there again,' said Ludo. 'I don't want any more to do with this.' He unconsciously rubbed his leg where he had been wounded.

'But there's so much we need to find out. Why is Dirk Tot in league with the Fifth Mystery? And why are the coloured men living inside the paintings? We need you, Ludo; you've been here longer than either of us,' coaxed Wren.

'Look, no one's going to force you to do anything you don't want to, OK?' said Mel. 'But we still have to get a good look inside Dirk Tot's study. You can help us with that, surely.'

'I don't know. What if we meet somebody while we're in the passages?'

'I'll go on ahead and make sure that the coast is clear. I know the way by now,' said Mel. 'You and Wren can follow on behind if it's safe.'

'I don't know . . .'

'Come on, Ludo,' said Wren.

Ludo looked at his only two friends. 'I suppose so. We're all in this together, aren't we?'

Five minutes after Mel had gone, Wren said, 'If he'd met anyone in there he would have been back to warn us by now. Let's go.'

'Wren, I . . .'

'Don't worry. I'll be right beside you all the way.'

Inside the passageway Wren could hear Ludo's breath coming rapidly and saw that he was sweating. He began to tremble. 'You're not up to this, are you?' she said.

'I want to, Wren. I really do . . .' Ludo looked sick.

'Come on, I'll let you out. You've been through a lot lately.'

Normally cautious, Wren would have opened the

door a crack to make sure they could emerge unobserved, but in her concern for Ludo's well-being she forgot this simple precaution.

'What're you two up to?' It was Groot and he was drunk. He grabbed them firmly by their arms as they emerged. 'What's in there?' He nodded at the open passageway. 'Where's Fegie? I've seen you in the refectory. You three are as thick as thieves.'

'Look who's talking,' said Wren under her breath.

'What?' Groot narrowed his eyes. 'He's in there, isn't he? *Isn't he?*'

'No. Mel was exhausted after all of that stupid scrubbing you've put him to. He's gone straight to bed,' said Wren. 'He's in the dormitory right now. Go and see for yourself if you don't believe me.'

Groot studied her face for a moment. He then looked again at Ludo, who refused to meet his gaze. 'That's just what I *will* do. You, get back to the kitchen, where you belong. I'll be telling Cook about this. And as for you, Ludo, I'll deal with you later. Leave the door,' he said as Wren tried to close it. He confiscated their candles and key and watched them until they were out of sight.

'Gone to bed? Like skeg he has,' he said to himself. He stepped unsteadily inside the open passage.

Mel could not read the nameplate on the door but he recognised the shape the letters made as belonging to Dirk Tot's study. He stooped and put his ear to the door. He could not hear anything inside so he opened it a crack. The room was deserted. He entered, leaving the door ajar in case he needed to make a quick getaway. He had no idea where to start or even what he was looking for.

He went to the desk and hauled himself into the steward's oversized chair. The desk was littered with papers and they were all covered in dense writing. He tried the desk drawers. One contained quills, a penknife, a ruler, sealing wax and sundry odds and ends. The others were locked. He sat back, exasperated. *Where have Wren and Ludo got to?* Then his attention was caught by the top shelf of books on the wall opposite, spotlighted by the rays of the setting sun streaming in through the window. To Mel it seemed too neat, too orderly compared with the other shelves, which were crowded and overflowing. A giant like Dirk Tot could reach it but it was too high for anyone else.

There was a chest under the window and Mel dragged it to the bookshelves. He manhandled the heavy guest chair towards it and struggled to lift it on top. He climbed his improvised ladder but it was still too short, so he removed some thick books from the lower shelves and piled them on the seat. He found that he could now reach the top shelf from his wobbly perch. *The books are dummies!* The spines from real books had been removed and glued on to a panel. The illusion was good but not perfect. One book looked slightly different to the rest, as if it had been used more than its neighbours. Mel reached up as high as he possibly could and just managed to get his fingertip to the top. He pulled it towards him. The bottom was hinged and it tipped forward. There was a low rumbling accompanied by a creaking noise and a section of the bookcase to his right swung open. *That's more like it,* he thought and climbed down.

He gazed into a long room much larger than the

adjoining study. Down its length were two trestle tables crowded with a vast array of scientific equipment. There were a great many different-sized glass vessels, some full of transparent, brightly coloured liquids that glowed like gemstones. Gas flames burned under several of the flasks, causing their contents to bubble. They were connected by a complicated maze of glass tubing in loops and spirals, inside which tiny beads of moisture were condensing. Alongside them lay open books filled with long lists and calculations, indecipherable to the youngster. In the far corner stood a large copper boiler with many pipes of its own. Vapour escaped from a valve with a quiet hiss. Next to it was a small, unlit furnace.

Mel walked slowly down the room, inspecting the apparatus. He stopped at one and watched as a blue-black liquid slowly dripped from the mouth of a retort through a muslin filter into a beaker. Next to it were a pestle and mortar and several large jars full of pigment in the familiar household ultramarine. If it was as valuable as Dirk Tot had said, then the contents were worth a fortune. Nearby were other jars full of different coloured pigments. More were arranged on shelves around the room. He also found a sheaf of the wooden flowers similar to the ones he had seen in the fugitive garden. *Wren and Ludo have got to see this.*

Wondering where they had got to, Mel left the laboratory and shut the door. He dismantled and replaced the components of his ladder, relit his candle and left through the service door.

He walked swiftly back towards the others and soon saw the light from their candle coming from around a bend farther down the dark passageway.

'Wren, Ludo, you'll never guess what I've found,' he called as loudly as he dared.

'And what's that, Fegie?' said Groot as he rounded the corner.

Mel stopped dead in his tracks.

'There's no one else around now. It's just you and me. And very soon there'll just be me. Fegish scum like you should never have been allowed in here in the first place to study with your betters. Your scrotty drawing isn't going to help you now and neither is your friend Blenko.' Groot advanced towards Mel, grinning wickedly, and drawing a knife from his belt.

There was no way Mel was going to get into a knife fight with someone as big and vicious as Groot. He turned and ran. He knew the passageway better than the head apprentice and the distance between them soon increased, but he could never hope to lose him completely as the light from his candle constantly betrayed him. He ran on and up but habit unconsciously led him back to the door to the master's studio. It was right at the top of the mansion and the passage went no further. His only escape was through the door and he pushed it open. The room was unoccupied and Mel rushed to the window. He looked out but there was a sheer drop to the courtyard far below. He was left with only one way of escape. As the service door flew open and Groot lurched into the studio, Mel made the secret gesture and found himself inside the painting.

The Irascible House

Munchie was waiting for him. Most of her tail was missing and she was ferociously angry. Her tongue shot out and lassoed his legs and she began to reel him in like a fish on a line.

'Oh, no you don't,' said Mel. He snatched out his bodkin and stabbed her tongue.

Munchie uttered a howl of pain and let go, her tongue recoiling as if spring-loaded. Mel scrambled to his feet and backed away but bumped into something solid. He looked behind him and saw that he was trapped against a rock face. The incensed vermiraptor leapt at him. Mel raised his hands and cowered but Munchie's leap was checked in mid-air and she dropped, choking, to the ground a few paces from him. Against all the odds she was still attached to the leash, which remained fastened to the tree. She screamed in frustration and lashed her bloody tongue once again at Mel. He had his bodkin ready and parried her attack and was able to retreat to one side, beyond her reach.

A moving scene of pure malice erupted across her hide. Mel saw a stylised representation of himself being torn apart by the vermiraptor. It would have been fascinating had it not been so horrible.

He looked beyond her, but the wall of mist had vanished. He moved around in a wide arc, careful to stay outside the range of her tongue, and the mist came back into view. It was as he had thought – the way home was only visible from a head-on angle. With dismay, he realised that Munchie, at the limit of the leash and with her long tongue, commanded the way out of the painting. He imagined getting her to chase him round and round the tree until her leash shortened as it wound around the trunk, but then remembered the way the flow of time was altered inside the pictures. He could stay here a week and Groot would still be waiting for him when he came out. *What I need is another exit.*

Mel made his way down to the shore of the lake and stared across at the strange house for a while. He could not escape the feeling that the house was staring back at him. He stepped on to the bridge, which unexpectedly felt as soft and pliant as a thick carpet, and crossed into the building. It not only looked human from the outside, the interior also mimicked the inside of a mouth. He found himself in a cavernous hallway with a vaulted, red brick ceiling. Underfoot was a rich, red carpet and the walls were loosely draped with scarlet tapestries. At the rear of the space was a huge spiral staircase leading down. Suspended immediately above the stairwell was a great chandelier made from a multitude of sparkling rubies. *It must be so perfectly imagined that even the bits the master didn't paint are as detailed as the bits he did.* Mel approached the staircase and shouted down into the void.

'Hello, anyone down there?'

'. . . down there . . . down there . . . down there,' his voice echoed back.

He did not like the thought of descending into wherever that led and withdrew. Then a vibration began under his feet that grew and grew until the entire space trembled. The rubies on the chandelier tinkled loudly. An almighty wind filled the chamber, accompanied by a roaring belch and a nauseating smell. Mel was blown off his feet and catapulted out of the entrance. He somersaulted over and over as he was hurled down the bridge. The soft surface left him shaken but otherwise unscathed. He picked himself up and, as he approached the entrance once more, the ivory white portcullis dropped shut with a heavy thud.

'Bog off!' came a deep, gruff voice. 'Yer needn't think yer coming back in 'ere.'

'What?' said Mel, startled.

'I said bog off. How would you like it? Something crawling around inside yer gob like a spider. S'orrible. Sling yer 'ook. Scarper. Vamoose.'

'Who's there?'

'What're you, blind as well as stupid?'

'Who said that?'

'Ruddy deaf too. *Struth!*'

'I . . . I . . .'

'*And* the little scut stutters. What 'ave I done to deserve this?'

With a shock, Mel realised that the *house* was talking to him. He looked up at the two great windows and saw the overhanging thatch rumple as if the facade was frowning. 'I'm sorry if I've offended you but –'

'*Huh!*'

' . . .but I'm lost. I need to find my way back home.'

'Right behind you, Sonny-Jim, past yer pet crocodile. Couldn't be plainer. Just do a sweet little one-eighty and Bob's yer uncle. And while yer at it, tell yer pet to put a sock in it. That racket's doing me 'ead in.'

'I can't go back that way, there's . . . I can't go that way.'

'Not my problem, squire.'

'Look, I can't go back that way. I need to find another way. Can you help me?' pleaded Mel.

The house did not answer.

'If you won't help me then I might as well stay here.'

No response.

'In fact, I think I might pitch camp on this bridge.'

'*Tongue!* It's not a bridge, it's me tongue.'

'Whatever. I think I might make it my home.'

'No, you skegging won't.' There was a long silence. 'All right, Pip-squeak, if I tells yer where to find another way back will yer bog off and leave me in peace?'

'That's all I want. I'll be out of your face as quick as you like.'

'OK. See that hill over there to the right? My right, blockhead, not yours. Well, just beyond that there's another way out. Climb to the top and yer'll see it. But yer not going to like it.'

'Oh? Why not?'

'Look, d'yer want a way out or not?'

Mel was about to press the irascible building further but thought better of it. 'Yes, I do. Thank you. I'll be on my way. Goodbye.'

He returned to the shore and set off for the hill. After he had gone a little way the house called after him. 'Out of yer face. I like that.' It gave a little chuckle. 'Out of yer face. That's a good 'un.'

When Mel climbed the hill and reached the summit, he understood the house's warning.

There was a town at the foot of the hill. It looked to be completely in ruin and the shells of the buildings were burning fiercely. Thick black smoke rose and made an already overcast sky as dark as night. There were a great many semi-naked people running about, pursued by misshapen demons that were scourging them with whips or prodding them with long, many-pointed spears. They were herding them towards an enormous, yawning chasm which had opened up in the earth. It spat gobbets of incandescent, molten lava high into the air. Nearer at hand, tall poles had been erected, the tops of which supported cartwheels with more bodies spread-eagled on them. They moaned pitifully. A broad river with the remnants of a bridge bisected the town. Some of the hunted had swum out to seek refuge in the cool waters or on an island but, as Mel watched, dark creatures rose from the depths to snatch them and drag them below.

On the far side of the river, beyond the town and some open ground, just as the house had said, he saw the wall of mist and his way home. *How am I going to get all the way over there?* he thought in despair.

Several figures ran up the hill towards him. As they drew nearer Mel was surprised to see that they were imperfectly formed. They had only the most rudimentary faces, almost like a child's drawing, with just two dark holes for eyes and a gash for a mouth.

Their limbs – such as they were – were in proportion but without any detail, giving the illusion that they were hastily fashioned from modelling clay by an inexperienced hand. They silently mouthed something to Mel.

'What? I can't hear you.'

Mel jumped out of the way as an equally ill-formed demon rushed past in pursuit. The demon ignored him. *I hope the others show as little interest in me*, he thought as he started down the hill. Other people fled past him as he descended and he saw that their features were more defined the farther he advanced. Then it struck him that these figures were in the background of the scene, furthest from the wall of mist and the picture plane. He had entered this canvas from the rear.

By the time he had reached the outskirts of the town everyone that he saw was perfectly formed and detailed. The place was hideous but of one thing he was sure: this place wasn't made by Ambrosius Blenk. The technique and the subject matter were unfamiliar. Mel had stumbled into someone else's depiction of the underworld.

Whether from anxiety or from the noxious fumes oozing out of the ground all around him, Mel began to feel unwell. *I need to get out. But how to get across the river? How?*

There were demons everywhere and they took a huge variety of forms, amongst them snail-like fiends with warty skins and huge shells on their backs. Tubes led from these, with which the demons squirted gouts of flame at the damned. Mel saw that some of their shells had become floppy and realised that they weren't actually part of the creatures. They were soft and more like bladders attached to their backs. Near the river's edge a couple of demons knelt and refilled these with the gas that bubbled to the surface. When they were inflated once more, Mel noticed that they leapt much higher now because the gas in the bladders made them lighter.

I wonder . . . He saw two snail-fiends who had been overcome by those they were tormenting, their bladders now as slack and as lifeless as their bearers. He crept towards them and removed the sacs, which were attached to their backs by shaggy ropes, and dragged them to the edge of the river. Tying them securely to a large rock, he began to inflate them with the gas bubbles as he had seen the others do. The gas made him feel increasingly nauseous and he tried to hold his breath as the sacs filled. When they were full, Mel grasped the ropes firmly with one hand and cut himself free. He rose into the air. Now he could get across to the wall of mist.

'Yaaahhh!' *I'm flying. I'm actually flying.* It was a mixture of terror and pure exhilaration.

The wind took him in the direction of an island. Then, to his horror, as if from nowhere, a flock of airborne demons swooped down at him. They had lizard-like bodies and weasel heads, with snapping jaws full of sharp teeth. They were borne along on bat wings that were incongruously patterned with butterfly markings. 'Get off! Get off, the lot of you!' Mel kicked wildly at them as they attacked him, but one soared over his head and tore a long gash in the underside of one of his balloons. Foul-smelling gas gushed from the puncture, making him feel even sicker and he began to plummet downwards. His exhilaration was instantly replaced by stomach-churning panic as the world beneath his feet rushed up to meet him. He only just made it to the central island before the balloon deflated completely. He landed with a jarring bump as another wave of the flying creatures dived on him, forcing him to release the other bladder, which floated away.

Marooned, he looked around him among the bleak vegetation for a hiding place; then he began to feel movement underfoot. The island wobbled and lurched as it began to rise, dripping glutinous river water as it did so.

'What the –' Mel soon saw that what he had taken to be an island was the carapace of a grothling like the one he had seen in the bestiary. He lost his footing on the slimy surface and began to slide down towards the river, trailing the tattered remains of his balloon, which snagged on encrustations and slowed his descent. The creature's long, antlered head broke surface and snapped at the flying demons. *Those must be – whatcha-macallits? Megaphines!* thought Mel as he desperately tried to stop his headlong slide. The grothling blew a mighty jet of dirty water from a blow-hole on top of its head. Mel slid towards this and when he reached it, jammed the limp balloon into the beast's air passage. For a moment nothing happened, and then the creature gave out a series of choking, gurgling noises and uttered an enormous sneeze that blew the obstruction – and Mel – high into the air. As Mel began to fall back to earth and certain death, the ripped balloon opened above him with a sharp snap and became a parachute that glided him slowly down on to the far bank of the river. His panic vanished as relief flooded his body. He felt an absurd urge to laugh out loud.

Grinning like a madman, Mel abandoned his parachute and ran through the far side of the town towards the wall of mist. A band of demons gave chase. He vaulted a low wall on to the open ground but after he had covered a short distance, the surface became boggy and sucked at his feet. He was in a swamp fed by the waters of the river that heaved and bubbled with gas. He cast an anxious look over his shoulder and was surprised to see that his pursuers had stopped. They just stood there watching him. In a sign of defiance he thumbed his nose and blew a raspberry at them. It felt good. Then a giant mud-bubble burst at his feet and he caught a lungful of gas that smelt like rotten eggs and caused him to retch.

He heard it before he saw it. There was a repeated squelchy rumble like hundreds of rubber plungers being pulled from blocked sinks. The ranks of demons parted and a strange contraption mounted the wall and rolled out on to the bog after him. It moved on four broad paddlewheels studded with suckers. Inside each of these wheels sat a muscular demon peddling furiously. Mounted on top was a double-decker platform. Several more fiends with spears and ropes crowded the lower one while above that was mounted a larger version of the flame-squirter crowned with a towering, conical gas bladder. The machine was bedecked all over with human scalps and skulls and a carved prow with a hideous figurehead projected from the front. It advanced over the boggy surface as easily as a boat over water.

Mel turned. The wall of mist was now only a short distance away, but it might as well have been a mile at the rate he was able to progress. With a roar, the flame-squirter fired and Mel felt a searing heat at his back. Nearby bubbles of swamp-gas ignited, which in turn lit others, and then still more, until the whole surface of the bog was alive with leaping columns of flame.

Then a squadron of megaphines arrived, diving at him and snapping their cruel jaws. Mel waved his arms about his head to fend them off whilst his feet made a disgusting sucking sound as they pulled free of the mud. The flying creatures wheeled off and circled above him, regrouping for another diving attack, just as he reached the wall of mist. He made the unlocking gesture and leapt at the wall just as a lasso fell over him. But the strength of the portal pulled him through.

Unfortunately, it also pulled the demons and their entire swamp-machine through with him.

The far side of the portal was in pitch darkness, broken only by the feeble glow of the fire drizzling from the end of the demons' flame-squirter. This then spewed a long tongue of fire that swept in a wide, roaring arc, brilliantly illuminating the surroundings. The demons spotted Mel and began cackling wildly.

He could now see that they had arrived in a huge hall. He could make out decrepit articles of furniture and walls hung with rotting tapestries. The flame-squirter fired again. Several of the flying megaphines were caught in the jet and burst into flame. They flew about the space screaming and colliding with objects and the remainder of their flock that also caught fire. As the flickering light of the conflagration increased, Mel glimpsed the painting they had all emerged from, seen this time from the viewpoint the artist had intended. It was terrifying. If he had seen it from this perspective he would never have attempted to travel through it.

He felt a sharp tug on the lasso as he was yanked helplessly towards his tormentors. The panic he thought had gone came out of hiding and made itself at home in his stomach. It took control of his muscles and they refused to work properly. The flame spat again, this time aimed directly at him. The heat was intense but did not reach him. The rope caught fire and, as Mel struggled against it with his remaining strength, snapped. He threw off the smouldering remnant and took to his heels, in a kind of racing stagger for the safety of the darkness. It felt like he was running in slow-motion. The demons were right behind him, shooting more gouts of flame and throwing their spears as they stampeded after him, jabbering with excitement. He ran as fast as his trembling limbs would allow, but after a short distance he was overcome by nausea. His legs turned to jelly and he collapsed forward on to his stomach. He raised his head and something in front of him caught his attention.

Tiny pinpricks of light like a swarm of fireflies hovered in the darkness. These sparks grew bigger and brighter and with a great, whistling swoosh shot over his head, followed by a rapid series of wet thuds and screams. He turned and saw that each of the demons had collapsed with a flaming bolt embedded in them. They shrieked as they were engulfed in fire. Mel looked back in the direction the bolts had come from and, out of the darkness, emerged twenty or more figures carrying discharged crossbows. They were illuminated by the flickering light of the burning fiends.

'We meet again, Mel.'

The Rainbow Rebellion

The green man walked into the light. This time he was accompanied by a whole palette of coloured comrades, who finished off the screaming demons with their swords.

Mel vomited violently.

'You're pleased to see us, then.' It was the blue man Mel had met before.

'You'd better start by telling us how you got here,' ordered the green man.

Mel raised himself to his knees and wiped his mouth on his sleeve. He pointed a shaky finger back at the painting.

Blue let out a long whistle. 'I'll say this for him; he's got guts if he's been in there. That's a Flink.'

'How long were you in there?' asked Green.

'I don't know. A while. Before that I was in the master's picture. That's how I got here. Wherever here is.'

'That's why you're feeling sick,' said Green. 'You

can't stay too long inside the pictures before it gets to you. Believe me, I know. It starts with the body but before long it gets to work on the mind. It's a good job you got out when you did.' He helped Mel to his feet. 'You'll be feeling better soon. Come with us now. You've got a lot of explaining to do.'

Mel was not blindfolded this time; there was no need. Several of the men lit torches from the bodies of the blazing demons and the wreckage of their chariot and set off after their leader in single file. From time to time, the flickering torchlight of their procession lit the walls of crumbling galleries hung with paintings, but it was too dark for Mel to see what they depicted. There were other abandoned treasures too – statues, furniture, huge ceramics and tapestries. Everything was rotting and festooned with cobwebs.

After about half an hour they stopped.

'This is our camp,' said Green. 'You'll be safe here. We'll rest for a while – you look like you could do with it.'

'I'll get the fire going,' said Blue. 'Killing demons always gives me an appetite. How about you, Mel? A nice greasy hunk of rat?'

Mel thought he might be sick again. 'No, thanks.'

Several of the men joined in Blue's laughter.

The large fire cheered Mel but failed to illuminate the space. It must have been vast for the light from such a blaze not to touch the walls or ceiling. The fire was fed with pieces of broken furniture, and a number of skinned rats and a haunch of some unidentifiable meat were put to roast on a spit. Mel gazed around at his saviours, who were lit by the stark chiaroscuro of the firelight like brilliant stabs of colour on a black canvas. It illuminated green, blue, yellow, red, mauve and orange faces and an extraordinary collection of clothes. Their garments had been fashioned from carpets, tapestries and curtains held together with crude stitching and lengths of rope. They had armour improvised from silver and gilt plates or salvers, and bowls for helmets with candles stuck to them. Some wore an assortment of over-sized jewellery around their necks recycled from crystal chandeliers and interspersed with the skulls of small rodents. The owners of this motley wardrobe all eyed Mel with suspicion.

'Now,' said Green, 'I want to know everything about how you came to be here – and I mean *everything*.' He stroked an odd, piebald creature of a type Mel had never seen before that came and sat on his lap. 'I'll know if you're lying to me.'

As if to reinforce the point, Blue began to sharpen his knife.

Should I tell him everything? thought Mel. He met Blue's icy stare and decided. *Yes.*

So Mel recounted his discovery of the secret symbol, his journey through the master's picture and then through Flink's underworld. He also told them what Wren had said about the coloured men.

After he finished, Green studied the multi-hued faces of his comrades before looking back at him. 'That's quite some story. So how many of your friends know about us?'

The sound of the knife being sharpened seemed very loud in the silence. 'Just two. I'm sorry.'

Mel's answer did not anger the man as much as he had expected. 'You've found out a lot and guessed much of the rest. You're right, all of us here once worked in the mines on Kig. One by one, we managed to escape before the worst symptoms of the Coloured Death became evident, but not before our skin became stained. We'll be like this for good. Now we must hide here, beneath the Great Houses.'

'*What?* You mean . . .' Mel gazed up.

'Yes, that's exactly where we are. Most people imagine that Vlam is built on three hills but those hills are only the ancient and abandoned cores of the palaces. They've just gone on building and building on top of them. It's taken more than a thousand years. The foundations are so extensive that down here they actually all join up. Right now we're beneath the House of Thrones. A few hundred feet above our heads King Spen is probably at his table. Tonight we'll also be dining in the palace.'

Everyone laughed.

'It suits us just fine, down here. There's always something to eat – if you're hungry enough.'

'Some rat?' said Blue, offering Mel his tiny drumstick.

Mel put his hand to his mouth.

More laughter.

'Nobody alive remembers these halls and no one ever comes down this deep. We scavenge the forgotten galleries for most of what we need: clothing, armour and even weapons. Very fine weapons they are too, originally crafted as collector's pieces and made to hang on walls. But they work just fine.' Green proudly stroked his jewelled sword.

Mel now saw that their crossbows were ornate and made from rare materials.

'We can travel under the city unseen and if we need to go anywhere in a hurry then there's the Mirrorscape.'

'The Mirrorscape? What's that?'

'It's the world within the paintings.'

'So you *can* get inside the pictures. All of them. Not just the master's. I *knew* it. They're all joined up, aren't they?' Mel's mind went into overdrive. If every painting was its own world then they could all join up to make another universe. A universe where anything artists had ever imagined became real.

'Only some,' said the green man. 'Those bearing the secret symbol. The mirrormark it's called.' He second-guessed Mel's next question. 'Not every artist can make the mirrormark, only the greatest. Ambrosius Blenk and Lucas Flink before him and a few others. Lesser artists can mark the canvas but it won't open a door into the Mirrorscape, and not every painting bears the mirrormark. The Mirrorscape recognises its own.'

Mel asked, 'How big is it?'

'I don't know; no one does. And it's getting bigger all the time. Whenever your master makes one of his paintings it grows.'

'And other masters will add their own bits to it in the future,' observed Mel. His eyes grew wide with wonder at the notion. 'But what happens if a painting is destroyed?' he asked, thinking of the ill-conceived world he, Ludo and Wren created. 'Does that piece of the Mirrorscape disappear?'

Green thought for a while. 'I don't know. My guess would be that it remains, but that the portal into it is closed. The only way you could get there again is from another painting.'

'That makes sense. Once something's imagined,

it can't be un-imagined. And is it all like . . . like inside the Flink?'

'Some of it is. Some of it's beautiful and some of it's dangerous – often it's both – and everything in between. It depends on the artist and what they painted. We have a rough map of some of the less hostile regions and we try to stick to those. But it's not always possible. And there's something else you should know about the Mirrorscape. The mirrormark, the seal that keeps people out, also keeps the inhabitants locked in. There's plenty in there that we most certainly don't want out here.'

'Like the demons.'

'Like the demons – and worse.'

'*Worse?*'

'You don't want to know, Mel. They're not like us, the creatures of the Mirrorscape; figments they're called. They don't obey the same laws. I'm not talking about man-made laws – I mean the laws of Nature. If some of those creatures ever got free . . .' He let the thought hang there.

You don't have to tell me, thought Mel. 'Time's different

too. It's frozen – compared to here.'

'The Mirrorscape's a very big place. In some parts time stands still and in others – well, it's different. More different than you can imagine.'

'And the insides of things, bits that you can't see in paintings, that the artist never painted. They're real as well.'

'You've noticed that, have you? I believe that some artists imagine things so clearly, so perfectly, that every tiny detail of their world is realised in the Mirrorscape. There's one more thing you should know. The seal's not permanent, it's fugitive.'

'Fugitive? Like colours that fade in daylight?'

'Yes. After a few hundred years it breaks down. In the very oldest and deepest parts of the Great Houses there are paintings that are so old the seal will be weak. It's a place you don't want to go.'

'How do you know all this?' asked Mel.

Green almost smiled. 'I just do.' Then, after a short silence, 'And as for us, we're just a small band at present; those of us here and a few more, but there're more joining the Rainbow Rebellion all the time.

There are a few people in Nem – very rich and powerful people – who sympathise with our cause.'

'Like my master?'

Green did not answer, but by the way he looked at him, Mel knew he had guessed right.

After a moment Green continued. 'And others. Despite what you may think, there are those in the Mysteries – yes, even in the Fifth Mystery – who are sympathetic to our cause: to put an end to their worst excesses. Lord Floris, the former governor of the Coloured Isles, for one. He helped us – while he could.'

'How?'

'Lord Floris is an art lover. He had a very fine Blenk in his quarters on Kig.'

'That's how you escaped,' said Mel.

Green nodded. 'And now, Mel, whether you like it or not, you're also one of us. In fact, it would suit us very well to have someone else who can travel about up top without attracting attention. Our topside ally is not exactly inconspicuous. I want you to keep your eyes and ears open in the mansion and to let me know if anything unusual happens.'

Who's this 'someone else'? Something told Mel not to ask. Instead, he said, 'I've been in Vlam for less than a week. I don't know anything.'

'You know a great deal, Mel. You're a very observant and resourceful boy. There're apprentices who've been in Ambrosius Blenk's studio for many years and haven't worked out the hundredth part of what you have in a few days. So?'

Green had saved his life – twice now. Mel felt he could trust him. 'I'll help you if I can. I owe you that.'

'Good lad.'

'Look, I'm feeling much better now and I really ought to get back to the mansion. Am I free to go?'

'Of course you are. We can escort you back by a different route. My mate here will show you the way.'

Mel stood up and Blue laid his hand on his shoulder. He winked at Mel and cocked his head, indicating that he should follow.

Mel looked at Green. 'How can I get in touch with you?'

'Can you get inside the big clock that overlooks the square?

'Yes, I can.'

'Good. If you need to talk to one of us tie a shred from your sash around the dragon.'

'The one that looks like the High-Bailiff?'

'He's quick, this one,' said Blue.

'Do that and we'll come and find you. We're closer than you think. Now, off you go.'

'Erm . . . what do I call you? I don't know your names.'

'Just call us by our colours. That'll do fine for now,' said Green. 'Now, skedaddle.'

Blue grabbed a torch and led Mel away from the fire until they came to a wall hung with paintings. 'You know how this works by now. Grab hold of my arm.' He performed the gesture that unlocked the mirrormark.

Mel felt the familiar tingling and found himself side by side with his guide in the midst of a city made entirely of ice. From there they travelled through a bleak landscape littered with the bones of enormous, long-dead animals and, after that, through some kind of botanical hothouse where all the plants had human faces. Then they stood before another wall of mist.

'This is where we say goodbye for now, Mel. We'll meet again, soon enough.'

Missing Persons

'How many of them were there?' asked Wren.

'I counted twenty-six, including Green and Blue. Green said there were a few others. And they've got a spy up here in Vlam.'

'Oh, if they've got a spy, then that makes *all* the difference,' said Ludo. 'What're they going to do, liberate a semaphore tower? Turn it into the Alphabet Republic?'

'So who is this spy?' asked Wren. 'The master?'

'No,' said Mel. 'I think the master's on their side but he's not the spy. Green said the spy's conspicuous.'

'How about Dirk Tot,' said Ludo. 'You can't get more conspicuous than him.'

'It *can't* be him,' said Mel. 'I know what I saw on the road to Vlam. It's got to be someone who hates the Mysteries.'

'That narrows the field a bit,' said Wren. '*Everyone* hates the Mysteries.'

'Everyone hates the Mysteries for good reason.

You've seen at first hand what they're capable of, Mel – and that was just because of a single Pleasure.' Ludo scoffed another mouthful of breakfast. 'Imagine what they would do if they caught someone who was helping the rebels. Better still, don't. Did they *really* eat cat?'

'Keep your voice down.' Mel gazed around the empty refectory. 'I promised I would. It wasn't cat, it was *rat*.' He looked at the remains of his breakfast and pushed it aside. 'What about you? What do you suppose Groot's going to do?'

'He was probably too drunk to remember he caught us,' said Wren as she cleared away the last of the breakfast plates.

'Don't count on it,' said Ludo. 'When it comes to being spiteful, he's got a memory like an elephant. Aren't you going to eat that?'

Mel pushed his bowl across the table to Ludo.

'We'll cross that bridge when we come to it,' said Wren. 'Now, eat up and get a move on, you two. You're already late. All the other 'prentices went up to the studio ages ago.'

'Yeah, I can hardly wait,' said Mel.

*

Later in the day, Ludo ran out of the materials he was using and went into the storeroom for more. As he was searching the shelves for what he needed, he heard the door close quietly and Groot's voice say, 'Here, you dropped this, Ludo.'

'I didn't drop anything.' He turned and saw the head apprentice holding a small paper parcel. He knew at once what it contained.

'You know what happens to snivelling little apprentices who steal pigment from the master, don't you? It'll be a shame to see you go. I've so enjoyed tormenting you.'

'Everyone knows who's been doing the stealing around here, Groot. I'm surprised you've not been rumbled before now.'

'Rumbled? Me? Oh, I'm much too careful for that, Ludo. I learnt from the best. You're forgetting who my family are.'

'A bunch of thieves?' said Ludo bravely.

'Why, you little scut . . . You know, I think we'll go to old Half-Face now. We'll see who he believes.'

'He's not the fool you take him for.'

'You think so? Can you be absolutely certain that you won't be packing your bags and heading home before the day's out? And, you know what; I think I'll ask my uncle Adolfus to open an investigation into the Cleefs. See if they can account for every single Pleasure they consume. And they do consume an awful lot of Pleasures, don't they? Shall I do that?'

'Leave my family out of this.'

'It's you who brought up families, Ludo, not me. What do you imagine a thorough audit might turn up?'

Ludo felt sick. His family, like many others, often bought additional Pleasures on the black market. 'You wouldn't.'

'Oh yes, I would. I most certainly would.' Groot paused for effect. 'Unless, that is, you were to tell me how he did it.'

'What?'

'Come on, Ludo. You know what I'm talking about. How did Fegie manage to vanish like that?'

*

That evening the office of the High-Bailiff of the Fifth Mystery was a happy place.

'Well done, Groot my boy, well done! You are to be congratulated. You've done us proud in the past with your snippets of information but this is a triumph!' The High-Bailiff held up Mel's sketch of the mirrormark. 'Look, he's even signed it for us. How did you manage it?'

'It was nothing, Uncle. After all, I learned from the best.'

Adolfus Spute treated his nephew to one of his repulsive smiles. Mumchance was happy too. With his master in such a good mood there was little chance of his receiving a kicking.

'Now, are you sure you've got this right? There's another world inside Blenk's paintings? And he uses this . . . this thingamajig to go there? And we can use it too? And those infernal rebels you say, under the House of Thrones?'

'Yes, Uncle.'

'You know, dear boy, this is the opportunity I've been waiting a long, long time for. Blenk has always been a thorn in the side of the Mysteries what with his wealth and influential friends. He's always been able to buy Half-Face out of trouble before now. I think we'll arrange a little surprise for him inside this Mirrorscape of his. Something to lure him in. But he won't be getting out again. Oh, no. As soon as Blenk is removed from the scene that repulsive giant will be mine for the taking. Once he's in my hands I'll make him pay for all the humiliation he's heaped on me over the years. I'll make him pay with interest.' Adolfus Spute's eyes glowed with an inner fever. 'This is wonderful. It's everything I could have wished for. Well, almost everything. You searched the Fegish runt's possessions thoroughly, I take it?'

'Yes, uncle. Including his hidey-hole.'

'And there was nothing else there? Nothing of mine?'

'Only his scribble.'

Adolfus Spute's brow darkened for a moment before his septic smile returned. 'You won't go unrewarded. We'll soon see if Half-Face has indeed been fabricating counterfeit pigments, as I've long suspected. There's always been too much blue in that household for my liking. Far too much. Even Blenk would have been stretched to afford that much. Then the monster and his silver hand will be packed away to end his days on Kig, and I will sit at the head of the Council table. Lord Spute! Everyone will be so grateful. There are great times ahead for you and me, dear boy, great times.'

'And Fegie, Uncle?'

'Who? Oh, *Smell*. After I retrieve my property, you can have him. You can do whatever you please with him. My gift. The first of many once I'm Lord-High-Master. The time is ripe for us to pay a little visit to Ambrosius, high-and-mighty, Blenk's mansion, don't you think? This is wonderful, simply *wonderful!*'

The following day, Mel returned to scrubbing a floor that had acquired a great many more stains overnight. Groot caught his eye and smiled a triumphant smile.

Mel edged towards Ludo. 'He's up to something.'

'Not now. Can't you see I'm busy?'

What's got into him? wondered Mel.

It was the most communicative Ludo was all day.

Normally, the master would have visited the studio in the morning to inspect and comment on the work in progress, but he failed to show up. By the afternoon, the household rumour-mill was again in full swing.

'The master's unwell.'

'*Rubbish!* He's never had a day's illness in his life.'

'A friend of a friend saw him going into the House of Thrones. They said one of his pictures is falling to pieces.'

'*Piffle!* There are no paintings better made than the master's.'

'He's locked in his studio, working on a secret commission.'

'*Nonsense!* In that case, why are the mistress and Dirk Tot also looking for him?'

He still had not shown up by bedtime.

Something's wrong, thought Mel. *Very wrong.*

*

Late that night, there came a fearful noise of pounding. 'Open up! Open up in the name of the Fifth Mystery!'

The commotion filled the courtyard and penetrated the dormitory, waking Mel. He got up and opened the window near his bed. The other apprentices crowded the windows that ran the length of the dormitory. He saw that Groot, Bunt and Jurgis were not among them. Neither was Ludo.

'Ludo, wake up! There's something going on down there.'

Ludo appeared to sleep on.

Mel watched as beneath his window two score of men-at-arms carrying lanterns burst into the courtyard and surged towards the main door. Then Adolfus Spute, with Mumchance in tow, strode out of the tunnel.

Minch, still in his nightshirt, emerged from the mansion and confronted the High-Bailiff. He attempted to block his way.

Mel watched as Mumchance crept behind Minch and got down on all fours.

'How *dare* you! You bucket of lard,' screamed Adolfus Spute. 'No one stands in the way of the Fifth Mystery. Especially not a flabby, offal-brained, privy-licker.' He pushed Minch, who fell over the crouching dwarf. Adolfus Spute strode into the mansion laughing.

'Mel. *Mel.*'

Mel looked round for the whispered voice.

'Over here.'

Wren's hand was beckoning him from the crack of the door to the service passage. Mel looked at the other apprentices but they were too engrossed in the scene below to pay any attention. He crossed to the passage and briskly stepped inside, closing the door after him.

'What's going on?'

'I don't know. They're ransacking the place,' said Wren.

'They've got a nerve. Is the master back yet? He'll give them what for.'

'No. No one's seen him since yesterday. Dirk Tot will throw them out.'

'You really think so?' Mel chewed his fingernail. 'What's up with Ludo? He won't talk to me.'

'Perhaps he's unwell.'

'Perhaps.'

'I think you'd better stay out of sight, Mel, till the High-Bailiff's gone.'

'You don't need to tell me. I'll hide in the clock.'

'The sooner, the better. Come on, follow me.' When they reached the door opposite the clock, Wren opened it a crack and quickly closed it again.

'What?' said Mel.

'They've got Dirk Tot. He's in chains. They're taking him away.'

'*What!*' Mel stole a look. 'Trying to, more like.' It was taking six burly men-at-arms to restrain the giant as they bundled him down the stairs. Several more followed, carting away laboratory equipment and boxes full of illicit pigment. 'Looks like they knew exactly where to go.'

'Still think he's one of them?' asked Wren.

'Yeah.'

'You don't sound so certain.'

That night, Mel slept in the clock waking on the hour, every hour.

In the morning the Mystery men had gone. Mel ventured from the clock, dressed and made his way up to the studio. Without anyone to tell them what to do, the apprentices stood around idle. All of them, that is, except for Mel, who was ordered to continue scrubbing, and Ludo, who said he was ill. He had taken to his bed and refused to talk to anyone.

Soon the skylarking began as balls of paper were flung about the studio. This quickly escalated into dollops of paint. When this paint fight was in full sway, and Mel's hopes of ever getting the floor clean were rapidly disappearing into infinity, Minch entered the studio, receiving a large glob of cadmium yellow full in the face. He wiped this from his eyes and pointed a fat finger at Mel. 'You. Mistress. *Now!*' he ordered.

Mel followed the angry, paint-stained servant up to the top of the mansion. *It's the monkey. I know it's the monkey. I'm going to be punished for what happened to Albinus.*

Minch knocked on the door to the master's private studio.

'Yes?'

Minch opened the door and ushered Mel in before departing. The mistress was sitting in a large upholstered chair with Albinus in her lap and her lady-in-waiting standing at her side. She was dressed in much more sober clothes than the last time he had seen her and she looked less frivolous and more noble, almost a different woman. Mel noticed that the master's canvas had its face turned to the wall.

'Mistress, if it's about Albinus, I'm really sorry,' gushed Mel.

'What? No, it's not about that. In fact, now that I've got used to him, I really rather like it. My husband made me a gift of some more. They've become quite the rage among my friends.' Turning to her companion she said, 'Thank you, Gerta. That will be all. You can leave us now.'

When they were alone, the mistress sat studying the apprentice before she spoke. 'My husband and Dirk Tot have been watching you for some time, Womper.

They tell me that there's more to you than meets the eye. Is that true?'

Mel did not know what to answer to this.

'They even think that you might know a secret. A secret that you shouldn't know. Well, how about it?'

'I'm sure I don't know what you're talking about, Mistress.'

'Close-lipped, I like that. Your circumspection does you credit.'

Mel was unsure how much he could give away.

'Look, my husband has vanished and I think that both you and I know where he might be.'

No reaction.

'Let's stop beating around the bush, shall we? Do you or don't you know about the Mirrorscape?'

The mention of the word caught Mel off guard.

'Ah, that's better. I can see from your face that you do. So, who else in this household knows?'

There was no point in pretending any more. Mel told her.

'Well, my husband has gone into the Mirrorscape and has not returned. I believe he's been tricked into entering his world and is being held there against his will. It can be no coincidence that as soon as he's out of Vlam Spute and his men ransack our mansion and arrest our steward. They would never have dared act that way if he was still here. My husband is one of the few people who is powerful enough to stand up to them. Ambrosius has been in the Mirrorscape for some time now. If he's remained within the part he created, then he won't get sick. But my fear is that he could be enticed outside and become as vulnerable as anyone else. I must remain here and attempt to hold this household together and try to fend off that odious High-Bailiff, should he return. But you know about the Mirrorscape and you know how to follow your master. I want you to go in there and to bring him back.'

'Yes, Mistress. If that's what's necessary, then I'll try and find him. But I'll need some help. Can I take Ludo and Wren?'

'You may. But before you and your friends get into this, there's something you should know. Something that may change your mind.' The mistress rose from her chair with a soft rustle of silk and went to the easel. She swung it around on its castors.

Albinus uttered a terrified shriek and ran up the curtains.

'What the . . .' Mel nearly choked. 'It's just not possible!'

The Temporal Labyrinth

Mel was out of breath by the time he had raced through the mansion and finally found Wren in the kitchen. On his way he had gone to the clock and tied his signal around the neck of the dragon for the Rainbow Rebels. He explained what had happened and told Wren about his interview with the mistress.

'So? Will you come?'

'Of course I will.'

'I was hoping you'd say that. Without the master there'll be no household and without a household there'll be no job. I know how much you need it.'

'It's not the job. There's a more important reason than that.'

'There is? What?'

'Friendship, you dummy.' Wren shook her head. 'Let's go and get Ludo.'

'You think he'll come? He's been acting really weird lately.'

As they approached Ludo's bed, he saw them

coming. He turned away and pulled his blanket over his head. 'Go away. I'm not well.'

'What's wrong, Ludo?' asked Wren as she sat on the edge of his bed. 'This isn't like you. Shall we send for a doctor?'

'Don't need a doctor. Just go away.'

'While you've been in bed, the whole place has gone to pot,' said Mel. 'Dirk Tot's been arrested. They found his secret laboratory and masses of pigment that he's been making. All the stuff I told you about.'

'You know, I think it's why he didn't want you to see his secret garden,' said Wren. 'He was probably testing his own colours there.'

'Yeah, and come to think of it, he must have been using it to top up the pigment Groot was stealing.' Mel looked down at Ludo. 'And the master's vanished as well. He's gone inside the Mirrorscape and he hasn't come out.'

Ludo groaned and pulled the blanket further over his head.

'The mistress has asked Mel to find him and bring him back. I'm going too. If you were feeling better then we'd ask you to come with us,' said Wren.

'Leave me alone. I don't want anything to do with the Mirrorscape any more. Or with you. Can't you see I'm not well?'

'But, Ludo . . .' pleaded Mel.

Wren put her hand on Mel's arm and shook her head. 'We're sorry to see you like this, Ludo, but we understand. We'll see you when we get back.'

'*If* we get back.' Mel bit his lip. *Stupid! Why did I say that?*

Wren shot him a withering look. 'Goodbye, Ludo.'

'Yeah, hope you're feeling better soon.' Mel rose and followed Wren towards the door. 'You go and get any stuff you might need and I'll meet you in the master's studio.'

After she had left, Mel opened his cupboard and removed the loose board to his cache. He thrust his arm into the space, searching for his sketch of the mirrormark, but it was not there. *Has someone taken it?* He thought about this for a moment. *No one knew it was there.* The chimes of the great clock echoed through the dormitory. He mentally shrugged. *If it's gone, it's gone. I can't worry about that now.* He worked his arm deeper inside the narrow space and his hand closed on the tiny box. He drew it out and looked at it. *Maybe I'm not coming back. I should take this with me.* He tucked it inside his doublet next to his bodkin. *I guess that's all I have.* He hurried off to meet Wren.

As soon as Mel had left, the door to the service passage opened with a creak and Groot stepped into the silent dormitory. He carried two bottles of the finest Volmish wine. Having discovered the passages, it had not taken him long to find his way into the master's wine cellar and he had since become a regular visitor. He had returned to the dormitory to hide his loot and had overheard the conversation. 'What a touching little scene, Ludo. You know, it almost brought a tear to my eye.'

'Go away, Groot. They were my best friends and now I can't even look them in the eye. Leave me alone.'

'Oh, I will. Very soon now. I've an appointment with my new friends here.' He clinked the bottles together. 'But there's one more thing I want you to do for me.' He sat on the edge of Ludo's bed, leant down and whispered into his ear.

Mel was not the first to arrive in the master's studio.

'Green! How did you get here so quickly?'

'The Mirrorscape might be dangerous but it's quick. So, what's up?'

'Dirk Tot's been arrested. Last night. And no one's seen the master since the day before yesterday. The mistress thinks he's being held against his will inside the Mirrorscape.'

'That's really serious news. I'd best get back at once and warn my men. Bad luck always comes in threes.'

'I'm going to look for him and bring him back.'

'What, in *there?*' Green looked at the master's canvas. 'All on your own?'

'Not quite on his own.' Wren entered the room. 'I've scrounged us some food. I didn't know how long we'll be gone.' She held up a small sack bulging with provisions.

'Wren! This is Green.'

'Nice to meet you, Wren. But it's hello and

goodbye, I'm afraid. I must hurry. We'll meet again.'
He left by the door.

'Mel!' Wren gazed aghast at the canvas. 'What's happened?'

Before, where the picture had been full of sunlight and bright, luminous colours, it now looked totally different. The smiling clouds had vanished, to be replaced by a leaden, overcast sky that seemed to hover only just above head-height. Swirling shapes within them suggested screaming heads. The delicate trees had been either felled or blackened where they had been burnt. The corpses of many of the fabulous creatures lay about, dismembered, and more rotting bodies floated in the now filthy lake. Vultures with blood-matted feathers picked at the bloated carcasses. The island in the lake was empty. There was no sign of the anthropomorphic house that had formerly stood there, just an enormous crater. It was an awful transformation. The scene looked like the last place they would ever want to go, but it was their doorway into the Mirrorscape. They must follow the master.

'How could that have happened?' asked Wren. 'Who'd do such a thing?'

'I don't know. Perhaps the person who stole my sketch of the mirrormark.'

'It's gone?' Wren looked alarmed. 'But how are we going to follow the master?'

'Don't worry, I've got it memorised. Now, I wonder if there's anything here that might help us find him?' Mel began searching the studio. He found a large leather satchel and placed some pencils into it. He added a telescope with curious dials and knobs along its length, which he thought might come in useful. He picked up a leather-bound book.

'What's that?'

'It's the master's sketchbook,' said Mel, opening it.

'Really? Let me see.'

'It's beautiful. I've never seen drawings as fine as these.' Mel traced the exquisite lines with his finger, imagining he was drawing them himself.

'They're drawings from his paintings – preparatory sketches.'

'Are you sure? That means they're drawings of

the Mirrorscape. We should take this too.'

'Well, there's no putting it off any longer,' said Wren. 'The two of us should get going.'

'Make that the *three* of us,' said a voice.

'Ludo!' they both exclaimed.

'What made you change your mind?' asked Mel.

'Oh, it was the thought of you two recounting your adventures after you get back and forever saying "You should have been there, Ludo". Besides, with you two gone, there's nothing left for me here. I'm sorry if I offended you.'

He sounded cheerful enough, but Wren noticed that he was avoiding eye contact. 'Are you *sure* you're feeling better?' she asked.

'Look, are we going or not?'

'What's got into you?' said Mel. 'First we couldn't drag you into the Mirrorscape, then you can't wait to go.'

'We're all going now. That's all that matters,' said Wren.

'All right, let's do it. You OK, Wren?'

'Not really. I'm scared.'

'Me too,' said Mel.

'When you two are *quite* ready,' complained Ludo.

The three friends looked at the painting for a moment and linked arms. Mel took a deep breath and traced the mirrormark in the air. The surface of the painting shimmered and they vanished.

'Come on, it's gaining on us,' shouted Adolfus Spute. 'Surprising turn of speed for such a big building, don't you think?'

Mumchance blew an extended trill on his whistle.

'I'll thank you not to rub it in, you rancid manikin. My plan was perfect – *perfect*. We had Blenk nicely trapped inside that peculiar house of his while we arrested Half-Face. The last thing anyone could have expected was for that jumped-up bungalow to get up off his foundations and come after us like that.'

Another blast.

'Now what?'

And another.

'You mean that crag over yonder? For once in your miserable little life that's not a bad idea. I doubt if that hooligan of a hovel can climb. Or maybe there'll be some cosy cave where we can hole up until it gets tired of chasing us through the Mirrorscape. Come on, Mumchance; whistle up the rest of the men. Let's go mountaineering.'

The first thing the friends found inside the Mirrorscape was Munchie's leash attached to the stump of a tree. It was bloody and had been cut or gnawed through. There was no trace of the vermiraptor – not that Mel was anxious to meet her again. He scanned the ground and saw a trail of footprints. *She's got away.*

'This is *amazing*,' said Ludo, gazing around. He knelt and touched the grass. 'Feel this. It's all so real, not at all like the world we made.'

'Amazing? It's *appalling*,' said Wren. 'Being real's what makes it even more horrible. Even down to the cries of those vultures. How can the master paint sound?'

'This isn't the master's work,' said Mel, 'not any more. It started out as his. It was just as real but smelt a whole lot better.'

'Death stinks wherever it is,' observed Ludo.

'When we first saw the painting it was so beautiful,' said Wren. 'How can it have changed so much?'

'I don't know. But I've a feeling that we're going to find out soon enough. Come on, you two,' said Mel. 'The master's not going to find himself.'

The friends hurried away, circling the lake. On the far side they came upon a huge, almost human footprint in the mud. It had left a deep impression.

Mel jumped down inside and examined it. 'I bet the house left this. It must be able to walk.'

'There's another one over there,' said Wren. 'And there're more leading off into the distance.'

Mel climbed out of the footprint. 'Look, we saw the master going into the house when we first saw the painting. Remember? Maybe he's in there again.'

'And maybe he's not,' said Wren. 'Maybe we chase it and just find the house.'

'At least that'll get us somewhere. When I was here before, the house helped me. Maybe it will again. Let's go.'

'You two go on, I need to pee. I'll catch you up,' said Ludo.

'I'm not sure you should be peeing on the master's painting,' said Mel.

'Sorry, I've got to.' Ludo emphasised the point by crossing his legs. 'Besides, it's already been ruined.' Ludo went behind the remains of a tree. When he was sure that his friends were walking away, he crouched down and took a small paper parcel from his doublet. He opened a corner and, on the blackened grass, drizzled a trail of orpiment. When he had finished, the yellow pigment traced a vivid arrow pointing in the direction they were headed. He refolded the parcel and tucked it away before running to catch up with his friends.

When they reached the fourth footprint from the lake, they found out who had been responsible for the desecration.

'Yuck, that's gross. What was it?' Wren shuddered.

'Not what, *who*,' said Mel. 'Judging by the red robes, I'd say it was a Mystery man. It looks like the house has deliberately squashed him.'

'Best make sure we don't annoy it if we catch up with it,' said Ludo.

'How do you suppose the Fifth Mystery managed to get into the Mirrorscape?' asked Wren. 'Could they have taken your drawing when they raided the mansion?'

Mel shook his head. 'I shouldn't think so. Even if they did, they wouldn't know what it was.'

Ludo looked away.

As they trekked towards the background of the master's picture the grass underfoot became progressively smoother until it was like walking on a hilly billiard table. The vegetation also became cruder and more stylised, and the trees like spheres perched on poles. They reached the top of a hill and stopped to survey the way ahead.

'It's different,' said Mel.

'Of course it's different,' said Ludo, 'unless we've been walking round in circles.'

'No, I mean it's been created by another artist.'

'It's a very subtle difference,' said Wren. 'What makes you so sure?'

'Texture. Brushwork. Technique. Whatever you like to call it, it's different.'

'You've missed the most important thing,' said Ludo.

'What's that?'

'Subject matter. The master's never painted anything like that.'

Before them towered an enormous green pyramid. It was so high that wispy clouds clung to the side here and there and the top seemed to be dusted with snow. All around it the Mirrorscape was as flat and plush as a well-tended lawn and dotted with weirdly shaped trees or large bushes. Mel fished out the telescope and studied the pyramid before he handed it to the others. 'What do you make of that?'

'Those steps are like terraces. They go all the way up,' observed Wren. 'Here, what can you make out, Ludo?'

'All that vegetation around it is formed from clipped bushes and trees. Topiary. They've been shaped like monsters or huge, deformed heads.'

The telescope was returned to Mel and he raised it to his eye again and idly twiddled one of the knobs. The image in the device grew dramatically. 'Neat trick. This gizmo's got a zoom. Hey, that's no ordinary pyramid.'

'So what's an *ordinary* pyramid?' said Ludo.

'You know what I mean. This one's a skegging great maze! A three-dimensional maze. The sides are made from some kind of clipped, evergreen plant. And the giant footprints lead right up to it.'

They set off across the Mirrorscape but stopped after only a short way.

'Where's Ludo got to now?' asked Mel.

'Perhaps it was something he ate?' said Wren. 'Ludo!'

'I'm coming. I just had to look at those topiary heads again.'

'Gardening a new hobby of yours, is it?' she asked.

'Just interested.'

They arrived at the great arch that formed the entrance to the pyramid-maze. It was guarded by two giant topiary monsters that towered above them.

'It looks like the house stopped here,' observed Mel.

'Do you think it went inside?' asked Wren.

'There's no sign,' said Ludo. 'Something as big as a house couldn't get under that arch. And it couldn't have leapt over. Maybe it went around the outside.'

'You two wait here. I'll go and see if I can find any

tracks.' Mel placed his satchel on the ground and followed the wall of the maze.

'See any, Mel?' called Ludo.

'That's odd!' said Mel.

They turned around at the sound of his voice and saw him coming towards them from the other direction.

'*Mel?*' Wren quickly turned and saw him walking away from them. He slowly became indistinct until he vanished. She turned back and looked at him again. 'Did you see *that?*'

'I saw it but I still don't believe it,' said Ludo. 'How'd you do that, Mel?'

'I didn't do anything. I was going that way and then you two appeared in front of me and I found myself back here.' He scratched his head.

'I don't like this place,' said Ludo.

'Let me have a go in the other direction.' Wren walked off and slowly disappeared. She reappeared from the other side. 'It's just like you said, Mel.'

Ludo had to try it before they became convinced. 'Well, if we're not able to go around, then neither was the house. It must have gone inside.'

They stepped through the arch into the labyrinth and looked to the right and the left. Both directions looked identical and the dead-straight path seemed to stretch away to infinity. It must have been miles long either way. They turned left and began walking. At regular intervals they passed tall lamp posts, but otherwise there was nothing to indicate how far they had gone.

'Listen. Did you hear that?' asked Wren.

'Hear what?' said Mel.

'Are you sure you didn't? Like a faint, low boom.'

'You're cracking up,' said Ludo.

After they had walked for about a mile he stopped. 'Look, this is hopeless. It just goes on forever. All we seem to be doing is walking around the base of the pyramid. We can't even see the end.'

Mel got the telescope out and looked down the path. 'Hang on, there's something up ahead. Let's take a look.'

It turned out to be a broad ladder. They climbed it and found themselves on another path identical to the first.

'See if you can find another ladder,' said Wren. 'At least that would take us further through the maze.'

'Let's see.' Mel raised it to his eye and fiddled with the knob to activate the zoom. '*What the . . .!*'

'What is it, Mel? Is it another ladder?' asked Wren.

'Yes. But not only that. It's *us!* See for yourselves.'

'Us? What do you mean *us?*' Wren took the telescope and saw the three of them in the distance. 'You're right. Here, Ludo, you take a look.'

'This gives me the creeps,' said Ludo, handing back the telescope.

'Me too. But at least we know there's another ladder down there. Come on.' Mel led them towards the distant ladder. It took a while, but when they got there he had an idea. 'I wonder . . .' He raised the telescope to his eye and looked back the way they'd come. 'It's us all right. Just as we were a little while ago when we saw . . . us.'

When they reached the next level, Mel surveyed the maze in both directions. He saw himself, still a great way off, waving.

When they finally reached that spot they found

another ladder. Before they climbed it, he said, 'Just a minute, there's something I need to do.' He waved back down the pathway.

'Now *he's* going off his rocker, too,' said Ludo.

At the top of that ladder, Mel said, 'If my theory's right, then we should see ourselves at the next ladder.' He looked in both directions with the telescope but the path was deserted.

'So much for your great theory,' said Ludo.

'I've been thinking about this,' said Wren. 'Time seems to be trapped in here somehow. It's as if . . . *There!* Did you hear that deep boom? I'm sure it's coming from inside the pyramid.'

'There's no sound,' said Mel. 'At least, none that I heard.'

'If you didn't hear that, then your ears need washing. Both of you. Now, time . . .'

'. . . Is something we don't have much of,' said Mel. 'We've been in here a while now. Before too long we're going to start to feel sick, remember. We'll need to find a way out soon. And we still haven't found any trace of the master. Come on.'

After they had walked down the path for a while, they came to the mouth of a tunnel, lit by more lamp posts, that led into the heart of the pyramid.

'Do you suppose they . . . we went down here?' asked Wren.

'Must have done. But there's only one way we're going to find out for sure,' said Mel.

'I'll catch you up,' said Ludo. 'I just want to see ourselves when we come into view. I'll give us a wave so we can find this place.'

They entered the tunnel and presently Ludo ran up to join them.

'Did you signal us?' asked Wren.

'What? Oh, yeah. All done.'

'That's funny, I didn't see you waving at us,' said Mel. He stopped and looked back down the tunnel. 'What's that?' He took the telescope from his satchel. Behind them, running in and out of the pools of light cast by the lamp posts, were a band of scarlet-clad men-at-arms, each with a drawn sword in his right hand. 'It's Mystery men! Let's get out of here.'

The friends took to their heels and sprinted down the long tunnel.

Suddenly it ended. The heart of the pyramid was one humungous, hollow space. It was lit by hundreds of spherical lamps that hung from the inward sloping ceiling high above. The walls looked, and certainly smelt, like earth and the huge, hairy roots of the maze protruded through into the interior, creating a sinuous jumble of twisted tendrils on an immense scale. Many more formed springs, wheels and ratchets that interlocked and moved with one another like a great machine. At the very heart of the pyramid swung an immense pendulum. It was so huge it moved slowly and took a long time to complete each swing. As it reached the limit of its arc, they heard the deep boom that had so puzzled Wren.

Mel's eyes soon adjusted to the gloom and above and below him he took in many more doorways similar to theirs that opened on to the interior. They were all joined together by a confusing tangle of slender walkways like rope bridges, formed from the same root material. They overlay, underlay and joined on to others like another vast labyrinth. Yet more, like rope ladders, joined them vertically. On this impossibly complicated cat's cradle they could make out dozens more of the men from the Fifth Mystery running to and fro. Each carried a sword in his right hand.

'They're all coming towards us,' said Mel.

There was an anguished shout.

'Where's Ludo?' said Wren.

Their tunnel was joined to its own swaying walkway. Mel and Wren ran out on to the flimsy structure and looked over. Below them, screaming and falling into the fathomless void, was Ludo.

Mirrortime

'*Ludo!*' Wren's cry echoed inside the cavernous space.

'No,' said Mel, almost under his breath. Then he shouted, '*No!* Maybe he . . .' Mel looked over the edge but any hope he might have had about Ludo landing on a walkway evaporated. There was no sign of him anywhere. 'It's all my fault. I persuaded Ludo to come with us.'

But before the loss had a chance to properly register, his attention was torn back to their immediate peril. Surging towards them from every direction along the walkways and in the tunnel behind them were the sword-wielding men-at-arms of the Fifth Mystery. Scores of them. Their scarlet robes billowed out behind them as they raced in the friends' direction.

'Wren. Grab hold!'

Wren's attention snapped back as the walkway lurched to one side. 'Mel! What're you doing?'

Mel was frantically cutting through the roots that attached their walkway to the inside of the pyramid.

'It's the only way. Grab a root. Just one more. Hang on!' He severed the final root and grabbed on to a free-hanging fibre. The pair swung down in a vertiginous arc into the heart of the pyramid, clinging to the stout tendrils. Above and behind them red-robed bodies, unable to stop in time, spewed out from the mouth of the tunnel into thin air. One after the other, they tumbled through the void, disappearing far below.

Mel and Wren crash-landed on to another walkway fifty feet below their starting point. It shuddered violently and groaned at their impact.

Winded, Mel picked himself up. 'We're not safe here,' he shouted. He sawed through the roots of their new perch. They swung down again and landed heavily on yet another walkway even farther down. The Mystery men skidded to a halt above them, but two of them lost their balance and plunged headfirst into the void.

'There's something very odd about them,' said Mel. He fished his telescope out and scanned their pursuers. He handed it to Wren. 'Take a look. Tell me what you see.'

'*Mel!* There's no time for this.' But she took it

anyway. 'Lots of armed men chasing us. What did you expect?'

'Look harder. Use the zoom.'

'They're . . . they're all the same. They're identical!'

'Yes! You remember how we kept seeing ourselves, as if there were lots of us? Well, I'm pretty sure it's only one man. Perhaps the invaders were here and he got left behind. The weird time in here has somehow multiplied him.'

'Maybe. But even if there is only one, he's really big. And he's carrying a skegging great sword.'

Just then their walkway started swaying as men-at-arms reached it and ran towards them.

'It certainly feels like there's more than one.'

'Here we go again.' Mel hacked through the roots of the flimsy walkway. This time their pursuers – or pursuer – were nearly upon them before the roots parted and they swung away and crashed on to the temporary safety of another, deeper walkway.

The Mystery men fell screaming from the slack gantry as it collapsed. Far above them, yet more men were scampering about, trying to find a new route to them through the rearranged tangle of walkways.

'This is hopeless, Mel. We could spend the rest of our lives swinging from one walkway to another,' said Wren in despair.

'If we don't, there won't be a rest of our lives. You know about time. What do we do?'

Wren collected herself. 'I don't know. This isn't like normal time. It's *mirror* time.' She looked around at the strange root-mechanism. Then it came to her. 'Mel, it's a *clock*! We're inside a clock. It's pretty strange but it's got a pendulum, gears, springs, escapement. Everything. If only there was a –'

'Wren, *look*! Down there.' Mel had been scanning the interior of the pyramid with his telescope. He had it fixed on a spot deep below. He handed it to Wren with a broad smile on his face.

'How can you smile at a time like this?'

'Just look, will you?'

Wren took the proffered telescope and followed Mel's pointing finger. A broad smile also spread across her face. She laughed out loud. 'It's us. It's you and me . . . and *Ludo!*'

'Think, Wren, *think!* How do we join up now, to the future, down there? What's the missing piece?'

'OK, we're in a clock, right? What we need is a regulator.'

'What's it look like?'

'It'll be a dial of some kind, probably with a knob or lever.'

Wren scanned the inside of the pyramid with the telescope but could see nothing. She tried again. She almost missed it, but then jerked the telescope back. 'There's something over there. Let's go. But this time, please, no swinging.'

The pair clambered along, through and down the swaying cat's cradle of gantries until they reached the spot Wren had identified.

'It could be a regulator but it's unlike any I've ever seen.' It was about the size of a dinner plate and covered with clinging earth. She brushed some away to reveal a broad circle of root with others arranged eccentrically inside. 'Lend me your bodkin for a moment.' With the blade she scraped away damp earth from the face and then used the point to dig out more, revealing a scale incised into the surface. There was a plus sign at one end and a minus at the other, with graduated markings in between. About halfway between the two was a kind of lever formed from a filament of hairy root. She grabbed it but it was stuck fast. 'Mel, I need your help. We have to move this.'

Mel also grabbed the lever. 'Which way?'

'Towards the minus sign, this way.' They heaved it together but it was stuck fast. Then the long walkway beneath their feet started swaying as twenty or more Mystery men reached it and began running towards them.

'It won't budge, Mel. If it was a real clock I'd give it a shot of oil.'

Mel knelt down, opened their sack of provisions and took out a flask of water. 'Here, use this.' He shot a worried glance at the scarlet men who were approaching rapidly.

Wren poured the water on to the regulator, turning the earth to thin mud that drizzled off. They both tried again, working it to and fro. Ever so slowly, the lever began to move. Time slowed down.

As if in slow-motion, the first of their pursuers reached Mel. He raised his sword high over his head and struck down.

With a jolt, the lever came completely free and went all the way to the minus end of the scale. The razor-sharp blade halted a bare hand's breadth from Mel's skull. It then rose away. Slowly at first, but gathering pace, the man began to move backwards. He reached his doubles and they too began to reverse their course down the walkway as the mirrortime unwound.

'That was close,' said Mel, rubbing his head.

'Come on,' said Wren, 'I don't know how long this'll last.' With a mighty wrench, she pulled the regulator off its support and stashed it in Mel's satchel. They grabbed their belongings and ran after the retreating men.

Then their whole pursuit went into rapid reverse. When they reached the dangling ends of the severed walkways that they had descended on, they grabbed them and were whipped up into the air. It happened so fast that they nearly lost their grip. This was repeated several times as they retraced their descent, until they found themselves speeding upwards towards the mouth of the tunnel where they had entered the interior. Just before the walkway reattached itself to the inner wall of the pyramid, eleven men-at-arms shot from the darkness below and into the mouth of the tunnel. Mel looked down the passage and saw them running backwards and then he and Wren following them – or preceding them; it was all very confusing.

He looked over the edge of the walkway and saw Ludo rising towards them at great speed. As he neared the walkway, he slowed down. Mel reached out, grabbed his friend and hugged him tight. The three of them watched for a moment as they saw themselves disappearing backwards into the tunnel.

'Ludo! It's so great to have you back.'

'Have me back? I haven't been anywhere – and let go of me.'

'Come on!' shouted Wren.

They hurried out on to the restored walkway. After they had gone a short way, it began to sway.

'We'd better hurry. You can't treat a clock like that and expect it to work normally,' said Wren.

'What are you talking about?' asked Ludo, puzzled.

'We'll tell you later,' said Mel and Wren together.

They rushed on, descending through the walkways as the entire interior of the pyramid began to vibrate. The noise of the pendulum – more of a 'moob' than a boom now – became increasingly frequent.

'Just a moment, Ludo,' said Mel as they arrived at the spot where they had seen themselves earlier. It stood at the entrance to another tunnel that seemed to lead out of the pyramid. 'Come here and stand by us. Look up there and wave.' He pointed back up into the heart of the swaying tangle of walkways.

'You've both gone mad,' said Ludo.

'Just humour us,' said Wren. 'It's for your own good.'

The three friends waved energetically, repeating the scene Mel and Wren had witnessed earlier.

'You're cracked,' said Ludo. 'Both of you.'

'You fell into the pyramid,' said Mel.

'We thought you were dead but then we saw us all standing here. We reversed time and got you back,' added Wren.

'Dead? *Me?*'

'We'll all be dead if we don't get out of here before the entire place shakes itself to pieces,' said Mel. 'Let's go.'

They were bouncing off the walls by the time they reached the outside. They emerged through a doorway at ground level and ran out on to the grassy plain beyond for some way before they stopped in front of an enormous topiary head and looked back. The pyramid went through an instant autumn as the leaves of the towering maze all fell at once, revealing a bleak terraced structure through the suddenly bare branches. This tottered and, for a moment, seemed as if it was about to implode. The terraces leant against each other at drunken angles and came to rest. Then, like a shockwave spreading out from an explosion, all the topiary figures on the plain also shed their leaves, leaving huge, skeletal vegetation behind.

The friends looked round, and beneath the bare vestiges of one of the giant heads that now resembled a skull was the entrance to a wide underground passage. Leading out from the tunnel entrance and disappearing towards the horizon was a trail of giant footprints.

'Well, that answers one question,' said Ludo. 'The house didn't go around, it didn't go over and it didn't go through. It went *under*.' They all peered down into the hole.

'Do you suppose the house knew about the tunnel?' asked Wren.

'Maybe the Fifth Mystery chased him here,' said Ludo.

'From what I know of the house it would have been the one doing the chasing,' said Mel. 'Are you two all right? You don't look well.'

'To tell the truth, I don't feel too good,' admitted Ludo.

'Me neither, Ludo,' said Mel. 'It's the Mirrorscape sickness Green warned me about. We need to get out for a break. Can either of you see a wall of mist anywhere?'

'You mean like that, over there?' asked Wren.

'That's just what I mean. Come on, you two.'

'I'll catch you up. I've got a pebble in my boot,' said Ludo.

The wall of mist shimmered and parted. On to the black and ruined shores of Ambrosius Blenk's lake stepped Groot, Bunt and Jurgis. They were wearing scarlet robes and each had the freshly shaved tonsure and pallid faces of the Fifth Mystery. Groot looked about with satisfaction at the work of his new colleagues. He folded Mel's sketch of the mirrormark and handed it to Jurgis, who tucked it inside his robes. They searched around until they found the yellow arrow.

Groot laughed. 'No strength of character, that boy. None at all.'

The friends found themselves back in Nem and feeling better after the onset of the Mirrorscape sickness. It only took a short while before the symptoms disappeared. They were in a small, octagonal room hung with paintings. Wren opened the sack and shared out some of their provisions.

As they ate, Ludo listened to their story of how they reversed the mirrortime but was incredulous. 'If I'd fallen down into the pyramid I'd know all about it. Look.' He rolled up his sleeves. 'Not a scratch.'

'But you *did*,' insisted Mel. 'And then Wren worked out how to rewind time – and you didn't.'

'You're just trying to confuse me. Either I did or I didn't.'

'What's this then?' Wren showed Ludo the shaggy regulator.

'How should I know? What is it anyway?'

'We used it to rewind time. It's something my father would be interested in. I'm going to show it to him. One day.' She put it away. 'Where do you think we are?'

'We must be in the House of Mysteries,' said Mel, pointing at the view through the windows.

'Figures,' said Ludo. 'The Mysteries have most of the best paintings. What's that one? Next to the pyramid.'

'It's called "The World Turned Upside Down",' said Wren, reading the nameplate. It portrayed a scene where birds swam in rivers, fish flew in the sky and horses rode their riders. 'But this is my favourite.'

Mel and Ludo joined her and gazed at a canvas of an artist's studio.

'Look, the perspective's impossible,' said Mel. 'You look at it one way and the wall's the floor and then you look at it again and it's the other way round. And there're figures going up the staircase and under their feet there're others coming down. It doesn't make sense.'

Ludo did a handstand. 'If you do this, it still looks wrong.'

Mel and Wren twisted their heads.

'I think I know how it's done,' said Mel. 'It's got three vanishing points, one for each way you can look at the picture. Let me show you.' He searched in his satchel for a pencil and the master's sketchbook.

'Not now, Mel. Show us after we've found the master,' said Wren.

Restored, and back in the Mirrorscape, the friends picked up the trail of footprints and they followed it until they came to a huge, smooth rock face at the base of a towering crag, where it stopped abruptly.

'Now what?' said Ludo. 'This time there's no tunnel and it obviously didn't go around.'

'Maybe it flew over,' said Wren.

'A flying house? I don't think so,' said Mel, craning his neck to see the top of the crag. 'Perhaps there's some explanation in here.' He took the master's sketchbook out from his satchel. The friends flipped through the pages but could find nothing.

'Oh, this is hopeless,' said Ludo. 'We might as well give up now. I don't know why I ever agreed to come along with you. The house – if it actually exists – has just vanished into thin air.'

'Perhaps it's gone inside the mountain,' said Wren, studying the smooth rock face. There, at head-height, was a sculpted, hemispherical boss of rock about the size of a thumbnail. Incised over it in small, neat letters was the word 'Deliveries'. 'Why don't we ring and ask?'

Mel shrugged. 'It's no crazier than anything else we've come across in the Mirrorscape.' He pressed the boss. There was the sound of a large bell striking somewhere far away. After a minute or so he pushed the boss again. Then there came a cracking sound, like someone snapping a bunch of twigs, and beneath the boss a pair of carved, human-shaped lips appeared out of the solid rock.

'All right, all right, keep your hair on. *Yes?*' said the lips in an irritated voice.

The friends looked at each other amazed. Mel said, 'Can you please tell us, has a house passed this way?'

'Speak up! What? Speak up I said . . . Oh, scrot. Just a minute.' There was another snapping noise and a pair of carved ears appeared either side of the boss. 'I can't hear you. Speak into the ears.'

Ludo leant closer and said in a raised voice, 'A house! We're looking for a house!'

'*Ouch!* No need to shout, I'm not deaf. Now, what was it you wanted?'

'A house,' said Mel in a more moderate tone.

'Do I look like an estate agent?'

'Err, no. But –'

'Then what're you bothering me for?' There was another snapping sound and the ears and lips disappeared back into the stone.

Undaunted, Wren pushed the bell again.

The snapping sound, much louder and angrier this time, was followed by the appearance of the lips and ears. '. . . don't put it there, it's bound to . . .' There came the muffled sound of something crashing to the ground. '. . . fall over. Why doesn't anyone ever listen to me? *Yes?*'

'Look, we're sorry to disturb you,' said Wren. 'You sound very busy but we're looking for a house. Did a large, funny-looking house come this way?'

'Who the skeg's that? Hang on a minute. Which switch was it?' There was a double crack and two carved eyes popped open just above the boss. There was now a complete, flattened-out face in high-relief with the boss as a nose and 'Deliveries' forming a long eyebrow. 'Ah, that's better.' The eyes blinked and surveyed the trio. Then in a curt tone, 'What now?'

Mel said, 'We've been following a house and he seems to have come here. We were wondering if you've seen him . . . it.'

'What's that say?' said the face, raising its eyes to look at its brow.

'It says "Deliveries",' said Ludo. 'But –'

'And have you got a delivery?'

'Not exactly . . .'

'Then what are you bothering me for? Haven't I

got enough to do without time-wasters?'

'Well, we might have one, if we knew what this place was,' said Wren. 'What exactly are you?'

The face huffed and rolled its eyes. 'We're a *mine*, ducky. What do you expect to find inside a mountain?'

'What sort of mine, exactly?' asked Mel.

'A mine of *inspiration*,' said the face in a tone that clearly suggested it was talking to an idiot.

'Don't you mean a mine of *information?*' asked Ludo.

'Where do they get 'em these days?' said the face in an exasperated tone. 'Whoever heard of a mine of information? Information's already out there. It's everywhere. You only have to open a book or a newspaper or talk to people. *Inspiration*, on the other hand, is much more difficult to come by. You have to delve for inspiration, ideas that no one's had yet. It's not just lying around anywhere now, is it? Inspiration's new stuff. Once it's been dug out and used it becomes information. Even an imbecile can work that one out, can't they?'

'Yes, I suppose so,' said Mel.

'Well? Have you got any or not?'

'What, inspiration? Between the three of us, I guess we must have,' said Wren. 'In fact, we've got lots.'

'Why didn't you say so in the first place? Come on in.'

There was a much louder cracking sound and a huge carved door appeared in the rock face. It opened with a hollow, scraping sound, permitting the friends to enter.

Groot watched Bunt and Jurgis being sick with morbid fascination. He did not feel too well himself, but he was not going to let it spoil his enjoyment at seeing his companions suffer. They had picked up Ludo's trail on the far side of the pyramid. Since the root-clock inside had ceased working they were able to simply walk around the outside. Groot knelt and picked up a hastily scribbled note anchored by a stone next to a yellow arrow. Having read it, he screwed it up and threw it away.

'Come on, you pukes. Apparently it's being in here that's making us feel unwell. We need to get out for a spell.' He led them away towards the wall of mist, which had been clearly marked by Ludo.

When they emerged into the small chamber in the House of Mysteries, Groot had an idea and sent Bunt to procure some paints, brushes and canvas. Jurgis was sent to the High-Bailiff to fetch the models. All he now needed was a studio to work in to bring his plan to fruition. He did not need to search far.

The Mine of Inspiration

'Are you seeing what I'm seeing?' gasped Ludo.

'It's hollow,' said Mel. 'The whole mountain's *hollow*.'

'It's like an enormous sculpture,' said Wren.

Bright shafts of daylight streamed down from openings high above in the ceiling. This was supported by hundreds of columns hewn from the living rock, each one different from its neighbour. One was shaped like a tall palm tree, its swaying fronds fanning out to form the ribs of vaulting where carved birds hopped about singing. The next column was a representation of a coil of rope, which snaked upwards with dozens of busy monkeys clambering up and down, and yet another was a great column of water that poured down from the capital in the shape of a tipping amphora. There were many more besides.

Between these columns, and covering most of the acres of floor space, were dozens of islands with square-rigged, stone ships plying back and forth. In the heaving, flag-stoned space between the islands – the

347

aisles between the isles – the ominous fin of a stone shark would part the rolling waves or a school of sculpted flying fish would break the surface with a noise like a grindstone and glide above the stone waters for a distance, trailing bright sparks behind them. The beaches gently rose to support a confusion of carved mangrove roots. Scampering among the roots were many creatures also crafted from the stone – snakes, iguanas, parrots, land crabs, walruses and many others. Nestling within the honeycomb formed from the leafless, twisted limbs of the mangrove trees were a mind-numbing assortment of items in every imaginable shape, size and colour. There were jellyfish and sycamore trees, clouds and unicycles, Ferris-wheels and dinosaurs, cathedrals and euphoniums. You name it, it was there.

High above the islands, suspended from a network of cables, hung bullet-shaped silver craft that cruised the upper reaches of the mine, occasionally stopping to descend and pluck or deposit yet more items from the higher branches of the mangroves.

At least, that's what it would all have looked like if

the house had not already been there. What the friends saw as they stood on a ruined pier that projected into the mine was altogether different. To either side, the mine still retained its original design, but right through the centre was a broad swathe of destruction. Many of the islands forming the archipelago had been flattened, and their inspirational contents were now so much flotsam and jetsam bobbing on the stone floor. Shipwrecked mariners clung to this wreckage or to the floating remains of their foundered vessels. Some of the sounder craft plucked their unfortunate colleagues from the mineral waves or fended off circling sharks. Several of the overhead cable cars had lowered rope ladders to the distressed seamen and were ferrying them to intact islands. It was a scene of great activity and utter confusion.

'*Ow!*' A rope ladder had fallen from above and hit Wren a glancing blow on her shoulder. Above them, swaying gently, was one of the cable cars. 'Perhaps we're meant to climb up into that contraption,' she said. 'It's the only way off this pier.'

Just then, the lips briefly appeared on the lowest

rung of the ladder. 'Come along now, don't dilly-dally. There's work to be done.'

'Hang on. Where's Ludo?'

'He was here a moment ago,' said Wren. 'Perhaps he's gone back outside.'

'I'm right here,' said Ludo, hurrying back to his friends. 'You needn't think I'm going down there,' he said, pointing out into the sea of flagstones and disorder.

'It looks like we have to take the cable car if we plan on finding out more,' said Mel.

When they reached the contraption, they found that the outside was covered in sheets of polished metal riveted together. It had sweeping fins, large air scoops and exhaust pipes along its sides, which anyone could see were just for show. Inside, the car was constructed like a rowing boat with several bench-like seats running from side to side. Where the rowlocks would have been there were stout pulleys which were attached to the cables from which the car dangled. At the front was a small, semicircular glass windshield and beneath it, at an angle, was a polished and riveted dashboard. In the centre of this was a button, above which were embossed the words 'Push for Attention'.

Mel pushed the button. There came the sound like a door opening on rusty hinges and the same face appeared, but this time formed from the polished metal around the button, with 'Push for Attention' for a brow. The rivets looked like pimples.

'Oh, there you are. You took your time.' It sounded harassed. 'So, what've you got?'

'Got?' said Mel, puzzled.

'Oh, *really!* You're making a delivery,' said the face tetchily. '*Remember?*'

'That wasn't too bad, was it?' said Ludo as he attempted to flatten his static-charged hair, which was standing wildly on end.

All three friends looked as if they had just received the worst fright of their lives. The cable car had taken them out to one of the undamaged islands. One by one, they had been lowered down to vacant cells in the sculpted mangrove tree. Inside each was an odd metal helmet that looked like an upturned pudding basin encrusted with coils, dials and coloured lights. As

351

instructed, they had placed these on their heads, closed their eyes and imagined something. The helmets had hummed, causing their scalps to tingle and the lights to flash and then, with a sound like a nightingale trapped inside an accordion, the object they had imagined materialised in front of them.

Wren had imagined a quintet of tortoise-like creatures of various sizes, their shells replaced by bellows. In place of heads grew brass funnels like the bells of trumpets. As the bellows expanded and contracted, they blew clear, golden notes in perfect harmony. Inspired by Wren, Mel had continued the musical theme. He had imagined a flock of multi-coloured ibises with their long, curved bills formed from clarinets, oboes, trombones and saxophones, and Ludo, who had taken a dislike to the grumpy face, imagined a large bass drum with the being's features emerging out of the drum skin. All around the circumference were bells, gongs and cymbals. He took great pleasure bashing the drum with a drumstick shaped like a fist on a stick.

When they were all back inside the cable car

once more, Mel pushed the button again.

'*Very* nice, very nice indeed,' said the face as it re-emerged. 'Although there was no need to test the drum quite so vigorously.' It grimaced. 'You may only have a single brain cell between the three of you but that's some quality inspiration, I must say. We could do with a lot more of that – to replace the damaged stock.'

'We wish we could stick around and help some more but we must be after the house,' said Mel.

'Perhaps you didn't hear me right. I said, "*we could do with a lot more of that*".'

'I'm sorry, but we haven't the time right now. We have to go.'

'Go? You're not going anywhere. Not until all the stock's been replenished. That house you seem to be so friendly with was the cause of all this damage. And now you're going to put it all to rights.'

'I thought you said you hadn't seen the house,' said Ludo.

'I didn't say I had and I didn't say I hadn't.'

'But we *have* to go,' pleaded Wren. 'We've already spent far too long here as it is. If you could just show us the way out, we'd be ever so grateful. *Please.*'

'Oh well, if you have to go, you have to go,' said the face, relenting. 'It's a pity. We sure could have used your inspiration. You don't see quality like that every day. Hold tight.' The face vanished and the cable car sped off with a lurching motion, into the heart of the mine.

They headed for an island towards the periphery of the flagstone sea. This one had a large, cone-shaped volcano on it rather than the ubiquitous mangrove trees. When the car was immediately over the volcano it came to a swaying halt and the face re-emerged from the dashboard.

'Here we are.'

'Where?' asked Wren. 'This doesn't look like a way out to me.'

'Way out, ducky? Whatever could have given you that idea?' asked the face. 'Like I told you, you won't be going anywhere until the mine's been restocked. I'll find out what's needed and come back for you. Until then, you can keep the other one company. He looks like one of your lot. *Alley-oop!*'

'What other –?'

Mel's question was cut short by a whirring noise as the pulleys all along one side of the car engaged and the whole conveyance abruptly tipped upside down. The friends spilled out of the car and through the air into the crater. Down and down they tumbled, landing on a great pile of junk that filled most of the interior. The debris broke their fall and they clattered, helter-skelter down the slope, landing in a heap on the floor deep inside the hollow volcano.

Mel looked up and saw the mouth of the crater, a disc of light no bigger than the full moon, high above them.

'That lying scrot,' said Ludo as he staggered to his feet, dusting himself down.

'Perhaps you shouldn't have imagined that drum,' said Wren.

'We shouldn't have been so inspirational.' Mel angrily kicked a piece of junk.

'What're we going to do now?' said Ludo.

'We need to find a way out – in a hurry. Before too long we're going to become sick, remember?' said Mel. 'Perhaps we can find something to help us in all this rubbish.'

'I suppose a ladder would be too much to hope for,' said Ludo, sorting through the junk.

'It'd need to be a really long ladder,' said Wren. 'Even from the top of the heap it'd never reach the opening.'

'This is all junk,' said Ludo. 'Everything's broken or useless.'

'It must be the mine's dump,' said Wren

'I've found a kettle. *Yuck*, it's made from butter.' Mel wiped his greasy hands on his doublet.

'Here's a chocolate frying pan,' said Ludo. 'And a teapot made from feathers. What have you found, Wren?'

'I've got a velvet cartwheel, an elastic spanner and a sewing machine that seems to be made out of smoke. Nothing here's the least bit useful.' Wren sat down on the scrapheap.

'There's got to be a way out,' said Mel as he knelt and unfastened his satchel. He withdrew the telescope and began to pan around the interior of the dimly lit volcano but there was very little to see in the feeble light filtering down from above. The far side of the volcano was obscured by the scrapheap. Even with the zoom, he could find nothing. The only way out was the mouth of the crater high over their heads.

'*Ahem!*' A polite cough sounded behind the friends. 'Young sirs, miss, if I might be so bold as to venture a small suggestion?'

'This is more like it, eh, Mumchance? Who's doing the running away now? Look at that cowardly cottage run!'

The High-Bailiff looked down from the cabin of his flying command vehicle at his men-at-arms far below, thundering across the Mirrorscape in their newly plundered conveyances. Fleeing before them in a cloud of dust was the house.

'Amazing what one can find inside a mountain these days. These machines are just the job.' Adolfus Spute gazed admiringly at his fleet of bizarre vehicles, plundered from the Mine of Inspiration. 'Mumchance, we're losing altitude. Adjust the buoyancy, my little man. Give us a trifle more elevation, if you please.'

The dwarf mounted a ladder and opened a trapdoor in the roof of their weird flying machine. From the outside it resembled the rotting carcass of a rhinoceros. He blew a violent blast on his silver whistle. Above his head flew a huge flock of birds attached to the passenger compartment with myriad fine wires. When his whistle blast had no effect, he reached inside his scarlet robe and withdrew a small catapult. Fitting a pebble into the sling, he took aim and fired into the midst of the flock. There was an enraged cawing and a cloud of shed feathers as his missile hit its mark. The birds flapped harder and the vehicle rose.

'Ah, that's better. Not long now, my manky miniature. Soon we'll have Ambrosius Blenk in our hands once more.'

Down and Out

Startled, the friends turned at the sound of the voice. He was about their height and dressed exactly like them in the Blenk household livery. But there the similarity ended. He was more or less human in shape, but his bald head was completely spherical and his face recessed into it.

'Perhaps I should introduce myself. My name is Swivel and I am Master Blenk's butler.' He inclined his round head in a bow.

'No you're not,' said Ludo. 'I've never seen you around the mansion.'

'Forgive me, young sir, but I serve the master here, in his residence in the Mirrorscape. Like all inhabitants of the Mirrorscape I am a figment. In my case, of Master Blenk's imagination.'

Mel quickly made the connection. 'You mean you work in that funny-looking house?'

'Precisely, young sir. And it's rather important that I get back as soon as possible. The master needs looking after.'

'Then you'll know what's happened here?' said Wren.

'Indeed. Master Blenk was visiting his house by the lake when a large band of red-robed ruffians from the Fifth Mystery arrived and began vandalising the grounds and mistreating the wildlife. Then they attempted to enter the residence, quite without invitation. Such *appalling* manners.' At this point the strangest thing happened. Swivel's face, which up until then had been composed, swivelled around within his head with a metallic, scraping sound, to be replaced by another with a look of disdain on it. It then swivelled back and he continued. 'Billet, who you rather questionably refer to as "that funny-looking house", took umbrage at this and, after excusing himself to Master Blenk, set about teaching that rabble how to behave towards their betters. But they wouldn't be told. It was all most regrettable.' He sighed and his face rotated in the other direction to display one of resigned sadness before flipping back. 'They fled and he . . . we gave chase. To cut a long story short, we ended up here, at the Mine of Inspiration, where things took a turn for the worse. Up until that time, Billet had the upper hand and the hooligans were in full flight. But once inside the mine they managed to appropriate several important articles of inspiration and caused quite a furore. I'm sure you've seen the result. Not to put too fine a point on it, the tables were turned. Master Blenk and Billet were expelled from the mine, this time with the hooligans in pursuit. Unfortunately, during the unpleasantness, I was accidentally ejected and left behind. I believe I may have been held to blame by the management for the unfortunate events and found myself sequestered here.'

'It looks like the master needs our help now more than ever,' said Mel. 'The question is, how do we get out of here?'

'I was just about to suggest something, young sir. But first, if you'll permit me?' Swivel's hand concertinaed up into his sleeve and when it came back out had a clothes brush attached. He began to brush the dust from Mel's velvet doublet.

'Never mind that now. What's your suggestion?' asked Mel.

'As you wish. It's just that I see you have the omniscope.'

'The what?'

'The omniscope, young sir.' The clothes brush hand withdrew into Swivel's sleeve and his open hand popped back out. 'May I?'

Mel realised that he was referring to his telescope. 'This thing? I've used it but I can't see a way out anywhere.' He passed it to the butler.

'But perhaps the young sir is not aware of its rather special attributes.'

'You mean the zoom?'

'Forgive me, but the omniscope does rather more than that. You have perhaps been wondering about the various attachments along its length, only one of which is the special enlargement facility – the zoom, as you put it. This control here, for instance, allows for better illumination of the subject and this one here –'

'Let me see,' said Ludo, snatching the object from Swivel's hand. '*Wow!* You should see this, Mel. Everything's as bright as day.'

He handed Mel the omniscope and Mel began to re-inspect the interior.

'Excuse me, young sirs, but you won't find a way out there. I've already looked.' At this, Swivel's face rotated again, this time from his chin upwards, revealing a face with huge, nocturnal eyes.

'*Ah!*' Its ghastly appearance made Ludo jump.

'I'm sorry if I startled you.' The butler's face swivelled back to his normal one.

'So there's no way out,' said Wren, disappointed.

'Perhaps if I may continue? This control *here* will permit you to see a distance *through* things.' Swivel indicated another knob on the omniscope.

Mel returned the apparatus to his eye and twiddled the knob. At first nothing seemed to change, but as he turned the knob further, the walls of the volcano paled and vanished and he could clearly see the surrounding islands and ships. 'That's *amazing*, but I still can't see a way out of here.'

'*Ahem!*' The polite cough once more. 'Perhaps the young sir is looking in the wrong direction?'

Mel lowered the contraption and looked at

Swivel quizzically.

The butler nodded towards the pile of junk.

Mel turned the omniscope on it and looked down deep into the heart of the scrapheap. 'There's a great big hole in the floor, right in the centre, like a massive drain or something. But it's blocked. There's a big whatnot wedged in it. Perhaps all this junk's supposed to vanish down there.'

'Exactly,' said Swivel. 'You see, I myself have something of the omniscope's functionality built into one of my many faces. If you will allow me to demonstrate?'

'Please don't,' said Ludo quickly. 'That last mug of yours was horrible.'

'As the young sir wishes.'

'But that still doesn't help us much,' said Mel. 'There must be hundreds of tons of junk in this pile. We'll never shift it.'

'Maybe this'll help.' Wren held out a battered and dented helmet similar to the one they had used to produce their inspiration. 'I've just found this on the scrapheap. It's been through the wars but perhaps we can get it to work.'

'How very enterprising of you, miss. If you'll permit me?'

Wren passed the helmet to Swivel. He held it in his left hand and his right withdrew into the sleeve of his doublet and re-emerged as a stubby screwdriver. He tightened a few screws, changed his hand for a pair of pliers, remade a connection or two, changed his hand back to normal, blew some dust off the helmet and handed it back. 'That might serve tolerably well, although I sincerely doubt it will function perfectly. After all, it had been thrown away.'

'Go on, Wren, you found it, you use it,' said Mel.

Wren put the helmet on and closed her eyes. Her brow furrowed in concentration and the lights flickered and then glowed dimly. This time the sound was more like fingernails scraping on a blackboard, and something amorphous began to materialise on the floor in front of Wren. At first it was vague and transparent and then it started to fade away altogether.

'*Do* excuse me, miss.' Swivel whacked the side of

the helmet with his hand. 'Most frightfully sorry, and all that.'

Wren recovered from the blow as the lights glowed brighter and, with a pop like a champagne cork, a python with the head of a flamingo sprang into existence.

'Well done. That's fantastic. It works!' said Mel, slapping Wren on the back.

'No, it doesn't,' said Wren, disappointed. 'I tried for a rope with a hook on the end. Something we could use to drag this junk aside.'

'At least we're getting something,' said Ludo.

Wren tried some more and then Ludo and Mel took turns, but after an hour of attempts at imagining something useful all they had produced was another pile of worthless junk. More by luck than design, they had created several more or less round wheels, lots of nondescript tubes and more than a fair share of useless and malformed animal parts before the helmet gave up the ghost with a flash, a bang and a puff of multi-coloured smoke.

Mel removed the smoking helmet. 'Well, I guess that's it.'

'What now?' said a downhearted Ludo.

'We're not necessarily finished yet, young sirs, miss. Between the items you have imagined and the scrapheap here, we now have at our disposal a rather large quantity of raw material. A kit of parts, as it were. If you were to describe exactly what you were aiming for, with my skills I might just be able to fabricate such a device.'

Mel retrieved a pencil and the master's sketchbook from his satchel and turned to a blank page. 'What about some kind of excavating machine?' He sketched out what he had in mind. Wren and Ludo made some helpful suggestions which he incorporated before handing the finished design to the butler. Swivel set to work.

Swivel was amazingly industrious and, after going through an impressive repertoire of different faces and hands, had Mel's machine fully assembled. It would have been finished a lot sooner if he had not stopped periodically to tidy up after himself. The friends inspected the finished machine.

The main part of it was built from the ribcage of an enormous fish. Inside was a four-seater tandem bicycle frame. This was bolted on to a flat bed that was articulated at intervals, and from beneath which protruded a multitude of feet. Some were human-looking (with and without shoes), while others were distinctly animal in origin. There were also more than a few mechanical ones built from small pistons, bolts and springs. For the excavating end there was a huge dinosaur's head with a formidable array of sharp teeth. Its eyes had been replaced with lanterns. It was anchored in front of a rather dangerous-looking steam engine, topped with organ pipes of varying length. The excavated waste was to be channelled along the machine by a complicated tangle of intestine-like flexible pipes and finally expelled from the rear via something that resembled an oversized sousaphone. This emerged from a great big bottom. All in all, it looked as if it would be rather more dangerous to the operators than to the scrapheap.

'Look, I'm not so sure this is a good idea after all,'

said Ludo, studying the machine. 'I think I'd rather stay here having inspiration than getting in that jerry-built thing.'

'Excuse me, but I rather think you are labouring under a misapprehension,' said Swivel. 'When the Mine of Inspiration wishes to uncover a large amount of inspirational ore, it uses what any other mine would given the same situation.'

'Oh, and what's that?' asked Ludo.

'Why, *explosives*, young sir.'

Ludo was the first to climb on board the strange machine. He took the rear saddle with Wren in front of him, then Mel, who fastened his satchel to the crossbar. Swivel, who knew how to operate the contraption and had the advantage of his omniscopic vision, sat in the driving seat immediately behind the steam engine. As they built up a head of steam the organ pipes began to whistle musically. The butler started the excavator and it rose on its feet and edged forward like a huge, weird centipede.

'And just what do you think you're doing?' The face emerged with a metallic *boing* from a malformed gondola at the edge of the scrapheap. It was evidently angry.

'With your permission, young sirs, miss?'

'Be our guest,' said Ludo.

Swivel pulled one of the many levers arrayed along the handlebars and the head of the machine turned and crushed the boat with its massive jaws.

The face immediately reappeared on the other side, this time on a church steeple that appeared to be constructed from dried moths. 'Oh no, you don't. I know what your little game is. I'll fix you.'

The face vanished and moments later the gloomy light inside the volcano dimmed even more.

'What's that?' said Wren.

Mel looked up. 'Whatever it is, it's bad news.'

They all gazed up through the ribs of the excavator and saw that a black cloud was obscuring the mouth of the crater.

'I didn't expect them to have weather in here.'

'That's not weather, Wren,' said Mel as he trained the omniscope on the cloud. 'That cloud's made from *beetles*!'

'Let's get out of here!' shouted Ludo.

Swivel pulled a lever and the jaws of the machine bit into the scrapheap. The friends could hear a clanging noise in the pipes as the masticated morsels of junk were channelled along, to be expelled behind. Suddenly, the interior of the excavator was invaded by the beetles. Their bodies were as big as goose eggs and their scratchy legs began crawling over the occupants, nipping them painfully with their pincer-like jaws.

'*Aaahhh!*' Wren screamed as several of the huge insects became entangled in her hair.

'Keep going, Swivel. I'll deal with this,' shouted Mel over the combined din of the swarm and the steam engine. Flailing his arms to bat away the beetles, he jumped off his saddle and grabbed one of the flexible pipes running alongside the excavator. 'Everyone cover your faces!' He wrenched the pipe and it came away. He used it like a machine gun to hose down the insects with the shredded junk that shot from the end with great velocity.

By this time, the excavator was wholly inside the

scrapheap and trapped smoke from the engine was mingling with the beetles. No more insects could get in and those behind were being pelted with the debris thrown out from the rear of the machine. Within a short time Mel had shot them all. Then the bucking pipe and its inspirational ammunition became more of a menace to the occupants and, after a short struggle, he managed to reattach it.

The friends tended to their painful bites between coughing back the choking smoke as the excavator chomped on into the heart of the scrapheap. It was very dark and the only light they had was that reflected back from the furnace beneath the steam engine plus a little from the lamps in the head, shining on the walls of the tunnel they were excavating.

After a while, the butler turned and reported their progress. The face he was using had a stubby omniscope in place of one eye and a respirator over his mouth. 'Not far now, young sirs, miss.' His voice was distorted by the mask. 'There appears to be a large cavity all around the drain.'

The cavity itself was formed by the upturned hull

of a truly enormous galleon. Most of the decks were missing, exposing its ribs and keel, and the gigantic masts and yards had crumpled and were wedged crossways in the drain, causing the blockage.

The friends could all breathe more easily now that the smoke was escaping into the cavity, but even above the rhythmic noise of the steam engine and the musical pipes, they could hear the ominous creaking of the countless tons of rubbish above them bearing down on the hull.

'The scrapheap's about to collapse!' cried Ludo.

Swivel navigated the excavator through the jungle of fallen rigging and spars that littered the floor. As he manoeuvred up to the drain, he worked a handlebar lever that engaged a circular saw. It bit into the debris that was causing the blockage, sending a fountain of bright sparks high into the air. Then, suddenly, the obstruction tumbled down into the drain. Without hesitation, the butler drove the excavator forward and into the hole, just as the hull above them ruptured. The friends in their machine tipped over the lip of the drain and the entire contraption fell headlong into the void.

Their cries formed an anguished counterpoint to the overworked organ pipes.

After a brief, vertical plunge, the passage of the drain evened out into a steep, downward slope. Swivel wrestled with the controls as they dived deeper and deeper.

'You won't be getting away that easily.'

'Look!' cried Wren in alarm.

The face had appeared out of the wall of the drain. It was much bigger and angrier than before and was moving along at great speed, keeping pace with their descent.

'That brain cell of yours is getting a real workout,' it sneered. 'But you won't be getting out of the mine just yet.'

Muscular arms emerged from the wall and their powerful hands grabbed two of the excavator's ribs, snapping them apart as if they were matchsticks. One hand thrust into the excavator and made a grab for Mel. Mel leapt from his saddle as the hand crushed the bicycle frame, and his satchel fell to the floor. It burst open and the contents spilled out. Wren grabbed the regulator, and Ludo the sketchbook with one hand and the omniscope with the other. Mel lunged for the pencils but they rolled out of the machine. The hand reached in again and seized Ludo and Wren.

'Help! Help!' cried Ludo.

Ludo and Wren wailed in pain and struggled vainly to free themselves from the face's grasp.

Mel reached down, grabbed one of the snapped-off ribs and thrust it out of the excavator and into the face's left eye. 'Let go of my friends!'

The face howled and dropped the youngsters. 'You vicious little tyke!' spat the face, rubbing its wounded eye. It formed its other hand into a fist and punched hard into the machine, catching Mel a hefty whack that bowled him across the floor of the excavator. He made a fruitless grab for one of the ribs on the far side as he was hurled out of the machine just as it reached a fork in the drain. Mel fell into one side-branch, while the excavator with Swivel, Ludo and Wren careered on into the other.

Mel tumbled head over heels until he managed to

force himself on to his back so that he was sliding feet-first. Fortunately, the lining of the drain was smooth, but this also prevented him from slowing himself down. He veered wildly from side to side striking his elbows, ribs and, occasionally, his head, sending sick-giddy shockwaves through him. One half of his mind fought against mounting panic while the other half tried to concentrate on avoiding any more collisions. He slid for ages until eventually the light in the dark drain grew and then, as he rounded the last of a series of bends that slowed him down somewhat, he came to a halt with a jarring thud. He was stopped by a heavy grille blocking the end of the drain. Through its criss-cross bars he could see a long slope of ejected scrap and, beyond, a green, flat landscape.

The face appeared from the opposite wall of the drain and stared balefully at Mel with its uninjured eye. The other one was swollen and closed. 'I'm going to wring your ruddy neck, you whelp. *Come here!*' The muscular arms emerged from the drain wall and made a grab for him.

Mel jumped back and the face's powerful hands

closed on thin air just in front of him.

'Come here, you little blighter.' The face vanished and reappeared on the opposite wall but it still could not reach him, as Mel jumped back the other way. It then flowed sinuously around the inside of the drain and on to the floor like quicksilver. Mel leapt on to the circular grille and climbed to the centre just as the face smashed its great fist into the wall where he had been standing only an instant before. The face made another vain attempt to grab him, this time from above. But Mel was just beyond its reach. As long as he stayed put right in the centre of the grille, the hands could not touch him.

Then he heard it. A clanking rumble was echoing down the drain. There was no mistaking what it was. It was getting louder and louder and the drain began to shake. A sizeable proportion of the monstrous scrapheap was hurtling towards him where he was perched like the bull's-eye on a target.

'Now we've got him. There's nowhere left for him to run to.' Adolfus Spute rubbed his hands together.

'We've got him and his atrocious abode surrounded. Mumchance, my leprous leprechaun, signal the men to attack. This is finally the end of Ambrosius Blenk.'

The Excavator Excavated

'Slow down!' yelled Ludo as the strange excavator hurtled on through the dark and winding network of drains.

'No, go faster! Or we'll all be crushed,' shouted Wren as the rushing scrapheap grew increasingly louder behind them.

Then, with a sense of alarm (and a face to match), Swivel detected a heavy iron grille over the end of the drain ahead of them with his omniscopic vision. 'The young sir is correct, miss. We really need to brake.' He frantically engaged another lever on the handlebars, and the feet beneath the machine dug in their many heels in an attempt to brake. But this only served to create sparks and make the excavator unstable.

'There's the end of the tunnel. We're going to crash!' Ludo raised his arms to shield his face.

'No, look!' said Wren. 'It's opening.'

The grille covering the tunnel exit began to rotate upwards and outwards with a nerve-jangling, mechanical squeal.

'I do believe the way ahead's clear,' said Swivel, just as the colossal bolus of debris reached the rear of the excavator. The machine shot out of the end of the drain into thin air, along with the geyser of junk.

They had emerged on the far side of a crag high above a wide, deep pit. The butler operated another of his levers and a pair of scruffy wings unfolded from the top of the machine, flapping wildly. This was just enough to get them out of trouble and the contraption landed with a jarring bump more or less intact in the bottom of the pit, just a few yards beyond the end of the outflow.

'Phew, that was close,' said Wren. 'I thought we were done for when the face grabbed us. You saved us, Mel. Thanks. Mel? Where's Mel?'

'He was just behind us. Mel?' Ludo looked around for his friend.

'I'm sorry, young sir, miss, but your companion parted company with us some way back,' Swivel informed them.

'*What?* You mean he's still in there? We have to go back and get him,' said Wren.

'That's impossible,' said Ludo flatly. 'That drain was miles long. We've just seen that the excavator can't fly and there's no way we could climb back up there. Besides, the grille's closed again. You saw how many other drains branched off to the side. He could have gone down any one of them.'

'The young sir's right, miss. I'm afraid we've lost him for good.'

'We can't just abandon him. Perhaps he's come out of another exit. We have to try and find him,' pleaded Wren.

'But where, Wren? We don't know if there *is* another exit. We don't even know where *we* are,' said Ludo.

Wren looked desperately from one to the other. Their faces told her what she was refusing to admit to herself. She sat down on the edge of the excavator and felt tears begin to well up behind her eyes. After a moment she choked them back. 'No. *No!* That's not going to help us find Mel. He's still alive; I know he is. And blubbering's not going to get us out of here. We came into the Mirrorscape to do a job and we owe it to

Mel to complete it. We must go on and find the master.'
She stood and wiped her eyes with the cuff of her sleeve.

'I agree, miss. The young sir struck me as an eminently resourceful chap. Why, he's probably got out of the mine and is searching for us right now. He'll surely make his own way to the master.' The butler seemed to have a face for every occasion. This time it swivelled to display one with a sad but hopeful smile.

Wren was grateful for the reassuring gesture but felt no better. She knew as well as the others that the odds were against Mel.

'At least we've still got the satchel and most of the stuff. We stand as much chance as we did before of finding the master,' said Ludo.

The party studied their surroundings. The pit had steep rocky sides, from which the occasional gnarled tree grew out horizontally. Perched on them were strange junk-eating birds that made forlorn cries that echoed off the walls. There was a long, sloping pathway that spiralled around the inside of the pit all the way to the top.

'It's an awfully long way up to the rim,' said Ludo.

'Why don't we take the excavator?' suggested Wren.

'A splendid idea, miss. However, our supply of fuel has diminished considerably. Perhaps if you and the young sir would be so kind as to search the scrap and procure anything that is in any way combustible, to fire the boiler, we might proceed.'

Impatient at the delay, Wren and Ludo rushed around collecting anything from the ejected junk that might burn.

As they set off, neither Wren nor Swivel noticed the yellow arrow pointing up the path behind them.

When they finally reached the top of the pit, Swivel brought them to a halt.

'Any idea of where we are? Which way do we go?' asked Wren. She glanced back towards the grille in the pit far below them, and the scavengers picking over the junk. 'Where are you, Mel?' she said under her breath.

'I believe it would be constructive to consult the omniscope,' answered Swivel. 'As I intimated, it has a number of remarkable features.' He watched as Ludo took it from the satchel. 'If you were to try this knob here, for instance, we might learn something to our advantage.'

Ludo put the omniscope to his eye and twiddled the control the butler indicated. 'I can't see a thing. Everything's gone black.' He removed the contraption and looked at the lens, but it was unobstructed. 'Maybe it got broken in the mine.'

'Perhaps if the young sir were to pan around in the other direction.'

As Ludo swung around the light in the device increased and he could see clearly. He continued panning and the image darkened again before he swung back to where it appeared brightest. He saw a barren and featureless landscape and – could it be? He fumbled with the other knobs until he found the zoom.

'There it is! There's not just a single track of footprints but a great churned-up mass of them leading away. We've found the trail.'

'That particular function of the omniscope is somewhat like that of a compass, young sir; a rather intelligent compass. It is always brightest in the direction of what one is searching for. In this case, the master.'

'Then why can't we use it to search for Mel?' asked Wren.

'We can, miss, but not yet. It can only point in one direction at a time. You may have noticed that our master is rather . . .'

'Absent-minded?' suggested Ludo.

'. . . Liable to go off at a tangent, shall we say. Therefore, I took it upon myself some time ago to set the omniscope to always point the way to the master. Once that's been achieved it can be reset to look in another direction,' explained Swivel.

'So let's hurry up and find him,' said Wren.

They set off across the Mirrorscape, leaving the comparatively delicate footprints of the excavator alongside the broad furrow ploughed up by Billet and his pursuers. They made good time on the flat terrain and soon Swivel called back to Wren and Ludo. 'I can see a cloud of dust up ahead. Why don't you two see what you can make out?'

The friends clambered up and on top of the rapidly

moving excavator. When they were seated side by side on the dinosaur head, Ludo used the zoom on the omniscope to study the cloud.

He raised his voice so that Swivel could hear him above the musical tune of the pipes. 'I can see the house – I mean Billet. He's surrounded by a whole herd of them.'

'A whole herd of what?' asked Wren.

'Here, see for yourself.'

Wren took the omniscope and trained it on the distant cloud. She recognised Billet from the master's canvas, and milling around him were huge shapes made indistinct by the dust. Occasionally, a burst of light erupted within the cloud, followed seconds later by the low rumble of distant thunder. As they got closer, she could make out progressively more detail. 'There must be a dozen strange contraptions circling Billet.'

'Yeah, and each one is crammed with men-at-arms,' said Ludo.

Each contraption seemed to have been cobbled together from disparate items plundered from the Mine of Inspiration without the slightest regard of how they fitted together. Some spat bolts of lightning, and had succeeded in setting fire to the thatch that crowned Billet's head. Other machines sported huge iron fists or a variety of wickedly sharp blades of various shapes and sizes. Still more war engines were like long-legged steamships that fired nets and miles of sticky string that tangled Billet's feet and prevented his escape. One machine, which seemed to be in command, hovered in the air above the battleground. It was suspended from many wires attached to a great flock of birds of all shapes and sizes that were flapping manically to keep it aloft. It was directing the evil dance of the machines below. The omniscope now clearly showed the High-Bailiff and his dwarf peering out from between the exposed ribs, organising the assault and telegraphing instructions to the ragtag squadron with a small semaphore machine hanging beneath them.

'It looks like we got here too late,' said Ludo.

'There must be something we can do.' Wren anxiously scanned the scene with the omniscope, trying to make sense of the melee. 'Wait a minute. I can see . . .'

'What? *What?*'

'Ludo . . . it's the master! He's alive! He's on the roof trying to beat out the flames. We're not too late.'

'We've found him. Swivel, we've found the master and he's alive,' said Ludo.

'*Ahem!*'

'What now, Swivel?' said Ludo. 'Don't tell me you've thought of some urgent tidying up to do.'

'In a way, young sir, I have. It occurs to me there's an awful mess down there surrounding the master that simply must be attended to. I can't abide mess.'

'What did you have in mind?' asked Wren.

'Might I suggest that it is not beyond your decidedly superior creative abilities and my more humble, workaday skills to engineer, as it were, a way out of this predicament?'

'He's right, Ludo. We're not exactly defenceless; look what we did to the scrapheap.'

'Yeah, and look at what the scrapheap nearly did to us. We might not be so lucky this time.'

'Ludo, only when this lot are tidied away, can we begin to look for Mel. Full steam ahead, Swivel!'

'Yeah, full steam ahead,' echoed Ludo, with markedly less enthusiasm.

Swivel set the excavator on automatic pilot. The smoke from the steam engine that had previously been such a hindrance now worked to their advantage. The butler rearranged some pipes that blew thick clouds from the mouth of the excavator to mask their approach. The moth-eaten wings fanned this towards the enemy.

Through the smoke and din of battle they could make out Billet's booming voice. 'Call that a slap, yer limp-wristed twerp? I've been hit harder by snowflakes.'

Before the attackers knew it, the excavator was in amongst them and using its powerful jaws to hamper and maim the assailants. Blinded by the smoke, the inspirational monsters were unable to receive instructions from the High-Bailiff hovering above in the rhinoceros. In the confusion they began to set about each other.

'Our smokescreen seems most effective,' said Swivel. 'Now, if we remove the enemy's head we might be able to make inroads into his body.' Swivel launched a carefully aimed circular saw blade at the flying contraption from an improvised catapult. The spinning projectile found its mark and severed many of the lines that attached it to the flock of birds.

'Good shot!' Wren and Ludo cheered as the rhinoceros crashed into the midst of the monster-machines, sowing yet more panic.

While the enemy contraptions were busy laying into each other, Swivel manoeuvred the excavator right up to Billet and dismounted. 'A spot of gardening is called for, I believe.' With a sickle attachment on his hand he began to cut away the entanglements that bound the house.

But before he had managed to achieve much, Ludo and Wren noticed that the smoke was beginning to clear. Adolfus Spute had climbed from the wreckage of his aerial vehicle and mounted a tortoise contraption. It had a tall steel pylon on its domed back from which swung a spiked, iron ball on a chain like a rotor. The High-Bailiff used this to blow the smoke back towards the excavator.

'There goes our smokescreen,' said Wren. 'Time

for another of Mel's machine guns, I think.'

'Two are better than one,' said Ludo as the pair grabbed pipes to use like Mel's improvised weapon.

'But what are we going to use for ammunition?' asked Wren. 'There's no scrapheap here.'

'There's one thing,' said Ludo. 'The excavator!' He tried several of the handlebar controls until he found a combination that set the excavator to begin devouring itself. It started to gyrate like a puppy chasing its own tail. Beginning with the sousaphone and then moving steadily along the length of its sinuous body, it chomped while the friends stood to one side and aimed the remains at Billet's attackers like firemen dousing flames.

'It's working,' said Ludo, 'but not fast enough.'

'We're running out of ammunition,' said Wren. They could see that the excavator would have totally consumed itself before the assailants could be put to flight.

'We might not need much more. Look!' Wren nodded towards Billet. Swivel had finally cut the house free from its entanglements.

'Right, yer bogey-chewing sticks of rhubarb. Let's be having yer!' bellowed Billet as he weighed into the melee, adding his considerable resources to the battle. 'How d'yer like *that!*' Those monsters he could not flatten with his enormous feet, he butted with his head. From one of his great windows, the master rained down pieces of furniture and other household items.

'We're winning!' said Ludo, seeing the High-Bailiff in the tortoise-machine wheel around and flee the battlefield, followed by his men in the remains of their battered contraptions.

With a final and seemingly impossible contortion, the excavator munched its own head and the last of the debris was fired from Wren and Ludo's truncated hoses as parting shots before they became limp and useless in their hands.

As the dust settled, the friends were able to get a clear view of Billet. He was much as they had first seen him in the picture, except that now he stood on two giant bare feet that seemed to be attached to his great head without the aid of very much in the way of legs in between. Strangely, he had no arms, and much of his exterior was understandably battered about and in need of redecoration.

'That showed 'em! That showed 'em good,' roared Billet. Then, noticing his smouldering thatch for the first time, 'Cripes! Me barnet!'

While the house was complaining loudly to anyone who would listen, Swivel led the two friends in through a postern door in Billet's heel and guided them up innumerable stairs.

'It's much bigger in here than it looks from outside,' observed Wren.

'That's because Billet is a figment. Each part can be any size his creator imagines,' explained Swivel.

As they ascended, they passed many doors that opened on to all kinds of rooms. One or two were secured with formidable locks. Near the bottom they passed a dark, smelly chamber that seemed to be full of fat pipes and drains.

'Poo! What's in there?' asked Ludo.

Swivel explained. 'Just as Billet has a more or less human countenance –'

'Rather less than more, if you ask me,' interrupted Ludo.

'. . . So his interior has many functions that also

equate to the human body. Here, near the bottom –'

'Thank you, Swivel. We get the picture,' said Wren.

As they mounted higher they passed a kitchen and several well-stocked storerooms.

'Stomach?'

'Just so, miss.'

'And this must be the studio,' said Ludo as they climbed higher. They looked in on a lofty room lit by the two tall windows of Billet's eyes, with a splendid view of the Mirrorscape beyond. The contents were in total disarray following the skirmish.

At the very top, and out of breath, they came to a panelled, book-lined library. Many of the books lay scattered on the polished floor and a tall library ladder had toppled over. Amidst this mess, sitting in a comfortable leather armchair, was the master. His skull cap was askew and by the light of a green-shaded lamp he was consulting a large book open on a low lectern before him.

The butler gave his habitual polite cough and the master looked up. His pale face had sooty smudges on it and his beard was singed. 'Ah, Swivel, there you are.

Where've you been? I could have used your help a while ago. I was just consulting my atlas of the Mirrorscape, trying to find exactly where we've got to. We've come far off the beaten track. There's a long way to go before we can get back out into the mansion.' He removed his reading spectacles and looked up. 'And by my giddy aunt, we have guests. Young Cleef, isn't it?'

'Yes, master.'

'And . . .?'

'Wren, master. I work in your kitchen.'

'Upon my word. Now, what are you two doing here? And where's your friend Womper? But forgive me, I'm forgetting myself. You must be exhausted after the fracas. Swivel, tea for my guests.'

As they sat in the library sipping tea, Ludo and Wren recounted the arrest of Dirk Tot, the ransacking of the mansion and their journey through the Mirrorscape searching for the master. As they spoke, they watched Ambrosius Blenk's face darken. He twirled his long beard round and round in his fingers and fixed them with his piercing blue eyes.

'The impudence of Brool! This explains why Spute

and his men have been preventing me from returning. With me out of the way there's no one to prevent the Fifth Mystery from doing as it pleases.' As the master continued to stare at the friends his expression lightened. 'That sounds like quite an adventure you've had. Dirk Tot and I suspected that young Womper might know a little. Now I see that he knows rather a lot.'

'Excuse me, master, but Mel's sure that Dirk Tot is working for the Fifth Mystery.'

The master began to laugh but stopped himself. 'Young lady, nothing could be further from the truth. Believe me.'

'But he saw him meeting with some Mystery men – when he was coming to Vlam.'

Ambrosius Blenk smiled. 'Did he now? Or did he just see my steward with some men in red? The kind of red you get mining cinnabar?'

Wren and Ludo looked at each other, the light of realisation in their eyes.

'Now, does anyone else know about the Mirrorscape?'

'There are the coloured men, the fugitives,' answered Wren. 'They do.'

'The coloured men, you say?' The master grunted. 'So you've met them, have you? They've more reason than most to hate the Mysteries. Anyone else?'

'I don't think so, master.'

Ludo looked down at his feet and shook his head.

'Very well. That still doesn't tell us how the Fifth Mystery managed to get into the Mirrorscape in the first place.' He twiddled his beard and thought some more for a while. The only sound was the rhythmic sighing of the ventilation that sent wafts of fresh air around the room from an ornate brass grille set low in the wall. Somewhere below, the sound of Swivel tidying up drifted towards them.

Then the master clapped his hands and rubbed them together. 'All right, there's much to be done. We must get back home as quickly as possible and see about freeing Dirk Tot. The confounded nerve of the Mystery to ransack my mansion like that!'

'But what about Mel? We can't leave him here,' said Wren.

'Quite right, young lady. We really ought to find young Womper and take him with us. I can't have my apprentices going astray now, can I? You say you lost him in the Mine of Inspiration?'

Wren nodded. 'We don't even know if he's . . .' She couldn't complete the sentence.

'If only I'd thought to bring my omniscope with me.'

'It's here. We have it,' said Wren.

Ludo produced it from the satchel and handed it to the master.

'My giddy aunt. Thank you. How very prescient of you.' The master smiled and stroked the contraption fondly. 'Let me explain a little about the omniscope. Do you know that each of these knobs and sliders along its length operates one of its many functions? This one, for instance, enlarges the subject and –'

'Please, sir, we know all about the omniscope. It helped us get here. But I –'

'I'll thank you not to interrupt me, young lady!'

Wren lowered her eyes and blushed deeply.

'Now . . .' The master paused and stared hard at the youngsters. 'Now, I'm sure you don't know *all* about the omniscope. You may have fathomed that this wondrous instrument can enlarge things, can illuminate things, can see through things and can even indicate a desired direction, but there's one function that I'm sure you have *not* discovered. As well as perform all of these undoubtedly useful services, it can also peer some distance into the future. Make it appear a little closer, as it were.'

'You mean we can use it to see if Mel's all right – or going to be all right?' Wren's face shone with renewed hope.

'In a manner of speaking, yes. But first we need to know where to look. Come over here.' Wren and Ludo followed Ambrosius Blenk to a dormer window in the corner of the library. 'Before anything else, this needs to be reset. There, that should do it.' Attaching the omniscope to a heavy brass tripod, the master bent and put his eye to it and turned what the friends now knew to be the direction-finding knob. He swung the instrument back and forth and settled on a direction. He stood up. 'Are you sure you wish to see this? It may tell us something we don't want to know. Once something's been seen it can't be unseen.'

Wren and Ludo looked at each other. They

looked back at the master and nodded.

'Very well.' He bent again, put his eye to the omniscope and operated the chosen control. Suddenly he coughed, and the colour drained from his face. 'Oh dear. This is much worse than I imagined; much, much worse.'

'The World Turned Upside Down'

A warm breeze blew softly across Mel's face, lifting the fine, fair hair off his forehead and waking him ever so gently. It carried a familiar scent, comforting and evocative; the smell of home. He stirred. He did not want to open his eyes, not yet anyway, not while he was enjoying the delicious floating feeling. The sunshine felt so good, but he knew he had slept too long. He lay there listening to the birds singing and the insects buzzing in the grass. But he must be getting home. His parents would be wondering where he had got to. He slowly opened his eyes and looked up through swaying branches at insubstantial white clouds. Such a blue, blue sky. Bluer than blue. The clouds could almost be angels smiling down on him.

Mel sat up and his head reeled – he had certainly slept too long. The world swayed as he got to his feet, and he needed to brace against the bole of the tree to steady himself. After a moment he felt better. But there was something nagging at the back of his mind. Something he should remember. Or maybe something he was trying to forget. But that could wait until later. Everything was too beautiful for him to be troubled with mundane thoughts. *This must be what heaven's like.* The thought brought a smile to his lips. He looked round, oriented himself with the spire of the fane and set off for home. He passed through a glade dappled with sunlight and stopped to pick some bluebells for his mother. Her favourites. These were the best bluebells he had ever seen. Such big and succulent flowers and every one of them perfect. She would be delighted and he could draw them later.

When he reached the fane he turned left and took the familiar path for home. But after he had gone a short way he found himself out in the fields again. And such fields! Acre upon acre of blue-flowered flax, lush and heavy, stretched away to the flat horizon. It would be a bumper crop this year and no mistake. He turned and retraced his steps and continued past the fane. *How odd!* The way home lay to the right. He had certainly befuddled his brain with too much sleep to have made a silly mistake like that. *Why did I take the left-hand path?*

He skirted Kop, passing the back of the houses so as to take a more direct route home. Someone was drawing water from a well and he waved, but his greeting was not returned. He passed another house and saw someone at an upstairs window. He looked harder but could not recognise them. He had not heard of strangers in the village. Could it be someone visiting from Bols? He would have to ask his mother when he got in. She knew all the comings and goings for miles around.

He saw his cottage bathed in an ethereal light, with no harsh shadows anywhere. Two storeys tall, with carving around the gables, and a weaving shed at the bottom of the garden. *When had Dad added that?* He tried to remember but his head ached so. He approached down the well-tended road and swung open the gate. *Is that another addition?* His father *had* been busy. Mel entered through the front door and went down the corridor to the kitchen.

His mother looked up from preparing food in her well-cut tabby dress. 'Hello, Mel. Are those bluebells for me? You are a thoughtful lad. Just leave them there. How was your day?'

'Oh, fine, except that I . . .'

'Yes?'

'I . . .' He shook his head to clear it but without success. 'Oh, nothing. Where's Dad?'

'He's still weaving in the shed but he'll be up in a minute. It's nearly supper time. You've time to go up to your room and change.' She smiled at her son and pushed back a lock of hair behind her ear with a ringed hand.

Mel smiled back uncertainly, noting that his mother had taken to wearing make-up a little too heavily applied. He climbed the stairs, but when he came to the landing he could not remember which his room was. *How could I forget something like that?* He pushed open the first door he came to and saw all his drawings pinned up around his bed. *Of course – this is my room.* He went in and looked round. It was all strangely unfamiliar. Then he caught sight of himself in the mirror. The mirror? *What is it about mirrors?* Nothing looked out of the ordinary as he studied himself. His white hose and blue doublet looked dusty but apart from that . . . what? He went closer and, on a whim, breathed on the glass and idly drew a circle with his finger in the misty condensation. *The mist?* He then elaborated the doodle and drew some more swirls within it. *Why does that remind me of something?* It certainly felt like it should.

He looked at his reflection. What was that on his forehead? He touched a scab of dried blood and traced it up into the matted hair on his scalp. No wonder he was feeling groggy. He felt a wound there, still bleeding, and suddenly pain exploded through his skull. For an instant a great rush of thoughts dashed unbidden through his brain. He saw a studio full of boys dressed just like him and the floor covered with spots of paint. There was a boy smiling at him and a girl with auburn hair. Then it was gone.

'Mel! Supper's ready.' His mother called up the stairs.

When he entered the dining room, his parents were already seated and he said hello to his father. Willem smiled back at his son and then stood and began to carve the roast chicken while his mother served the vegetables. He could not remember his mother cooking chicken before and he wondered what it tasted like. He was disappointed; it was completely tasteless. He could have been eating warm cardboard. After the meal was finished and his parents had drunk the last of their wine, his father leant back in his chair. Strange that they had not mentioned the wound on his scalp. Mel felt confused.

'Mel, there's something I need you to do urgently.' His father's voice was oddly distant.

'Yes, Dad, of course.'

'You must take this message to Dan Feen. He lives in the old house beyond the fane. Go straight there, as fast as you can. Will you do that for me, Mel?' He handed his son a folded piece of parchment sealed with red wax and the Womper crest.

'Old house? Dan Feen?' His head hurt.

'He's new to the village, sweetheart, but he buys lots of your father's cloth,' said his mother. 'He's become our best customer. Hurry along now. That letter won't deliver itself.'

Mel walked out of the house in the direction of the

fane. As he approached, he heard another familiar voice.

'Mel, my boy. Where are you off to in such a hurry?' Fa Theum emerged from the doorway. It was almost as if he had been waiting for him.

'Hello, Fa. I have to deliver this message for my dad. It's very urgent.'

'If you'll slow down a bit, I'll come with you.'

The pair walked on in silence for a way before Fa Theum spoke again. 'So, Mel, what have you been doing lately?'

'I've been . . . I've been . . . I can't remember, Fa.'

'Never mind. You've probably been up to no good. It's best I don't know.'

'It's just that I . . .' Mel touched the bump on his head again. More pain, accompanied by a confusing flood of images. Men in red robes and jars full of bright colours. And something else. There was . . .

'What, Mel?'

'I don't know. Nothing really. It's just that I don't recognise where we are.'

'Don't worry your head about that, my son. Dan Feen lives this way.'

'How did you know I'm going to Dan Feen's?'

Fa Theum did not answer.

Mel looked around and saw that the landscape had changed completely, as if in a dream. The expansive flatness of Feg had been replaced by steep-sided hills covered with bare trees. Had they really come so far, so soon? Down the valley echoed the haunting song of a whale, answered by others from farther away.

Ahead of them lay a bridge across a broad stream. As they were crossing, Mel looked to his right and saw a silvery pike perched on the branch of a riverbank tree. It was such a peculiar tree. As if it had been uprooted and stuck back into the ground upside down. It looked like the roots had become its branches. Roots? *What is it about roots?* Was it a dream he had? He watched as the fish dived from the branch into the swift-flowing stream, only to emerge a moment later clutching a struggling blackbird in its jaws and regain its perch. Why did it seem so odd?

'Penny for them, Mel?'

'What, Fa?'

'Wool-gathering again?'

'Doesn't it seem strange to you that . . .?'

'What, Mel?'

'That fish back there . . .' He looked up at the wise old face of the priest. 'Fa, is this heaven?'

The priest smiled down at Mel but said nothing.

The lane led on until it joined a broad road. Mel and Fa Theum turned left and continued on their way. There was a noise to their left and a small flock of lobsters scuttled out from beneath a hedgerow and made off into the long grass on the other side of the road.

At the sound of running feet behind, Mel turned. Coming down the highway towards them was a brightly coloured cart drawn by six dapple-grey men. The horse driving the vehicle raised its beribboned hat and shouted a friendly 'Good day' as he passed. Fa Theum waved and Mel, feeling as if he was somehow doing something wrong, did the same.

'Well, would you believe it? Here's a fog bank. What is the world coming to? Such strange weather here lately. You know, Mel, I have a secret charm, taught to me by the Maven himself. It's a charm for dispelling fog. Would you like to try it for me? Here, take this piece of paper. On it is a charm that you must draw in the air. That way the fog will vanish.'

Mel stared at the symbol. It looked like his doodle on the mirror. It made him think of so many strange things. Of houses that looked like people, of underground clocks, of volcanoes and faces that appeared out of walls. Impossible things. Things he would rather not think about. He handed the paper back. 'Please, Fa, I don't like this. I feel unwell.'

'Go on, Mel. Do it for me.'

Mel put his hand to his bump again. It was coming; the thing he was supposed to remember. It was . . .

'Come on, Mel. Do as Fa Theum asks.' It was his father's voice.

Mel turned, and his parents were standing right behind him. 'Dad, Mum, how did you get here?'

'Mel, be a good boy,' said his mother. 'We followed you to make sure you delivered the letter. It's very important. Draw the symbol and make the fog go away. Go on.'

Mel felt confused. His head hurt. He raised his hand again and touched the painful bump. Pain, bright lights and then he remembered. It all came flooding back like the sudden unblocking of a drain. A drain full of inspiration!

He had been clinging to the grille just out of reach of the face in the mine when the debris from the scrap-heap had exploded into the drain in front of him. He barely had time to leap into the fist-shaped depression the face had smashed in the wall. He had curled up tight inside as the thundering wall of rubbish hurtled past, hurting his ears and making them pop. It seemed to go on for ages until the flow eased and then came to a stop. When he peered out of the hollow, a tardy item of inspirational junk – an enormous amoeba whose sticky mass had slowed its descent – had struck him from behind with a wet *thwack*. He was propelled out of the drain, over the outflow of debris and into the Mirrorscape beyond, smacking his head hard against the trunk of a tree.

'Mel! Do as you're told,' his father barked at him.

'*No!*'

'Don't speak to your father in that tone,' said his mother sharply. Then in a pleading tone, 'Please, sweetheart. Do it for me. There's a good boy.'

'No, I won't. This is all wrong.' He looked closer at his parents, so familiar and yet so strange. His senses came alive and he saw that his father's face was the same but his clothes fitted too well. And his mother's complexion was too florid. He studied her hair, searching for the strands of grey he had noticed as he fled Kop with Dirk Tot. There were none. And the jewellery. She never wore jewellery, for the simple reason she had none.

'Come on, Mel,' said Fa Theum. 'Behave yourself and do as your parents command.' There was subdued anger and threat in his voice.

'You're not real. None of you are real. This is all wrong. What's going on?' Mel looked around, increasingly desperate. He had been here before – or, at least, seen it somewhere. Then it came to him. It was a painting! 'This is "The World Turned Upside Down"!'

'Mel, my son, you're talking nonsense,' said Fa Theum. 'You're not well. Just make the sign and deliver the letter.'

Mel looked at the letter in his hand. The Wompers

did not have a seal. None of his family could read or write. He broke the seal and tore open the letter. It was blank. He looked at his parents but their faces were expressionless.

'Mel, that's enough of your tomfoolery. You're to go through the fog this instant,' ordered Fa Theum. When Mel did not move he grabbed him by the wrists. 'You're going through there even if I have to drag you.'

Mel struggled in the old priest's grasp, which was surprisingly strong. He got one hand free and grabbed the dangling diaglyph, yanking it downwards. The corner of it caught the priest's habit and tore a broad, diagonal rip across his chest – his bare canvas chest. '*None* of this is real!' Mel kicked the apparition in the shin and struggled free.

The phantom that was supposed to be his father made a grab for him, but Mel pushed him away. He felt sticky. He looked at his hands. They were smeared with wet, tabby-coloured paint and he could see raw canvas on his father's chest. Mel began running back the way he had come.

'Where do you think you're going, Fegie?'

Groot, Bunt and Jurgis were standing across the road, barring his escape, and dressed in the scarlet robes of the Fifth Mystery.

Mel stopped. *I see it all now. I need to pass though the wall of mist to escape after all. That would take me back to the octagonal chamber in the House of Mysteries. Then, all I have to do is unlock the picture with the pyramid and the temporal maze – and I will be able to follow Wren, Ludo and Swivel. They're probably waiting for me now.*

'What did you think of my depiction of a Fegish village, Fegie? I just painted the most sordid hole I could imagine. And how about your skegging parents? Pretty good, eh?' asked Groot.

'It was pathetic. Poor observation and sloppy technique. A classic Groot.'

'It fooled you easily enough, Fegie. Or else you wouldn't be here. And where do you suppose I got my models from?'

Mel felt a sickening feeling in his stomach. Groot's sloppy depiction of Kop would not have fooled him if he had not been so groggy. But the portraits of his parents and Fa Theum were too good. They could only have been painted from life.

'Look at his face, Bunt. He's only just worked it out.'

'Where are they?' Mel's voice trembled as he asked the question.

'Wouldn't you like to know. Let's just say that my Uncle Adolfus is looking after them. Isn't that kind of him? So what do you think of my technique now, Fegie? It was easily good enough to fool you.'

It was true. There must be something else going on here, otherwise he would have seen through Groot's shoddy work sooner. Then he remembered what Green had told him: 'You can't stay in the Mirrorscape too long before it gets to you. It starts with your body but it soon gets to work on your mind.' The image of Kop must have been formed as much in his own mind as by Groot's brushwork.

'So when did you join the Fifth Mystery?'

'Oh, I've always been a member, Fegie. They like to keep an eye on everything, especially where colour's concerned. It's a family tradition.'

'What is? Treachery?'

'I've had as much as I can take of you, you little scrot. I can't say it's been fun. And now I have more important things to do.'

'Like what? More second-rate paintings?' Mel glanced to one side as a flock of startled octopuses took to the air.

'Like take over old Blenko's studio. That and everything that goes with it.'

Out of the corner of his eye, Mel tracked the octopuses as they flew towards him, their soft bodies expanding and contracting as they pulsed through the air. He stooped and picked up a rock.

'Throwing stones, Fegie? That's a child's weapon. It's no match for a knife. Especially not for six knives.'

'I only count three of you, Groot.'

'Count again. Look behind you.'

Mel shot a glance over his shoulder. The images of his father, mother and Fa Theum were also wielding knives and advancing towards him. He looked back to Groot. 'Perhaps you should do the same,' Mel said. He flung his rock at the lead octopus. It landed with a rubbery thud on its soft body. The octopus's blue-green spots flashed a fiery red in warning as it dived, infuriated, towards its attacker. Mel turned and ran back towards the wall of mist.

Several of the molluscs descended on Groot, Bunt and Jurgis like fleshy umbrellas. Jurgis screamed and hacked with his knife at a tentacle clinging to his face. It fell away, revealing a livid pattern of circles left by its suckers. Mel dived flat on the ground just as the lead octopus attacked. The flying creature swooped over his head and collided heavily with the image of Mel's father. A dense cloud of ink filled the air like smoke, masking Mel as he ran headlong for the way out of the Mirrorscape. He made the mirrormark in the air as he leapt at the shimmering mist. But something was different. The air seemed as thick as porridge and he seemed to move through it in slow-motion. It felt as if invisible hands were tugging him back. He hung there for several moments. Then the resistance faded and he was through.

But the painting was no longer hanging on the wall in the octagonal room. It had been moved. It was now propped on the window ledge high above Vlam and it was facing outwards. As Mel emerged, his back foot was on the window sill, but his front foot and all of his weight was resting on . . . *nothing!* He pitched forward and began to fall down towards the city far below. He was back in the real world; back in Nem. There was no topsy-turvy mirror-logic to save him now. There was just thin air and gravity pulling him down with irresistible force to certain death.

'The Garden at the End of Days'

Wren pushed past the master and approached the omniscope on its gleaming brass tripod, afraid of what she would see. Her hand trembled as she put her eye to the instrument. It only took a moment for her to take in the vertiginous scene. She drew in her breath sharply and took a step backwards. She looked at the master and Ludo. A great, desperate sob escaped her throat.

'That's quite enough of that, young lady. Tears never solved anything.'

The master's words checked her and she fell silent.

Ludo came forward and looked through the omniscope. He put his fist to his mouth and uttered a stifled cry. 'This wasn't meant to happen.' He sat down hard on the floor, his head in his hands. 'What've I done?'

Wren looked confused. 'What're you talking about?'

'No one's done anything,' said the master. 'What you saw *hasn't* happened. But it will if we don't do something to prevent it. The important thing is I recognise where Womper is.'

'You mean that we can still save Mel?' Wren sniffed loudly.

The master produced a red silk handkerchief from his sleeve and handed it to Wren. He consulted the slider on the omniscope to determine how far into the future he had looked and glanced at a clock on the wall. 'We can certainly try. You must have noticed something about the way time flows in the Mirrorscape.'

'It's frozen,' said Wren.

'That's not entirely true but time does flow at a different rate relative to Nem – in most places, that is. We can make use of that.'

The master crossed to a bunch of flexible speaking-tubes arranged side by side in a labelled rack on the wall. He selected one, unplugged the stopper and spoke into it. 'Billet, we must be off. Take us in the direction of "The World Turned Upside Down".' He put it to his ear to hear the reply. 'What? I don't care how sore your feet are. You can rest them later.' He listen again as Billet responded. The master sighed. 'Billet, I'm not about to argue with you. Will you do as you're told?' The speaking-tube went back to his ear. 'And the same to you!' He re-plugged it and slammed it back on its rack. 'What nerve! Why does he have to argue about everything? The next time I'll create a more compliant residence.'

Wren smiled. 'Still, he is rather good when it comes to the rough stuff.'

'I don't know where he gets it from. It certainly doesn't come from me. Now, you two are going to need all your wits about you for what I have in mind,' the master said as Billet set off.

'What do you want us to do?' said Ludo.

The master ran his hand along the shelves and pulled out a large catalogue of paintings bound in deep red leather. 'Now come here and look at this. And *do* pay attention.'

The master explained his plan and then insisted they rehearse it. But however many times they repeated it Ambrosius Blenk was never satisfied.

'Oh dear,' said the master, shaking his head, 'it's not going to work. You're just never going to be able to move fast enough. It's all a matter of physics, you see. There's simply not enough time.' He chewed his fingernail in frustration.

'But there must be some way we can get it to work,' said Ludo.

'The regulator!' exclaimed Wren. She retrieved the hairy object from the satchel.

'Where did you get that?'

'I kind of found it.'

'Did you now? You weren't thinking of taking this back as a souvenir?' The master shook his grey head. 'What belongs in the Mirrorscape must remain in the Mirrorscape. You can't imagine the trouble you could cause if anything ever got out.'

Ludo and Wren exchanged a glance. They knew only too well.

The master looked at the regulator again. A smile blossomed beneath his beard. 'Swivel! Ah, there you are. I'll need you to help us with this.'

The rehearsal recommenced, now with three

participants, and it soon became apparent that it might work.

'Now, have you got this straight?' asked the master.

They nodded.

'We're to wait by the wall of mist until you give the signal,' said Wren.

'Once we cross back into Nem coordination will be lost,' said Ludo, 'so we must wait for you to tell us the plan's working before we go into the picture.'

'And if we fall into the hands of the Fifth Mystery, we're on our own,' added Wren.

'Good,' said the master. 'Everything depends on you and Swivel. If we get the timing right – precisely right – we might just get Womper out of this fix.'

'We are approaching "The World Turned Upside Down",' said Swivel. 'If you'll excuse me, I'll go and prepare.'

Presently, the house stopped moving and one of the speaking-tubes whistled for the master's attention.

'Very well, Swivel. You know what's to be done. Good luck.' The master replaced the tube and selected another. He unplugged it and spoke into it.

'Billet, you're to take us to "The Garden at the End of Days" – as quickly as you can. You know very well where it is and it's not that far. Lucas Flink will not mind in the least if we briefly trespass in his garden for a worthy cause.'

From where they sat, even Wren and Ludo could hear the curses issuing from the tube. They learnt several new words in the space of just a few seconds. Even the worldly master learnt one.

'*Just do it!*' Red in the face, Ambrosius Blenk hung up the speaking-tube and took several deep breaths to calm himself.

The butler slipped through the small door in Billet's heel and closed it behind him. He climbed high into the roots of one of the strange, upside-down trees next to a bridge over a stream. He settled himself and swivelled his face to display the one with the omniscope. He watched as Billet disappeared in a new direction before he turned his attention back to the Mirrorscape below him and waited.

And waited.

And waited.

Little by little, his face began to slip down back into his head. Then, with a soft click it disappeared altogether, to be replaced by one with closed eyes and an open, gently snoring mouth.

Wren and Ludo stood in the library window watching the Mirrorscape fly by through the leaded panes as Billet strode towards their destination. There was a palpable tension between the two friends.

'Ludo, what did you mean back there when you said "What've I done"?'

Ludo turned away from the window and stared at his feet. 'Oh, it's just that I feel responsible . . . for . . . for Mel falling out of the excavator like that. If I'd been quicker, I could have grabbed him.'

'Are you sure that's all?' Wren touched his arm. 'Why won't you look at me?'

'Wren, please don't . . .'

'Come on, you two,' said the master. 'This is not the time for idle gossip. We're almost there.'

*

Swivel's omniscopic face sprang back into place with a sharp jolt. Approaching over the bridge was Mel with an elderly priest. When they had passed Swivel's tree, he climbed down and followed them. At one point he disturbed a small group of lobsters that had been feeding, and he froze as they scuttled away under the hedgerow and across the dusty road in front of Mel and the old man. To his relief he saw that their attention had been distracted by a cart driven by a horse in charge of a team of dapple-grey men. When he felt it was safe, he continued to follow them. Presently, they came to the wall of mist that the master had explained to him led to a chamber high in the House of Mysteries. A couple of tabby-clad peasants came up unseen behind Mel and the Fa. Then some kind of argument broke out between them and Mel. Mel turned and ran back in the direction they had come from. This was not part of the plan! He was supposed to go through the wall of mist. This would ruin everything!

Swivel set off in pursuit, shielded by the hedgerow. As he ran, he jumped into the air and caught a fleeting glimpse over the top of the hedge of three members of the Fifth Mystery. What was he to do? He had to get Mel running back towards the wall of mist. Still running, he jumped again and landed heavily in a nest of grass-green octopuses. The disturbed molluscs instantly shed their camouflage, ejected a cloud of ink, rose angrily into the air and flew off. He waited for a moment and then parted the hedge again, just in time to see Mel throw a rock at the lead octopus. *Good thinking, young sir.* In the ensuing confusion, Mel turned on his heels and began to sprint towards the wall of mist.

Now was the time. Swivel withdrew the regulator from his doublet and planted it in the ground. He knelt and retracted his arm into his sleeve and it re-emerged with a watering can attached. He quickly sprinkled the regulator. He peered back through the hedgerow and saw that Mel was halfway to the wall of mist. Swivel looked back at the regulator, willing it to take root. Then, with a face displaying relief, he saw slender tendrils emerge from the side and burrow down into the soil. It was working, but had he left it too late?

When he felt the rapidly growing roots were established, he took hold of the regulating lever and tugged it towards the minus end of the scale.

For a moment, the fishes ceased singing in the trees and the scudding clouds halted in their tracks. The next time Swivel looked, Mel had vanished.

Ambrosius Blenk stared hard at the ornate clock on the library wall. 'Come on, come on. Can't you say anything except tick and tock?' He listened for a moment. 'Obviously not. Come on, Swivel. Do your stuff. Plant the regulator and slow down time.' He peered out of the window at Wren and Ludo far below, waiting impatiently in front of the wall of mist in 'The Garden at the End of Days'. He looked at the clock again. 'It's not going to work. I've miscalculated. By now, Womper will be decorating the rooftops of Vlam. Shut up, you old pessimist. Of course it's going to work!' He looked again at the clock. The pendulum was definitely slowing down. Slower and slower . . . and then it stopped! He leant out of the window, his megaphone already at his lips. '*Now!*'

428

'Come on, Ludo! Just like we rehearsed,' said Wren.

Ludo made the mirrormark but in his haste fumbled it. 'Scrot, it's not working!'

'Here, let me try.' Wren concentrated, then traced the mirrormark in the air – and they were through.

'It's not the same, Wren. The gallery's much bigger than the space we rehearsed in the library.'

'There's no time to worry about that now. There's "The Garden at the End of Days". Help me unhook it.'

'Ooofff! No one said how heavy it'd be.'

The two friends staggered backwards, almost overbalancing, as the canvas came free.

'Careful! Don't drop it. Have you got it?'

Wren nodded. 'Let's get it up on to the window sill. *Heave!*'

They struggled to lift the upright painting on to the sill, and slid it forward.

'It's stuck! The window's too small!'

'What now?' Wren shoved the canvas harder.

'Stop. You'll wedge it. Lean it at an angle. So it's diagonal to the window frame.'

It *just* went through, scraping some of the gilding

from the frame in the process. Once through, there was enough room on the sill for it to be laid flat, picture-side uppermost. The friends clambered on to it and their weight held it in place like a diving board jutting out over the void.

'We've done it! We've done it!' crowed Ludo.

'I've just thought . . .' said Wren, turning serious. 'What if Mel doesn't realise what's going on and hits the surface without making the mirrormark? His weight will catapult us out into the air and . . .'

'. . . we'll *all* die.'

The rushing air tore at Mel and roared in his ears as he fell. As the rooftops of Vlam raced up to meet him, he thought of his parents and, briefly, of his friends. Then he started to hallucinate. He saw a wonderful garden appear below him. Tiny at first, it grew rapidly as he rushed to meet it. Perhaps it really was heaven this time. But this vision of heaven had a great house in it shaped like a human head. *Billet!* In an instant, he understood what it was. He just had time to form the mirrormark in the air before he tumbled head over heels into the garden inside the Mirrorscape. He picked himself up from between the giant feet of Billet, laughing hysterically.

Wren and Ludo were not launched into the air. The blur that was Mel fell into the picture as smoothly as if he were diving into water.

'He did it. Mel did it!' shouted Ludo. 'Come on, let's go.'

'Not yet, Ludo. We must stay put. The plan – remember?'

A few moments later, another blur – Swivel – fell into the canvas without a splash.

'Now!'

The friends hauled the huge canvas back into place. Wren made the mirrormark once more and the gallery was empty. Only an eddy of dust motes swirling in the still air and a glint of gold on the window frame betrayed that anyone had been there.

'Come on. Get inside, the four of you,' called the master from the library window. 'And *do* stop giggling. You can congratulate yourselves later. We must be getting back home without delay.' The megaphone made his voice sound loud and distorted.

'Mel, we're so glad to see you again. We thought you were . . . we thought we'd lost you for good.'

'Me too, Wren. When I saw the funny-looking house in the picture I couldn't believe my eyes.'

The friends reached the top of the stairs and burst into the library.

'Well, Womper, I'm glad to see you back safe and sound and all in one piece. Your friends here have been to a great deal of trouble to get you back. And now –'

The master was interrupted by a shrill whistle from outside. Everyone crowded round the window. Far below them stood Mumchance.

'What's *he* doing here?' said Mel.

'What's that he's waving?' asked Ludo.

'It looks like a white flag,' said Wren.

The master's face bore a puzzled expression. 'I do believe he wants a truce.'

The Crystal Bridge

Swivel cleared his throat and read aloud from the scroll the dwarf had presented. 'To Ambrosius Blenk, artist and master, greetings. Let it be known that I, Lucas Flink, artist and master, late of the city of Vlam in the land of Nem, Lord of the Mirrorscape and proprietor of "The Garden at the End of Days" do hereby challenge you to a duel . . .'

The master almost choked. '*A duel!* What's the man talking about. He's my oldest and dearest friend. Go on, Swivel.'

'. . . The reason for this said duel being that Ambrosius Blenk has given shelter and succour to the enemies of our gracious friends the Fifth Mystery, whose faithful service and magnanimity we greatly respect. These felons include, but are not limited to, one Dirk Tot, steward and counterfeiter, and one Melkin Womper, apprentice and thief . . .'

All eyes in the room fixed on Mel. He shifted uncomfortably from foot to foot.

'. . . Moreover, Ambrosius Blenk has also permitted his residence known as the Mansion, located in the city of Vlam, to be used for the preparation of and dissemination of substances injurious to the benefices of the aforementioned Mystery. Namely, counterfeit pigments of a most inferior quality. This duel to take place forthwith, with weapons to be mutually agreed.'

Mel laughed nervously. 'It's a joke, right? Lucas Flink's been dead for two hundred years.' He glanced at Ludo, who nodded.

'Dead? Now there's an interesting concept, Womper. In fact, he's as alive and well as you and me here in the Mirrorscape. You see, great artists never really die. They live on forever in their work. "The Garden at the End of Days" is Lucas's retirement home, in a manner of speaking.'

'So it's not a joke.'

'No, Womper, it's no joke. Lucas would never make light of a thing like this. One thing's for certain though; he didn't write that overblown piffle of a challenge. Come on, Swivel, let's go and get to the bottom of this.'

'Sir? If I may be so bold? A duel requires two seconds.'

'Don't you mean a second and a third?'

'Two *seconds*, sir,' repeated the pedantic butler. 'Protocol demands it.'

'All right. One of you must come with us. Not you, Womper, there's a price on your head. Nor you, young lady, I think. Cleef, you'd better accompany us.'

'*Me?* A duel sounds dangerous. Please don't make me go.'

'There's not going to be any duel; not if I've got anything to say about it. Come on, Cleef! The sooner we get this over with, the sooner we can get back to my mansion.'

'Go on, Ludo,' said Wren. 'You helped save Mel. You can do this.'

Dragging his heels, Ludo followed the master and Swivel as they left Billet. He was certain the High-Bailiff would give him away.

'Do try and keep up, Cleef,' called the master as they marched down a shaded tree-lined avenue.

For a moment Ludo almost forgot his fear as he

gazed down on to a beautiful valley tightly enclosed by tall, coloured mountains. Its steep flanks were peppered with irregular holes, making them look like monumental sponges. At intervals, the cliffs were etched with terraces. Sparkling waterfalls cascaded from these in intricate patterns, feeding a circular lake below. The effect was of entire mountainsides embroidered with liquid, silver filigree. Everything in the composition led the eye to Lucas Flink's magnificent house by the shore. It stood alone on its own promontory that jutted out into the lake. The building was made of the purest crystal and took the form of a giant sea anemone. Its many spines flexed gracefully against each other in the breeze, softly chiming like bells. The sunlight that fell on this structure was multiplied by the prismatic walls, and rainbows sprang from them like flying buttresses down to the surface of the lake. Silver-scaled flying fish glided back and forth in their glow.

'Ever the showman, old Lucas,' observed the master.

'Indeed, sir, most artfully contrived,' agreed the butler.

'Are those what I think they are?' asked Ludo, pointing upwards.

'Indeed. They're angels,' said the master as a pair flew overhead. 'An artistic conceit, of course, but a nice touch.'

As they reached the crystal house, Lucas Flink emerged. With his long, grey beard, Ludo thought he looked like Ambrosius Blenk, although from his deeply lined face he was evidently somewhat older. He was dressed in a grey robe in the high fashion of two centuries ago. Ludo was sure he looked embarrassed. Accompanying him in his scarlet robes was a smirking Adolfus Spute. Ludo tried to make himself as inconspicuous as possible behind his companions.

'Lucas, my old friend,' said the master, 'what's all this nonsense about a duel?'

Mel and Wren sat cross-legged on the library floor.

'What did that challenge mean when it called you a thief?' asked Wren.

'Does the Fifth Mystery ever need a reason for

anything it says or does? They took your father without a reason.'

Wren's shoulders slumped. 'Yes, they did.'

'And now they've got mine as well. And my mother.'

'*What?* How do you know?'

Mel told her. 'That's why we've got to get back to Nem as soon as possible. I don't know how, but I've got to rescue them. But right now something else is worrying me.'

'What's that?'

'I've been thinking. First the master's lands in his painting are wrecked to lure him into the Mirrorscape and then he's trapped here. With him out of the way, Dirk Tot is arrested, the mansion ransacked and the artificial pigments that pose such a threat to the Mystery are seized. Everything the Fifth Mystery's been doing since is to prevent the master from returning to Nem.'

'You think they're still trying?'

'Yeah, I do. And another thing. The master's been in the Mirrorscape ages and he hasn't got sick. The mistress said that while he's in a part that's created by his own hand, he's protected.'

'And now, he's been lured outside. Into Lucas Flink's bit of the Mirrorscape – where he can get sick if he stays too long.'

They both said it at once: 'It's a trap!'

Mel and Wren crouched behind the trees at the end of the avenue and peered down into the valley. In the pristine air they could clearly hear the conversation taking place below. Ambrosius Blenk reasoned with Lucas Flink, while the High-Bailiff and Mumchance stood to one side. If there was a trap Mel could not see where it was coming from. Then they saw Adolfus Spute bend his tall frame and whisper something to Mumchance. The dwarf raised his silver whistle to his lips and blew a long, shrill blast.

For a moment everything was still. Then Mel and Wren saw the mirror-like surface of the lake begin to shimmer. The faint ripples grew bigger until waves began to lap on to the shore. Bubbles began to erupt from the surface and an indistinct shape, hung with dripping lake-weed, rose out of the roiling water. It kept on coming and coming until an enormous tortoise-like contraption stood clear of the lake on long spider legs billowing filthy black smoke from its funnels and polluting the unspoiled air. It stalked towards the shore.

'It *is* a trap!' said Mel.

'It's a machine like the ones that attacked Billet,' said Wren. 'They must have cobbled it together from the leftovers of those we destroyed.'

From the space where the tortoise-monster's head had been, a watertight door squealed open and a gangplank emerged that thudded down on the shore. From the body of the machine ran a score of scarlet-clad men-at-arms of the Fifth Mystery. They surrounded the two old masters and Ludo and Swivel, crossbows aimed at their throats.

Wren got to her feet. 'Come on. We've got to help them.'

Mel grabbed Wren's arm and pulled her back. 'No, there're too many of them. Let's stay hidden until we can work out what to do.'

'What's going on?' said a strange voice from behind them.

Alarmed, the friends turned and there, radiating light in the shaded avenue, stood a white-robed angel. From above them came the soft flutter of wings and a second blond-haired angel landed beside its companion, casting its own pool of light. They were identical.

'Here, let me see,' said the second angel.

Wren's mouth was hanging open. 'I should be used to the Mirrorscape by now, but *angels*. Are you *really* angels?'

'Of course we are. What did you think we were, shuttlecocks?' said the first.

'There's our master,' said the second.

'Lucas Flink?' said Wren.

'Certainly. But who are all those other people?'

'That's *our* master, Ambrosius Blenk – and the funny-looking one's Swivel, his butler,' said Mel.

'And the boy's our friend, Ludo. The ones in red are from the Fifth Mystery,' added Wren. 'And they've taken them all prisoner.'

'Why?' asked the angels together.

'Because . . .' began Mel. 'Look, it'd take too long to explain. The important thing is that we need to rescue them. Will you help?'

'Will it involve any . . . you know . . . *devilry*?'

'I'm afraid it will,' said Mel.

'In that case, I'm your angel. How about you, Farris?' asked the first angel.

'Count me in, Bathor,' answered the second. 'I'm always up for a spot of devilry. It's so boring flying around all day looking angelic.'

'But what good can just four of us do?' said Wren.

'I've got a plan,' said Mel. Turning to Farris and Bathor, he asked, 'Tell me, how well can you two fly?'

Ludo, Swivel and the two old masters had been left in a room high in Lucas Flink's crystal house. It did not seem to have any walls. Or a ceiling. Or a floor. Ludo could feel the solidity of the building beneath his feet but his eyes told him he was standing in mid-air. It made him feel very queasy. The room had a panoramic view of the lake, and if he looked down he could see the men-at-arms milling about on the shore.

The High-Bailiff and Mumchance were clumsily ascending what must be a staircase. They kept missing their footing and bumping into things.

He's going to give me away. Ludo looked around. *Where is there to hide in a crystal house?*

'*Now* do you see that you've been misled?' said the master, attempting to convince his old friend that he had been the victim of a cruel deception.

Lucas Flink shook his head. 'But surely there's some mistake, Ambrosius. The Mysteries are a force for good.'

'Don't you see? Your view of them is over two hundred years old. Since your day they have become corrupt.'

'But they say it's *you* who's become corrupt. The High-Bailiff assured me he had evidence that you'd been fabricating synthetic pigment in your household. Is this true?'

'Yes, Lucas, it is. We've been making pigment that ordinary people can afford. Colour belongs to everyone, not just a few. In your time everyone could afford colour in their lives but now the price of the Mystery's Pleasures has become exorbitant.'

'Pleasures?'

'So Adolfus Spute forgot to tell you about those, did he? Well, Pleasures are –'

'Pleasures are what make the world go round; my world, that is.' The High-Bailiff and Mumchance entered the room. 'And this old fool and his half-faced servant have stolen more Pleasures than your feeble brain could possibly imagine.'

'How dare you talk to me like that!' said Lucas Flink. 'And in my own house.'

'Now I have your skeg-bellied friend here, you and your house have served their purpose.'

'*Now* do you believe me?' asked the master.

Ludo edged towards what he thought was the farthest corner of the room.

'Stay where you are, my little stool pigeon,' ordered the High-Bailiff. 'Trying to fly the coup, were you? Wouldn't you like to stay and sing us another song, Birdie?'

Ludo suddenly felt hot. Beads of perspiration broke out on his brow. He looked about for somewhere to hide. Anywhere. And then he saw it. '*Look!*' he shouted.

Everyone turned. Out over the lake, two angels had begun an aerobatic display. Ludo looked down and saw that all of the Mystery men had seen this too and stood transfixed by the spectacle.

'Yours?' asked the master, nodding towards the angels.

'Mine,' confirmed Lucas Flink. 'Misbehaving again.'

'It's *fantastic!*' said Ludo, thankful for the distraction.

Mumchance blew his whistle and pointed to the lakeshore below, where the men-at-arms were jostling each other to get a view of the performance.

'Fools,' said Adolfus Spute. 'Gawking when they should be plundering. Come with me, Mumchance. We'll soon put an end to these shenanigans. *Ooph!*' He had walked into an unseen wall. It took two more collisions before he succeeded in finding an exit.

Just then, the angels began an especially spectacular series of loops, whirls and arabesques that elicited gasps of wonder from their audience below.

'Do they often do this?' asked Ludo.

'If ever they get the chance,' said Lucas Flink. 'Sometimes I wonder why I created them.'

'I have the selfsame problem with Billet,' said the master.

Ludo's eye was caught by something else. He nudged Swivel, who turned his morose face towards Ludo.

'Yes, young sir?'

'Don't look now but . . . I said, don't look now.'

Below them, snaking their way upwards on an invisible staircase towards the rear of the house crept two figures – blue figures!

A smiling face swivelled into place. '*Ahem!*' Swivel coughed his polite butler's cough.

The masters glanced up and the butler nodded in the direction of the back staircase, where they saw Mel and Wren reach their floor.

With his finger to his lips, Mel silently beckoned them towards him.

'Womper, how good of you,' whispered the master. 'You too, young lady.'

'Did you put those angels of mine up to this?' asked Lucas Flink.

'I hope you don't mind,' said Mel.

'Mind? If I'd been as quick as you, I wouldn't find myself in this pickle. I see now that I've been deceived by the Fifth Mystery. I think we should leave.' He led the small party through an invisible door on to the landing. For an instant, Ludo's eyes strayed to the angels' exhibition outside and he slammed hard into a transparent wall and cried out in pain.

'Birdie! *Smell!* Stay where you are, all of you, you lizard-drool!' bellowed Adolfus Spute from below. '*Guards!*'

A loud blast from Mumchance's whistle reinforced the alarm.

'Come along. Walk exactly where I do,' ordered Lucas Flink. He led them, single file, through imperceptible doors and along invisible corridors. They saw the building below them fill up with men-at-arms running in from the shore, turning the diamond crystal of the house into the blood-red of a ruby.

'We're trapped,' cried Ludo.

'*Now* how do we get out?' said Mel.

'Lucas?' said the master.

'Oh, dear. I was hoping things would never come to this.' Lucas Flink removed a fine gold chain from around his neck. Hanging from it were three small tuning forks. He unthreaded them and knelt on the floor, where he struck the largest fork and stood it upright. Its clear note hung in the air and then the whole structure began to sing in sympathy.

'It sounds like that trick you can do with a wine glass,' said Wren.

Mel looked around. 'It's coming from everywhere at once.'

Lucas Flink then opened an invisible door and stepped through and took a few paces into thin air.

'We must take the crystal bridge to the far side of the lake.' So saying, he strode off. 'Quickly now. You'll be in no danger just as long as you follow me precisely.'

The friends edged out cautiously, feeling their way as they went.

'Come along, don't dawdle,' called Lucas Flink.

'You heard the man; keep up,' said the master as the two artists strode ahead.

Mel, Wren and Ludo were barely halfway across

when they saw Lucas Flink kneel down ahead of them, tap the second of his tuning forks and set it upright on the bridge. All around, the noise swelled and became discordant as the structure began to vibrate unpleasantly.

Out over the lake where the angels were continuing their aerobatic display, the friends saw a lightning bolt shoot from the tortoise-monster and detonate in the air. As they blinked away the after-image all they saw was a shower of white feathers drifting down to the lake.

'Farris! Bathor!' cried Wren.

Suddenly, there was a sharp tattoo like hailstones hitting a glass roof as crossbow bolts struck the underside of the bridge, leaving star-shaped crazing where they had ricocheted off.

'Don't stop,' said Ludo. 'Keep moving. We're protected by the bridge.'

Again there came the blast of a whistle behind them, and Mel turned to see the High-Bailiff and Mumchance edging out on to the crystal bridge. Adolfus Spute smiled broadly and began to stride towards them.

'It's as if they can see the bridge,' said Mel.

'They're going to catch us up before we can reach the other side,' said Ludo.

'What's that?' said Wren. 'It looks like a trail of yellow powder on the bridge.'

'Ludo, it's coming from you,' said Mel.

A trickle of powder fell from Ludo's doublet like superfine yellow snow. 'It's . . . it's pigment. I, er, thought we might need some. The parcel must have burst back there.'

Wren looked puzzled. 'What's going on, Ludo?'

'Nothing.' Ludo's eyes darted from side to side. 'Nothing's going on.'

'How much have you got?' asked Mel.

'Not much,' answered Ludo, producing the crumpled paper parcel. 'Please, let's get out of here.'

Mel grabbed it. 'Come on, follow me.' He opened the corner of the parcel and gently threw some before him. 'There. We can see where the bridge is now.'

They hurried on after Lucas Flink, the master and Swivel, who had already reached the far side of the lake and were disappearing into one of the caverns in the cliff face. Mumchance's whistle sounded very close behind.

'Come on!' shouted Mel, flinging the parcel aside. 'Run for it!' They dashed straight for the opening and ran inside.

'Ah, there you are,' said the master.

'If you'll just step up off the bridge,' said Lucas Flink. He tapped the last of his tuning forks on a rock and stood it upright on the end of the crystal bridge. The dissonance was now unbearable and the bridge began to shake violently. Great cracks appeared in it. The sound echoing around the cavern was very loud and everyone covered their ears.

Mel looked back along the length of the bridge and saw that the High-Bailiff and Mumchance were nearly upon them. Then, as the sound reached an ear-splitting climax, the entire bridge shattered into crystal dust. On the far shore, the crystal house imploded. The music stopped abruptly and the two scarlet-clad figures plummeted feet-first into the lake.

Everyone cheered.

They saw Adolfus Spute and Mumchance bob to the surface, spewing water.

'Now I wish I'd stocked my lake with sharks. Come along, follow me.' Lucas Flink led them up an irregular flight of steps. The tunnel led deeper under the mountainside. Eventually, they emerged into the light at the far end of the avenue. Waiting for them in front of Billet were two very dishevelled angels.

'That *was* fun,' said Farris.

'Beats being angelic any day,' said Bathor, smiling. Their gowns were in shreds. Both had singed hair and eyebrows and their angelic faces were covered in black smuts. There were featherless gaps in their wings and their inner radiance now flickered on and off as if it was short-circuited. They looked up and saw their master standing there. They hung their heads shamefacedly.

Lucas Flink shook his head. 'You needn't think I'm going to paint you all over again.'

'What happened to you two?' asked Wren.

'Direct hit with that lightning gun by the look of it,' said Ludo.

'Come along now,' said the master. 'Let's get inside Billet and repair his damage.'

'The sooner, the better,' said Mel. '*Look!*'

Iconium

A vivid flash of lightning erupted, followed by an instantaneous explosion as the tortoise-machine hauled itself up on to the avenue and opened fire on Billet.

'My giddy aunt!' said the master. 'If the studio's been hit we're really in trouble.'

Everyone ran to Billet and raced upstairs. The lightning bolt had blown in one of the windows and wrecked the place.

The master swore under his breath. 'This is simply terrible. Every pot of colour's been smashed. I was counting on having sufficient materials with which to create something to confront that abomination out there.'

'You mean paint something?' said Wren.

'Something that would come alive in the Mirrorscape, like your other creations,' added Mel. 'But surely that would take time?'

'Too long, perhaps. But it was our only hope,' said Ambrosius Blenk. 'Now, without any materials . . .' He shrugged.

'So now what do we do?' said Ludo.

'Might I suggest we ponder that while we are on the move?' said Lucas Flink. 'This is not perhaps the most conducive place at present for a spot of dithering.'

'Of course. Quite right. Swivel, a chair for my friend – if you can find one intact.' The master navigated the debris and took up a speaking-tube. 'Billet, I think you should put some distance between us and that infernal contraption out there.'

The lightning gun spat again and everyone staggered to maintain their footing as Billet lurched under the impact.

'Surely there must be something we can use amongst all this,' suggested Lucas Flink.

'Ludo, did you bring any more pigment?' said Mel.

The master turned to Ludo. 'You have some pigment, Cleef?'

Ludo shifted uncomfortably. 'It's all gone.'

'Pity. There must be *something* we can use. Everyone turn out your pockets onto the table. Let's see what we've got between us.' From his own capacious pockets the master produced a small notebook, a pencil stub, a two-headed silver piece, a threaded conker, two biscuits and a jay's feather.

Swivel, Farris and Bathor had nothing (figments rarely do) but Lucas Flink found a pair of spectacles with one lens missing, a piece of coloured glass, a dried seahorse and a diary two hundred and seven years out of date.

From Wren's pocket came a seashell, a pine cone, a pressed poppy, a small selection of tiny cogs and gears and a pendant watch with cracked glass on a silver chain. On its tiny face was a double portrait of her parents.

Ludo's haul amounted to a few scraps of crumpled paper, a half-eaten sugared almond covered in fluff, a split pebble with a fossil inside and a small purse embroidered with his family's coat of arms. From the clunk it made on the tabletop it evidently contained a sum of money.

All the while, Mel became increasingly anxious. *Everyone will know I'm a thief now.*

'What do you have, Womper?' said the master.

Dreading what Wren and Ludo would think of him, Mel laid his bodkin and the little box on the table.

The master picked the box up. 'What's this?'

'It's . . . a box. Just a box.'

'A rather beautiful one it seems. What's in it?' The master held it to his ear and rattled it gently.

Mel shook his head. 'Nothing really.'

'It's noisy for nothing really.' The master tried to open it. 'It's locked. Let's see if I can prise it open with the bodkin.'

They have to know sooner or later. 'No need. It opens like this.' Mel pressed both ends at once and the lid sprang open. Inside, glowing with its own colour-shifting iridescence, was the strange powder.

The master gasped. 'It's not possible! Lucas, is this what I think it is?'

Lucas Flink gazed at the shifting colours. 'Where did you get this, young man?'

I found it. It was given to me. I won it. I'm looking after it for a friend. All of these thoughts raced through Mel's mind. What he said was, 'I kind of stole it.' And, anticipating the next question, 'From the High-Bailiff.'

The two old masters looked at each other. Then they burst out laughing.

What's so funny? thought Mel.

Wren and Ludo stared at each other, equally confused.

The old masters' laughter was the kind that would have carried on for ages if it had not been interrupted by a flash and another lightning strike nearby.

'So that's what "Melkin Womper, apprentice and thief" meant in that challenge,' said Wren.

'I'm sorry,' said Mel. 'I didn't mean to be a thief.'

'I know that,' said Wren. 'Anyway, I bet Adolfus Spute stole it himself.'

'Is someone going to tell us what it is?' said Ludo.

'It's our salvation. That's what it is! Eh, Lucas?'

'Young man, what we have here is iconium.' There was a boyish sparkle in Lucas Flink's old eyes. 'I have only ever seen it once before – more than two hundred years ago – and never such a large quantity as this.'

'It's unbelievably valuable,' said the master. 'Why, with what's in this box you could buy as many Pleasures as you wished and still have money left over.'

'Can I see?' Ludo craned his neck for a better view.

'Just think of the devilry we could cause with that.'

Farris nudged Bathor and their eyes twinkled.

'Many years ago,' continued Lucas Flink, 'when I was no older than you youngsters are now, a meteor fell from the sky near the western shore of Kig. A fragment was retrieved by the Fifth Mystery and it was found to contain this extraordinary pigment. A little more was extracted, but unfortunately the impact of the meteorite made the substrata of the island unstable. It was already fragile, due to the extent of the mining. It triggered a number of earthquakes, which caused great fissures to open up. The meteor was swallowed by one of these and was lost.'

'Then the iconium that had been extracted from the meteor also vanished; no one knows where. It's never been seen since.' The master tapped the box and watched the play of the shifting iridescence.

'But how did the High-Bailiff get his hands on it?' asked Wren.

'That's a good question, young lady,' said the master.

'There doesn't seem to be very much of it,' said Ludo.

'"Much" is a relative term, Cleef. "Much" is probably all there is in the world.'

'Yeah, but how's it going to help us?' asked Ludo. 'There's nowhere round here where we can sell it.'

'Sell it?' said Lucas Flink. 'We must *use* it. Iconium has almost miraculous properties. It can –'

'Make pictures all by itself?' said Mel.

'Just so, young man. This apprentice of yours, Ambrosius, has a rare head on his shoulders. Is he as nimble with his hands as he is with his mind?'

'Indeed he is, Lucas. I expect great things from Womper. That is, if we ever manage to get back to Nem.' The master smiled at Mel. 'I myself have never seen iconium. It is reputed to be highly fugitive. Is that so, Lucas?'

'Yes. It is the most powerful *and* the most fugitive of pigments. Whatever is created with the iconium lasts but a short time – minutes, no more.'

'So, Womper, what are we to do with this serendipitous substance?' asked the master.

'Well, we could make our own creations to destroy the tortoise-machine. Using iconium they'd be done in no time at all.'

Ambrosius Blenk looked at Lucas Flink and they

both smiled. 'That's exactly what we would do. Come on, to work – all of you.'

'We've stopped moving,' said Wren.

Ludo pointed. 'No wonder. Look out the window.'

Beneath them, and curving away to either side, was an enormous chasm. It had sheer cliffs and was perhaps a mile wide and just as deep. Even though it was full daylight, the sky above the far rim was darkest night seeded with brilliant stars. Deep below, at the bottom of this natural barrier, flowed a glowing river of molten lava.

'Ah, we've reached my moat,' said Lucas Flink. 'I created it to surround my valley and keep unwelcome guests out. Now it rather looks as if it's keeping us in.'

'How do we cross it?' asked the master.

'There's a causeway. Unfortunately, it's behind us, on the far side of the valley. This is regrettable, to say the least, for just over there is my latest addition to the Mirrorscape, "The Empire of Sleep", the painting I gave to you recently, Ambrosius.'

'The one in your studio,' said Mel.

'The very same,' said the master.

Lucas Flink pointed to the far side of the chasm. 'On the other side of the moat is the way back to your mansion.'

'Well, maybe Billet can hold the monster off for long enough.' The master clapped his hands. 'Come on, time's against us. To work!' He carefully removed several blank sheets of paper from his sketchbook and handed them round. 'We must take turns with this pencil stub. And be quick. Just lightning sketches.'

'Lightning sketches. Very good, Ambrosius. But you can't expect us to work in all this mess.'

'Of course not, Lucas. We'll repair to the library. Swivel, why don't you tidy up?'

'Farris, Bathor, lend him a hand,' said Lucas Flink.

'Do we *have* to?' said Farris.

'Why can't we do a bit more *devilry?*' said Bathor.

Lucas Flink sighed and rolled his eyes.

Once in the library, everyone in turn made a quick sketch. By the time it was Mel's turn the pencil stub was almost too small to handle.

'Now, let's see what you've come up with,' said the master. 'Lucas, that's classic.' The monster he had conceived was indeed horrible, with massive, hairy arms and razor-sharp horns that extended in front to form a deadly crescent.

'Yours too, Ambrosius.' Lucas Flink stood there, admiring the master's sketch. 'It's a giant Pyrexian vampire-orchid, a natural predator of tortoises, if I'm not mistaken. Let's create both – just for the heck of it. I'd love to see them in action.'

'Is that wise with so little iconium? What have the others created? Fine work, Cleef. What exactly is it?'

'I call it a forceposaur, master. See, it uses its long, pointed jaws to force open the tortoise-monster's shell and expose its soft body inside.'

'Very imaginative, Cleef.' Turning to Wren, the master said, 'I had no idea you could also draw, young lady. This sketch is not unlike the dragon that adorns my clock.'

'Yes, master. I designed it.'

'You did? Remarkable. Are you related to Thomas Delf, the clockmaker?'

'He's my father.'

'Indeed.' The master looked hard at Wren.

'Now, what does this dragon of yours do?'

'The usual dragon trick. It breathes fire. But this one bores into the shell with its corkscrew snout and injects the fire. The monster cooks from the inside out.'

The master was delighted. 'Any one of these inventions would be the equal of that old humpback.' Ambrosius Blenk placed them on the table with the others. 'Now, what have you come up with, Womper?'

Mel showed them his sketch. It was a bridge. He explained how it was going to work.

'That's great, Mel,' said Wren.

'I wish I'd thought of it.'

'It doesn't matter who thought of it, Cleef. We now have a way out of our dilemma.'

'Two birds with one stone, eh, Ambrosius?'

'I think we're all agreed that this solution is the best. Lucas, as you're the only one here who has experience of the iconium, perhaps you would like to realise young Womper's sketch while we all watch and learn?'

Swivel had salvaged a battered canvas, an easel, some brushes, a palette and a selection of oils from the wreck of the studio. Farris and Bathor helped him to set them up near the window.

Lucas Flink explained. 'To use the iconium one simply mixed it with two media: oil and imagination.' He selected a large brush, prepared some iconium and began to apply it to the canvas in broad strokes. As he worked, he could not suppress a broad grin. The first marks he applied initially looked like nothing more than multi-coloured smears but as they watched, the blurry stains organised themselves, swirling about the surface of the canvas until they came to rest as a perfect representation of the view through the window.

Wren and Ludo gasped out loud. Even Mel, who had seen the power of the iconium before, felt a great surge of excitement as the image swam into place. Ambrosius Blenk seemed outwardly detached but his hand was trembling, obviously itching to get to grips with such a wondrous medium.

Farris nudged Bathor. 'If we had some of that . . .'

'Enough of that, you two!' warned Lucas Flink.

As the first marks of Mel's design began to appear, Wren called out, 'Look at *this!*'

Through the window they saw the painting

becoming real as the first faint outlines of Mel's bridge appeared in the air, soaring out towards the middle of the chasm. As Lucas Flink continued, they saw the outlines fill in and the great bridge begin to take shape. Impossibly tall piers rose from the depths of the moat to support the wide spans. Along its length, colourful towers and graceful arches sprang into existence, interspersed with tall statues. Banners fluttered from pinnacles and the surface of the roadway was patterned with bright mosaics featuring giant serpents that intertwined with each other. The entire bridge looked, and indeed was, magical.

Billet shook with the impact of another lightning bolt. The smell of burning invaded the library.

'Time we were off,' said Wren.

'Lucas, you'll have to complete it as we advance.' Taking up a speaking-tube, the master said, 'Over the bridge, Billet. No dilly-dallying. Next stop home.' Then to the youngsters, 'Come with me. I know where there's a better view to witness the fun. You angels had better stay and help your master.'

He crossed to the far corner of the library and

swung open a section of bookcase that concealed a narrow staircase just wide enough for them to squeeze up. Beyond a small door at the top was a large attic. As their eyes adjusted to the dim light, they made out the rafters of Billet's sloping roof, with narrow shafts of daylight piercing the slats and damaged thatch. The attic itself was covered in a thin film of dust, and cobwebs hung everywhere.

'Here, help me with this,' said the master as he dragged a large trunk across the floor, leaving tramlines in the dust. He climbed on it and opened a trapdoor in the roof. Bright light flooded in. 'Come up here and watch the second part of Womper's plan. You won't want to miss this.'

Mel, Ludo and Wren mounted the trunk and, side by side with their master, they all looked back along the bridge as Billet strode on.

'*Duck!*' Mel's shouted warning was just in time as a searing lightning bolt detonated just above their heads. 'That was close.'

Ears ringing, they raised their heads again to admire the rapidly forming bridge.

'It's . . . it's *incredible!*' said Mel. He had merely suggested the towers that flanked it in his sketch, but Lucas Flink had elaborated these into fantastic pieces of architecture complete with tracery, statues and gargoyles.

'You must feel very proud, Womper,' said the master.

'I'd feel better if it wasn't for that.'

Close behind came the tortoise-monster, pitter-pattering after them on its spider legs. They could hear the lightning gun recharging.

'Master, it's gaining on us!' exclaimed Ludo.

'Calm down, Cleef. I'm sure Lucas has made provision for such a likelihood.'

As the pursuing monster reached the first arch, the row of stone gargoyles that sat atop it came alive and sprang on to the contraption. Several squeezed into the lightning-gun port and began attacking the occupants. Others clambered up the tall tower, breaking off anything that protruded with their powerful arms.

'Look at the statues,' said Wren. The figures that lined the bridge also came alive and, agile as monkeys, began to scale the long legs of the machine.

'Now it's the mosaic,' said Ludo, jumping up and

down. 'Look!' The pattern of snakes reared up from the surface of the roadway and began to entangle the machine's many legs. Soon they had stopped it dead in its tracks. 'Looks like chucking-out time.'

As they watched, they saw red-robed figures being flung from the machine by the gargoyles and statues.

'Oh dear,' said the master. 'The iconium is much more fugitive than I expected.'

'The bridge is fading away behind us,' observed Mel. 'I hope Billet gets a move on.'

They watched as the bridge paled and vanished beneath the tortoise-monster and it toppled into the chasm. As it fell, they could just make out the top of the tower open and a flock of birds fly out. Hanging from them by thin ropes were two figures – one very tall, the other very short – being carried away.

'Who's the birdie now?' said Ludo.

'Birdie?' said Mel. 'Oh, I see what you mean.'

'Rats deserting a sinking tortoise, eh, Mel?' said Wren.

'Yeah, scum always floats.'

'*Ahem!*'

'Yes, Swivel?' The master turned from the action.

'The library, Master, when you have a moment. Master Flink has encountered a slight technical problem. He would be grateful for a word with you.'

The master led his butler and the friends back down to the library.

'Swivel tells me that you've hit a snag, Lucas. Anything I can do to help?'

'A snag? Yes. I'm afraid that I've er . . . run out of iconium. I know I should have eked it out but I rather got carried away and used too much and now . . .' Lucas Flink showed them his almost empty palette, '. . . there's not enough left to get us to the far side.'

Child's Play

'A simple causeway might have been the prudent option, Lucas,' chided the master.

'Yes. I'm sorry. But I felt inspired by the lad's sketch, truly inspired, and this iconium is fantastic to work with. If I had more I could –'

'But you don't have more, old friend. The question is, what do we do now?'

'How about stilts for Billet?' said Wren. 'There might be enough iconium left.'

'Mile-high stilts?' said the master. 'To walk in molten lava? A trifle impractical, I think.'

'What about a tightrope? That wouldn't need much either,' suggested Ludo.

'Billet is many admirable things; but a funambulist he is not. In any event, I don't think the tightrope's yet been made that could bear Billet's weight.'

'A safety net then,' persisted Ludo. 'At least we'd still be alive.'

'That might save us for a while,' observed Wren,

'but it wouldn't last for long. Is there enough left for a flock of birds? They worked for the High-Bailiff and the dwarf.'

'We would need a flock each, and a simply enormous flock for Billet. I don't think that's an option,' said the master sadly.

'Excuse me, Master Flink,' said Mel hesitantly, 'but I was in one of your paintings, the one with the bladder-demons . . .'

Lucas Flink's old eyes lit up. 'You know, young man, I think you might have it.' His brush searched the entire surface of the palette and collected what little iconium there was left. With it, he painted as large a disc as he could in the air over the rapidly fading bridge. He trailed the brush and with the last vestiges of the wondrous paint flicked in a fine line with the point. 'That's it. It's all gone now.'

Before their eyes, the mark transformed itself into a spherical balloon and the fine line into a dangling rope.

'*Ahem!* If you'll permit me?' Swivel nodded towards the open window where a stout, hooked line had appeared. He extended a concertina-like arm and attached the line firmly to the window frame. The shadow cast by the large balloon above them dimmed the room.

'I hope for all our sakes your idea works, Womper,' said the master.

As they gazed from the window, they saw the last of the bridge become dimmer and dimmer and dimmer until it faded away altogether.

Then Billet started falling.

'*Scrot!*' wailed Ludo. 'It's not working.'

'Language, Cleef!' scolded the master.

'The balloon's giving us *some* buoyancy,' said Mel, 'but the trouble is, we're too heavy. Why don't we throw anything we don't need out the window?'

'Yes, Womper. Everyone jettison all the useless stuff. Start with the studio.'

There was much debris from the attack that the friends were able to eject from the damaged studio window, while the angels threw a similar amount of weighty items from the kitchen. Swivel emptied the house of all his cleaning materials, which lightened it considerably. Everyone rushed back to the library.

'Our rate of descent has slowed but we're still falling,' said the master. 'All right, now for the furniture. We don't have much time. Soon the balloon will begin to fade.'

By the time the last of the furniture had been thrown into the chasm, they hung stationary in the air but altogether too near the lava for comfort – especially Billet's. They could hear the yelps of pain as his feet toasted.

'It's no good. There're just too many of us in here,' said Lucas Flink. 'Some of us will have to leave.'

'*Leave!*' said Ludo. 'You can't throw us out.' The friends looked at their master, the alarm evident on their young faces.

'He means us,' said a delighted Farris. 'Come on, Bathor.'

'*Yahoo!*' they shouted as they leapt from the window.

The angels' tattered wings were not up to any serious flying, but with them spread wide they were able to soar in wide spirals on the powerful thermal currents rising off the lava. Immediately, Billet began to rise.

'Great,' said Ludo. 'All we've done is increase the distance we'll have to fall. We're still no nearer the far side.'

'Womper, you seem to be the one with all the bright ideas,' said the master. 'If you've got another one tucked away, now's the time to produce it.'

'Only this.' Mel picked up a jar of turpentine from beside the easel and dashed it against the canvas. The image of the balloon smeared and began to run down the canvas in tear-like streaks.

'What're you doing?' cried Lucas Flink. 'That's all that's holding us up.' Then, after a moment, 'We're falling!'

'No time to explain.' Mel rushed at the canvas and, with both hands, began to stir the loosened iconium into a great spiral. Round and round flew his hands, and as they did so a roaring noise swelled and entered the library. The room grew dramatically darker.

'What's happening?' shouted Ludo. He put his hands to his ears as the air pressure dropped dramatically.

Wren rushed to the window. 'Look, everyone!'

As they all peered out, they saw the air continue to

darken and a towering tornado materialise around them. Then it seized Billet in its powerful vortex. Slowly at first, then faster and faster, they revolved in the irresistible current. It drove Billet towards the far wall of the chasm and then back the way they had come and then forwards again. But, as its speed increased, it began to exert a lifting force. Billet spun helplessly in the overpowering spiral and everyone in the library was hurled around as if they were blobs of paint flicked from the end of a brush. Books flew about like missiles.

As Mel dragged himself to his feet and fought his way back to the easel, a hefty volume caught him a glancing blow on his forehead. Clinging on to the easel with one hand, he kept working the spiral with his other. He could feel the iconium rapidly drying. The whirlwind would only last as long as he could keep the pigment in motion.

Wren struggled to the window and saw the rapidly approaching wall of the chasm. '*Mel!*'

Mel saw it too and redoubled his efforts. Then, just as it seemed they would all be smashed against the wall, the tornado lifted them the last few feet and they were over the solid ground of the far side. The iconium finally dried beneath Mel's fingers and faded. The wind outside dropped suddenly. So did Billet.

'Me feet. Me skegging plates!' he shouted as he landed with a bump.

'Womper, you've saved us,' said the master. 'Who would have thought that we'd be rescued by a spot of finger painting? Call Farris and Bathor back in. The way home is clear, if I'm not mistaken.'

But the master *was* mistaken.

A hot breeze caused the candles to flicker as the brocade drape that formed the tent flap to Lord Brool's pavilion was drawn aside. Through the flap could be briefly glimpsed a desert view of the Mirrorscape. Lord Brool's secretary, Skim, entered and bowed his emaciated frame low before his grotesquely fat master. 'We have found Groot Smert, my Lord. He was in the House of Mysteries, drunk as a boiled owl, celebrating the demise of Blenk's Fegish apprentice. We have sobered him up and he is being put to work straight away as you ordered. He has the Mystery's finest bestiary to work from. All he now needs is the pigment. I'll stay with him to ensure he uses it wisely.' The secretary glanced at a casket standing open on a table beside his master's chair. It was so full of iconium the lid would not shut. 'And the High-Bailiff and his assistant have just arrived. They crave an audience.'

Lord Brool spat some half-chewed sweetmeat on to the carpeted floor at the foot of one of the easels that supported two large paintings. He reached out and selected a candied snail from a dish on the table. He crunched it noisily and gave a flick of his scarlet-gloved hand as a signal to bring them in.

Skim bowed again and left, taking the casket with him. Normally a rigidly controlled man, the thought of the inconceivable wealth represented by the shimmering pigment he cradled in his skinny arms induced a fit of hiccoughs. 'The Lord-*hic*-Master will see you now.'

Adolfus Spute's stained and creased robe hung shapelessly from his tall frame. His white make-up was streaked and his natural, grey-tinted flesh showed through. Mumchance looked no better.

'*Spute!*' bellowed Lord Brool. 'Don't just stand there; you're letting that confounded desert air into my pavilion.'

The High-Bailiff and his dwarf entered, but the former's eyes were transfixed by the casket. He only found his voice when Skim closed the flap with a *hic* and left. 'That's . . . that's . . .'

'Yes it is, isn't it? Amazing what one can find if one knows where to look.' In spite of the heat, Lord Brool was beginning to enjoy himself for the first time since he entered the Mirrorscape. 'You see, that piddling quantity of iconium you collected for me is no longer the only iconium that the Mystery possesses. Ever since I became Lord-High-Master I have had a team of my own miners searching Kig for the fallen meteorite. And, while you were away extracting that titbit from Floris, they found it. Not that I really expected you to return it to me. At least, not all of it.'

'I don't understand . . .'

'Of course you don't, Spute, of course you don't. That is why you are merely the High-Bailiff and I am the Lord-High-Master. I, on the other hand, understand a great deal. A little bird told me. Just as you have had your little songbird listening to the goings-on in the Blenk mansion, I have had my own little bird singing to me about the goings-on between you and your nephew. Some might go so far as to call it a conspiracy. He has been keeping me up to date with all your scheming. Isn't that so, little bird?'

Groot's sidekick Bunt emerged from behind the drapes. With his layers of puppy fat, scarlet robes, white make-up and freshly shaved tonsure, he seemed a younger, reduced version of the older man. He stood grinning next to Lord Brool.

'And my little bird made a copy of that device that your little bird took from the Fegish boy. Which is how I came to be here. I knew all along that you would bungle things – you always do. I thought that I should be here to make certain that events turn out for the good of the Fifth Mystery, that is to say, for *me*. I've known all along what you've been up to, Spute. Everyone conspires against me. Why should you be any different?'

'Tweet, tweet,' said Bunt with a mocking smile.

Suddenly there were far too many birds in Adolfus Spute's world, as he realised he had been out-manoeuvred.

'You know, I do believe you have outlived your usefulness, Spute. However, as a treat – a *final* treat – I think I will allow you to witness the little reception I have arranged for Ambrosius Blenk. You've failed miserably to thwart his power and influence in the past. Now I'll show you how it should be done. It'll be child's play. Here, Bunt, help me up. The fun is just about to start.'

Billet hobbled on scorched feet over the brick-red sand of "The Empire of Sleep", complaining volubly. The night sky above was overpopulated with stars that bathed the arid wilderness in a crepuscular light. All around, towering sandstone heads emerged from the desert floor as if they were the tops of giant statues buried up to their necks. Burning wicks protruded from the crowns of these heads, adding a flickering counterpoint to the starlight and casting puddles of dancing yellow light at their base. Other heads seemed to have burnt down like candles, their stony features distorted like melted wax.

The three youngsters lay curled up on the library floor, sleeping soundly. Exhaustion had overtaken them now that they were so close to home. Swivel dozed in the corner, leaning against a bookcase, while Farris and Bathor were quietly preoccupied with preening each others' wings, which were nearly whole once again. The old masters stood side by side at the window, gazing out admiringly over Lucas Flink's creation.

'I wonder what the world would be like if there was more iconium available. If you could just think a picture into existence would there be any need of us artists, do you suppose?'

'I'm sure there would, Ambrosius. Technique is always hard won but surely it's our imaginations that make us different.' They both ruminated on this for a while in silence. 'That's odd.'

'What is, old friend?'

'*That*. That's not part of "The Empire of Sleep".'

The master followed Lucas's pointing finger.

Silhouetted against the distant wall of grey mist that marked their exit from the Mirrorscape and the portal back into the mansion, was a large, squat shape.

He picked the omniscope from the floor and steadied it against the window frame.

'My giddy aunt! It's a *baby*. It's an enormous baby.'

At least that is what it looked like. But as they drew closer he was not so sure. It certainly appeared to be a baby, and a rather ugly one at that, but its vast size suggested otherwise. It sat cross-legged on the sand, occasionally making jerky movements with its chubby limbs and looking from side to side. A thin trail of drool hung from its chin. Closer still, and they could see a large scarlet tent, with many smaller ones off to one side. The black-eyed, red banner of the Fifth Mystery flew from the centre of this camp, and a group of men-at-arms moved through it bearing flaming torches. The baby spotted Billet as they came nearer. Its face first registered a look of curiosity, which soon changed to one of consternation and then petulance. It screwed up its podgy features and opened its mouth wide in a howl. But no noise came from its throat; something else did.

A monster!

Behind the emerging creature's swordfish snout was a warty, lizard body tipped with a venomous scorpion sting. It was borne aloft on butterfly-patterned bat wings.

'That looks like –'

'I do believe it is, Ambrosius. It's one of my monsters.'

The baby screamed its silent scream again.

'And one of yours too.'

The second monster that flew at them definitely had some stag beetle and dragonfly present, but the overall theme was undoubtedly spider, with more than a hint of wasp in its pointed abdomen.

'They're setting our own creations against us!'

'Monster time, again is it?' boomed Billet. 'All right. Let's be 'aving yer, yer flying fatheads.'

The creatures flew twice around Billet and then attacked. The first monster hurled itself towards them where they watched from the library window. Billet shook with the impact as its long snout penetrated the wall, barely missing the masters and stopping just inches from the sleeping friends. Mel awoke with a start, but had the presence of mind not to leap up. He lay on his back, staring at the lethal spike just above him. Then the library window shattered as the creature's tail thrust into the room, its deadly tip thrashing and searching for something to sting. Drops of amber venom dripped from its end, searing the floorboards like acid. There was another impact away from the window, followed by the ominous sound of gnawing. The second creature was using its powerful mandibles to chew through the wall and expose the occupants.

'*Ahem!* If everyone would care to move to the far side of the library.' Swivel's face rotated to one wearing welding goggles, and a cutting torch appeared from his sleeve. Its flame roared into life and a cone of fierce blue light stabbed the twilight. Carefully avoiding the probing sting, the butler crossed to where the sword-like snout of the creature pierced the wall and, amid a shower of bright sparks, deftly cut it off. There was a great howl of pain and the monster dropped to the desert floor.

The butler's masked face swivelled away and he

extinguished his torch and drew it into his sleeve, replacing it with a long auger. He crossed to the wall and put his ear to it, gauging where the gnawing sound was loudest. Satisfied he had found the spot, he set the augur spinning and began drilling through the wall. He lurched forward as the drill reached the far side. There was another wail as the giant insect felt its bite and fell off the house.

Wren hesitantly peered down from the broken window at the two bodies lying on the sand before they were crushed by Billet's feet. 'They're dead. They've lost their colour and . . . they're *vanishing!*'

Mel joined her. 'It looks like someone else has got their hands on some iconium.'

'Yeah. And rather more than we had,' said Ludo. '*Look!*'

From out of the gaping mouth of the babe came another monster; bigger, uglier and infinitely more dangerous.

'We're so close to home,' said Wren. 'And this time we've nothing left to fight back with.'

'If only we had some ordinary materials,' said the

master. 'It'd take longer to create our riposte, but at least we could go down fighting.'

Mel looked at the wall of mist. *It's not far. I can do it.* 'Let me try to get through, Master. I know how to use the mirrormark. I could bring back the materials.'

'Me too,' said Wren. 'I can help. Between us we could bring back easels and brushes and oils and colours – as much as you like. Ludo will help us as well. Won't you?'

Ludo nodded unenthusiastically.

'Ambrosius?' said Lucas Flink. 'It's probably our only hope.'

'Very well. You've all been in the Mirrorscape a while now. If you're not feeling unwell already, you will be soon. You need to get out for a spell anyway. Take Swivel with you.'

'I believe Swivel will be of more use here. Take my angels.' Lucas Flink turned to his creations. 'You two, keep an eye on them.'

'*Great!*' said Farris and Bathor as one. 'A chance for more mischief.'

'Right, off you go. But take care. I don't wish to lose

you now; not after all we've been through.' The master smiled at the three friends.

Mel, Wren, Ludo, Farris and Bathor raced down the stairs. At the bottom, Mel signalled them to halt. 'It's dark outside. Two shining angels are going to give us away. Here, put these on.' He unhooked two hooded travelling cloaks hanging next to the door.

An enormous two-headed dragon was busy attacking the house from the front as the small party dashed from the postern door in Billet's scorched heel. They ran to the wall of mist, using the deep shadows cast by the giant heads as cover.

'Look at the baby,' gasped Wren.

Its giant profile towered over them. As they watched, they saw the whole of its side becoming transparent. There were two people inside, lit by a dozen tall candelabra. A tall, skinny man loomed over Groot. The head apprentice stood before an easel copying monsters on to a large canvas from a book open on a lectern to one side. To his right was a smaller easel with the image of the baby on it.

The thin man looked up and pointed to the

transparent patch. 'If you concentrated as much on keeping us hidden as you do on your monsters, I'd feel a lot happier.'

Groot glanced up. For a terrible moment Mel thought he had seen them, but soon realised that he was only regarding the flaw in his masking illusion. Groot spooned some iconium from the nearly full chest at his side. He mixed it and applied some to the portrait of the baby with one desultory swipe of his brush. 'Happy now?' The giant baby became opaque again, but not before Mel saw Groot pocketing a handful of the priceless pigment while the other man's back was turned.

'It's *Groot* creating the monsters,' said Wren.

'He's just copying them from a book,' said Ludo. 'No originality.'

'Yeah, but more importantly, did you see how much iconium he's got to work with? Come on, we must hurry.' Mel led them, crouching, to the wall of mist, made the reverse mirrormark and they were through.

Their sense of relief was palpable as they re-emerged into the daylight in the master's studio directly opposite the canvas through which they had left. The knot of anxiety that had been in Mel's stomach ever since he entered the Mirrorscape unravelled. They began to laugh and they felt the strength returning to them as the Mirrorscape sickness flushed from their bodies. Wren quickly led them to the service passage and ushered them inside before the angels could think up some new mischief.

'Wait; we'll need some candles,' she suddenly remembered.

'Allow us,' said Bathor. The angels removed their hooded cloaks and lit up the narrow space, enabling Wren to lead them to the entrance hall. From there they entered the clock without being seen. Just then the hour struck and the automata sprang into life. When the chiming ceased, Bathor immediately began touching and prodding the delicate models with glee as they filed back in. In his excitement, he dislodged the figure of a knight and it fell to the floor. Its head snapped at the neck and rolled off.

'Oh, no,' said Wren.

'Now look what you've done!' said Mel. Bathor

looked crestfallen and Mel immediately felt guilty for his outburst.

Wren knelt by the broken figure. 'I'll need to fix it before the clock chimes again. Its absence is bound to get noticed and someone will come to investigate.'

Seeing how upset Wren was, Mel suggested, 'I don't know about either of you but I'm starving. Why doesn't one of you raid the kitchen and find us something to eat?'

'I'll go,' said Ludo.

'Use the service passages,' said Wren. 'Meet us in the master's studio.'

'We'll go with you,' said Farris.

'To light the way,' added Bathor.

When they were alone, Mel retrieved the head, which had rolled under the machinery. 'They're beautiful figures. Did you really design them yourself?'

'Certainly I did. I designed them and my father cast them.'

'They're lighter than they look.' Mel picked up and hefted the body of the figure in his other hand.

'They're hollow. Look in the knight.'

Mel suddenly remembered what Wren's father had said. '"Look in the knight?" *Wren*, that's the message your father gave me for you. Remember?'

'I thought he meant night, like in night-time,' said Wren, looking inside the hollow head. 'There's something in here.' She withdrew a paper and unfolded it. 'It's my father's handwriting.

'"Dearest Wren. If you are reading this, it means that a great misfortune has befallen our family and I am no longer around to care for you and your mother. A while ago, Lord Floris, a great lover of clocks and a good friend, gave me something precious to look after for him. I do not understand its nature but I know that it is of great value and power. He told me that if ever something bad were to happen to him, or if I found myself in danger of arrest, then I was to pass it to Ambrosius Blenk. He can be trusted to use it for the good of everyone in Nem. I now know that that time is near. A close friend of Lord Floris's in the House of Mysteries has warned me that I am about to be taken. I do not know why and I do not have much time. I have tried and failed to pass this thing to Ambrosius and now

I fear I will be caught with it still in my possession. Under no circumstances must it be allowed to fall into the hands of the Fifth Mystery. I have hidden it here in the certain knowledge that you will be looking after this great timepiece that you love so much and will eventually find it. It is too late for me, but I beg you to pass it to the great master. Know that wherever I am, my thoughts are with you. Kiss your mother for me. Your loving father, Thomas Delf.'" Wren stared at the letter in silence.

'I'm sorry, Wren.' Mel placed his hand on hers and gave it a squeeze. He looked in the body of the figure. 'There's a bag in here.' He pulled the small sack out and loosened the drawstring that fastened it, tipping a little of its contents into his open hand.

'Mel! It's . . .'

'Yeah, it is.' Mel carefully poured it back into the bag, refastened it and handed it to her. 'Here, you take it. We should go.'

When they arrived at the master's studio, the door was ajar and sitting in the ornate chair was Green. His head was bandaged and he looked haggard. In his lap rested the bloody and lifeless figure of his tiny, piebald creature. Mel pushed the door open a fraction more. Standing next to Green were Ludo and the angels. Ludo looked up at him in alarm.

'Run, Mel! They're going to kill you!'

Out of the Frying Pan . . .

Mel grabbed Wren's wrist and pulled her back down the corridor but blocking their way was Blue, with two other rebels. They had their crossbows levelled at the youngsters' heads.

'That's far enough. Back inside, *traitor*,' said Blue. 'Keep your hands where I can see them.'

Green shifted painfully in his chair. 'You've got a nerve to turn up here. But it saves us having to hunt you down like the two-faced cur you are.'

'I don't understand.' Mel looked around feeling suddenly very afraid. There were four more wounded rebels leaning in the corner. They were so bloodied that he hardly recognised them. They stared at him with a fierce, unblinking gaze, charged with malice. On the floor between them, bound and gagged and struggling, was Jurgis in his red robes. His face still bore sucker marks like oversized measles.

'Don't play the innocent with me. We know what you've been up to. I should have let Blue slit your gizzard the first time we met.'

'I think there's been some mistake. I've not been –'

'Oh, there's no mistake. I have a confession signed by your own hand.' Green produced a crumpled sheet of paper from inside his bloodstained jerkin and held it up for all to see. It was Mel's sketch of the mirrormark.

Ludo said, '*No!*' He was as white as a sheet.

'Your friend's guilty all right.' He pointed to the signature in the lower right-hand corner. 'Your name's Melkin Womper, isn't it? Or are you going to deny that too?'

'No, the drawing's mine.' Mel fought to control his breathing.

'So you admit it?' said Green. 'You *are* a traitor.'

'No. Someone stole it from my locker in the dormitory.' Mel heard himself. He sounded very lame.

'He's lying,' said Blue. 'How else would the Fifth Mystery have known where to find us? He's the only one to have been to our hideout.'

'The Fifth Mystery found you?'

'Don't pretend you don't know,' said Green. 'They were waiting in ambush for us beneath the House of

Thrones. They killed most of my men. We're all that's left. Eight of us. The entire Rainbow Rebellion is here in this room. Now you're going to pay for it. You'll pay for it in blood.' He laid the still body of his creature on the floor beside him.

'This can't be true,' said Wren.

Ludo's eyes darted around the room. He was sweating.

'But I didn't tell anyone!' Mel was seized from behind and forced to his knees. His hair was grabbed and his head yanked backwards. A hand – Blue's hand – came from behind. It held a knife at his bared throat. Mel whimpered as he felt its cold, sharp edge and a trickle of warm blood run down his neck as the blade was pressed against his flesh. 'We're on the same side. Why won't you believe me?'

The angels tried to push forward.

'You two. Stay where you are,' ordered Blue. He twitched the knife. Mel's eyes grew wide with terror and an involuntary moan escaped his lips.

Wren cried out. *'Don't!'*

'Shut up! Or are you in this too?' asked Green.

'No one's in this. Not me and especially not Mel.

He's been with us all the time. He couldn't have betrayed you.'

'She's covering up for him.' Blue pressed his blade harder against Mel's throat, making him cry out.

'No, I'm not. If you only knew what Mel's been through, trying to rescue the master. If we don't get back to him soon he'll be killed.'

Green looked hard at Wren. His expression was stony. 'I don't believe you.' Then to Blue, 'We're wasting time. Kill him.'

'*No!*' screamed Ludo. 'Mel didn't betray you. *I* did!'

'*What?*' said Wren.

'Ludo?' Mel's jaw dropped and he tried to turn his head towards his friend before it was yanked back by Blue.

'It won't work, son. Your friend's going to die.' Green nodded at Blue. 'Do it!'

'No, it *was* me!' insisted Ludo. 'Groot made me do it. He's been blackmailing me. His uncle was going to arrest my family if I didn't help him. I'm sorry, Mel. I took it from your hiding place. That's how Groot got into the Mirrorscape.'

'I thought you were our friend,' said Wren.

'I'm *sorry*, Wren. I had no choice. Groot followed us all the way. He must have shown Mel's sketch to his uncle. Ask *him* if you don't believe me.' He pointed at Jurgis.

Green nodded at the men guarding the renegade apprentice and one of them bent and loosened his gag. 'Well?'

'He's lying. Fegie's one of us, has been all along. He gave Groot the sketch with his own hands.' Jurgis's eyes darted shiftily from side to side.

His guard drew his dagger and held it at the apprentice's throat.

'Let's hear it again. The truth, this time,' said Green.

The dagger bit deeper. 'All right, all right. Don't hurt me. It's true. Fegie's got nothing to do with it. Ludo's been helping Groot all along. Just don't hurt me.' He started crying.

Green looked at Jurgis long and hard. 'That's better.' Then to Blue, 'Release Mel. There's our traitor.' He pointed at Ludo.

Blue let Mel go and grabbed Ludo savagely by the

throat. 'Why you little . . . Don't think I have any qualms about killing youngsters.'

'*Stop!* Don't do it.' Mel tried to force himself between Blue and Ludo. Another rebel dragged him away.

'Give me one good reason why not,' spat Blue. He gripped Ludo harder still until his eyes bulged.

'*Please* wait,' pleaded Mel. 'We all know how the Fifth Mystery works. This is just what they want; to see us destroying ourselves. Put yourself in Ludo's place. What if they threatened *your* family? And there's a battle going on in there.' He pointed emphatically to the canvas of "The Empire of Sleep" leaning against the wall. 'The master is fighting for his life while we're here fighting amongst ourselves. We have to get back to him at once.'

'We need brushes and oils and easels,' said Wren. 'And we need every artist we have to fight what's in there. Including Ludo. The Fifth Mystery's got a terrible weapon.'

'That's right,' said Bathor, 'terrible.'

Farris nodded.

'You'd better believe it,' said Mel. 'They can create as many monsters as they want. If we just stay here they'll have won. With the master out of the way, the Mysteries will never be stopped.'

'So, they got hold of the iconium after all,' said Green.

'You know about that?' said Mel.

'We knew they were trying to get some,' he said. 'The most recent escapees from Kig told us of Brool's special mining team. There's only one thing they could have been looking for. So, Ambrosius Blenk's in danger, is he?'

Mel looked anxiously at the canvas and then back at Green. 'He's as good as dead if we don't act at once. Him and Lucas Flink and Swivel. If we go now we'll be behind the Mystery men. You can take them by surprise – ambush them like they ambushed you. They'll be so busy attacking the master that they won't be expecting you. But we must go at once. *Please.*'

Green shifted uncomfortably in his chair, his forehead creased with pain and indecision.

Blue looked at his leader, uncertain what to do. 'Boss?'

Green looked at Mel. 'Ordinary colours are no match for iconium – but you're right. We've got to try. He nodded at Blue. 'All right, let him go.'

Blue relaxed his grip and Ludo gulped in air.

Green said, 'We can deal with this one later.' He looked at Ludo. 'But someone better stick by him, just in case.'

'Let me,' said Blue. 'If he so much as looks the wrong way, I'll put his eyes out.' He released Ludo, who slumped to the floor, clutching his throat and gasping for air.

'No. I'm more badly hurt than you. I'll stay with him.' Green got painfully to his feet. 'OK, Mel. Gather what you need quickly and let's go. You, come here.' He grabbed Ludo roughly by his collar and used him to support himself.

'Is this why you've been acting so strange ever since we entered the Mirrorscape?' said Wren. 'You should have told us earlier. We could've helped.'

'I couldn't,' croaked Ludo. 'I just couldn't. I'm so sorry.'

Mel looked at his friend. 'I know how you feel. The Fifth Mystery's got my parents.'

'*What?*' gasped Ludo. 'How do you know?'

Mel told him what he had told Wren earlier. 'The only way we're going to get them back is to see this thing through to the end.'

'I had no idea, Mel,' said Ludo. 'I've been selfish. Tell me what I can do to put things right. I'll do anything. *Anything.*'

'It's all right, Ludo. Let's just finish this thing together.'

'Mel's right,' said Wren. 'Let's stick together from now on.'

'Right,' said Green. 'Blue, you take the men and attack the Mystery. I'll go with this lot and get the materials to Ambrosius. Good luck.'

As soon as they stepped back through the canvas, they could see that the enemy was winning the battle. Dozens of flying, wraith-like creatures were surrounding Billet. They were attacking and retreating, only to attack again. Their forms were vaguely human and looked to be made from red-hot coals bound together with dirty cobwebs. Wherever they touched was seared black.

Billet looked to be in an advanced state of demolition. One of the great studio windows that served as his eyes, and most of the wall surrounding it, was missing, the interior open to the desert air. Flames and black smoke billowed from the other. He was stamping his giant feet in the hope of crushing his attackers but it was haphazard, and obvious he could no longer see. 'Is that the best yer can do, pip-squeak?' croaked Billet. His voice was nearly unrecognisable. It was sheer bravado.

Blue took advantage of the distraction and led his men silently behind the baby to await their moment to enter the camp from the rear.

Groot had made no effort to disguise the back of his hide, nearest the wall of mist. Mel could clearly see him and his companion in the strange studio inside the hollow baby.

'Here, do this creature next,' said the tall man as he turned the pages of the bestiary.

'How dare you tell me what to do, you emaciated streak of snot! I'll decide what to paint next, not some jumped-up flunky.' Groot threw down his paintbrush and folded his arms, stubbornly refusing to continue.

'Have some more wine. It might improve your temper,' said Skim, proffering the bottle. 'No? If you don't want any more then I might as well pour it away.'

'Wait!' Groot held out his goblet and sank it greedily once it had been filled. 'More.' He held out the drained vessel again.

'Can we continue now? Or have you run out of inspiration?'

'What would the likes of you know about art?'

'Not much – but I know what I like. And what I like is more monsters. What I *do* know about is serving wine. Now, if you want some more let's see another one.'

Mel could see from the way Groot now tipped the chest to recharge his palette with the iconium that he had used up most of it. 'Come on,' he said, 'we've seen enough here.' He led the others towards Billet, making use of the giant heads as cover. Carrying their bundles of materials, they got as close as they could without being observed.

'We're not going to make it across the last patch of sand without being seen,' said Green.

'We will if we're quick,' said Wren. 'Look at the wraiths.' As she spoke, the highly fugitive pigment that had created them started to fade and, one by one, they blinked out of existence. 'Come on.'

Mel, Ludo and Wren bolted for the postern door. Much to Farris' annoyance, Bathor left his fellow angel to help Green while he spiralled up into the air and wreaked some serious devilry on the last of the fading wraiths.

There was so much smoke drifting over the desert battlefield that the Mystery men could not have seen them from their camp. When they entered Billet, they found his interior was also filled with smoke, but they made it up the stairs to the library where Swivel had constructed a barricade in one corner from a mountain of books.

'Hello! Master?' At Mel's shout three smoke-blackened faces appeared over it.

'Womper! We thought you'd never get back. Did you bring all we need? Who's that with you?'

'It's me, Ambrosius.'

'Green? Is that you? Damn this smoke. Did you bring your men?'

'They're out there now – what's left of them – preparing a nasty surprise for Brool and his men. Things don't look good, Ambrosius.'

'It's just as well you came. We could use another artist.'

'You're an *artist?*' said Mel.

'Green used to be my apprentice,' said the master, 'just like you. Billet's in a bad way. I see you've brought the materials. They'll be a poor match against the iconium, but now at least we can try to fight back. Even if we fail, we'll have given a good account of ourselves. Swivel, set up the easels here. Brushes and oils next to them. Where're the colours? Womper, you didn't bring any colours.'

'No, Master, we brought this instead.' Wren produced the small sack. 'Lord Floris gave it to my father.'

The master took the proffered sack and eased the

drawstring to look inside. 'Oh, my giddy aunt! Lucas, look! More iconium!'

'No one has seen it for hundreds of years and suddenly we seem to be awash with the stuff,' said Lucas Flink.

'Now we're in with a real chance,' said the master. 'To work! All of you.'

Swivel set up the five light easels with blank canvases, while Ambrosius Blenk divided up the iconium into equal portions.

'I'm not about to let you have all the fun this time around, Lucas.'

'Please don't rub it in, Ambrosius,' said Lucas Flink.

'How about you, Green?' asked the master. 'Are you up for this?'

'Iconium? Just try and stop me.'

'I'm sorry, young lady,' said the master. 'There are not enough easels or brushes for you.'

Wren smiled bravely to conceal her disappointment. 'I think this work calls for real masters and apprentices.'

Once it was shared out, there was much less of the pigment than Mel had supposed. 'There seems barely enough for one good monster each.'

'As long as they're good monsters, it's all we'll need,' said Ludo.

'Right. Lucas, Green, Womper, Cleef. An easel apiece, I think.' The master handed them a brush each.

Mel looked at his canvas, the brush in his hand and the iconium. He was about to paint the most important picture of his life with the rarest of pigments, alongside two of the greatest artists who had ever lived. *Mum and Dad, this is for you. And Fa Theum.* He had his picture already worked out in his head. He held his brush poised over the iconium.

Then he lowered it. 'Here, Wren, you take my place. Groot's got lots more iconium than we have. We're never going to match him monster for monster. If I can't steal his supply, then I can at least destroy it.'

'You can't go back out there.'

'I must. It's the only way to even things up.'

'Then let me go. The best artists are needed here.'

'You're one of the best artists. Besides, I've unfinished business with Groot.'

He dashed from the library.

'Be careful, Mel,' said Wren to the empty doorway. 'Be careful.'

Mel had just made it to the cover of the nearest head when it began. From the mouth of the massive baby flew a host of monsters. They were horrifying, but Mel could see they were sloppily imagined and imperfect. Groot was obviously drunk. Mel retraced his steps until he was abreast of the baby again. The giant illusion of the baby was vanishing before his eyes. Its creator could no longer be bothered to renew the small image on canvas that maintained the phantasm.

Then there came cries of alarm from Lord Brool's pavilion as smoke billowed and flames blossomed. Blue and his men were beginning their attack. Mel watched as the tall man said something to Groot and ran through the fading image of the baby, back towards the camp.

'It's just you and me now, Groot. And pretty soon there'll just be me.' Mel felt in his doublet and withdrew his bodkin. He stood up straight and walked towards the head apprentice.

'Groot. *Enough!*'

Billet was beyond fighting back. He was visibly crumbling away, and it was all he could do to remain upright. His cries of defiance now sounded like creaking timbers and falling rubble, the words lost in a chaos of decrepitude.

A ghoulish croak split the air as a new creature approached, intent on delivering the coup de grâce. A great toad-like apparition with evil, hooded eyes swooped towards them on green, webbed wings, its back poxed with poisonous warts. Immediately, Lucas Flink counter-attacked with a writhing mega-serpent. It formed in the air above the house and encircled the attacker, wrapping it round and round in its muscular coils and crushing the life from it as it tightened its mortal grip. The toad-creature suddenly burst apart like an overripe melon and the air was filled with flying gobbets of flesh and milky strands of toad spawn. The slimy ribbons fell over the remains of Billet, the black embryos within stirring menacingly. They rapidly swelled and burst forth. Thousands of newborn tadpole-monsters renewed the attack. Fat, rasping tongues tore chunks from the house as Billet began to dissolve like a sugar cube in hot tea. Huge holes appeared in his facade, and the occupants in the remains of the library were dangerously exposed as they worked at their canvases.

Ludo's and Wren's inventive creations – a heron-headed crab and a voracious parrot-fish – attacked the tiny tadpoles, destroying them by the dozen, but the numerics of amphibian reproduction were against them. Hundreds of the squirming creatures were being wiped out, but even more remained and continued the relentless assault as they visibly grew into toadlets. They swarmed over the crocodilian creature Green had created, smothering it by sheer numbers.

Ambrosius Blenk's riposte was in the form of a giant, rainbow-hued hummingbird. It hovered in the air next to Billet, its wings noisy blurs, picking off the attackers with its long bill and sticky tongue. The desert below was fanned into towering dust-devils by the downdraft. But even this inspired conception was inadequate to tackle the sheer number of the creatures. A great many invaded the wreck of the library, where the fierce turbulence of the hummingbird's wings whipped them into their own darkly swirling vortex amid a storm of paper from ruined books. Within this miniature tornado, the toadlets fused and combined with one another until a new and powerful monster dominated the remains of the room. Overall it was human in outline, with an ovoid toad head attached to massive shoulders covered in toxic carbuncles. Powerful arms ended in webbed claws. Its pot-bellied torso was supported on two legs with fat, amphibian thighs and splayed feet. Its black tongue darted in and out, scenting the air for prey.

'The iconium's spent,' shouted the master. 'Everyone back to the barricade. Where have those angels got to now?'

'If you'll permit me?' Swivel, cutting torch redeployed, shielded the master and his companions but was effortlessly brushed aside by one swipe of the monster's powerful arm. He lay in the corner twitching, his many faces swivelling out of control one after the other.

The creature's predatory instinct was to go for the

weakest and it seized the injured rebel leader. Green swung his sword to defend himself but this was snapped like matchwood by the monster and it shook him as if he were a child's plaything.

'*No!*' cried Ludo as he climbed on to the barricade. 'Let him go!'

'Ludo, don't!' screamed Wren.

'I must. Everyone's suffered enough because of me.' He leapt and encircled the creature's neck and they whirled around in a macabre piggyback dance. Some of the carbuncles burst under him and the acidic poison they released burnt through his doublet. Crying with pain, he hung on and his fingers scrabbled over the toad's face, seeking its eyes. When it found them, he clawed deeply. The toad-monster howled with pain and dropped Green. It spun round, smashing Ludo against the library wall.

Still the apprentice clung on, tormenting the apparition with his probing fingers. The beast swung again as it attempted to rid itself of its clinging tormentor. The wall cracked and rubble cascaded from the ceiling. Then the monster lurched backwards, its intent to crush the life from its assailant by sheer force. The wall gave way and the creature, Ludo still clinging to it like a limpet, fell through the gap and plummeted to the desert floor.

'Ludo!' Wren ran to the gaping hole and stared down. There, far below, lay the lifeless, spread-eagled body of the toad-creature. Of Ludo there was no sign. The master and Lucas Flink joined her.

'Where's Cleef?' said the master as the monster began to fade.

'There he is,' said Lucas Flink. As the dead creature grew more and more transparent they saw a terrible sight. Lying beneath it, mauled by the monster, shattered by the wall and crushed by the fall, lay the unmoving form of Ludo.

'Ludo,' said Wren. 'Oh, Ludo.'

... and Into the Fire

'Groot. *Enough!*'

The head apprentice turned at the sound of Mel's shout. At first, his drunken eyes refused to focus. He blinked rapidly several times and looked harder. Wide-eyed, he dropped his palette and backed clumsily into the easel. The canvas toppled to the ground. So did the small chest. What little iconium there was left, disappeared into the desert sand, to be trampled underfoot as he fought for balance.

'*Fegie!* It can't be. You're . . . you're dead.' Groot put out a hand to steady himself. The easel fell and so did he.

Mel said not a word.

Groot scrambled to his feet. 'Stay away from me.' He turned and fled into the mayhem.

Mel followed him across the burning camp and into Lord Brool's pavilion. He was met by a solid wall of heat as if he had walked into an oven. Anything that was not already burning freely was smoking. Overhead, the ceiling appeared to be made of a rippling mass of smoke.

Groot rushed, coughing, to one of the large paintings, its surface cracking and blistering in the heat. He made the mirrormark and pushed at the canvas, thinking that he could pass through it as easily as a door. He screamed with pain as the molten paint on the unyielding canvas stuck to his hand. He had chosen the wrong picture. He crossed to the other. Its surface was also beginning to bubble. He turned for one last look at Mel and, as he did so, the hem of his scarlet robe brushed the side of the tent and caught light. Groot tore it off and threw the blazing missile at Mel. Then he turned, made the mirrormark and vanished.

Disentangling himself from the burning robe, Mel made for the painting that had swallowed Groot. Its surface was now so badly blistered that it was impossible to discern what it depicted. No matter: Mel made the mirrormark.

He fell face down into soft snow. Blessed, cooling snow. Coughing uncontrollably, he rolled over, extinguishing his smouldering clothes and soothing his burnt head. He grabbed a fistful of snow and brought it to his mouth to suck, chasing away the acrid taste of smoke and soothing his scorched throat. His coughing fit subsided. For a moment more he lay there, enjoying the blissful, cleansing iciness. Then he heard a fluttering sound and felt a chill breeze on the back of his head, and he lifted it and looked around to get his bearings. Behind him, he could feel the heat coming off the wall of mist and through it the faint sounds of battle. As he rolled over, it bubbled and disappeared. In its place was a seamless continuation of the silent, snowy scene all around. He knew then that the painting had at last been consumed in the flames on the far side. There was now no way back. If he was ever to get home, he would need to find another exit.

He moistened a corner of Groot's charred robe in the snow and used it to wipe his face. The icy shock temporarily banished his fatigue. He got unsteadily to his feet in the lightly falling snow. He did not need to guess which way Groot had gone. His footprints led off into the distance as clearly as marks drawn on paper. Mel followed them with his eyes and saw a stumbling figure, black against the pristine whiteness, running as fast as the deep snow would allow. But there was more than one set of footprints. Several people had left mute testimony to their recent passing. Mel wrapped the remains of Groot's red robe around his neck as a scarf and set off to follow them across the too-perfect terrain of the Mirrorscape.

He soon lost sight of Groot, but continued to follow the trail. After a while, the tracks veered off to one side. Mel followed them until he found himself in front of a thick, impenetrable wall of thorns. The high hedge seemed impassable. Groot and whoever else he was tracking had evidently felt the same way, and the footprints set off in a new direction.

Presently, he arrived at a flat area that was obviously a frozen body of water. The footprints led out on to this but after a short distance stopped in a confusion of imprints next to a hole in the ice. Someone seemed to have fallen through. It could not have been too long ago as the surface had yet to refreeze completely. There was a flattened area nearby where someone had been hauled out, evidently with some difficulty. Then the trail led off again back towards the shore and, later, in yet another direction. After several of these random changes of course, Mel came to the conclusion that whoever he was tracking was hopelessly lost.

He began to feel hungry. The food that Ludo had gone in search of in the mansion had failed to materialise and the last thing he could remember eating was dinner with the phantasms of his parents.

Mel wished his friends were there with him now. Ludo would have something funny to say and Wren would have practical advice. With his friends by his side, his trek would be that much easier. But they were not there. He was alone. He shivered.

Mel trudged on, following the footprints as they led into a wood. His breath formed pale clouds in the air in front of him as he laboured through the deep snow. A little way into the wood, Mel's attention was caught by a large, solitary icicle sparkling where it hung from a branch. He went closer. As he gazed at it, the colours refracted through it changed. The pure white of the snow and the blue of the shadows vanished as if a curtain had been drawn over them. A curtain the colour of blood.

'Lost are we, Smell?'

Mel's reaction was instantaneous. At the sound of the High-Bailiff's voice, he turned to flee but tumbled headlong over the body of the dwarf crouching directly behind him.

'The oldest trick in the book and he fell for it, Mumchance. That's a joke, you may laugh.'

The tiny man blew an ululating trill on his whistle as he sat on his captive's back. He ripped off Mel's tabby sash, bound his hands tightly behind his back and dragged him to his feet. He patted him down and found the bodkin.

'We've so looked forward to renewing Smell's acquaintance, haven't we, Mumchance? There's so much to catch up on. So much unfinished business. There's even a debt to be repaid. Repaid with interest. Of course we don't have our Instruments of Interpellation, but we can always improvise. Why even a delicate thing like this icicle here,' the High-Bailiff snapped it off, 'can work wonders in the right hands.'

Adolfus Spute held the glistening point at Mel's eye. The cold air between them was filled with clouds of condensation, Mel's coming rather more rapidly than his captor's. 'What do you think, Mumchance? Up for a spot of improvisation, are we?'

The dwarf blew a questioning note on his whistle.

'Do you really think so?' asked the High-Bailiff with surprise.

Another blast.

'You know, that's not a bad idea. Not bad at all.' He looked Mel up and down with an appraising stare. 'Come along, Smell. Things to do, people to see. No dilly-dallying.' He strode off through the snow, hitching up the hem of his long robe with one hand as he steadied himself with his multi-coloured staff of office. Mumchance followed behind, urging Mel forward with the bodkin.

A chill colder than the icy Mirrorscape ran through Mel's body. The first time he had encountered the High-Bailiff, Dirk Tot had saved him and the second, Green. Now he was on his own. All he could do was hope that an opportunity to escape presented itself.

This thought sharpened his senses. He felt his mind ease into the same state as when he drew. He began to study his surroundings with his artist's eye.

He noticed at once that something in the texture of the scenery around them had changed. It was not very evident in the thick snow, but there was less detail to be seen in the Mirrorscape. It was the kind of simplification seen in the background of a painting. Even the light was different: it had stopped snowing and had grown darker. He was sure they had crossed into another painting. At one point there was a muffled thud behind them as snow fell from a high bough. A flapping of wings told them it had been dislodged by birds and no one paid it any attention. Eventually, the wood thinned out and they looked down on to a natural hollow surrounded on all sides by jagged mountains. The sun was setting and the evening star was visible. Nestling in the lee of a rocky outcrop was a group of strange-looking buildings. Their exact shape was difficult to see, as they were draped in thick snow. As they approached, Mel could see yellow lamplight spilling from one on to the ground outside its door.

Adolfus Spute entered and Mumchance forced their prisoner inside with the point of the dagger. As soon as his eyes had adjusted to the dim light, Mel could see that they were inside the frozen carcass of some huge animal, its ribs and backbone like the vaulting of a great building. At one end of the long space a fire had been built. Smoke snaked upwards and escaped through a hole in the ceiling. Incongruously, there was a table and two long benches. They seemed to be made from frozen entrails and discarded bones. Seated around it, close to the fire, was an obscenely fat man draped in the outer garments of the other two people who sat shivering in their shirtsleeves nearby. One was hiccoughing repeatedly. A huge set of scarlet robes were propped in front of the fire, steaming as they dried.

The fat man sniffed loudly. 'Ah, Spute, about time. And who's this?'

'Introductions. Of course, how remiss of me.' Adolfus Spute bowed. 'This is Lord Brool, the Lord-High-Master of the Fifth Mystery and his private secretary, Skim. I believe you are already acquainted with my nephew, Groot . . .'

Groot cradled his burnt hand.

'. . . and, of course, my assistant and I need no introduction.'

'Yes, Spute, very nicely done. But who's this?' asked the fat man impatiently.

'This,' said the High-Bailiff with a theatrical flourish of his hand, 'is *dinner*.'

'*What?*' choked Mel.

'There's not much of him.' Lord Brool eyed Mel up and down. 'When I sent you out to trap something I was thinking more along the lines of a nice, juicy deer. That unintended dip in the lake has left me famished. Oh, well; if that's all there is on the menu. A leg for me, I think – and maybe the kidneys for garnish.'

Mel was dragged outside and Mumchance tied him to a tree. He drew Mel's bodkin from his belt and felt its edge. He seemed dissatisfied and held up one gloved finger as if to say *don't go away* and went towards a nearby rock. As he crouched down with his back to his prisoner, Mel could hear the ominous *shick-shick-shick* sound of the blade being sharpened.

Mel felt the last reserves of his courage ebbing

away. He could see the glow from inside the building growing brighter and thick smoke issuing from the chimney as the fire was stoked. The sound of the sharpening knife grew more insistent. Mel struggled frantically against his bonds.

'Stop fidgeting or I'll never get these knots undone.'

'*Farris?*'

'No, I'm Bathor. Farris is waiting up by the trees.'

'Where did you two come from?'

'We've been following you since we left Billet. Our master distinctly told us to stay close and to look after you. We thought you would have noticed. We made enough noise. Besides, we thought you might be up to some . . .'

'Devilry?'

'Exactly. There, that's it. This way. We've found one of those walls of mist. It's up here.' Bathor led Mel up to some trees where Farris was waiting.

'So you found him,' said Farris. 'What kept you?'

A shrill whistle blast sounded behind them, followed by shouts from Groot and the others. The snow had drifted deeper there and Mel struggled to lift his feet higher and higher as they made their way uphill. He was puffing loudly and great clouds of steam came from his mouth. He looked back. Mumchance and Lord Brool were having as much trouble with the deep drift as he was, but Adolfus Spute and the partially clothed figures of Groot and Skim had overtaken them and were gaining on him rapidly. Mel stumbled.

'Oh humans. *Really*,' said Farris and Bathor in unison. They each grabbed one of Mel's arms and rose into the air. Their wings caused a mighty wind that fanned the snow into a blizzard in front of their pursuers, who cowered in the downdraft as the angels flew off.

Mel felt exhilarated, but his flight was short and they soon landed in front of the wall of mist. With the angels still holding his arms, he formed the mirror-mark in the air. There came the familiar sensation of tingling as the snowy world around them whirled and they were through.

They emerged into a strange space. A long gallery stretched away to the right and left, its wall hung with many paintings.

'The pictures . . .' said Farris.

'They're leaking light,' said Bathor.

Light flooded the floor in front of the canvases and strange vegetation grew out of them. Water splashed from the pictures on to the floor and flowed away down the gallery. Suddenly, Mel recalled Green's warning about the Mirrorscape: 'The seal's not permanent. After a few hundred years it breaks down.'

Mel said, 'We must be in the oldest part of one of the Great Houses.'

'What's that mean?' asked Farris.

'The portal between the worlds is open . . .'

A distant roar echoed from the darkness at the end of the gallery.

'. . . and things can come and go.'

'*Look!*' Bathor was staring back at the painting of the snowscape. It was the only picture in the gallery with its seal still intact. Bathed in the light shed by the angels, they could clearly see the painted images of the High-Bailiff, Groot and Skim near the foreground as they ran towards them. Further behind them, in the middle ground, was Mumchance and behind him waddled the gross figure of Lord Brool, now back in his red robes. 'Why don't we wait for them here? Then, when they come through, we can get up to some . . . you know.'

'There's no time for that now,' said Mel. 'Come on.' No sooner had the words left his lips when the animal roar came again, closer this time. The trio ran, splashing, following the direction of the water as it flowed down the gallery.

By the time they had reached the darkness at the end, they heard Mumchance's whistle behind them and then Adolfus Spute's enraged voice. 'After them! Don't let Smell get away. After all he's done to me, I've plans for *him*.' Their pursuers were through.

As they ran on, the stream became stronger as tributaries joined it from other dark corridors that they passed. Ahead, they could hear a continuous thundering sound growing louder with every step. The passage they sped along ended abruptly and they skidded to a halt.

They had arrived at a cavernous stairwell, the top and bottom lost in darkness. By the angel-light, they could see many staircases, some clinging to the side of the space, and others vaulting the void to landings on the far side. The steps were carpeted in running water that cascaded in foaming cataracts, each adding to the others until they met in a deafening cacophony of roaring, white water far below.

Farris and Bathor flew up into the great void, the spray forming luminous rainbows around their glowing forms. But rather than define the space, the light of the angels only emphasised its vastness. By their glow, Mel could dimly make out the intricate carving of the crumbling masonry. Stone faces and mythical beasts looked down on them disapprovingly. A great many old paintings lined the stairs. The angels glided back down to rejoin Mel.

'Which way?' Mel looked back along the corridor they had entered by and saw bobbing lights. His pursuers had made flaming torches. '*Up!*' he shouted, reinforcing the only option left with a stabbing finger. The angels smiled, grabbed his arms and took off. They had not risen far before a great black shape swooped down at them from the darkness. Its horrific roar could be heard even over the thundering water. Mel was able to make out huge wings, a gaping maw and massive eyes with a glowing blue light at their nexus. The angels flew to a landing on the far side of the stairwell and set Mel down. He had to grab a carved banister to help him stay upright in the swift flowing current.

Just then, the High-Bailiff and the others emerged from the corridor into the far side of the stairwell and their torches fizzled out in the spray. The shining angels marked Mel out for them clearly. They began battling up the stairway that connected them to the landing where Mel stood. They linked arms and formed a chain as they hauled themselves against the rushing water. The dark shape of the winged creature circled menacingly overhead.

Mel looked round for an escape route. There was no corridor leading off the landing and only one exit suggested itself. The large painting hanging behind him was cracked and its surface was beaded with spray. Mel made the mirrormark, but nothing happened. He tried again but without result. All the while, his pursuers were drawing nearer. Why was the mirrormark not working? Again, Green's words came back to him: 'Not every artist can make the mirrormark. Lesser artists can mark the canvas but it won't open a door into the Mirrorscape and not every painting even bears it.'

Mel heard Mumchance's whistle over the crashing water. Then, from the depths of despair, rose the shining bubble of an idea. Mel unwound the remains of Groot's robe from his neck and frantically searched the pockets. His hand closed on something powdery. The last iconium in the world. He dipped his finger in, and with it drew the mirrormark on to the surface of the inert canvas. 'The Mirrorscape recognises its own.'

There was a great whoosh and a loud roar as the black creature swooped.

'*Farris! Bathor!*' But the angels had gone, plucked from the landing by the beast. Mel watched, horror-struck, as they spiralled into the air, the angels struggling against the black beast. For a fleeting moment, he caught a glimpse of the angels' faces. They were laughing and had a devilish glint in their eyes.

Then down, down, down in a mortal spiral until they disappeared into the thundering foam below. Mel stood for a moment in the sudden darkness, feeling more alone than he had ever felt in his life.

A piercing blast on the whistle told him how close his pursuers were and jerked him back to the moment.

Mel turned and traced the mirrormark in front of the canvas. As he completed the gesture, he felt a tug on the robe he still held.

'*Smell!*'

Then he was through. But the daisy chain of his enemies was also drawn through by the power of the mirrormark.

Mel was the first to recover. They were in a dismal landscape shrouded in mist, a grey world with indistinct shapes. It reminded him too much of his own ill-conceived world. The shapes of his enemies stirred nearby as they scrambled to their feet on loose shale. Wrapping his scarf back around his neck, Mel began running up a steep hill. A shape at the summit, dark grey against a paler background, resolved into a ruined semaphore tower. Its skeletal arms hung uselessly, creaking in the breeze, and a rusty weathervane on top squealed as it turned slowly. A large bird perched on the tower cawed a melancholy cry. Behind him, he could hear tumbling rocks as the clumsy posse climbed after him.

Mel reached the tower. As he ran his hands over the rough, clammy stones, two thoughts occurred to him simultaneously. One, that sooner or later his enemies would gather there at the only landmark in the desolate wasteland. Two, how was he to find the wall of mist again in a land of mists? He had to find it soon before the iconium faded. He heard sounds; a muffled shout, an answering whistle and a foul curse as the High-Bailiff stumbled. Then there was the sound of a hiccough off to his right. *Time to move.* He descended the hill on the far side and lay flat on the ground. As he looked back up the hillside, dark shapes assembled at the ruined tower.

'Smell, I know you're out there. I know you can hear me. Show yourself,' called the High-Bailiff. 'There're five of us and we've got all the time in the world.'

Oh no, we haven't, thought Mel.

Adolfus Spute seemed to be looking in his direction and Mel carefully edged to one side. But not carefully enough. Loose stones beneath him rattled away down the hillside. Adolfus Spute gestured with his arms and three other shapes, two tall and one short, spread out and slipped away to each side.

Mel scuttled, crab-like, to the side, always keeping the outline of the tower as a fixed point. At the sound of falling stones, he froze. A tall figure was coming towards him. He grabbed a stone and threw it over the shape's head. It landed with a clatter behind the shape.

'Fegie? I can hear you. I know where you are.' Groot's shadow stalked off in the direction of Mel's missile. A little later there came the sound of a scuffle. 'Got you, you little scrot!' There was a whistle blast. 'Sorry, Mumchance. He must have gone the other way.'

The same ruse worked a second time as another tall, hiccoughing figure was sent chasing shadows. Mel continued to circle the indistinct form of the tower, hoping that he would find something – anything – that would indicate where the wall of mist was. Then he heard it; the faint roaring sound of cascading water. As he edged in its direction, it became louder. When it was at its loudest, he began to back down the hillside. Soon he felt resistance behind him. He turned. 'The wall of mist!'

'We thought we'd find you here, Smell.' Adolfus Spute and his nephew emerged from the greyness to Mel's left.

Groot shouted, 'Over here. We've got him!'

Mel turned, the wall at his back. He could feel the resistance of the mirrormark that sealed them in press against him like invisible hands. He could hear Mumchance's triumphant whistle blasts and the wheezing complaints of Lord Brool as Skim helped him over the rocky ground towards where Mel stood cornered. He stooped and picked up a stone. The High-Bailiff shook his head as if disappointed with this last, pathetic show of resistance. Mel threw the stone high over the heads of the High-Bailiff and Groot.

'Missed, Smell.'

'I don't think so.' There was a clang as the stone hit the weathervane, followed by an angry cawing and flapping of wings from the direction of the tower. In the dank air it sounded like the beat of angels' wings. As the two men turned, so did Mel – but in the other direction. He made the reverse mirrormark in the air.

But nothing happened. He had left it too late. The iconium had faded. He pushed against the force field and it gave slightly. He pushed harder, almost willing himself through. It was like walking into a wall of treacle.

'Oh no, you don't,' cried Adolfus Spute. '*Got you!*'

Mel felt his scarf seized and strong arms hauling him back. He strained against it with all his might. Then it suddenly slipped from his neck and the additional momentum propelled him through the wall.

He fell to his knees in swiftly flowing water. It was dark. As dark as night.

Almost.

He held his hand in front of his face and could see its outline. Lying on the crumbling balustrade before him, he found the source of the feeble light. A single glowing feather: an angel's feather beaded with spray. He picked it up, turned and held it to the canvas, wiping away the moisture with his other hand. By its light he could see several murky figures in front of the ruined semaphore tower. They were looking back out of the painting, their hands gesturing wildly in the air as they struggled to trace the mirrormark. The mirrormark that was no longer there.

Mel watched the frozen image for a while. Then he turned from the canvas and, by the light of the glowing feather, began the long climb up the staircase towards the world above.

Epilogue

Far away in Borealis, the northernmost of the Seven Kingdoms, the first snows dusted the flanks of the mountains like sprinkled icing-sugar, while farther south in Nem the faint whisperings of autumn could already be heard by those that cared to listen. But for the time being, the days remained warm and bright, the blue canvas of the sky only lightly scumbled with small white clouds.

A large crowd had gathered in the square outside Ambrosius Blenk's mansion. They were dressed in their Sunday best and a carnival atmosphere prevailed. They jostled one another in a good-humoured way for a position that gave them the best view, and some of the more adventurous youngsters had even clambered on to the fountain, not caring that they got wet in the process. Word had been circulating all week that the famous clock adorning the facade had been refurbished. It had been stopped for two days as craftsmen had toiled inside to replace key elements in time for its inauguration at noon that Sunday. The crowd had begun gathering shortly after dawn to ensure a good place from which to witness the event. Throughout the morning this had grown until, as the hands of the great clock stood at five minutes to midday, the square positively thronged with citizens.

There was a loud buzz of conversation among the assembly. They had much to talk about.

'I can't believe you've not heard. It's been the talk of Vlam for the last few weeks. Where've you been – Pyrexia?'

'Not nearly so far. I've just this hour returned from Issle.'

'So you won't have heard. There's been a secret election in the House of Mysteries. Everything's changed. The High-Council of the Fifth Mystery's fallen and the other Mysteries have tumbled along with them.'

The traveller looked sceptical. 'If the election's so secret, how come you know?'

'I just do. Lord Brool, the High-Bailiff and other

influential members of the High-Council have been voted out of office and gone into exile. Every last one of them.'

'You're pulling my leg. If that's the case, who's running the Mysteries?' asked the traveller sceptically.

'Lord Floris is back and . . .'

'And what? What's put such a smile on your face?'

'. . . all of the most outrageous Pleasures have been abolished!'

'*What?*'

The hands of the clock moved one minute nearer the hour.

'Hello, neighbour,' called a pasty-faced woman. 'I didn't expect to see you and your family here, what with travel being so difficult of late.'

'It would take more than a lack of trams to keep us away.'

'I heard they'll be back to normal soon enough. My cousin's friend's brother's been employed dismantling the treadmills in the winding sheds, and he has it on good authority that they are to be replaced with a new kind of engine that runs on boiling water.'

'Boiling water? Whatever next.'

A wheelwright and his family passed close by.

'Mummy, why have those men got red hands and faces?' asked their smallest child.

'Hush, poppet. Don't point,' said her mother.

'They're released prisoners, sweetie,' said her father. 'They used to work in the mines on Kig but they're all free men now.'

'My friend says there'll be no more colour from now on,' persisted the child. 'Is it true?'

'Bless you, no,' said her father. 'Quite the opposite. The Fifth Mystery's warehouses have been thrown open. They've been stockpiling pigment for years. There's colour enough for everyone now. Pigment that we can all afford.'

Every strata of Vlamian society seemed to be represented in the throng.

'There are Lord and Lady Cleef and their youngest son, Ludolf, the one in the wheelchair,' whispered a baker to his companion. 'I heard that he was injured in a fall. But he's mending fast.'

'So who's the green man pushing him?'

'Search me.'

'You mean you don't know?' said a stranger interrupting. 'He was once one of Ambrosius Blenk's apprentices. He had a run-in with the Fifth Mystery and ended up on Kig. Don't tell a soul, but I heard,' the stranger leant closer and lowered his voice, 'that he was the leader of the Rainbow Rebels.'

'I don't believe you. How could he have escaped from Kig?'

'Apparently there was an original Blenk hanging in the Governor's quarters and there was some kind of hidden doorway behind it . . .'

'You mean, like a secret passage?'

'Of course. What else? Anyway, several more prisoners used it to escape before Lord Floris was removed as Governor.'

'And then what?'

'I heard that some important man was helping them. Supplying them with money and documents. Someone big – *very* big.'

'I think you're having us on. I don't believe a word of it.'

Nearby, a prosperous burger leant close to his plump wife and said, 'I know for a fact – for a *fact*, my dear – that Lord Smert's son, Groot, has finally graduated from Ambrosius Blenk's studio and has gone to seek his fortune elsewhere in the Seven Kingdoms as a journeyman artist.'

'About time too.'

Vlam had become a city of rumours.

Alongside the well-to-do there were also people from other strata of Nemish society and from much farther afield than Vlam. Marked out by their clothes were a provincial weaver and his wife.

'I hear their son's one of Ambrosius Blenk's apprentices,' commented a fashionably dressed woman. 'And quite talented for a Fegie, by all accounts. But look at them, my dear. You never see tabby in Vlam. It's so dowdy.'

'Do you really think so, darling?' said her companion. 'You know, I'm getting fed up with all this colour. Now that the Pleasure's been abolished, even the hoi polloi will be able to afford it. Can you imagine? I rather like what they're wearing. It's so restrained, so natural, so *unaffected*. I think I'll ask my dressmaker to see if she can source any tabby – especially if it's as well-made as theirs. Mark my words, it'll be all the rage by next season.'

Overhearing this, an astute merchant introduced himself to the Fegish couple and enquired about the availability of tabby of such quality as theirs. The merchant was also introduced to the couple's companion, an elderly priest in a wheelchair.

'So you're to work in the Maven's library? You'll certainly have your work cut out. I've heard that his collection of books is the biggest in the entire Seven Kingdoms,' said the merchant.

The clock now stood at three minutes to the hour and a murmur spread through the crowd as Thomas Delf, the clockmaker, entered the square. He and his workshop were responsible for the revamped timepiece they had all come to see. People stood aside and greeted him warmly.

'Is that his daughter, do you suppose? The one in the Blenk livery?'

'Surely you've heard. She's been admitted to

the Blenk studio – as an apprentice.'

'A girl apprentice? Whatever's the world coming to?'

'Don't be so fuddy-duddy. Personally, I think it's a splendid idea. I'm sure we'll be seeing more female artists in the future.'

Times certainly were changing in Nem.

The windows of the houses on the three sides of the square that faced the mansion were crowded with people, the owners in the upper floors and their servants below. The younger and more energetic of both classes had climbed to the rooftop turrets and even crowded into the semaphore machines that crowned several of the grand edifices. They watched sweetmeat-sellers with handcarts as they worked the square below, selling foods concocted from delicacies that only a short time ago would have been prohibitively expensive due to the Pleasures levied on them. Now they were selling like the hotcakes they were. Hurdy-gurdy men strolled about, playing newly Pleasure-freed tunes to the delight of the crowd.

'Look! There's Ambrosius Blenk. Up there at the window.'

'Who's that with him?'

'That's his wife and Lord Floris.'

The master waved an acknowledgement to the throng.

'And look. There's whatshisname.'

'Dirk Tot. Come closer. Swear you won't tell, but he's the man who's invented all the new and cheap pigments that you can now buy.'

'Really? Such beautiful colours from such an ugly man. Who'd have thought it?'

'I hear he lost half his face and his hand while he was experimenting with those new pigments.'

As the hands on the clock reached one minute to the hour, an expectant hush fell throughout the gathering. The street musicians fell silent and all that could be heard was the musical gurgling of the fountain. Everyone turned expectantly to face the mansion.

Then the moment arrived. The minute hand eclipsed the hour hand and the familiar carillon began echoing across the square. The many doors around the clock face swung open and from them appeared what everybody had come to see. The first figure to appear was a minstrel. It was as if he was singing a ballad of the figures that were to parade beneath his window. Then a giant emerged, pursued by a scarlet carriage. Halfway across the clock face, the rear wheels of the carriage fell off, causing a wave of laughter to ripple through the crowd. Then three small blue-clad figures led a strange creature on a leash across the face. Suddenly, in a coup de théâtre, the mechanical beast sprung apart and transformed itself into a larger and more frightening creature. There was applause as the three figures succeeded in dragging it to the far side and disappearing back into the clock.

Then there came an interlude in the automated tableau as dozens of tiny scarlet automata chased a band of multi-coloured figures across the clock face, only for the tables to turn and for them to be chased back again. It ended with the humorous spectacle of a green figure repeatedly kicking a skinny red figure in the behind.

Then came the finale. It was a grand battle involving a veritable bestiary of monsters. The first out was a skeletal creature with a dinosaur's head and many feet, its huge jaws opening and closing rapidly as it chomped a bevy of hybrid monsters that seemed to be as much machine as beast. A window on either side of the clock opened to reveal a bearded artist in each, working at their easels. Below them processed a strange, human-looking house assailed by monsters. First the monsters would gain the upper hand, only to be thwarted by the house before everything was reversed. Repeatedly, a figure with many rotating faces lent a hand. As the mechanical battle continued, more and more of the house dropped away until finally it was gone. Then, in a final flourish, a masterpiece of the clockmaker's art, the pieces of the house suddenly flew back together until it was whole, and it triumphed over the monsters.

All the while, two illuminated angels flew round and round overhead, harrying the attackers and generally behaving in a very un-angelic manner. As the house, the swivel-man and the angels bowed to the onlookers, they were carried back inside the clock and the chiming ended. Only those with the sharpest of eyes for detail noted that during the whole of the mechanical performance three small, blue-clad figures, two male and one female, remained on stage playing their own part in the conflict. Throughout the entire spectacle, the stars and planets whirled overhead as they always had done and always would. When everything finally disappeared back into the clock face, the crowd broke into spontaneous cheering and applause.

Hardly anyone noticed a blond-haired, blue-eyed apprentice dressed in the Blenk household livery in the corner of the square. While everyone was lost in baffled admiration of the clock and its enigmatic procession of figures, he was busy sketching the scene. He held open a new sketchbook of expensive paper and cradled a pot of the very best ink in one hand. With the other he held his drawing instrument. The finest he would ever own. It was a quill made from a brilliant white feather that appeared to glow with its own inner light. It seemed to dance in the air as it moved across the page.

Only once did he pause and look up from his work. That was to exchange a wave and a knowing wink with a couple of friends in the crowd.

Glossary of Terms in the Seven Kingdoms and the Mirrorscape

Allopecopithicum – A fox/monkey hybrid

Arachnophant – A spider/elephant hybrid

Armadillo – A hedgehog/tortoise hybrid

Arpen – The capital of the province of Feg

Bestiary – A book describing animals

Bols – A village in Feg

Borealis – Northernmost of the Seven Kingdoms

Cameleopard – A camel/panther hybrid

Catoblepas – An imaginary beast

Chicevache – An imaginary beast

Chromophage – A colour-eating worm

Cockatrice – An imaginary beast

Coloured Death, The – A wasting disease that colours the victim's skin

Coloured Isles, The – Chain of pigment-producing islands off the west coast of Nem

Crocotta – An imaginary beast

Diaglyph – Religious symbol worn by Fas

'Empire of Sleep, The' – A place in the Mirrorscape

Fa – The title given to a priest

Farn – The river that runs through Vlam

Fas (pronounced Fars) Major – Second echelon of priests, above Fas minor

Fas Minor – Lowest echelon of priests

Feg – A distant province of Nem

Fegie – An insulting term for an inhabitant of Feg. A bumpkin

Fifth Mystery, The – Guild governing the sense of sight

First Mystery, The – Guild governing the sense of touch

Fourth Mystery, The – Guild governing the sense of taste

Frest – A port in Nem

Fugitive Garden, The – Experimental garden in the mansion

Fustinbule – An imaginary beast

'Garden at the End of Days, The' – A place in the Mirrorscape

Great Houses, The – The House of Spirits, the
House of Thrones and the House of Mysteries

Grothling – An imaginary beast

Gryphon – An imaginary beast

Harlequin-Mangabey – An imaginary beast

Hierarchs – Third echelon of Priests, above Fas
Minor and Major

High-Council, The – Ruling body of the Mysteries

Hill of Mysteries, The – Hill beneath the House of
Mysteries

Hill of Spirits, The – Hill beneath the House of
Spirits

Hill of Thrones, The – Hill beneath the House of
Thrones

Hippardium – A horse/panther hybrid

House of Mysteries, The – Palace of the five
Mysteries

House of Spirits, The – Palace of the Maven

House of Thrones, The – Palace of King Spen

Iconium – A magical pigment that fades rapidly

Inspiration, Mine of – A place in the Mirrorscape

Interpellation, Instruments of – Torture implements

Issle – A province of Nem

Kig – One of the Coloured Isles. Home of the pigment mines

Kop – Mel's home village in Feg

Mansion, The – Ambrosius Blenk's house in Vlam

Manticore – An imaginary beast

Maven, The – The spiritual leader of Nem

Megaphine – An imaginary beast

Mines, The – Pigment mines on Kig

Mirrormark, The – The secret symbol that unlocks pictures

Mirrorscape, The – The world inside paintings and drawings

Mirrortime – The strange flow of time in the Mirrorscape

Mysteries, The – Five guilds governing the senses

Nem – Westernmost of the Seven Kingdoms. Mel's country

Nemish – The language of Nem

Omniscope – An optical instrument with special powers

Pleasures – The rights to anything beyond the bare necessities of life

Pyrexia – Southernmost of the Seven Kingdoms

Second Mystery, The – Guild governing the sense of smell

Service Passages – Secret passages that riddle the mansion

Seven Kingdoms, The – Nem and its neighbouring kingdoms

Tabby – Plain, uncoloured cloth

Temporal Labyrinth, The – A place in the Mirrorscape

Third Mystery, The – Guild governing the sense of hearing

Thringle – An imaginary beast

Vermiraptor – An imaginary beast that feeds on chromophages

Vlam – The capital city of Nem

Volm – A province of Nem. Home province of Vlam

Western Ocean, The – Ocean off the west coast of Nem

Some Artistic Terms

Achromatic Colours – Black, white and grey

Apprentice Piece – A picture made by an apprentice
to graduate as a journeyman

Azurite – A blue mineral pigment

Background – Distant elements in a picture

Body Colour – Opaque colour

Canvas – Linen or cotton fabric used to paint on.
Also a finished painting on canvas

Cartoon – A preparatory drawing

Cartridge Paper – Inexpensive white drawing paper

Charcoal – Drawing material made from burnt wood

Caricature – Exaggerated depiction of a person

Chiaroscuro – Bold depiction of light and shade

Cinnabar – A red mineral pigment

Collage – Picture made by sticking elements on to it

Composition – The visual organisation of a picture

Craquelure – Crazing on old paint or varnish

Easel – Stand or support for a painting

Foreground – Pictorial space close to the viewer

Foreshortening – The compressing distortion caused by perspective

Format – The shape and size of an artwork

Fugitive (colour) – A colour that fades in daylight

Gallery – A room or building used to display pictures

Gesso – White ground used to paint on

Gilding – Application of gold leaf

Glaze – Transparent colour

Golden Mean or Golden Section – Harmonious ratio for dividing a picture

Gradation – Smooth and gradual change of tone or colour

Graticulation – Grid used to enlarge, reduce or otherwise distort a drawing

Hatching – Tones formed by closely spaced parallel lines

Impasto – Thick, layered use of paint

Indian Ink – Dense black ink

Journeyman – Stage between being an apprentice and a master

Landscape – Picture of an outdoor scene

Landscape Format – Wider than it is tall

Lapis Lazuli – Blue semi-precious stone. Basis of
ultramarine pigment

Linseed Oil – Oil commonly used as a medium with
oil paint

Local Colour – The inherent colour of an object

Malachite – A green mineral pigment

Masterpiece – A picture made by a journeyman to
graduate as a master. A picture worthy of a master

Medium – Liquid mixed with pigment to make paint.
Also, materials used to make a picture

Middle Ground – Pictorial space between the
foreground and background

Nocturne – Depiction of a night-time scene

Ochre – A rich brown or yellow natural earth pigment

Oil Paint – Paint made from pigment mixed with oil

Opaque – Impervious to light

Orpiment – A yellow mineral pigment

Outline – The drawn boundary of an object or colour

Painting Knife – Small-bladed knife used to apply
paint

Palette – Surface on which paint is mixed. Also, a
range of colours

Palette Knife – Flexible knife used to mix paint

Perspective – Artistic technique for depicting depth

Picture Plane – The surface of a picture

Pigment – Natural or synthetic colouring matter

Portfolio – Folder for transporting drawings

Portrait – Picture of an individual

Portrait Format – Taller than it is wide

Primary Colours – Red, yellow and blue

Profile – Something rendered from a side view

Quill – A sharpened feather used as a pen

Realgar – An orange mineral pigment

Scumble – Pale, broken colour over a darker one

Secondary Colours – Green, orange and purple,
made by mixing two primary colours

Sepia – Brown colour derived from cuttlefish ink

Sfumato – Technique of softly blending tones or
colours

Sgraffito – Scratching through a layer to reveal
another beneath

Size – Liquid glue used to prime a surface

Sketch – A rapid drawing

Spectrum – Red, orange, yellow, green, blue, indigo and violet. Also, a range of colours

Stretcher – Wooden frame on which canvas is stretched for painting

Studio – Workplace of an artist

Swatch – A small sample of colour

Tertiary Colours – Colours other than primary and secondary colours

Tone – The lightness or darkness of a colour

Translucent – Allowing light through

Turpentine – Common solvent for oil paint

Ultramarine – Deep blue colour made from lapis lazuli pigment

Vanishing Point – Imaginary point in a drawing where parallel lines converge

Varnish – Transparent protective layer on top of a painting

Wash – Diluted paint or ink

Watercolour – Water soluble paint

Turn the page for more adventures in the Mirrorscape
in the exciting sneak preview of

Mirrorstorm

Published in October 2008

Prologue to Mirrorstorm

A fierce, scalping wind blew across a featureless
wasteland devoid of any tree or blade of grass.
Funnelled through hollow, wind-blasted rocks, it
howled an eerie drone. The sky, the same leaden colour
as the stone-strewn ground, seemed low enough to
touch.

Across this desolation moved a line of three, squat
figures with the unmistakable, wide-legged gait of
gnomes. They were swathed in heavy cloaks against the
chill blast and had cowls pulled low over their deep
crimson faces. Large, open-topped baskets were
strapped to their hunched backs. Each carried a
glowing crystal rod in one hand, a beam of light
shining from the end and crisscrossing the way before
them. Their glittering black eyes moved as regularly as
pendulums, following the beams as they searched back
and forth over the barren ground. From time to time
one of the group would stoop, pick up a rock and split
it with his small hammer. Most of the shattered rocks

were thrown aside with a curse but, occasionally, one revealed a shining crystal within and was tossed over the finder's shoulder into his basket with an ugly cackle of delight. Onward the trio moved, stopping neither to eat nor drink, although they were aware that night would never fall in that weird, twilit land.

The ground began to rise and, against every rule of nature, a thick clinging mist started to seep from the rocks beneath their feet, rendering everything indistinct. The gnomes moved closer together but their search for the stone-gripped treasure did not slacken. Then their leader halted and called to his companions. They picked their way up the slope and peered down at his find. It was a tall skeleton, white against the grey rocks. Then, on the headwind, came the sound of voices and the smell of cooking. The gnomes knew this smell. It was the odour of roasting human flesh.

Cautiously now, crystal rods dimmed, they continued up the slope, their mineralogy for the moment forgotten. Ahead of them glowed a fire haloed by the mist into a red-orange blur. Three indistinct figures were silhouetted against the dancing flames:

two adults and, possibly, a child who blew intermittently on a musical instrument. To one side stood a makeshift tent made from mismatched articles of clothing stretched between upright stones and the bloody remains of another butchered carcass. The strange Mirrorscape wind that was powerful enough to sculpt rocks but permitted mist to form blew the group's words apart so that their sound reached the gnomes' ears in brittle, fractured shards.

'. . . return to the Seven Kingdoms and take back . . .'

'. . . he may be Blenk's youngest apprentice but . . .'

'. . . just to see him die slowly . . .'

'. . . and his meddling friends . . .'

'. . . if only we had an ally . . .'

'. . . someone who's hungry for power and untold riches . . .'

'. . . to help us lure them into a trap . . .'

'. . . plant a traitor in their midst . . .'

'. . . lead them to us once we have . . .'

'. . . but what hope is there of ever finding . . .'

'. . . not while we're marooned here . . .'

The head gnome had heard little but he had heard the words dearest to a gnome's black heart. He exchanged a meaningful look with his companions who nodded back. He climbed through the mist towards the fire.

'If there's riches involved, I have the answer to your dilemma.'

Acknowledgements

This picture bears my signature but others have made huge and indispensable contributions in getting it from a blank canvas to the finished work you see here. My literary agent, Ivan Mulcahy, saw some of the original rough sketches and gave me valuable early criticism and advice. Later, my publisher Cally Poplak and editor Rachel Rimmer of Egmont Press made priceless comments concerning composition and technique. Wendy Birch brought her design skills to frame the picture. I would also like to thank Ben and Louise Jenkinson for their Latin scholarship and my friend Carol Smith for her unflagging support.

EGMONT PRESS: ETHICAL PUBLISHING

Egmont Press is about turning writers into successful authors and children into passionate readers – producing books that enrich and entertain. As a responsible children's publisher, we go even further, considering the world in which our consumers are growing up.

Safety First
Naturally, all of our books meet legal safety requirements. But we go further than this; every book with play value is tested to the highest standards – if it fails, it's back to the drawing-board.

Made Fairly
We are working to ensure that the workers involved in our supply chain – the people that make our books – are treated with fairness and respect.

Responsible Forestry
We are committed to ensuring all our papers come from environmentally and socially responsible forest sources.

For more information, please visit our website at
www.egmont.co.uk/ethicalpublishing